"He was aware of the ring he himself had offered pressing uncomfortably into one clenched fist and sought for her sake to collect himself, stalling for time, wrapping the object he had offered in love most carefully in its soft covering before he put it away.

'Martin, I swore not to tell, I swore on a crucifix Wat had. And now I have broken my word, but I could not let you go on hoping. Please - please, you will not tell Father?'

No, he would not tell her father because he would not for the world have laid another burden upon him in the last weeks of his life. Nor would he tell Cecily that if she waited until she were white-haired and bent, Wat would never come to claim her, fortune or no fortune. He had command of himself now, and turned to face her again, and silently he made a promise. If it meant he had to meet him and kill him, so be it: Wat should never cause Cecily one single day's unhappiness. It was a vow foreign to his nature, which was kind and gentle, but at that moment he undoubtedly meant it, and marvelled at the steadiness with which he said, 'No need to speak to your father yet. He gave us fourteen days, did he not?' . . . "

Margaret Birkhead has written for pleasure for many years but *Trust and Treason* is her first published novel. She lives in Hertfordshire and is currently working on her second novel, about the Gunpowder Plot.

TRUST AND TREASON

Margaret Birkhead

CORGI BOOKS

The poem from *Five Hundred Points of Good Husbandry* by Thomas Tusser, 1580, is taken from the Oxford University Press edition, 1984.

TRUST AND TREASON
A CORGI BOOK 0 552 13585 2

Originally published in Great Britain by
The Bodley Head Ltd

PRINTING HISTORY
Bodley Head edition published 1989
Corgi edition published 1990

This book is set in 10/11 pt Ehrhardt
by Falcon Typographic Art Ltd

Corgi Books are published by Transworld Publishers Ltd, 61-63 Uxbridge Road, Ealing, London W5 5SA, in Australia by Transworld Publishers (Australia) Pty Ltd, 15-23 Helles Avenue, Moorebank, NSW 2170, and in New Zealand by Transworld Publishers (N.Z.) Ltd, Cnr. Moselle and Waipareira Avenues, Henderson, Auckland.

Printed and bound in Great Britain by
Cox & Wyman Ltd, Reading

Good neighbours I have had and I have met with bad: and in trust I have found treason.

Elizabeth I, speech to Parliament, 1586

For Thomas and Katherine

Part I

1558 – 1578

CHAPTER I

1

For a man judged by his own father to be a lazy dog, it was Sir Herbert's complacent opinion that he had done well by his three sons. Within the year all would be married to suitable young women of his choosing, even Edward, who was proving to be surprisingly stubborn about the matter. He allowed himself a satisfied sigh and settled deeper into his saddle, looking forward to the end of this journey he had planned with so much enjoyment. Thomas, riding shoulder to shoulder with him as befitted the eldest-born, was scowling between his horse's ears. No spirit of adventure there, thought his father, of whom the same had been said often, none at all!

The dull purple of the short twisted heather, the grey-gold lichened rocks that rose from it, the occasional patch of vivid green, so pleasant-seeming yet so dangerous, that was bog bordered by cotton grass bobbing white heads in the sharp breeze, held no more attraction for Thomas Woodfall than had the flat, damp fenland through which the party had picked its precarious way only a week earlier. Ahead, visible from time to time between the banks of the deeply rutted track that was the road to Scotland, the blue sky faded to white in the heat and he caught glimpses of swelling hills, forest-black at their bases, rock-strewn and scarred. As if it were draining away through his finger ends he felt the easy sophistication of university life, his enjoyment of fashionable London pursuits, leaving him with every passing mile.

He shook his cloak to loosen the accumulated dust of a day's journey, caught his father's considering eye upon him and managed to summon up a grin as if, given a choice, he could have thought of no better way to spend four weeks of high summer than travelling from one end of the kingdom to the other to see a young brother married.

Far enough behind to allow the worst of the dust to settle before they in their turn stirred it up in the faces of escort and pack animals, Lewis Woodfall rode whistling alongside his twin brother Edward. It would take more than a tedious journey to worry Lewis. Within a week, if they made their way safely through this benighted countryside, he would be a married man, at the age of seventeen.

'I doubt the lad would notice if we rode across the landscape of the moon.' Sir Herbert's voice was dry, so that Thomas, laughing, turned in his saddle to raise a friendly hand to his young brothers.

'Easy enough to tell one from the other today, sir,' he observed and his father's brows twitched together with more concern for others' feelings than was his wont.

'Aye, this is hard on Edward.'

The three brothers got on well together, although Thomas had his own life, his own circle of friends. His birth had been followed by other children who had not survived infancy and Thomas had already been a sturdy four-year-old, promoted from baby clothes to his first pair of breeches and receiving early lessons from a tutor, when Lady Woodfall gave birth to Edward and Lewis, who not only survived but passed through childhood without a single day's serious illness. After them had come another space of years when puny infant after puny infant was born and died so regularly that neither lad thought it strange.

As befitted the heir to Highwoods, Thomas had gone to grammar school, to university, and, until he had declared his education finished this year at the age of twenty-one, the time he spent at home had been short: a week at Christmas, perhaps two at Easter, so that he finally returned, a worldly-wise man (in his own estimation), to find two grown brothers as unlike him in pursuits and thinking as it was possible for them to be. Lady Woodfall had prevailed upon her husband to allow the twins to be educated at home, and in the life they spent together the natural bond of twinship had grown so close that often one knew what the other was thinking without a word spoken. Somewhere along the way any idea of their going to university had faded; the life of Highwoods, its lands and people, seemed sufficient. The outside world Thomas found so compelling did not call them, and certain it was that even if he applied his mind to it, which his father feared was unlikely, he would never know as much as they about the estate he would one day inherit.

Just what Edward would do once Lewis's forthcoming marriage parted them by several hundred difficult miles had exercised Thomas's easy-going, kindly mind of late. Superstitiously he hoped that thus dividing twins did not mean that one or other of them must dwindle and die. It seemed to him that he had heard of such things. If he had been on easier terms with his half-sister, Agnes, he would have asked her; it was the sort of thing she would be sure to know about.

At sight of his twin's set face, Lewis stopped his whistling. Their parting was the one thing that marred his complete happiness, but his attempt to comfort was oblique: well though he understood it, he would no more mention the real cause of Edward's ill-temper than Edward would expect him to.

'It will be worth all this, I promise you,' he said and Edward, pushing down within himself the envy of which he was ashamed, smiled and so set his brother's mind at rest.

The fair, handsome Woodfall looks had passed by the twins, who were of their mother's slight build and mid-brown colouring. They were not so regularly handsome but, as Lady Woodfall had been laughingly wont to observe, quite personable underneath all those freckles. From her also they took the high spirits that made Thomas seem almost stolid by comparison.

Knowing their father's determination that the sons he had raised to manhood should consolidate the family's position in the county of Sussex by the simple expedient of advantageous marriages, everyone had been amazed at the lack of opposition Lewis encountered when he announced that he wished to marry Anne Harrington, with whom he had fallen headlong in love at one brief meeting in London. True, land was there for him to add to the Woodfall acres, but it was on the borders of Scotland, and the Harringtons, moreover, were staunchly Roman Catholic. The brothers could only conclude that in the restlessness of the times, the heads of both families perceived that to keep a foot in each camp was no bad thing. Queen Mary was known to be in failing health; she was childless, despite countless rumours of pregnancy since her marriage to Philip of Spain and if, when she died, as soon she must, the Princess Elizabeth should succeed her, the Protestant Woodfalls, who during the present reign had found no weight of conscience preventing them from devoutly attending Mass, would merely revert to the new ways they had so easily followed during the brief reign of the young Edward VI. But the doubt in many minds was whether the Roman Catholics at Mary's court would easily be displaced at her death. Philip might prefer to live in Spain, but his troops were strong in the Low Countries and invasion from that quarter was not unforeseen, nor could the possibility of trouble with the Scots or French be ruled out, in which case a connection with a family professing the Old Religion, and with never a taint of Protestantism about them, would be of great use to Sir Herbert, whose only care was that his land and possessions remained intact.

Lewis cared neither one way nor the other so long as there was no bar to the marriage he wanted more than anything he had ever wanted in his young life. He saw no reason why he should not adjust to life on the Border. Someone was needed to take the place of the only Harrington son, lost repulsing a cattle raid by moss troopers the previous year. The thought of being so far from Edward troubled him but, if he were honest, that was for Edward's sake rather than for his own.

Thomas himself had never found fault with the match

arranged for him. Until two months earlier, when their betrothal service had taken place, making the contract between them as binding and indissoluble as would the wedding service itself, he had known his future bride only as a girl seen from time to time since the provisional promises had been exchanged in childhood. Even now, although he had kissed her most dutifully when they had given and accepted rings, he would have been hard put to reply had anyone asked him for a description of the lady with whom he was to spend his life. She would bring as her dowry land abutting the Woodfall estate that would almost double its size, and that was what mattered. His Oxford friends had confirmed him in the belief that one married for material advantage and, if one's wife were not wholly agreeable, set her to constant childbearing whilst seeking pleasure elsewhere. The selfishness of this attitude did not strike him and that Eleanor Coulton might view matters differently had never, thankfully for his peace of mind, occurred to him.

What had further amazed the young Woodfalls was the eagerness with which their father agreed to Lewis's marriage taking place at Anne Harrington's own home that summer, with all the menfolk of their immediate family in attendance. Summer it might be, but what roads there were leading so far to the north were dangerous not only for their surfaces, or lack of them, but because they were beset by roving bands of footpads and tramps. Thomas's tentative suggestion that his father should not be away from home during the busy weeks of harvest, when he was wont to keep a stern eye on tenants and peasantry alike, was overridden.

Sir Herbert's mind was made up and like a boy setting out on his first long journey he mapped out their route, calculating the miles they might expect to cover each day, recalling old friends who lived on or as near to the beaten track as made no matter and who would, he knew, be delighted to provide a chance-come party with accommodation. It was time, he said, that Bailiff Steadman earned his keep. Anything weighty could be referred to Master Henry Stratton, a lifelong friend and neighbour, who willingly agreed to take over his duties as Justice of the Peace. And with Agnes to oversee day-to-day matters there was little fear of anything going awry.

Lewis and Edward were sure of that. The way their half-sister was deferred to by man, woman and child on the estate afforded them endless amusement. More than once they had seen their father treat her as another son rather than a daughter. 'Mistress Agnes will speak to you' had speedily settled more than one argument that had seemed likely to be endless.

The twins had been ten years old when their father, white-faced and showing more emotion than had ever been seen in him before, came home one day with a dark, thin girl of some fifteen years riding pillion on his lively chestnut mare. Lady Woodfall had greeted her, long known about, half-expected, with warmth, introducing her to Lewis as matter-of-factly as if illegitimate children of his father arrived every day to live with them. It was not long before servants' gossip made it known that her gypsy mother had that very day been burned as a witch in the market square at Downfelton, and only the respect in which all held their master and mistress prevented an effort to expel one who might be a fledgling witch herself.

The girl had still been standing before Lady Woodfall, unresponsive despite much gentle coaxing, when Edward returned home from a round of his rabbit traps. Intrigued beyond measure by what an excited servant told him, he forgot the training that would usually have urged him to make some small attempt to rid himself of evidence of the afternoon's outing and crashed into his mother's parlour without so much as knocking on the door. The addition to his family was made known to him; they regarded each other for a moment silently, considering, then he smiled the smile that at times seemed wide enough to split his freckled face in two and held out filthy, bloodstained hands in spontaneous friendliness. Lewis who, although greeting her politely, had remained decidedly aloof, watched his brother's impulsive action begin to unfreeze the horror of what the girl had seen and heard over the past days. For weeks after that she followed Edward like his shadow, seldom speaking, yet in growing content, until – and Sir Herbert and his wife never knew for certain quite when it happened – Agnes was as much part of the family as if she had always been there.

Thomas, introduced to his half-sister at his next home-coming, had taken as little notice of her as possible; he was of an age to find an older sister of such antecedents an embarrassment. And with Lewis there was a slight holding back which Edward had found impossible to overcome, try as he might. 'She won't turn you into a toad,' he said scornfully, but Lewis had never been able to consider the matter so lightly.

All Sir Herbert and his wife had to say about Agnes and her mother had been said between themselves years before; now Lady Woodfall accepted the girl's coming as if she herself could see into the future. She passed on instructions regarding the way Sir Herbert expected his house to be run for his comfort, seeming gradually to ease herself away from day-to-day cares and Agnes, quick to learn, soon adapted to her new life. Agnes had been at Highwoods just over a year when, one cold winter's morning, her stepmother died in childbirth and thereafter the half-gypsy girl carried out all the duties she had been taught so well that Lady Woodfall's personal maid crossly avowed that her dear mistress might never have lived, so easily did Sir Herbert take her loss.

Now, as the small cavalcade ambled on and Edward allowed his thoughts to wander, Lewis, with the telepathy that existed between them, said, 'Edward, are you certain she is not a witch?' and Edward, not needing to ask of whom he spoke, frowned, seeing the first two fingers of the hand that rested on his brother's knee crossed, as if even at all these miles' distance Agnes might, if the idea occurred to her, cause trouble.

'Quite certain.' Edward's tone was confident. 'Just different, that's all.'

'You are right. You *must* be right. She meant nothing by it.' Lewis was desperately trying to convince himself of something.

'By what?'

'When – when we left she took hold of my hands and stared at me. I felt – strange – and more to cover that than because I thought she would tell me, I asked her what she foresaw for Anne and me.'

'Well?'

'She said "great happiness and many babies".'

Edward threw back his head and laughed. 'What more do you want? I see nothing to worry you there.'

'She said nothing about long life, Edward, and when I turned back to wave she was still looking – very – very solemn.'

Edward reined in close, caught the bridle of his twin's horse and whispered in confidential manner, as if he were senior by years rather than the ten minutes in time that in fact separated them, 'Many babies take many years, little brother. How come you are so close to marriage and the inheriting of a castle without knowing that at least?'

The cloud left Lewis's face at once. He flushed, laughing in return so loudly that the noise raised a flock of birds feeding in the high bracken by the side of the track, sending them wheeling and swooping through the blue sky until they landed once more, at a safer distance.

'Anne says that on the Border anything built in stone with more than two rooms one atop the other is called "castle"! I'll race you to that twisted tree!' and as he spoke he kicked up his horse and was gone, leaving Edward to follow in his dust as best he might.

Because of his head start Lewis won and like two children he and Edward were still disputing the fairness of such a proceeding when their father and Thomas caught up with them and the former enquired, somewhat acidly, pointing to the jagged stones that stuck up through the road's surface, whether Anne had told him that she wanted a bridegroom with a broken neck.

Although Lewis's worry seemed soothed, he returned to it obliquely two days later. Happy and contented after a most comfortable night spent at the house of a friend of Sir Herbert's university days, they were riding side by side, as ever, on the last stage of their journey when, staring at Thomas's broad back, he said mischievously, 'At least Thomas has no need to ask Agnes what his life will be. This time next year he will be married to Eleanor Coulton, heaven help him! – and the year after that, at most, will be completely under her thumb. I wonder if he knows how strong-minded she is?' He paused. 'As to children, unless he can find some way to bear them himself, I doubt there will be *many*. The lady is too proud of her figure to spoil it year after year for the sake of squalling brats!'

The laughter that united the twins died away as Edward said feelingly, 'Poor old Thomas. Sacrificed for the sake of more acres to add to the Woodfall estate.'

Lewis shrugged. 'So long as she feeds him well and allows him to hunt as often as he wishes, in season, she may have her own way without any difficulty.'

A sideways glance showed his brother looking unusually serious, and he could not resist adding, 'Tom's marriage I may miss, but the moment I hear that *you* have finally made up your mind, I shall start for home. Anne may come with me or not, as she chooses.'

Edward's smile was forced. 'I hope she will choose to come, and that she may not be so large with one of your many brats that she finds it impossible to travel!'

More sensitive to his brother's feelings than he appeared, Lewis said gently, 'Benedicta Williams will make you a good wife, brother.'

Edward's horse jinked sideways as if hands had suddenly snatched at the reins. '*I* will not be a party to Father's schemes. Let him be content with what Mistress Coulton shall bring, without my being sold for a few paltry acres more.'

'I hardly call Master Williams's holding "paltry",' observed Lewis. 'There is no son to stand in your way any longer. And the girl loves you.'

'But I do not love *her* – I do not even like her! It wasn't until her brother fell headfirst from that tree that Father even thought about her suitability as my wife. Tom and I must further his pet schemes whilst you marry a lady you

17

fell in love with at first sight! It would serve you right, Lewis Woodfall, if she told you to go away because she had found someone she loved better!'

The last words were flippantly spoken but Lewis felt Edward's frustration and resentment and hastened to repair the damage he had so unthinkingly caused.

'If you had your choice, Edward, what would she be like? Like Mother? Like Agnes?'

Edward was ashamed of his display of temper. Until Lewis found his Anne he had given little thought to women. He knew for certain who he did *not* want to marry, that was all. Now, for Lewis's sake, that they might part in harmony, he made an effort, saying jauntily, 'Let me see, small enough for me to keep in order easily, that's most important, and dainty – she must be dainty. Gold hair, I think, fine as cobwebs so that it sparkles in the sunlight, and eyes as blue as ours.' His voice grew full of longing. 'And, oh, Lewis, we shall laugh and be happy together until the day we die, be the time long or short and whether we have many children or none.'

There was a moment's silence before Lewis reached out a hand to squeeze his brother's shoulder. Beneath his breath he muttered, 'Poor Mistress Williams!' Aloud, aware that Edward had embarrassed himself by his declaration and that the time had come to turn the subject, 'Molly – without the pockmarks!'

At mention of his boyish escapade with a most willing milkmaid, Edward reddened, but said more naturally, 'Thank the Lord for Pigman Joseph. If he hadn't taken her away she would have declared for certain that I was the father of the child, even if the eyes were all wrong and squinting like a crow!'

Lewis was diverted. 'Agnes would soon have seen her off for you,' he said.

Next day they reached Barndale Castle, which had considerably more than the two rooms Anne had laughingly promised, although its grimness was, if anything, worse than the brothers had anticipated. Its windowless ground floor was little more than a vast storeroom designed, at need, to take foodstuffs, animals and implements. The living apartments on the first floor were approached by an inside staircase but even here light entered only through windows no larger than arrow slits, partly for protection, partly to keep out the biting cold of winter. Although it had no moat, its grey walls were surrounded by a wide tract of open land which made it impossible for visitors to approach unseen by the men who constantly manned the castle's two watchtowers. Beyond the bare open ground was such a wilderness of crag and moorland that Thomas, already hankering after London, was horrified, and Edward, as he thought of the winters they must experience here, the weeks upon weeks when snow would make it impossible to stir more than a few yards from the building, shivered.

Formality took over and as they waited their turn in the introductions to the bride's immediate family – Sir Richard Harrington, his wife Elizabeth and little Tabitha, their only living child besides Anne – Edward felt Lewis's impatience like some tangible thing, caught the look he exchanged with Anne who stood so demurely behind her parents yet managed to look as if she were about to jump up and down with joy, and the anger against which he had been fighting, ever since Lewis had returned from his trip to London scarcely able to talk of anything but the wonderful girl he had met, rose within him in bubbling, searing jealousy. He saw her receive, as if they were the costliest things in the world, the knots of white silken ribbon Lewis had carried all this way to trim her wedding gown, heard their happy laughter and wondered how he could bring himself even to be civil to her when they met more informally.

Yet when the time came and they had a few quiet

moments to themselves, he found it quite easy. Slim and red-headed and glowing, she stood with her hand in that of her future brother-in-law and smiled up into his eyes, with her head tilted to one side like the bird Lewis teasingly named her.

'Almost the same,' she said, and her voice was merry. '*Almost!*'

And Edward, aware at once of what his twin saw in her, asked, 'You do not think you could mistake me for Lewis and marry me instead?'

She answered seriously. 'Oh no, there is – something – I do not know yet what it is, but I shall always be able to tell you apart. Lewis is . . .'

'Lewis is Lewis,' said Edward lightly, 'and you are fortunate to have found each other.' As he spoke he kissed her hand, and she surprised him by putting her free hand on top of his bowed head. Although she could not entirely dispel his tumultuous feelings, he was soothed for the time being. Fortunate, fortunate Lewis!

Three days later, before friends and neighbours from miles around, Lewis Woodfall and Anne Harrington were made man and wife in the small, cold chapel that was the family's private place of worship. Sir Richard's view that marriage was sacred and solemn in all its aspects had stripped the occasion of much that Thomas had been looking forward to. Feasting there most certainly would be, extending over three whole days, but although the nuptial bed might be blessed by the priest, the bride and her groom would retire privately to their chamber. No public bedding, none of the bawdy ritual that so enlivened other weddings he had attended. And when Anne arrived to stand beside Lewis at the altar, although she wore his ribbons on her dress and a circlet of tiny white flowers surmounted her hair, left long and flowing as became a virgin, there were to be seen none of the garlands of flowers intertwined with ears of corn to symbolize fertility; her father condemned those as pagan.

And in that chapel, of all places, Edward Woodfall met his love. She was not golden-haired, her eyes were most surely not blue, and he gave no thought at all to whether they would laugh until the day they died. He first saw her as she stood as maid-of-honour behind Anne, and from that moment the ceremony faded into a meaningless drone of sound, the white and gold of the bridal couple's array blurred and merged into a haze in the light of many candles. He was conscious only of an empty feeling within himself and scarcely even noticed the moment when the priest's words joined Anne and Lewis to each other for the rest of their lives. At the feast that followed he ate richly spiced foods, drank wine and tasted nothing. He talked to his neighbours at the high table; that he knew, for later his father proudly told him that he had been complimented on the manners of all three of his sons. The one person who existed for him sat far away down the length of the high-ceilinged hall and his world righted itself once more only when he became aware that Anne was murmuring in his ear, 'Mistress Rosamund Emory, may I present Master Edward Woodfall . . .'

Lewis, his eyes following his new wife in all she did, caught the look in his twin's eyes as he bowed over the hand extended to him by a girl who was small and dainty to be sure, but whose hair, flowing long as the bride's, was black as night against her white skin, and thought suddenly that just so he must have looked at his Anne on first meeting. The mouth that smiled at the formal words Edward murmured was thin-lipped, with little of kindness about it, and with dismay Lewis noticed that already her eyes, strangely light grey with dark-rimmed irises, had strayed, lifting over Edward's bowed brown head to exchange a silent, encouraging message there was no mistaking with a man standing nearby – his brother Thomas!

Forcing down a spurt of anger, Lewis told himself that Edward was old enough to take care of himself, and allowed Anne to pull him away into the laughing throng. It was not until much later, when they were slipping away, leaving their guests to continue the merrymaking, that he saw Edward again. He stood alone, leaning against a pillar at the end of the hall, and the look on his face was decidedly stormy. Thomas Woodfall and Rosamund Emory were nowhere to be seen.

Questioned about the girl who had so fascinated his brothers, Anne said that Rosamund Emory was the daughter of a distant neighbour who had taken part in the wedding only because the priest who performed the ceremony was her brother, their own chaplain being sick. Lord Percy thought very highly indeed of the family but Rosamund – and Anne's eyes were primly downcast – was extremely worldly, which was why her own father had frowned on any close friendship between them. Then she looked up, brown eyes glinting, and demurely wondered aloud whether all bridegrooms spent the first night with their wives discussing the virtue of other women; her old nurse had not mentioned this aspect of married life to her.

Lewis's behaviour thereafter was exemplary, so Anne assured him later, amid happy laughter, and next morning she gladly gave him leave to seek out his brothers, refusing to go with him, professing herself well pleased to have an hour – but certainly no longer! – to herself. He had explained carefully that he must try to warn Edward, to persuade him that he was mistaken if he thought that he had found his heart's desire. Thomas was very much more experienced, if all he had let drop to his brothers were true, and he could take care of himself.

By asking questions in what he hoped sounded a non-chalant way, he learned that his brothers had left the castle one after the other some time before. When finally he found them in a rocky clearing well away from all eyes he was too late; whatever talking there had been was over. Stripped to the waist, they were fighting each other with, on Edward's side at least, grim determination, whilst at the edge of the clearing, well out of their way, sat Rosamund Emory, her teeth clenched on her bottom lip, her arms hugged tight about her updrawn knees and her face contorted into such a look of savage enjoyment that Lewis was appalled at the sight.

There was no hope of separating the combatants, but he did not feel the need. He had never seen lazy Thomas fight but he knew what Edward was capable of, had no doubt that before long the elder brother would measure his length on the bracken-strewn earth and the lady would leave on the arm of a triumphant Edward. But even as the thought came to him he realized that that was not what he wanted; Edward must lose for his own sake, if what Anne had told him about Rosamund Emory were correct, and he set himself to will Thomas on.

He might have spared himself the mental effort. Seething anger possessed Edward, shortening his breath, hindering judgement, sending wild, swinging blows wide of their target, but Lewis soon had to admit that even had both men been ice-cool the result could have been no different. Thomas, taller and heavier, was after all a better fighter. It was obvious, too, that the contest was none of his seeking. He had no difficulty in parrying his younger brother's furious charges and he stood there, with an ease Lewis would not have believed possible, seeking no more than to give Edward time to work off his anger and exhaust himself. Then, at a remark from Rosamund, his expression darkened, came a flurry of return blows, a dull thud as he hit home once and for all and Edward sprawled on the ground, flat on his face, and lay there, his sweat-soaked body heaving and panting whilst victor and lady scooped up garments and walked away without once looking back.

Furious though he was with Thomas for this piece of callousness, it was Lewis's firm belief that his twin was well out of an entanglement with Mistress Emory, but now was no time to tell him so, any more than it would have been opportune to run after Thomas to remind him about Eleanor Coulton. Very quietly he sat down, almost on the spot where Rosamund Emory had watched the fight for her favours in such unholy glee, and waited for his twin to recover.

Slowly, very slowly, Edward dragged himself up on to hands and knees, stayed thus a moment, head hanging, then got to his feet. Lewis also rose, took up Edward's doublet and shirt and held them out to him. He said no word: none was necessary. Almost blindly Edward took his clothing, eased himself into it and stumbled away. The only sign he gave that he knew of Lewis's presence was a swollen, blood-stained hand half-raised in his direction as he passed.

It was Anne who helped Lewis, when a white-faced Edward returned to the castle later that day, to bathe his twin's bruises before they put him to bed, with the excuse that he was feeling the effects of the previous day's festivities. A few hours' rest would soon put him to rights.

It was, Lewis told Anne miserably, a fine way to begin a marriage. He begged her to believe that the Woodfalls were not a parcel of ill-conditioned louts, and it came as an immense relief when with a fierce frown she laid the blame for the whole incident squarely at Rosamund Emory's door. She told him what she had not felt it seemly to voice the night before, that it was not the first time that men, young and old, had come to blows over her. It was widely believed that a youth from some miles away had deliberately ridden his horse over a cliff and killed himself when she refused his offer of marriage. It was Anne's opinion, given in face of Lewis's incredulity, that anyone could prefer Thomas over Edward, that it was Thomas's position as eldest son that attracted; Edward would soon recover, she added sagely, and find someone more suitable.

Not even to his beloved wife could Lewis speak of Edward's dream, but deep within himself he knew, from the suddenness and force of his own love for Anne, which he had seen mirrored in Edward, that the matter was not so simple.

'The girl must be a witch!' he said bitterly, remembering her face as he had seen it in the clearing. 'Thomas is as good as married; she has no hope there. If she looks for position, perhaps someone should point out that my father is a widower!'

Anne held out her arms. 'Forget her, my love, and leave your brothers to live their own lives. She will trouble neither of them long. In two days' time she sets out, at the Queen's command, to join Princess Elizabeth's household at Hatfield.'

'God save the Queen!' said Lewis, with such relief and fervour in his voice that it made them both laugh; then he and Anne had their arms about one another and family troubles were, for the time being, entirely forgotten.

It was a measure of Thomas's physical superiority, and possibly of his reluctance to fight, that having had time to pick his target, he had struck at Edward's body rather than at his face, so that no damage showed. When, after two further days of celebration, the guests departed, Rosamund Emory rode away behind her parents, at the side of her silent, priestly brother, showing no sign of regret at parting from anyone, whilst Thomas having, as he thought, given Edward's anger time to cool, sought him out to make up their quarrel, in the belief that to his brother, as to himself, it had been no more than a passing flirtation. He found Edward once more in control of himself but so changed from the cheerful youth he knew that he was shocked and before the other's rigid face and hard, accusing eyes found himself stammering out explanations that sounded feeble even in his own ears, in a way that would have amazed his contemporaries. A lady might surely make her own choice; it was no great matter after all since they would neither of them see her again; it had been harmless and enjoyable while it lasted.

Edward had sufficient sense not to lay himself open to ridicule by saying that he would love Rosamund Emory until the day he died, no matter how she treated him, and contented himself with pointing out to Thomas that he owed something to Eleanor Coulton and, with a great effort, made an attempt to heal the breach by attributing at least part of his own behaviour to the thought of his coming parting from Lewis.

And to Lewis he refused to mention the matter at all, saying farewell when the time came as light-heartedly as if nothing had happened, bidding him think longingly of his old home when the snow was up to the windows and he was marooned for weeks, or marauders came storming over the Border to run off his horses. Lewis, an arm about his bride, thought that perhaps Edward was not so much affected as he had feared and responded in kind, promising to send Agnes the skin of the first wolf he killed, and the Woodfall party rode southwards apparently happy in each other's company, leaving Lewis to contented contemplation of his new life.

But the courtesy was for the sake of the Harringtons only. Scarcely half an hour into their homeward journey Sir Herbert, not being as blind to his sons' behaviour as they had believed and hoped, enquired of Thomas what the devil ailed young Edward, riding so sullenly behind them. It was unfortunate that at his father's unexpected query Thomas, who thought the matter was now closed, looked back smiling, thus making the topic of their conversation obvious. For Edward it was the last straw. He urged his horse alongside his father and informed him politely but in a voice that trembled that he would ride on ahead; the sooner one of them reached Highwoods the better.

Sir Herbert waved a hand before his face in a vain attempt to dispel the cloud of dust raised by his young son's precipitate departure.

'Well?'

Thomas's smile was complacent. 'Truth to tell, sir, we fought over a lady who – preferred my company. Nothing serious, but the boy is younger than I remembered.'

Sir Herbert grunted. 'Is that all? Well, the ride will cool him down.' Briefly into his mind came the respect that the twins, despite their liveliness, had always shown towards their tutor in matters of importance, and he added comfortably, 'Agnes and Peter Acres between them will have him sorted out before we arrive.'

CHAPTER II

1

Long before he came to the late summer woods that marked the boundaries of his own lands, Sir Herbert Woodfall was a man well content. He had ridden the length of the kingdom and back, a journey that would tax the stamina of a man half his age, and was returning unscathed and fitter than he had felt for years. No harm, either of nature or men, had befallen any member of his family or their baggage.

The easy life he loved awaited him and he smiled at first sight of the old grey stone manor house with the late afternoon sunlight striking gold upon the glass in its recently enlarged windows. There young Edward would be waiting, sorry for his show of temper, having worked every hour of daylight as penance. The first steps towards draining the moat, perhaps; they had discussed that during the previous winter's weary evenings. No longer any need for such fortification, and relief from the stench of its waters would be welcome. He wondered if the lad had arrived at a solution to the problem of what to do with the sewage outflow.

There, too, would be Agnes, tall and graceful as her mother, ready to render him a full report on happenings during his absence. It would not be long, if he had read the signs aright, before he and Master Stratton met to arrange the girl's betrothal to young John Stratton.

Within half an hour he would have his boots off and be at rest in his large, padded chair, a tankard of ale in hand

and no reason at all why, once the first talking was over, he should not close his eyes and slip gently into sleep until time came to eat.

'Life is very good, my boy,' he said complacently to Thomas. 'Very good indeed.'

The half-hour passed: Sir Herbert, striding to and fro, ignored his padded chair. Ale was brought and the tankard was struck clattering aside in greater anger than he had shown for years. Ben, who proffered it, quailed and ran to fetch Master Thomas from the stables, leaving Agnes, undisturbed by her father's wrath, to stand motionless before him, hands folded across her stomach, awaiting the arrival of her brother.

Thomas came at a run, his only thought to find out what ailed his placid father, and it was the groom who received the benefit of Ben's demand as to what they expected when the master did go to the far end of the world to marry off Master Lewis when he could have been wed and living close to home like any decent Christian body.

'Read this!'

Sir Herbert held out to his eldest son a piece of paper, all too obviously torn from one of Edward's Latin books, and Thomas, whose own writing had been called appalling by tutor after tutor, had not half so much difficulty in deciphering the scrawl as in believing its purport. There was no greeting; the writer, under great stress, had launched straight into what he had to say.

'I am going away. If you change your mind about Benedicta Williams and I hear of it, I will come home. I can earn my living well enough.'

A gap followed, then, very much as an after-thought, 'My respects to you, sir. Please try to understand.' It was unsigned.

'Where did he go, and when?' The question was directed to Agnes.

'He arrived four days ago, said he had quarrelled with Thomas and that he was only come to collect his things. He stayed an hour at most and rode away without another word. There was no time even to fetch Master Peter to reason with him, and he would not listen to me.'

She turned to Thomas. 'You hurt him very badly, it would seem, brother.'

Thomas ignored his half-sister and her calm, accusing voice. To his father he said, 'I told you, sir. He acted like a young idiot.'

Sir Herbert sighed. He had accepted Thomas's explanation without difficulty. He knew him well enough to believe that he would not lie: sometimes he doubted he was clever enough! Far more worrying was the problem of how he would manage the estate with the quicksilver twins both gone. He had allowed Thomas to go his own way unhindered since his mother died, with the result that he had an heir who cared for Highwoods only insofar as it provided him with money to live the life he chose. Sir Herbert's euphoria disappeared. He had been counting on Edward. The journey had taken its toll after all, he decided.

To the only son he had left he said heavily, 'It is no fault of yours,' and in relief Thomas bowed, and turned to the door.

His father's voice, sterner than was its wont, followed him. 'I can get you settled, at all events. You will marry Eleanor Coulton as soon as it can be arranged.'

Thomas bowed again. He expected nothing else, saw no reason to protest. Two months, at the very least, it would take before all the elaborate preparations could be made, and two months was a long time.

Sir Herbert dropped into his chair at last. 'Sit down, my dear.' He spoke to Agnes as to one of his own age. At a loss for words to frame what he must ask, he began several times, not once looking directly at her, never getting out more than three or four words at most until, taking pity upon him, she smiled.

'What you are trying to say is that although you believe me when I say Edward left without saying where he was going, you think I know all the same. As my mother would have known.'

'Yes.'

For once she lost the calmness that was her strongest characteristic. With a quick gesture that seemed almost despairing, she ran across the hearth before the huge, cavernous fireplace and knelt in the rushes at her father's feet, turning an imploring face up to his.

'Ever since the day you brought me here I have tried so hard not to know things as she would have known them, because I want to be like other people, but especially because I am afraid that what – they – did to my mother will happen to me.'

Shocked into consideration of something he had never even suspected, Sir Herbert put his hands on her shoulders. 'You are my daughter and the daughter of this house. Nothing bad will ever happen to you. Believe me, my dear.'

Agnes sighed, smiled up at him wryly. He was doing what he always did, closing his eyes to things he found disturbing. But he was her father and she loved him, so she said, 'For all my efforts, all I seem to have achieved is to make the knowing imperfect, so that although I do not know where Edward is now, I can tell you that before long he will be back here, alive and well.'

'Then – then if I . . .?'

The blue eyes lost their strained intensity, regarded him steadily. Her confession was already dismissed. It was the first time in all the years she had lived in this house that either of them had mentioned her mother's strange powers and the fear that haunted her constantly was beyond his understanding, despite what he had seen that long-ago morning in Downfelton market square. She wanted to implore him never to mention the possibility of 'sight' to anyone, but knew that if he promised he could well forget, for his mind was on Edward and no-one else.

'If you go to Benedicta Williams's father and say that you have allowed Edward to travel for a while – to compensate for losing his twin, if you will – and that he will come back to claim her, all will be well. The girl will wait for him willingly. I truly do not think her father could beat or starve her into accepting anyone else, she loves Edward so.'

'And the lad will change his mind?'

'I believe so.'

Relieved, Sir Herbert nodded. 'I had to know.'

She rose to her feet, curtseying dutifully, and would have left him to his rest but he caught her by the wrist. 'And you, daughter? What about you?'

She shrugged and there was sudden weariness in her voice. 'I have had made plain to me what I have always known in my heart. Master Stratton came here often and talked to me whilst you were away – perfectly politely, but always on business until, one evening, he told me that John had gone away. It was as kindly done as might be, but I knew that what he was really saying was that no son of his would ever marry a half-gypsy bastard, even if her father were his oldest friend.'

There was silence before Sir Herbert said, 'I had hoped with John being a younger son, not the heir, his father might have seen things differently.'

'Unless I go back to my mother's people, marriage is not for me.' A smile glinted in her eyes. 'They are less concerned about mixed blood.'

Awkwardly Sir Herbert pulled her to him, put an arm about her shoulders. Fiercely he said, 'Your home is here. No talk of – of other people, please. I – I . . .' He cleared his throat. 'Damn it, girl, whatever would I do without you? I love you, that's a fact!' And having thoroughly discomposed himself by such an uncharacteristic outburst, he let her go and turned to glare at the unfired logs in the grate as if they were responsible for every misery that beset him and every uncomfortable thought that plagued his mind.

Agnes rose to her feet. 'I will stay with you, sir, for as long as I can, that I promise. What did they quarrel about?'

'The boy did not tell you? What else but a lady? Trivial enough, as Thomas says, but Edward was on edge to begin with. Not very taking from what I saw of her. Skinny little thing with eyes so pale they looked almost white. No telling what will appeal to some men!'

Late that evening, when all the house was still, Agnes made it in her way to meet Thomas where they could not be overheard.

'A word with you, brother, if you please.'

Immediately he was on the defensive. 'If it's about young Edward, try to keep Father from worrying. I start out tomorrow. If he's anywhere to be found I'll bring him home.'

Blue eyes glinted brightly on a level with his own. It would, he thought, be so much easier to deal with her if she were not so tall. Such height was not seemly in a woman.

'No doubt your track will lead you Londonwards?'

He nodded.

'Then,' said Agnes crisply, 'you will please carry a message to Gilbert Lovelace from me . . .'

2

Gilbert Lovelace sat sprawled at ease in his London lodging and threw back his head in a wild shout of laughter.

'So she could not help but tell you! Ah, Thomas, these women! Two visits, two only. I was passing the weary hours until you returned, that was all.'

Ever since they had met at Oxford Thomas had envied, had tried to emulate, Gilbert Lovelace, who did whatever he wished with grace and elegance, without let or hindrance, undisturbed by others' opinions or wishes or the hurt he caused. Now he laughed in his turn, lest Gilbert think him foolish, mumbled into his tankard words to the effect that he had only delivered a message after all, and found that his friend had already dismissed the topic from his mind.

'And what happened to you in our northern wilds, my Thomas?'

'Nothing!'

'Oh, come, man! You were gone six weeks or more – and very dreary weeks I found them. Even in the fastnesses of wherever-it-was there must have been at least one woman you found attractive? Remember, I know you as well as you know yourself.'

For a moment Thomas sat turning his tankard between his hands. The sight of Lewis with his Anne had stirred unaccustomed feelings of discontent, so that for the first time he wondered if the relationship between himself and Eleanor would be like theirs. He acknowledged to himself that his deliberate upstaging of Edward had, if he were honest, risen out of boredom and a desire to show people who lived at the back of beyond that he was a man of the world. He had never intended to hurt his brother, and one day spent in Rosamund Emory's demanding company had been more than enough for him. Perhaps, he reflected ruefully, he had done Edward a service by keeping him away from her! That thought brought another, even more difficult to face. The choice had not been his at all. Rosamund Emory had beckoned and he had followed, just as he always followed Gilbert Lovelace, as if he had no will of his own. But it was his father's face, shrunken and old with worry beneath his first fury at Edward's departure, that disturbed him more than all, that left him with an uneasy feeling that because of his own unthinking behaviour nothing would ever be the same again.

He became aware of the lengthening silence, saw Gilbert's knowing smile, and was not surprised when he said, 'I scent a mystery, my friend! I shall not rest until you tell me everything.'

Nor would he, and the desire to please his friend rose anew within Thomas. He thought of Rosamund Emory and how intrigued Gilbert would be by such a dark, strange lady. With a swiftness and decisiveness that would have surprised his father he reviewed what had happened, selected those parts that did not concern Edward, embellished and told them. By the time he finished Gilbert's admiring gaze had worked its old magic and he added that the lady was now at Hatfield.

'You must have made a great impression, my Thomas! You'll go, of course. Too good an opportunity to miss.'

'Oh, yes.'

'Foolish boy! You don't sound over-anxious. I'm tempted to take your place.' Gilbert's voice was silken smooth. 'Go

33

this very day – no, not today, it's the play tonight. Take my advice, Thomas, make hay before the lovely Eleanor's steel claws close around you for good.'

Thomas hated the way Gilbert spoke of his betrothed. So far as he knew, the only time they had met was at the betrothal feast, yet Gilbert's words implied that he saw something in her, something none too pleasant, that Thomas did not. In vain he tried to assert that married or no he would find no difficulty in getting away whenever he wished; Gilbert's mirth was unabated.

'It will be something to be able to say that you've bedded a maid-of-honour to a princess of the realm.'

As ever, Gilbert could make it sound adventurous, but even with the true reason for his searching out of Rosamund Emory, Thomas had his doubts as to what would happen when he reached his destination. The Princess Elizabeth was well guarded, everyone knew that, doubtless even more so now that she appeared nearer than at any time to the throne of England. It was hardly likely that a stranger would be allowed to ride up to the Palace demanding to see one of her ladies without answering a great many difficult questions. Gilbert might achieve it; he had an uneasy feeling that he himself would be thrown out. For the first time ever in Gilbert's company irritability whispered in his ear that this was how it always was, he did things and his friend sat back and mocked them. When had Gilbert last told him about an exploit of his own?

3

Gilbert's taunting, 'Nothing ventured, my dear fellow . . .' seemed still to be ringing in Thomas's ears next day when, shortly after noon and clad in his finest clothes, his purse lighter by the gold Gilbert had so carelessly borrowed, he came to the gatehouse at Hatfield Palace.

Sight of the guards before it and a glimpse of the people

thronging the courtyard beyond the arch caused his newborn courage to fail him. He had never imagined so large and impressive a household. It was, he told himself, unlikely that Mistress Emory would know where Edward was; he was wasting his time. And Gilbert, question he never so shrewdly, need not know that he had not seen her. A description of an old adventure – and there had been several – with here and there a detail changed, would serve well enough when he was called to account.

Arguing thus within himself, he allowed his horse to make its own way, and it was not until the animal stopped altogether, dropping its head to crop the grass, that Thomas realized that he was well and truly lost. The road had become a track, the track had petered out. There was no sign of buildings of any description, but the patterned layout of trees in lush, green meadowland suggested a park rather than common countryside. He was hungry, too; he became aware of the fact suddenly and, gathering up the reins and kicking his reluctant horse into movement once more, made his way towards a clump of tall oak trees, whose tops reared over a slight rise in the ground. As he neared them he was pleased to hear the sound of water running over stones. Food and drink; afterwards he could cast about for direction. He dropped to the ground, intending to lead his mount to the water before he quenched his own thirst, when he became aware that he was not alone.

On the bank of the stream, beneath one of the trees, stood a woman. In her hands she held a thin, whippy oak branch from which, one by one, she was ripping leaves, throwing them into the water with movements that were almost vicious in their intensity. Thomas's first thought was that there was no need to disturb her. The meadow was large enough; he would move further along. But at that moment his horse kicked a loose stone, sending it down the short slope to land with a plop in the water. The young woman whirled round and in that instant Thomas had a glimpse of her unguarded face. Unimaginative he had always been, but he recognized fear when he saw it. The next moment, as if she had put on a mask, it was expressionless and she was facing

35

him in a way that made him swallow an oath and go down on one knee before her, head bowed, heart pounding. His horse, let free, made its own way to the water and began to drink.

How long he remained crouched there Thomas had no idea, nor what would happen next, for he dared not raise his eyes.

A clear sharp voice said, 'What are you doing here, sir?'

Heart still pounding, Thomas mumbled something unintelligible even to himself and she said, 'In the Lord's name, man, stand up! How can I tell what you say if you mutter to your chest?'

Throwing back the brown cloak she wore over a dress that seemed to him nowhere near rich enough for a princess, she stood before him, hands on hips. No-one, in his opinion, could ever call her beautiful, but she had one of the most interesting faces he had ever seen. Everything about it was thin, its very shape, its nose, even the lips that he imagined he saw twitch slightly as he stared.

'You know who I am?'

'Indeed, madam – Your Highness – the Princess Elizabeth. I saw your father once, when I was small, and he stood just as you are doing now – as if he owned the world. You are very like him.'

The twitch turned into an outright smile. If he had sought all day for something that would please her he could have found nothing better, although he did not at the time know it.

She put out a long, white hand and he bowed over it, suddenly strangely at his ease – thanks to Agnes. The idea flashed across his mind fast as a kingfisher's flight, startling him. This lady, who stood so near to the throne of England, had that controlled stillness about her that invested his half-sister. Later, when he had time to think it over, he believed it came from living in a society that might, for either of them, turn hostile at any moment. The mothers of both had died violent deaths. The princess had lived with fear of death all her life, had in fact several times been imprisoned. For the first time he realized that Agnes Woodfall could well, if harvests failed and another culprit were not nearer to hand when hunger bit and cattle and weakling humans began to die, be dragged off as a witch to imprisonment and worse, just as her mother had been. Strange that it should take a meeting with a princess to make him understand his half-sister's predicament.

'And you are?'

'Thomas Woodfall, madam, of Highwoods, in the county of Sussex. Your very humble servant – and very lost.' He ventured a rueful smile and looked round.

'You are in Hatfield Park, Master Woodfall; trespassing.'

Thankfully he noted that she did not sound annoyed. 'I apologize most humbly, madam. If you could tell me which way lies the road . . .'

'I have not the faintest idea.' The long hazel eyes looked him up and down, obviously, although he was not in any condition to realize it, appreciating what they saw.

'I have only to shout and twenty men will come running to arrest you.'

'Because I asked you the way to a road?' He was suddenly indignant. 'It would be your word against mine.'

'And mine would be believed.'

'True, madam, especially now that . . .'

'Go on, Thomas Woodfall. Finish what you were about to say.' Her voice was sharper than ever.

He swallowed hard. He had gone too far to back away. 'I have been in London, madam. They – the talk is that the Queen is very ill and that before long you will succeed her to the throne.'

To him it was gossip concerning a thing so far removed from everyday life as to pass his understanding, and she wondered what he would say if he knew of the almost-court that had grown about her at Hatfield for the past months, of the great and would-be great who had come to seek a suddenly valued opinion, to offer themselves for a more than rosy future in her train. She was unable to keep the amusement at his naivety out of her voice. 'Go on!'

Thomas floundered. 'Everyone I heard speak of it seemed pleased.'

It was borne in upon him that he was being laughed at, and in an attempt to retrieve his dignity he said, 'If you intend to shout for help, I will remain. If not, I ask Your Highness's permission to leave.'

In the attempt he sounded younger, less sure of himself than ever, and listening to the somewhat petulant tones of his lazy voice she found herself liking him. Her laughter under control now, she waited silently for his next remark.

'Is it necessary for me to walk backwards from your presence?'

Thin red brows arched in silent enquiry and he added, 'If so, Your Highness puts her obedient servant in considerable danger!'

She followed his glance, taking in the state of the cowpat-strewn grass over which he had ridden, then she laughed, loud and long, in a way that many a man might have envied.

'For shame, to mind so small a matter, and you a countryman!'

'But a countryman in fine boots only two days old, madam.'

Still chuckling, she inspected the leg, clad in soft black leather, that he held out towards her, and he later thought that their friendship, if such he might presume to call it, dated from then.

'Stay, Thomas,' she said. 'You intended to eat here? Will you share your food with me?'

He went to his grazing horse, returning with a satchel that had hung from the pillion. 'Bread and meat only, madam.'

'Excellent!' She looked about her for somewhere to sit and with a flourish of gallantry that would have reduced Gilbert to fits of laughter, Thomas untied the cord of his short cloak and laid it, velvet side uppermost, upon a fallen tree for her to sit upon.

'Not only the boots,' she commented smoothly, as he broke bread into pieces and offered it to her on its linen wrapping, together with already-carved slices of beef. 'It would appear, Master Woodfall, that you dress very well

38

to ride about the countryside. Unless . . .' her voice took on an edge, 'unless you have lied and came this way hoping to catch a glimpse of me. One of the latest of those who begin to beat a path to my long-neglected door now that they think mine may be the star to follow?'

If she had doubted, she was completely reassured by the wave of red that swept over his face. The man was up to something, doubtless, but nothing devious.

He looked her straight in the eyes. 'I came hoping to see Mistress Emory, one of your ladies,' he said bluntly, and awaited an explosion that did not come, although she echoed the name as if it were most distasteful to her.

'*Rosamund Emory?* What have you to do with her, sir? Come, the truth!'

In face of her manner he could have told her no less even had he wanted to, and he did not. The tale of how they had met at Barndale came tumbling out. This time there were no omissions: he gave details of Lewis's marriage, the fight with Edward and the return home to find him gone. His hope was that Mistress Emory might have seen him again, could tell him where the lad was gone.

'Barndale? Percy territory! So then you come from Papist stock? I had thought Sussex to be Protestant in large part.'

'So it is, madam, so it is. But my brother fell in love with Anne Harrington and nothing would satisfy him but to marry her. Which is why I – and the rest of my family – have spent the last few weeks riding to the Border and back.'

That he had not enjoyed the expedition was clear from his voice and the princess had need to hide another smile by bending her head to brush crumbs off her somewhat worn skirt.

'I see,' she said, 'and may I ask what . . .'

She stopped in mid-sentence, gave voice to an oath he had not thought ever to hear on a woman's lips. 'We are found out! Mistress Ashley is here.'

Thomas scrambled to his feet before a stout, middle-aged lady, plainly dressed, who favoured him with one suspicious look before, sounding hot and cross, she said, 'My lady, Master Cecil awaits you. You must come at once. You cannot receive him in that dress. Just how you managed to get out here without being seen I cannot imagine!'

'By being my usual devious self, dear Kat! I will come, but first you must greet Master Thomas Woodfall. He came seeking Rosamund Emory, and met me instead.'

Mistress Ashley curtseyed perfunctorily to Thomas, and the princess held out her hand for him to take upon a sleeve and bow over as she said, 'I have enjoyed meeting you, sir.' She hesitated. 'You still wish to speak with Mistress Emory?'

'I do, madam, for my own peace of mind and my father's.'

Slowly she nodded. 'I will see what I can do for you. Be here tomorrow, at about the same time. Good day, Thomas Woodfall.'

Prisoner she might yet be, spied upon without doubt and her every known movement reported upon, but she was well used to having her wishes gratified. She left, giving him no time for objection.

He stood gazing after the two women as they walked away, seeing them talking, before he bent to pick up his cloak. Had he overheard their conversation he would not have been flattered.

'The man is harmless, Kat, quite harmless. He reminds me of Edward Courtenay, although nicer, much nicer. Nothing without the guidance of a strong woman! I wonder if Master Woodfall has one in mind?'

Mistress Ashley shivered as she remembered the danger they had dwelt in some four or five years earlier when the young Edward Courtenay, Earl of Devonshire, after a childhood spent in the Tower, had been released and restored to favour. His early hopes of winning the hand of Mary Tudor dashed, he had turned his attention to her younger sister, convinced by those about him that he and a princess so obviously English would prove far more acceptable to the country than a middle-aged queen, herself half-Spanish and married to the King of Spain. Nor had Elizabeth, in correspondence at least, appeared unwilling. Courtenay's further imprisonment in the Tower, subsequent exile and mysterious death had come as a distinct relief to Kat Ashley. She glanced sideways at her mistress, but it had been a chance-made observation; already the princess had her mind on things of the present.

William Cecil had come to office in her brother Edward's reign and his extraordinary abilities had enabled him, when Mary came to the throne, to maintain his position when others had fallen. Now that Mary was dying he had put before Elizabeth proposals that would make the transition to a new ruler as smooth as possible. Elizabeth trusted the man entirely, for much the same reason that her sister did. No doubt if she came to the throne and died three months thereafter Cecil would work as wholeheartedly for her successor as he now did for her. He was one of very few men about the court to whom the thought of personal advancement, whilst acceptable, was not paramount. It was for the good of the country he worked, and Edward, Mary and Elizabeth Tudor to him were each of them England. She lengthened her stride so that Mistress Ashley had to run to keep pace with her and Thomas Woodfall passed, for the time being, from her thoughts.

Thomas took a room in a nearby village inn and next day was early for his appointment beneath the oak trees. One way or another he hoped to have word for his father before the day was out. Of only one thing he was quite sure. If Her Highness saw fit to send Rosamund Emory herself out to him, she would not beguile him as she had at Barndale. Charm she never so well, he would ask his questions and depart. On the whole, however, he hoped that a messenger would come and spare him any embarrassment. So deep in deliberation was he, staring down into the clear, swiftly running water of the stream, that he was startled by the voice that said crisply, 'Good day, Master Woodfall!'

He swung round and dropped to one knee almost at the same moment. Today Mistress Ashley had come with her, standing two disapproving steps behind, and the princess's clothes were more what he expected of a great lady. Dark green velvet made her fair skin look almost translucent, yet still he saw little of physical attraction, because he saw no possibility that he might interest her. To him she was only a possible source of obtaining the information he needed.

Obeying her gesture he rose, waited until she had seated herself on the tree trunk by the water, then joined her. She kept him in no suspense.

'Rosamund Emory knows nothing of your brother,' she said abruptly. 'I am sorry to have no better news for you, but she is telling the truth, that I'd swear.'

'Thank you, madam. I am not surprised. The boy could be anywhere. I – I had not expected to see you again, madam. I thought – a messenger perhaps . . .'

'Or the fair Rosamund herself?' Elizabeth's eyes glinted. 'You have done me a great favour, Thomas. You must realize that my sister is in the habit of placing amongst my household certain ladies who report to her on my doings. Rosamund Emory is the latest in a long line. But spy or no, she must make some show of obeying my orders and because of certain things concerning her recent – shameful – behaviour that you brought to my notice, she is confined to her room for three days on a rigorous diet. Oh, Thomas, I *did* so enjoy telling her that. It is the first time I have ever seen her mouth drop open in astonishment!'

The princess's own mouth opened wide as laughter took her. It was a small revenge but it had pleased her, and despite his disappointment Thomas was glad. As she sobered down, she asked, 'And where will you search now?'

Thomas had already made up his mind. 'Nowhere, madam. If the boy were in London I could look for weeks and never come across him, and that is only one place. I shall be better employed, I think, going home and helping my father. Heaven knows, I've done little of that in the past and now, with Edward and Lewis both gone, he needs me.'

The resolution about him pleased her; she guessed – and rightly – that it was new, and she found herself loath to let him go.

'Do you suppose, Thomas, that your father would spare you to me for a day or two?'

'Madam?'

'No longer than that, I promise. It will not be long before those about me realize that I am disappearing regularly and contrive to put a stop to it, but until then . . . To have someone to talk to who is not connected with my everyday life would be most pleasing. And Mistress Ashley will be delighted to accompany me.'

Even as he bowed dutifully, Thomas knew quite well what that lady thought of her mistress's proposal: disapproval showed in every line of her body.

'I should be honoured, madam,' he said.

4

Each day they met beneath the oak trees. The time varied and always Mistress Ashley watched them, but she had to admit that this young man was not like those who of late had come hoping to win her mistress's favour. The princess was right; he wanted nothing, expected nothing. He paid no extravagant compliments, he talked of things she had never seen and thereby brought her closer to the people over whom she soon would rule. Kat Ashley bent her head over sewing she had brought with her and let the two young people talk.

It was not, Thomas knew, a friendship. How could it be, between a country gentleman of minor rank and a future queen of England? Therefore he ceased to worry. He would remain until, as would soon happen, she tired of his company, then he would go on his way. They talked incessantly, or rather the princess questioned adroitly and Thomas talked. Before long she knew all about his life to the present – with the omission of certain Gilbert Lovelace-inspired passages that suddenly seemed sordid, although at the time he had thought them enjoyable – about his family and his forthcoming marriage to Eleanor Coulton.

'Do you love the lady?'

'She was my father's choice for me, madam.'

'Aha! She brings a goodly dowry therefore?'

'Land!' said Thomas briefly, and the princess nodded in understanding.

'Such marriages work as well as any.' Her tone was tart and it was on the tip of his comfortably unguarded tongue to observe that she herself must know more of such things than he, but he caught Mistress Ashley's warning look in time and said nothing. Gilbert had told him it was common talk that once Queen Mary was dead King Philip had it in mind to woo her sister. Thomas looked at the thin, strong face beside him and thought that more than one person was in for a surprise if this young lady ever came to the throne. He thanked God that he would not be near enough to see the fireworks!

That was as near as they ever came to talking about her life. Pity welled in his unimaginative heart at what she did not say. To hear of people living under threat of death, to be told that they were imprisoned, released, imprisoned again, meant nothing after all. One said one was sorry, and secretly gave thanks that it was all happening far away. Actually to meet and talk with someone who had been used thus for the greater part of her life was a different matter. For the first time Thomas felt for someone else more deeply than for himself.

Only once did he attempt to joke.

'How old are you, Thomas?' she asked one day, out of the blue.

'Twenty-one, madam.'

'I am twenty-four.' He could see no reason for question or answer; almost it sounded like a child's boasting and, without thinking, he replied, 'In age, as in all things, you excel me, madam.'

The next moment the space between them was no more; the royal palm struck hard across his face and he sat there gaping, with red fingermarks down one cheek. It was the one time he met the Tudor temper and the only time he heard Kat Ashley laugh. So surprised was he that he did not apologize, nor did the princess appear to expect it, for she immediately turned the conversation and once again they were on to everyday topics. The incident served to demonstrate to Thomas the ever-present line between royalty and common folk: he was most careful never to cross it again.

Three such meetings they had, and the weather favoured each, but on the third day the princess announced, regretfully, that the pattern of her movements had aroused suspicion.

'Go home, Thomas,' she said gently. 'Marry your – Eleanor, was her name? – but remember me.'

Thomas bowed, smiled. 'I do not think that anyone who ever met you could forget you, Your Highness.'

'And you will be able to tell your family of our talks.'

Shocked, he replied, 'Most certainly not! What has been said here remains between us. It is for no-one else.'

The firmness in his tone was stronger than usual and she said, 'You are a true friend, Thomas. Come to my coronation when I send for you.'

'No,' he said slowly. 'At least, if you command I must obey, but I would ask you to excuse me. I should be sadly out of place, you know. But I will pray for you and I promise that if ever you need me I will do all in my power to help you.'

It was the weak offering assistance to the all-powerful, but it was sincerely meant. His bright blue eyes shone, and there was no hint about his lips of the ingratiating smile she saw so often in others. Therefore on impulse she slipped from one finger a simple gold band with three red stones and, as on the day he had first met her, he went down on one knee before her.

'Will you carry it on a chain about your neck for my sake, Thomas?'

'No, madam, I will not.' He looked down at the jewels glowing against his broad palm, and he did not fail her. 'For then someone might see it and ask questions. But I will keep it safe.'

The suspicion that life had bred in her made her say,

only half in jest, 'It is a keepsake, no more. You are not to send it to me one day in hope of receiving a favour.'

He was indignant as only a simple man could be, and for a moment she thought he would hand the ring back to her. Whilst he hesitated she put out a long, white hand and stroked his fair hair back from his forehead.

'Forgive me, Thomas. I am unused to people willing to do anything for nothing. The thought was unworthy. Goodbye, my friend. Perhaps one day we shall meet again.'

With the words she turned and strode away across the meadow, holding her skirts high to avoid the long grass and the cowpats that had made her laugh at him during their first meeting. Then, for the first time, Kat Ashley gave Thomas more than a curt word or nod.

'Thank you, sir. You have been a kind friend to my lady when that was what she needed most.'

Thomas rode away to collect his belongings from the inn. Already he was finding it difficult to believe that the last days had been more than a dream. And never once in all that time, he realized with a shock of surprise, had he given a single thought to Rosamund Emory.

5

Thomas Woodfall would have been astounded to know that if thoughts could have killed, Mistress Catherine Ashley would have laid him out stiff and cold not many weeks after his visit to Hatfield Palace.

The Princess Elizabeth with whom he had shared his simple food, to whom he had talked as a – very respectful – friend, had been three months Queen of England when Mistress Ashley, now mistress of her maids-in-waiting, had been forced to bring to her attention the fact, long known by everyone else, that Rosamund Emory was pregnant. Already, before her condition became apparent, a message had been sent to Mistress Emory's home asking for an escort to come south and collect her; her services were no longer required.

Questioned by Mistress Ashley, with the Queen, at her own insistence, secreted behind a curtain, the girl was self-possessed, untroubled. Indeed she was pregnant. The father? Thomas Woodfall. Perhaps Mistress Ashley knew that he had come to her at Hatfield? He had, she believed, also spoken to the Queen herself during his visit. Calculations made it certain that the baby must have been conceived at about that time. Mistress Emory, steadfast in her intention to travel to Highwoods as soon as possible, in spite of being told that Master Woodfall had recently married, and certain that he would provide for her, was dismissed to her room until sent for.

Behind the curtain Mistress Ashley found what she had dreaded, and hurried to inform Her Majesty's ladies that their services would not be required that night. Much as she hated the sly, smirking looks that passed between them as they drew their own conclusions, Kat would for once have been glad had they been justified. She hastened back to her mistress who stood rigid as a statue, her face deathly white, one fist stuffed into her mouth.

Ever since, as Catherine Champerdowne, she had been appointed governess to the young princess, Kat had dreaded the flaming Tudor temper, but at that moment she would have given much to see it. If the Queen had thrown something at her – hard – she would have rejoiced. Anything rather than go through the night she knew lay ahead. Over the years she had guarded Elizabeth through such occasional paroxysms, had somehow kept them secret, confidently expecting them to disappear with maturity or when fear and uncertainty were no longer part of her mistress's life. Never once had they varied, and she dreaded the time when she would no longer be there to help, when someone else must be told.

There were no tears; only an overwhelming tortured anguish, pitiable to see, of which few would have believed their self-possessed and autocratic young Queen capable. And there was nothing Mistress Ashley could do to help the charge for whom she would have died, for whom once indeed, in more perilous times, she had been imprisoned in the Tower and closely questioned. She must stay where she was, let the battle progress as it always did. Knuckles gleaming with saliva, indented by teethmarks, left Her Majesty's mouth. Slowly, as if in church, she knelt. Her eyes closed; she brought her hands almost together, began familiar movements. She was telling an invisible rosary, each bead a prayer for a woman betrayed, women she had known personally, or whose lives had touched hers fleetingly, or of whom she had heard tell. She made no sound, but Kat knew the names too well not to be able to lipread them.

First, always first, came the mother she knew only as a portrait. Anne Boleyn, defamed, slandered; then others of her father's wives, his first, put aside in hope of a son, the later silly women pushed towards acceptance of a match they had not wanted by men who sought power through them. A young cousin, proclaimed queen and executed. A sister, never loving, seldom kind, who had grovelled pitifully for the favour of a husband whose only interest had been in her kingdom and who, before she was even dead, had let it be known that he would woo her sister as soon as propriety permitted. Then the head rocked backwards and there came the name she had added to the list at the age of fourteen, when things imagined turned to brutal reality as Admiral Thomas Seymour had taken his arrogant male way with an innocent girl under his wife's protection. Not dead this time, but alive to suffer and remember. Elizabeth Tudor.

In helpless curiosity Kat waited and in the coldness and stiffness that clamped her there wondered why. *Why?* Why did Elizabeth never pray that retribution be brought down on the men whose lust, ambition and sheer greed had caused so much agony and sorrow? Decani to her mistress's cantoris, Kat ticked them off on her own fingers, adding simple, unsuspecting Thomas Woodfall at the end, until she came in all honesty and regret face to face with her own part in the horror that had made Elizabeth unable to bring herself to respond to the love of a man.

It had been after the discovery of Thomas Seymour with

his young ward in his arms that his wife, pregnant and ill, had insisted that Elizabeth leave her house. Carrying her own unspoken fears with her, Kat had accompanied the girl to the house of Sir Anthony and Lady Denny at Cheshunt. Scandal had been scotched; not so the remarks of Lady Denny, who was Kat's sister Joan.

Sympathetic enquiries had elicited the information that the princess's monthly flow was most irregular, that as her flat figure showed, she had not fully matured. And holding that knowledge Joan Denny had put Kat's fear into words. What if the princess were pregnant? Was Kat *certain* that the Admiral had not – simpering now – had his way with her? Better be safe than sorry, dear sister, unless you wish to find yourself blamed for a situation impossible to right if much time be lost. Lady Denny could furnish a potion, proved to have worked in the past, that would make certain that the young princess was – to all intents and purposes – unsullied. For long Kat held out against the suggestion until, exasperated and fearful, her sister's persuasion gave way to spite. No doubt all was well. After all, the girl could not be called attractive. There was something almost – masculine – about her, had not Kat observed it? The living image of the late King, in mannerisms as in colouring. And whilst that put paid to the rumours that he was not her father, well . . . Of course, if ever she came to the throne there would be men and to spare around her, but then everyone knew men would do anything for power . . .

It was at that moment that Kat had caught sight of the thin, childish figure, the drawn white face in the doorway, but her outraged warning to her sister came too late. The princess said nothing, then or ever, about what she had overheard. Next morning she swallowed the nauseating draught given her by the two women. Whatever it did or did not prevent, it made her violently ill, so that Kat feared for her life. That illness lasted all summer, during which time came news of the death of Thomas Seymour's wife in childbirth. Whether or not Elizabeth was pleased that he was free, could marry her if the Lord Protector and Council so pleased, Kat could never find out, despite much probing, and ere long the Admiral in his lust for power over-reached himself, came to the block and was never mentioned in the princess's household again.

It was soon after that that Elizabeth began what Kat termed her 'game'. From an early age she had spoken of her decision never to marry, never to be used as so many women were, and whether or not she was serious at the outset, most certainly she was now. Humiliated by the frigidity she could not overcome, she yet found it worse to hear the world whisper that she was mannish, that men found her attractive only for the position that might one day be hers. So by the time she came to the throne she had been long embarked on the masquerade that, despite her occasional agonized attempts to turn it into something warm and real, was to last all her life.

To Kat's horror her mistress, one of the most accomplished women of her time when it came to matters scholastic, as adept at politics and diplomacy as any man, had shown as little discrimination as the most ignorant serving wench in her kingdom when it came to the choice of a romantic partner. Elizabeth had known Robert Dudley since childhood: their common bond was that he, too, when his family over-reached itself in its search for power, had known imprisonment and fear of death. He was of the same type as Thomas Seymour; large and lusty. Only the colouring was different, but the dark-haired Dudley was cleverer than the Admiral had ever been, far cleverer. He accepted a relationship that would never be other than flawed because by it he remained close to the throne. Kat was not the only person to wonder whether he ever seriously expected the desperate flirtation, which was to end only with his death, to turn to something more permanent and powerful.

Often he lived in close proximity to the Queen, he paid her extravagant compliments in public, she allowed him to touch her hand, and occasionally – in public – to kiss her. They exchanged most passionate letters and gifts of great price for all to see. Undoubtedly there was intimate friendship, but there were times when it seemed as if a sheet of ice came down between them. Kat had seen Elizabeth look at the courtier as if she had never met him before. When she was in command of herself, which was most of the time, she handled him as a wild-animal tamer with a whip. But suppose he came across her in the state of shock that possessed her now? Treacherous, like all his family, he might well see his chance and take it. And throughout all he remained married to a wife he seldom saw, took mistresses less sparing of their personal favours than was the Queen, making her insanely jealous when she found out about them. And because she was in love with him, or wanted to be, and needed to be seen to be, time and again she forgave him his promiscuous behaviour. He grovelled before her, promised to reform, assured her that she was the star of his life, and the dance began once more. Kat Ashley's prayers on the subject of Robert Dudley made those she spent on Thomas Woodfall almost kindly by contrast.

All through the night Kat waited for the first signs that the spasm was abating. The first white streaks of dawn were in the sky before she was rewarded. The young Queen's rigid hands dropped into her lap, her eyelids flickered and gently Kat said, 'It is day, madam. Let me put this robe around you.'

For a moment they were back in the days when she had been nurse and more than nurse. The regal head, the gilded ornaments of the evening before still fastened in its hair, turned to her, fell upon her shoulder.

'They are all the same,' mouthed the white, pinched lips. 'Not one to be trusted, not one.'

'The day is here, madam. Your country looks to you. You cannot afford to be ill.'

So many illnesses there had been in the long years when her fate hung in the balance and Elizabeth, with the fierce courage that enabled her to hide her fear from all about her, hated more than anything the way her body, with its swellings and its rashes and its fevers, betrayed her. She sipped the wine that Kat held to her lips and slowly returned to normal.

Recall the night she might not, but the Queen most certainly remembered what had provoked the shock that racked her. No reason now to wish for temper, to complain of lack of it.

An hour later Mistress Emory, haled half-asleep from her bed, her considerable self-confidence gone, knelt and trembled before the woman she had once been sent to spy upon. Even Kat Ashley was excluded from that interview, nor did she ever learn what had been said. Her father's courier, when he arrived, was told to return alone to the Borders to inform his master that Mistress Rosamund would stay at court until it pleased Her Majesty to allow her to leave.

When eventually she was dismissed, Rosamund Emory was very near her time, and exhausted after long, hard working hours. Thus she paid the price for destroying yet another of her Queen's naive attempts to find friendship with a man, binding, cloying friendship that called always for a man's complete and utter subjection, his renunciation of all other women, in exchange for nothing more than the royal smile and, if he were highly favoured, the brush of his lips across bony, beringed knuckles.

CHAPTER III

1

'If'n I'd bin a mite early, an' I might ha' bin this time o' year an' wi' Maister Thomas ahurryin' me an' all, 'ow 'ud ee ha' gone along then, ee tell I that! A-bin sittin' by the way yet, ee would!'

The chance-met traveller who perched so precariously on the load of turnips made no reply, and Luke Morris's voice took on a more bullying tone. 'Nobody else 'ud ha' come thisaways tonight, 'tis for certain. What 'ud ee ha' done? Eh? Ee tell I that!'

There had been times, after boyhood escapades for which Luke had always received the exceedingly painful blame, when he had thought that one day he would get his own back on the Woodfall twins. Yet his first – and continuing – feeling when, on stopping to give a ride to a tramp slumped by the wayside, he had discovered him to be none other than Master Edward, had been one of pity and dismay, and even whilst he hectored he was wondering what he could do to help. He must deliver the young master to the stables and call someone who would clean him up, rid him of crawling things and the overpowering stench of ingrained dirt and stale drink that clung to him, before his family saw him. He turned on his seat, looking over his shoulder, and at last received an answer.

'Walked. Would have walked, like always,' and there was a spark of laughter in the slurred voice that sounded for an instant like the Edward Woodfall of old. It was the only thing about him that had not changed in the year or more he had been gone. The gathering gloom beneath the trees showed the skin of the thin face bleached, its freckles faded to blotches. And Luke, when he lifted him on to the wagon, had been horrified at the lightness of his body. To cover his emotion he snorted, 'Where ee bin, tell I that?'

The only answer was a hunching of Edward's shoulders and Luke acknowledged himself beaten; albeit he took a parting shot. 'All I can say is, wherever 'twas, didn't do ee much good, 'tis a fact!'

Edward, staring unseeingly back along the track they had covered, was beginning to wonder dully if he should not order the wagon halted and make his way to some place where his family would never find him, when he was seized by a racking cough and for the next few moments needed what was left of his strength merely to remain where he was.

'Home!' he gasped, and closed his eyes.

'But I didn't take ee 'ome, that I did not,' Luke told his wife later that night when passenger and turnips had both been disposed of. 'Awaitin' 'er was, along o' 'er gate as if 'er knew 'e were acomin'. Mistress Agnes I means, woman.'

Peg had married Luke when they were both twelve years old and had since borne him a child each year. Against all odds every one of them had survived, even the two congenital idiots who did nothing but lie on their backs all day on piles of rags staring into some invisible world of their own, so that now six of them were packed into the two-roomed hovel and at times she wanted to scream. Already the seventh was beginning to move within her. She hated Agnes Woodfall, had no interest at all in her or her family. The woman, no better than she ought to be, as everyone knew, lived alone except for her maids, in a house that had rooms enough to take a dozen children.

Peg leaned over the fire and stirred the mess of grain and scraps of rabbit meat that formed the evening meal before she peered across the smoke-filled room and allowed herself to wonder what had come over her Luke. So he had given a lift to the master's son who had gone off just when it pleased him, and now he had come back to be met by the sister to whom anyone with any sense about them gave a wide berth. Her lips twisted; she would not give him the pleasure of being questioned, that she would not!

Luke, recognizing the symptoms his wife always displayed when she was pregnant, was not surprised at her attitude. Apart from being relieved that he did not have to deliver Master Edward to the manor house in the state he was in, what he had seen had affected him in some strange way he knew he could never put into words without embarrassing himself and making his wife roar with laughter. It had made him think of Peg before she lost her figure, when she still looked young and midwife Joan had put their first child into her arms. Nevertheless, with the mood still upon him, he tried: ' 'eld out 'er arms to 'im, 'er did, as if 'er was 'is mother and 'e went to 'er like some babby.'

Peg said viciously, 'Well, 'ers 'ad plenty to do in that direction lately. No wonder 'er father did throw 'er out!'

She broke off as her husband said sternly, 'That'll do, woman! Less o' that, unless you wants to be lookin' for a new place to live.'

Defiantly, determined for the second time that day to have the last word, he added, ' 'Er father did not throw 'er out. 'Er goes reg'lar to see 'ee. An' all I knows is that they looked right, so they did, right as – as could be!'

He knew, who did not, the tales that flew concerning Sir Herbert's only daughter, but she had never been other than kind to him, and he had watched in horror the great change that had come over her. It was a long time, he reckoned, since she had smiled as she had when he delivered her brother to her that day.

'Safe and sound,' Agnes had told their father when he had asked her if Edward would come home. So confident she had been, and here he was; safe, to be sure, but sound? It had taken this woman who thought she had no emotion left in her all her strength not to cry out as he slipped down from the wagon, balanced himself upon a pair of rickety crutches, and took one uncertain swaying step towards her; his left leg was missing from above the knee. But all she said, with a wealth of love in her tones, was, 'Welcome home, brother,' before, with a nod of thanks for the man on the wagon, she put her arms about him and supported him into the house.

Edward, with the effects of the ale he had drunk to bolster his courage rapidly wearing off, muttered, so that she could barely hear the words, 'The husks that the swine did eat,' and fought an overwhelming desire to turn his head on to her shoulder and cry.

She set him down on a settle by the fire in the central room of this building that had been a hunting lodge, and presently a maid brought a bowl of thick broth. At his sister's urging he drank, and by the fire's light she watched him take a degree of command of himself. Physical difference and starvation apart, whatever life he had lived had changed him so that at eighteen he looked old and drained. He peered up at the woman who was a tall dark shape with the firelight behind her, and managed, 'I'm drunk, Taggy, and I feel sick.'

He was very, very sick, bringing back all the nourishing broth he had taken, and he was in no state to eat or drink again. She held out her hands and he gripped them as if life might flow into his veins from her, opening his mouth to explain as best he could, but she forestalled him.

'Not now,' and her voice held that comfort, need for which had finally overcome pride and brought him home. 'First a good night's sleep, then we will talk. Come.'

She pulled him up, put a strong arm about him so that like a child he went with her into a small room, where she undressed him as once his nurse had done, covered him with a soft blanket woven from the wool of the sheep that ran on the estate. 'Drink this.' She held a cup to his mouth and obediently he swallowed. 'Rest quietly, Edward.' She bent over, kissed him gently on the forehead and left him.

'In the morning,' she said to the maid who awaited her instructions, 'you will burn all that bedding, except the blanket. That you will hang over the hedge until it is thoroughly aired. Good night, Abigail.'

He had been so tired all day – on the wagon, on

Agnes's settle, whilst he was drinking broth, even as he was undressed – that it seemed impossible to Edward that he should not sleep, yet he lay for hours in the first comfortable bed he had been in for months with his eyes wide open, staring up at the patterns flickering firelight threw on the beamed ceiling, every nerve on the strain. Whatever Agnes had given him to drink had not soothed him at all. 'Too tired to sleep,' as his mother had been used to say to him and Lewis after a day's rushing and exploring. Thoughts chased themselves round and round his brain. Lewis. He had not even asked after his twin, or his father. Nor, if it came to that, had he asked Agnes how she was herself or why she was living in this place instead of at Highwoods. Still more concerned for himself than for anyone else, as he always had been, he told himself angrily. Vaguely, alarmingly, he became aware that there was something different about Agnes; what, he could not say, and as he shifted position his amputated leg began to throb with pain right down to the end of the toes he no longer possessed. It had happened before, often, and if he had not had money to buy the drink that would deaden it he had ground his teeth and borne it, but now there was Agnes, who knew how to stop pain, who could give him something . . .

Very slowly he pulled himself up. Agnes had taken his filthy ragged clothes, and he did not blame her. Across the foot of the bed lay a full-length woollen robe that he seemed to remember his father wearing. Pulling it on, he struggled on to his crutches, wondering if the longing to walk as once he had would ever leave him.

There was no sound in the hall when, by the light of the dying fire, he at last made his way there. His sister and all her household had gone to bed. Dim and golden below the bottom of a door opposite was a light and he knocked as firmly as he could, hoping he would not find himself disturbing the giggling, embarrassed child who had brought his broth earlier. To his relief, Agnes's voice bade him enter and he walked into a dream; that was the only explanation his over-tired, pain-racked brain could produce, and as in a dream he unquestioningly accepted what he saw.

She sat in a rocking chair by a cradle and as if it were the most natural thing in the world said, 'Come in, Edward,' before she turned back to the swaddled babe at her breast.

'Close the door to keep out the draughts.'

Once, he dimly believed, there had been a time when he would have taken the initiative, would have asked questions, but now someone had fastened a cord about his head, had pulled it tight and stopped him thinking.

'My leg hurts, Taggy.'

'Of course. Sit down on the bed and wait until this young man is contented, then I'll help you. It won't take long.'

It was warm in this room, warm and softly bright with candlelight bathing tapestry-hung walls. Edward blinked, blinked again and found his eyes too heavy to keep open. His leg still hurt but the sleep that had eluded him until now overtook him suddenly, or perhaps Agnes's draught had worked at last. Slowly he toppled sideways on to her pillow and was instantly as deeply unconscious as he had ever been.

Gently Agnes laid the baby back in its cradle, pulled her bodice across her breasts and tucked the coverlet that had once belonged to his mother under her brother's chin. Nothing would wake him before morning, a morning she dreaded, when all that had happened since he had gone away must be explained. A day – she tried to distract herself by mundane thoughts – when there would be two beds to be cleansed instead of one!

2

The room was bright with daylight when Edward opened his eyes, and his head had cleared. He looked about him and remembered: he was home, or very near it. He had dreamed of a cradle beside a bed and of Agnes suckling a babe. He smiled at his stupidity. It had been a dream, of course, for there was no cradle. Slowly he pulled his robe straight, ashamed of what he had become and the story he must tell, splashed his face from a bowl of ice-cold water that stood on a chest and made his way into the hall that was also the lodge's main room.

And there was his dream that was no dream after all, for his sister stood by the window looking out at bare-branched orchard trees with a baby laid over her shoulder. As she stood she swayed from side to side so that even as he watched the child was lulled into sleep. Without looking round she said, 'Good morning, Edward. You will feel better today, I dare say!'

All thought of his own situation was driven from his head. Again she was but a dark shape outlined against light and fear snatched at him as he realized that never once since he arrived had he seen her clearly. They had met when his eyes were blinded by tears, she had been outlined by firelight, she had sat by her bed with her face invisible in dim candlelight, and now the sharp winter morning showed only a graceful black shape. He knew a sudden urgent need to see her, to find that something in his changed world was constant.

As fast as he could he stumbled over to the window, put himself between it and Agnes, and, 'Face me!' he ordered.

It was her turn to obey. She stood waiting patiently whilst he took in the change in her.

'Twelve months can be a very long time, brother.'

He gazed in horror at the once-beautiful face gone gaunt, at blue eyes sunk deep into black hollows, at dark hair streaked with grey. She looked older than their father, more haggard than he remembered his mother in her last illness. There was no wedding ring on her long, bony hand. He made a gesture that took in both her and the child she held.

'Whose child have you borne?' His voice was fierce.

'The child is not mine, Edward.'

'But I saw you suckle it last night.'

'This *it*, as you call him, is Robert, who came to me in place of my own little Angharad, who died.'

59

Edward said grimly, 'You are right, I have been away a long time. There are many things I need to know, Agnes.'

Outwardly calm, she faced the one person in all her world whom she would allow herself to love, and the grip of her fingers tightened so that the babe, although he did not waken, stirred and whimpered uneasily.

'I will put down Robert, and you shall hear all there is to tell.' She left him, to return scarcely a moment later and take a seat beside him on the high-backed settle before the hearth.

His head was clear again, the terrifying half-stupor, half-tiredness of yesterday banished by sleep and his own troubles forgotten at sight of his sister's, but Edward scarcely knew what to ask or where to begin. Not for the world would he hurt her – who had obviously already been hurt almost beyond endurance – by prying into places that were private to her alone. He must begin by asking about members of his family and lead on to other things, if she would permit him.

As if she knew what was going through his mind, she said, 'First things first. Father is well, although not as well as I have known him. Your homecoming will cheer him beyond measure. Thomas married Eleanor Coulton not long after you left.' A smile flickered across her face. 'She rules the house with a rod of iron. And the best news of all – you are an uncle! Lewis and Anne's daughter – another Anne – was born in the summer. Another one is well on the way by now, I dare say.'

He swallowed hard, bracing himself to be repulsed, half wishing to be. 'But what of you, Taggy, what of you? The – the child that – that died, the babe with the strange name, was it John Stratton's? But surely not, he loved you too well.'

'Her name was Angharad. No, not his.' She did not flinch and her voice sounded as unconcerned as if they were discussing some other person. 'If you will promise not to interrupt I will tell you everything.'

Edward shifted on the uncushioned seat, propping himself in its corner so that he could watch his sister's face.

'My baby's father was Gilbert Lovelace – no, *no!* – you promised not to interrupt! He came to the manor several times when you were all away and I asked Thomas to warn him away. That was a grave mistake. It only made him the more eager and at Thomas and Eleanor's wedding he – he came after me . . .'

The bright, homelike room on the edge of the woods melted before her eyes. There was no child in the adjoining room and her young brother was not watching her with horrified attention. She was once again back at the splendid festivities of the previous year that for her had ended in nightmare. Not for Thomas the austere celebrations insisted upon by the Harringtons. He and his bride were to be bedded publicly, to the accompaniment of the ribald jokes and coarse merriment that so delighted Thomas's cronies. Eleanor might disapprove – who could tell with a face as thin and frozen as hers? – but she had the sense not to protest. It was Thomas's last fling; after today he would do as he was told. He appeared not to know it, but to his companions of Oxford and London it was all too apparent. They drank and shouted, drank and joked and drank again until it seemed possible that bystanders could become drunk on the fumes of the wine and ale that rose about them, and always in the van, urging them on yet drinking little himself, was Gilbert Lovelace. Clad from neck to toe in dark red brocade that set off his golden hair and pale skin, he had seemed to Agnes evil in his beauty and vanity. All day – as had happened the day before – she was aware of his eyes following her wherever she went, and because of it she had taken precautions when the day was young.

As she dressed in the pale blue velvet that set off her coppery skin and highlighted shining blue eyes, she told her maid that she would not require her that evening and locked the door to her room that no-one might enter. All day long she carried the key, cumbersome as it was, in the pouch at her waist. When the shouts and catcalls that accompanied the bridal pair to their bedding grew faint behind her, she slipped away and ran the last few yards along the unlit passageway, let herself into the darkness of her room and turned the key behind her in the lock. Two steps and she reached a candlestick and tinderbox left in readiness. A candle to light, the fire to be rekindled in the grate and then to bed. She was safe: the morrow could take care of itself.

The kindling on the hearth caught fire readily and she had half-risen to her feet when something cold touched her bare shoulder, something that moved sharply downwards, scratching as it went like the claws of a cat. With a gasp she spun round, to find herself face to face, in the first leaping firelight, with a silently laughing Gilbert Lovelace, who between the fingers of one hand twirled the ear of corn, pulled from some wedding decoration, with which he had scored her. For an instant she had the better of him, for instead of turning to run as he had expected, she launched herself at him, her fingers rigid like talons to rake his face. But, his surprise over, he took the initiative, gripped one arm and twisted it up behind her back. The smile on his face, coldly, cruelly sober, turned her sick with fear. He might look effete, but he was far stronger than she; he held her effortlessly. Who would hear her if she screamed, or take notice if they did, in the midst of the revelry that filled the house?

'How did I get in after you so carefully locked the door?' he mocked.

'Please, oh please,' she whispered, but the face so close to her only approached the nearer.

'No need to beg, my dear,' he said in his silken tones, 'you shall have your due without that! No-one, *no-one*, do you hear, warns me to stay away, especially a gypsy bastard.' As he spoke he was forcing her over to the bed, his free arm unlacing her dress with practised ease.

Fighting panic, conditioning herself to inevitable submission, she told herself that what would please him more than anything was that she should plead for mercy, should show fear and pain. Accordingly, through what seemed an age of being beaten, bruised and hurt, she writhed and moaned and implored that he let her go, until she was not sure where pretence ended and genuine pleading began.

And all the time a crystal-clear corner of her mind was praying, praying to the God the Woodfalls worshipped and in whom she had never believed, that she should not hate this brute who was violating and spoiling her body, should not remember harmful phrases and words taught her by her mother long ago. For surely if anything befell him before his brief association with her were forgotten she would be deemed to have put the evil eye on him and would suffer as her mother had suffered. The old fear she had tried to explain to her father tormented her mind just as this man was tormenting her body. Therefore she tried to pray to a God of peace and love in whose name Gilbert had doubtless been christened.

At last, sated, Lovelace rolled away from her. 'You will know better in future,' he said, and she could tell from his voice that he had found no enjoyment in her.

'Will you put a spell on me, or did your mother die before she had time to teach you her tricks?' He mocked but she wondered if perhaps he were afraid, and as she lay there, making no attempt to cover her naked, torn body from his gaze, laughter took her, high hysterical laughter, so that, half-dressed, he stood and stared until she gasped, 'You are quite safe, Gilbert Lovelace, quite safe.'

Only once more she spoke to him. As he turned to leave she asked, 'Tell me one thing. Where did you get a key?'

He hesitated long enough to inflict a final wound and to enjoy her reaction. 'Thomas gave it to me.'

This time there was no play-acting in her moan of pain. Thomas, who had seemed so much kinder since Edward's disappearance, was mesmerized as he always had been by Gilbert Lovelace, by the desire to stand well in his eyes. He would do anything to please his friend, even to rendering up his half-sister's body for a night's easy amusement. She was conscious of only two things: the cold, heavy weight of the key beneath her body and, equally cold and heavy, a sterile hatred of Lovelace and of Thomas. Not yet, because of her fear, but one day when they had forgotten what had happened, as men so lightly forgot, she would be revenged upon them both and they would wonder what had brought about their downfall.

Quite how much she told out loud she did not know. Edward's horrified voice called her back to the present.

'Lovelace *raped* you?' and then, so that she knew she had said very little, 'Thomas dealt with him, of course.'

Very quietly Agnes said, 'No. Lovelace was gone before morning. No-one has seen him since. I kept the matter quiet until I knew I would bear a child. Father would have ridden to London himself then, but I begged him not to. Consider: Lovelace had been known to come here before to see me. I had told my maid not to come to my room that night. In the world's eyes I received a visit I was expecting and the outcome served me right! It would have been his word against mine, after all.'

Thomas had, not surprisingly, avoided her after the fateful night, apart from one stumbling attempt to apologize: he had been grateful for her seeming readiness to keep the matter from their father, for he knew Lovelace well enough to envisage the delight with which he would inform Sir Herbert just how he had gained access to Agnes's room. Once the matter was general knowledge, opinions in the neighbourhood were only what Agnes expected. She must have encouraged this man, must she not? Besides, what matter? She of all people knew how to rid herself of an unwanted child.

'Why did you not make a potion for yourself?' Edward was asking the same question. What would he have said, she wondered, if she had told him the truth, that she had borne an unwanted, never-to-be-loved child that she might raise it to further her vengeance on those who had betrayed her? That thought carried her, outwardly serene, through nine months; it was not then that her looks had changed.

'Father gave me this house for my own and I decided to bear my child. Eleanor was glad to be rid of me. Almost twelve months married and no sign of a child herself. I am a sore reproach to her!'

'But your Angharad died,' prompted Edward gently.

'My little chrisom child. For three short weeks she was mine, for four endless weeks she has been lost.'

His throat tightened at the sudden anguish that rang in his sister's voice. 'But you did not bear your pain alone. Tell me you were not alone. Please.'

Agnes patted his hand, kindly, reassuringly. 'I had all the help I needed at the birth, my dear, and when the time came that I needed real help there – there was Master Acres – dear Father Peter. He saved me from despair.'

Peter Acres, homeless after the dissolution of Highwoods Abbey, had been part of the Woodfall family life for as long as Edward could remember. He had taught the twins, had rendered easy the paperwork of the estate that Sir Herbert found so irksome and was loved by everyone – except Agnes. She, torn between two cultures, had watched her half-brothers tease the gentle quondam priest unmercifully and had vented her anger on him, scorning him for the soft life he had chosen. Later, when the time was right, Edward would ask what had brought about her change towards him; now his part was to listen, to comfort if he could.

Agnes continued, 'He christened my little one and when the time came and the thought of her locked in the dark emptiness of the family vault was more than I could bear, he found a sheltered corner in the abbey ruins for her little body. She was so small, Edward, so very small, and it seemed so much kinder and warmer for her there. Peter said once sacred ground, always sacred ground, no matter what men did to it.' She looked at her young brother anxiously as if seeking assurance.

'You can trust Father Peter, Agnes.'

She shook her shoulders as if to rid herself of some well nigh impossible burden. 'Better him than the new man in the village.'

There fell a silence between brother and sister. He thought of the baby – Robert – in the next room. Could she have taken a village child to fill arms emptied by the loss of Angharad? A strange name, perhaps one learned from her mother. Had she needed something small and helpless to tide her over her grief? Shocked as he was by

65

her story, much as he loved her, that the daughter of the lord of the manor should act as wet nurse to a stranger's child ran counter to his upbringing.

'And this child?' he asked at last, as she showed no sign of saying more. 'Where did he come from, and why to you?'

Agnes roused herself, looked at this young man who was now all she had to love or wanted to love. There was no way of breaking the news gently to him. 'He came to me out of the night. A dark, stormy night when the wind in the trees was so loud it seemed to shake the house. How long the woman had been at the door before Abigail or I heard her I have no idea, but there came a lull in the storm and she knocked again. She was dying of hunger and neglect, and the child was tied to her breast by a shawl. She was almost beyond speech and certainly beyond any help of mine. The child too was starving, but that was an easy matter. He took my milk as if he had been born to me. The mother died, Edward, that same night. She is buried in our family vault.'

'In . . .? A chance-come stranger?' Yet even as he asked, the look on his sister's face brought the dawning of truth.

'You knew her, brother, this woman from the storm.'

Edward said nothing, only reached for his crutches, swung himself across the room and into the bedroom, followed by his sister. Standing by the cradle he said harshly, 'Waken him! Make him open his eyes!'

Agnes drew a finger down the sleeping child's cheek. The round face above the tight swaddling clothes turned slightly in protest, then eyelids slowly opened. Edward leaned over the cradle and Agnes heard him catch his breath. She knew what he feared to see, but the child was too young to favour anyone yet.

'Rosamund Emory?' His calm matched hers now.

'Yes, brother.'

'Then his father is . . .?'

'Thomas. That is why she made her way here.'

With a small mewing cry the baby had gone back to his disturbed sleep and Edward, swaying between his crutches, gazed intently down at his small nephew. As from a distance he heard Agnes tell him that Thomas had been once to the house, too late to see the mother alive, had refused point blank even to look at Rosamund Emory's emaciated body although later, at his father's insistence, he had followed her to her burial.

Edward called a determined smile to his face. 'Fortunate child to be with you. Will you raise him or will Eleanor . . .?'

Agnes shrugged. 'No by-blows for Mistress Woodfall's household, as I am told she made very clear to Thomas! He stays with me unless his mother's family claims him, which is not likely.'

Edward had turned to go back to the hall before he said, 'It seems providential that this little one should come along so soon after your own child died.'

Behind him, Agnes's flat voice said, 'Angharad was still alive when Robert arrived. Two days later I lost her.'

'Dear God! No wonder you look so ill, Taggy.' Edward caught a ragged breath, turned from his sister's agony to his own lesser pain. 'Rosamund – was she still beautiful?'

Agnes resumed her seat beside him. 'You must understand that she had been a long time on the road . . . I could tell how beautiful she must have been when you met her.'

'She came all the way from Barndale to find Thomas? Her family disowned her?'

'No, oh no. She had been at Hatfield Palace, a maid-in-waiting to the Princess Elizabeth. Some time you must go to the church.'

Edward drew a great sigh, pulled himself together. 'No! She is gone and I owe debts enough to the living. If I had been here perhaps Lovelace would not . . .'

'That is my affair, brother. Nothing to do with you. There is one small thing I would like you to promise, however.'

'Anything, Taggy, you know that.'

'Then please never, never call me Taggy again. He always called me that.'

'John Stratton? Where is he now?'

'Sent away by his family shortly after you left for Barndale to break what they considered to be a most undesirable

connection. Since then I have seen him only once. He –
he . . .'

She broke off, her voice failing. She was nearer at that
moment to tears than Edward had ever seen her, but her
head went up and she forced herself to go on.

'He was in church when I did penance for my sin.'

'You did *what*? Father let you walk through the village
before anyone who cared to stare? Why did he not pay the
archdeacon's fine instead? That would have been sufficient,
surely, especially when the child was born through no sin
of yours.'

'I insisted.' Her voice was proud. 'One law for the rich
and another for the poor will not do in such matters. Besides,
nobody knows I was – forced.'

Another sacrifice paid at the altar of fear. Let the
peasants see her humiliation and they might laugh instead
of drawing aside from her and crossing their fingers when
she approached. But for Edward there was only the picture
of his dear sister, proud with the blood of her mother as
well as of the Woodfalls, draped in a loose white shift and
barefoot, being paraded into church to confess the bearing
of an illegitimate child.

'John was there.' She was sparing herself nothing. 'He
looked at me – so coldly. And there was a lady by his side
– the bride his father had chosen.'

'If ever I meet Gilbert Lovelace, he will rue the day!'
Edward's vow came from between clenched teeth. 'And I
shall have a word or two to say to Thomas about his choice
of friends.'

'There is nothing to say to Thomas: he knows it all. He –
he . . .' she paused, made herself continue. 'On that Sunday,
when I reached the churchyard, Thomas came and walked
alongside me. He stood with me all through the prayers,
his hand on my arm.'

'Bravo, Thomas!' For the first time since the start of
Agnes's story Edward felt friendship towards his brother.
He could not know how Agnes had hated Thomas for
his act of charity. Life must be black and white; there
was no room in it for villains who made kindly gestures,

68

who shattered, however briefly, the long-term pattern she was weaving.

She braced her shoulders. 'I have told you all this only to save you hearing some garbled, gossiping version elsewhere. I look forward, not back, brother. Edward – *Edward!*'

'It – it is nothing,' he muttered, 'my head swims, that is all,' but as he spoke he was losing his balance, sliding forward, head on chest, to the floor, his undermined strength finally used up by the emotions aroused within him during the past hour.

Over her shoulder, as she moved to support him, Agnes called for Abigail. 'You have heated the water? The tub, quickly, girl. He must be put to bed and I cannot afford to have more bedclothes ruined.'

To Edward she said, gently, 'The *whole* of you must swim, not just your head! Before you lie down, as you assuredly must, you will be clean, and I shall have a chance to examine that leg of yours properly.'

Her voice reached him from a far distance, high-pitched, unintelligible. When he came back to the present he was in bed, with Agnes bending over the stump of his leg, smearing it with cooling salve and wrapping it in strips of linen.

'Messy!' she said briefly, as she saw him watching her. 'As are the sores in your armpits. We shall have to find better crutches than those before you are up and about again.'

Edward put a hand over his face. 'I – I stole them. From a beggar lying dead in the street. I'm not very proud of myself.'

Agnes worked on. 'I should suppose not. I doubt if he missed them, however.'

Edward found a splutter of laughter he had not known was in him as his sister finished her work, straightened up and wiped her hands on a napkin. She pulled the bedcovers over his emaciated body, stroked his damp hair and tenderly kissed his forehead.

'Rest now, my dear. Sleep until it is time to eat. And I promise you that you will be – be up and about again in two or three days. *If* you obey my orders!'

She was turning to go but he caught at her wrist. 'Stay

with me. Do not leave me alone,' and she realized that until he had relieved his mind of the troubles that seethed within him he would never rest. She sat on the edge of the bed as if she had all the time in the world.

'From the beginning. When you left here, where did you go?'

'To make my fortune on the high seas.' His voice was slow and very careful, that the words might not trip one over another. 'We were scarcely out of the Channel when – when *this* happened. A mast snapped and I was too slow getting out of the way. My first gale and my last.'

'And then?'

'They put me on a homeward-bound ship – and ever since I've been trying to get up enough courage to come back here.'

'London, I suppose? All these many months?'

'Where else? It's where all the jetsam of life fetches up, isn't it? Especially when it doesn't want to be found. I begged for my bread. There was nothing else I could do. But I drank more than I ate. It helped me forget.'

'So I can tell! I had thought you had more sense!' Her voice was caustic. 'And now you've come back where you belong.'

He could not bear her kindness, not now. He had come home to abase himself and ask forgiveness, only to find that his running away had been the beginning of so much more damage than he had imagined. He reached out his arms beseechingly; tears poured down his thin face.

'All this – all that has happened to you was beginning that day I stormed in and announced that I was going away. Never a thought for anyone but myself! I doubt if I even looked at you. I shall never be able to forgive myself, never!'

Softly Agnes wiped his eyes with her handkerchief. 'All is well with me. No more torturing your brain now. Rest and become strong again, then go to Highwoods and make your peace with Father. It will not be difficult, that I promise you. I have sent word to the house that you are back but must not be disturbed for the present. You don't want dear Eleanor to see you with your hands shaking. You need all your strength when you face her. No! No more talking now. Close your eyes and rest. Other things, other days, my dear.'

Once more she kissed him and obediently he closed his eyes. Only as he began to sink into the comfort in which he was wrapped he murmured, 'Why Robert? There are none of that name in our family.'

As for Agnes, she went into the stillroom where she spent so much of her time and on the way looked in on her foster-son, asleep in his cradle. For a moment she stood beside him then, very gently, touched his soft cheek with the tip of one finger. He spent so much time asleep; almost as if he were storing up peace against a life that might not allow him enough of it later on.

'Born of a whore, suckled by a murderess! What chance do you stand?' she whispered. 'Ah, but I never thought that anything could hurt so much!'

CHAPTER IV

It was considerably longer than the two or three days with which Agnes had soothed him before Edward was anywhere near fit enough to present himself at the manor. They spent a quiet, healing Christmastide together, the two of them, until in the grey, drab light of a mid-January day, with his breath spurting visibly on to the frosty air, he sat on a fallen log in the orchard, at last well pleased with his recovery. An axe hung loosely between his hands and the trunk of the old apple tree he had reduced to logs lay splintered about him.

'The boy is progressing.'

At the sound of the thin, somewhat diffident voice Agnes looked up from her needlework and out of the window, in time to see her brother laugh as a squirrel landed on the ground before him, standing upright and waving its front legs as it scolded this human who did such terrible things to trees that did not belong to him.

'I think that is the first time he has laughed outright since he came home. Smiled, yes, many times; but never laughed aloud.' Her voice was tender. 'He is well enough now to go on his way.'

'Have you told him about his father? It will come as a shock to him if he knows nothing.'

'Hints only, Peter. What good would it have done to worry him before he was strong again himself?'

'True. You are wise, but the sooner he goes, the better

for all concerned. I care a great deal for Edward, you know, and owe much to his father.'

Agnes smiled at the bald, middle-aged man in shepherd's dress with an affection that had sprung into being suddenly on the night of her own deepest despair. He had been at Highwoods since long before she arrived and always he had seemed ineffectual, choosing to stay where food was plentiful and life easy, so that when he knocked on her door, offering her priestly comfort, she had screamed at him, 'What help can *you* offer? Go back to your sheep and to peasants who do not question!'

He had expected nothing else, yet with a strength he had not believed he possessed he had calmed her, had told her what no-one but Lady Woodfall had ever known in full: the story of a young seminary student, never more than average in attainment, who had gone into the Church only to find, once ordained, that the call of the secular world was far greater than he had known, that to keep his vows was well nigh impossible. Broken in health and spirit, he had left those who depended on him, those who came for aid he believed himself unqualified to give, and wandered until one night, exhausted and heartsick, he arrived at the gates of the Charterhouse of Highwoods, and thereafter found in the harsh self-discipline of the Carthusian life the beginnings of the true dedication and peace he so desperately needed.

After a time he adopted their heavy robes of natural wool, lived as the monks lived, praying alone in his cell, working his tiny plot of garden, always in silence and solitude, until the battles he fought with himself became less and there were times when, fleetingly, peace came to him. Yet he was not one of them, and this had been 1539 when the few remaining religious houses throughout the country were being visited by King Henry's vicar-general's teams of suppressors, who invited the leader of each community to sign an Act of Surrender which meant, in effect, compulsory closure and the making over of everything they possessed to the Crown. It was the end of the old monastic life in the land. Once the abbot had broken his vow of silence with the young Father Peter to voice his hope and ask his

73

prayers that this time, as before when smaller monasteries had faced dissolution in the interests of 'economy', their own abbey might be spared. In case this was not the will of God, however, the old man, having heard of the cruelty practised in the suppression of the Charterhouse of Smithfield and determined to save something, had given certain instructions which Peter swore on his life to obey to the letter, no matter what the cost.

So it was that one mild spring night, his heavy robes hampering his legs, sharp stones cutting into his sandalled feet, the young man found himself running as fast as he could go, away from the Charterhouse, through surrounding woodlands and into the grounds of Highwoods Manor, weighed down by a sack containing a jewel-encrusted chalice, a golden crucifix and the tall candlesticks from the high altar. Sir Herbert, newly come into his inheritance, took him in as if in accordance with some prior arrangement and hid the treasure so that, he said, none would find it.

The next morning Peter had returned to the Charterhouse in time to join the small huddle of monks and lay workers who stood in silence by the gates to watch Abbot Bernard riding away in the midst of a band of armed men. He had refused, they said, to sign the Act, as being against his conscience, but general opinion was that it was because the house's only known treasures were nowhere to be found – in their place had been standing ornaments of pewter that fooled no-one – that he had been dragged off to face his trial for heresy.

For the first time in his adult life, Peter forgot himself and his own needs in care for the saintly man who had given him sanctuary. Several weeks later he stood in the crowd and prayed as he had never prayed before for the soul of the abbot as he went calmly to the stake. There was no-one able or willing to pay for the faggots piled about him to be laced with gunpowder; it was a very long time before he died.

Grief and horror made Peter ill: always his mind was tormented by the thought that by surrendering the ornaments he could have saved the abbot's life. How he got back to

Highwoods Manor he never knew, but it was there that he awakened to the conscious world again, to find that a whole year of which he had no knowledge had elapsed since the execution, taking with it his always precarious health and what little self-confidence he had ever had. His hair had dropped out – it never grew again – he was skeleton thin and trembled uncontrollably when anyone spoke to him. He had, Lady Woodfall told him, lived in the room given him in a manner as like that at the Charterhouse as might be, fasting and praying all through his lost year, and he was to stay for as long as he wished.

Time healed him physically, but he was unable to face the world and it was only Lady Woodfall, who, several years later, saw in him a tutor for her lively twins. When the boys had no more need of him he had become one of Sir Herbert's shepherds; a job, he said, that would repay those who had shown him such kindness and that would allow time for contemplation and prayer. This was the man who had come to Agnes in her hour of need and, having bared his own soul, had succeeded in reaching hers. Timid soul had called to flawed and she had accepted the help she would not have taken from a stronger man.

Now he said quietly, 'My visits are not entirely for Edward's benefit; you know that, my child.'

'And am grateful for it.' Agnes rethreaded her needle and deftly knotted one end of the wool. After that one harrowing night, whenever he attempted to approach her personal feelings it was as if a door slammed in his face. 'All is well with me.'

'And although you were glad of my services for the child, for yourself they are not welcome.' His voice grew dry. 'Explain the difference to me.'

Once more the sewing stopped and Agnes met his gaze squarely. 'She – Angharad – was so small and innocent. For myself, I value your friendship and honour your confidence, and I am coward enough to go through the forms of worship in church each week so that none point a finger at me, but I must follow my own path. I think you know that. I am too old to change the ways in which I was raised.'

'At – how old are you? Twenty-two? Twenty-three?' Despite his worry, Peter Acres was amused. 'I shall not give up hope, Agnes. My prayers are with you always, and if ever you need me again you will send for me, will you not?'

Calmly Agnes said, 'I will send.'

'And you are reading the Bible I left with you?'

'I am.'

'Agnes, you must not set your heart too much on Thomas's child. If the Emorys agree, it is your brother's intention that he go to them.'

'He will stay here.' Agnes's voice was confident, and as if he knew that he was being talked about, at that same moment Robert's thin wail made itself heard. 'They will not send for him. Forgive me if I leave you for a while.'

Peter Acres, as he chose to call himself, watched her tall, graceful figure as she went to answer the child's cry for food and was horrified to realize that he had almost crossed himself as she spoke. In his years at Highwoods he had chosen to step aside from full-time search after faith, but the effect Agnes Woodfall produced in him was frightening. She had only to speak as she had just done for some superstitious part of him that should long ago have been conquered to struggle to the surface. She had accepted his help in recent sorrow; he must hold on to the belief that one day she would come again on her own behalf.

It was with relief that he heard the outer house door open and Edward's voice instructing Abigail to tell someone to collect together the wood he had chopped.

'Edward! This is more as you should be!'

'Sir! I am glad to find you still here.' Clumsily the young man sketched the bow of a pupil to his tutor.

'And alone, you mean?'

'Yes.' Edward glanced towards the bedroom door, lowered his voice. 'How is she, do you think?'

'Your sister? You are worried about her?' Master Acres felt a glow of personal pride – a sin for which he must later ask forgiveness. Edward and Lewis had turned out so much better, in his opinion, than had their elder brother, for all his grammar school and university training. He rejoiced that Edward's thoughts were not for himself but for his sister. Remembering the lecture on irresponsible behaviour he had read the young man when they met after his return, recalling the way Edward had stood to receive it, white-faced, unmoving, he loved him the more for his lack of resentment.

'Have you time to sit a while, sir?'

Waiting until they were side by side on the settle, Edward asked, 'Surely she is too calm? She – she told me what had happened when I first came and since then she has been much as she was in the old days, except for the difference in her looks.'

'You do not expect her to beat her breast and repeat the details to you day after day?' asked his tutor drily.

'Hardly that, sir! But we have always been close, she and I; in some ways more so now than ever, and she is too quiet, too strong. If only she grieved openly for her child I would feel that it were more natural. I – I am afraid that – that one day all she has kept pent up inside will burst out and she will do something terrible.'

'To herself, you mean?'

Edward frowned. Agnes treated him, even now he was fully recovered, with a tenderness, a motherliness he had never once seen her extend to young Robert. Him she fed and tended scrupulously, but she did not smile at him or croon as Edward, whose knowledge of small children was admittedly limited, had seen other women do to their babes. What would Master Acres say if he came out with, 'She does not love the child. Despite her desire to keep him, she does not love him. She wants him for some reason I cannot understand.'

Unable to bring himself to put his perplexity into words, feeling himself prey to the fears Lewis had always held, he said, 'I do not know. Yes, yes, it must be that. What can we – you – do to help her to peace, sir?'

'You came home when you were most needed, and if only your brother doesn't send that child to his mother's people, I think all will be well.' The older man hesitated. 'There is

77

something I can tell you – in confidence – that may ease your mind. Many a night at the abbey I have seen Agnes weeping on her knees beside her daughter's grave.'

He broke off suddenly as there came the sound of a door latch being raised. 'Have you made up your mind when you will move on?' he asked, as easily as if they had been discussing such matters for a time. 'Ah, Agnes! We must get this young man back on to his way in life as soon as possible.'

Edward knew it; his every instinct was to remain here in untroubled comfort, but honesty told him he could not. He owed his duty to the father he had deserted, who Agnes said needed him, and apart from providing – as he hoped – much-needed company for his sister, he knew that the work she found for him was only to keep him occupied. A woman as efficient as Agnes had long since had all the firewood she needed for the winter cut and stacked, just as she had meat salted and fruit and vegetables dried and preserved.

He had come home to ask forgiveness, so that he might take up his old position at the manor once more. It had not taken him long to realize that whatever his family might feel about his return – and a note from his father assured him of his welcome as soon as he was fit – life would not be as easy as that. In London, where he had begged and lived alongside beggars, he had rapidly become indistinguishable from hundreds of others, living in squalor, dodging the patrols who sought to send them back to whichever parish they hailed from, living in filth, eating filth. Here he was son of the lord of the manor, well-known and all his life liked, until the day he had run off for no very good reason that anyone knew of.

It had not been a good year for his family, what with his own absence and Agnes's trouble, and there were those who showed no slowness in blaming much of it on him. Sir Herbert was seldom seen about the estate these days. What passed for his instructions, although there were those who suspected that they originated largely from the new Mistress Woodfall, came either from easy-going Master Thomas, or through Bailiff Steadman, who commanded no-one's respect, nor ever had. There were times when Edward felt all eyes on him in censure because he had not been there when he was needed.

Agnes took her seat by the hearth and picked up her needlework. It was seldom that her hands were idle, even when she looked so tired that she could scarcely move. Her mouth curved into the loving smile that these days belonged to Edward alone.

'I have done my best to speed him on his way. Only creature comfort holds him. He has the means of transport.'

Both men laughed and Edward rushed into explanation. 'The main problem, sir, is how I am to get about most easily. As soon as this frost gives, the track between here and the manor will be impassable for me – on foot at least!'

So he could joke, thought his tutor, however hard it came. Good boy!

'And I can't see myself digging a wagon out of the mud if I get stuck, so horseback is the only way. Agnes's old mare is long past hard work. I doubt if she'd raise a trot if a bear were after her, but her pace suits me well. I've tried her along the track, and keeping my balance is none too difficult. I'm ready to go.'

Later that night, Edward sat opposite his sister in the soft light of candle and fire and tried to express his thoughts.

'I shall never be able to thank you, Tag – Agnes, for the way you've looked after me.'

'Nor do I expect you to.' Her tone was crisp. 'If I cannot look after my brother, whom I love, then it's a poor world we live in. You'll be no more than two miles away. I shall see you often.'

That Thomas had never once visited his brother whilst he was recovering Edward put down to reluctance to be near the baby Robert and the residue of guilt he must feel about what had happened to Agnes. Agnes, with no great opinion of Thomas's common sense, hoped that he would not betray himself on the subject of Gilbert Lovelace. So far no-one beyond the two of them knew the truth, unless Eleanor had wormed it out of him, and she would surely see that he kept silent. It had not taken his wife long to find out and turn to her own advantage the fact that Thomas was easily led if life, as a result, was comfortable.

Edward was brooding, as he often had of late.

'Will there be a place for me at Highwoods now, do you think? A *useful* place?'

'Father needs you, my dear. You have forgotten more about the land than Thomas could ever hope to learn, even if his heart were in it, which it is not.'

'He will hardly take kindly to my coming back and trying to teach him!'

If Edward had been looking at his sister as he spoke, instead of into the fire, he would have seen her smile as if she knew something he did not, but all she said was, 'Less imagination and more action, brother. Ride over there tomorrow.'

CHAPTER V

1

Edward, chilled through by the enforced slowness of his journey, turned Doll over to Agnes's groom and made his way into the lodge to confront his sister.

'You knew, did you not? All these weeks you have known!'

She made room for him before the fire, and said quietly, 'Good! You managed to ride there and back without falling into a ditch!'

'Agnes! For pity's sake, why did you not tell me about Father? He sent me back to you, said I could not stay there. *She* is a monster. How long has he been like that? And do you know what he said to me? Do you?'

'Not in so many words. Nor am I ever likely to find out if you do not calm down and tell me.'

Her manner communicated itself to him: sitting down beside her he forced himself to wait until his breath came more easily before he began to talk of his visit to Highwoods.

Men who had been filling in the emptied moat with rubble had stopped work and stared curiously at the altered son of the house come home as Doll plodded towards the manor house and Edward had felt a wide, rather foolish smile tugging at his mouth corners long before he was near enough to greet any one of them. It was, after all, the place where he had spent a happy childhood, and someone had carried word of his coming, for there was Ben, who had worked in the house for as long as he could remember, standing beside the open door.

'Welcome home, Master Edward, welcome.' The words were sincere but sounded more subdued than he had expected; the old man was avoiding his eyes. A twinge of unease caught at Edward.

In the time it took him to slither awkwardly down from Doll's broad back and unsling his crutches from across his shoulders, he had decided that Ben could only be worried at the reception awaiting him. Small wonder that his father had words to say to him; the sooner they were over the better.

He said, 'In the hall, Ben? As usual?' and was moving off when the servant said hurriedly, 'No, sir, I'm afraid not. Oh, the master's there right enough and waiting for you, but Mistress Woodfall wishes to see you first and it's as well not to keep her waiting. Please, sir.'

He escorted Edward to the room that had been his mother's parlour and with great ceremony announced, 'Master Edward is come, mistress.'

She was alone, standing tall and thin before the fire, and as he went towards her Edward was suddenly glad that Lewis was several hundred miles away. Even so, he almost laughed: she looked as if there were a very bad smell under her nose. To his credit his face remained straight. He bowed, had begun to make some pleasant remark, to hope that she was happy in her new home, when she cut him down, in a few words killing for ever what amusement she caused him.

'I will not ask you to sit, Edward, since you will no doubt be in a hurry to go to your father, but before you do I wish to tell you that pleased though we are, we *all* are, at your return, you must understand that things have changed in your absence. Thomas's word is what counts now. All orders come from him.'

'And my father?'

'Is failing, alas. For which you must accept the blame. You – and your sister, of course.'

Unable to take his eyes from her vicious, thin-lipped

mouth, Edward said icily, 'You show a rare talent for welcoming the family of the house, madam. I shall take up no more of your time. Good day.'

He gave way to a childish impulse to bang the door hard behind him in hopes of annoying his sister-in-law, and was about to make his way to his father when Ben reappeared beside him.

'I must accompany you, sir. If *she* found out that you'd been wandering about . . .'

'Like a stranger, eh?' completed Edward through his teeth. 'Is she always like that? I wonder my father puts up with her.'

Furtively the servant glanced back over his shoulder to make sure he was not overheard. 'A very difficult lady to please, sir. Likes things done properly.'

Edward said, 'Poor old Thomas!' and waited outside the familiar door to be formally announced to his own father.

'Not so well as he has been': Agnes had several times tried to prepare him for some change in his father's health, but he had not expected this. Not so well, indeed! Before him was a man who not much more than a year ago had ridden the length of the kingdom and back with no ill effects, and now – now, at the age of forty-eight – he was old. Greying fair hair hung thin and lifeless about hollowed cheeks and he sat hunched forward in his great padded chair by the hearth, hands hanging limp between his knees.

In childhood, summoned to answer for some misdemeanour, Edward had dreaded this walk from door to chair, it was so far, so very far. And on the way here he had remembered it afresh, had wondered what he would say, whether his father would shout at him before he was halfway there, as had been known. But Eleanor Woodfall had done him a better turn than she knew. Anger carried him, chin up, across the floor, and concern for his father relieved him of all worry about himself.

To his horror he saw Sir Herbert's eyes fill with tears, and making his filial bow as best he might, said, 'Forgive me, sir. I've been a damned idiot.'

So much for the polished speech he had rehearsed for

over twenty-four hours to present to a father whose first concern, on old showing, was likely to be that his peace of mind had been disturbed. Now that same father, with a tremor in his voice, said, 'Well, stop being a damned idiot now! I've needed you, lad; you've no idea how I've needed you lately. Sit down – not over there! Can you drag the chair here so that we can talk in comfort?'

No sooner was Edward seated by his side than he went on, 'You've seen her, have you?'

'I have! Heaven help us all, sir, if she's often like that!'

'The worst day's work I ever did, marrying Thomas to that shrew, not that he seems to mind, mark you. She'll be the death of me, boy.'

'In your own house, sir?'

'Mine no longer. Thomas jumps when she says "jump" and I've had my own way too easily for too long to know how to assert myself over a termagant like that now. If I shout she declares it's an old man's tantrum and ignores me. Your mother would have dealt with her!' He paused, nodding at an obviously pleasing thought. 'Or Agnes. *She* would have coped. It takes another woman, y'know. Poor Agnes. She comes to see me often. Madam stays in her room then, as a mark of disapproval.'

'But you're ill, sir. There must be something we can do. Agnes . . .'

'I'm tired. These fevers take time to pass when you're my age. It's been a hard year, what with Agnes and you – you . . .'

For the first time he seemed to take a good look at his younger son. 'The Emory girl wasn't worth it. But you'll know all about that; Agnes will have told you. Not that I blame you. A young man is entitled to his fling. Are you well again, really well?'

'Yes, sir.' He ignored his disability, just as his father did.

'How was the sailor's life? Enjoy it, eh?'

Edward's old grin showed for the first time that day, rejoicing his father's failing heart. 'So Agnes told you! To tell truth, sir, I did not. I was seasick from beginning to end. It was days after I landed before the ground stopped going up and down!'

His father put out a hand, patted his arm rather conspiratorially. 'If only you could stay here – but I won't have it. I'm not letting her ruin the lives of two of my sons. Best live with Agnes for the present.'

'I think you need me here. You might find I can deal with her, sir.' Edward's tone was grim and he was rewarded by a gleam in his father's eye.

'You look so much like your mother, lad. So much like . . . But no, no, it wouldn't do. The only good thing about Agnes's terrible affair was that it got her out of the house. Now, listen. Over the months, as that harridan has been issuing her orders, I've been making my plans, ready for when you came home, as Agnes told me you would. What I propose to do is to give you the abbey lands, lock, stock and barrel, for your own. What do you say to that?'

Edward said nothing. That his father was prepared to carve out of the very heart of his cherished lands the acres acquired when the abbey was done away with and give them away – albeit to a member of his family – showed only too clearly the way things were at Highwoods.

Into Edward's mind flashed a picture of the old abbey ruins, the cottages huddled about them and the river close by, running through unspoiled flat meadowland.

'But that is some of your best pasture,' he managed at last, 'and the village stands on it.'

'And,' his father's voice was complacent, 'that stretch of the river has the best fishing for miles around. If you're still as interested in sheep breeding as you used to be . . .'

'I shall need money to build a house.' Edward, delighted by the prospect, spoke without thinking, reddened at sight of his father's raised brows.

'Benedicta Williams would bring a good dowry. Seems a better prospect to you now, does she?' Sir Herbert's voice was sly.

Edward jerked his head in the direction of Mistress Eleanor's parlour. If he had walked into a snare it was baited with something he could not resist. 'Better all the time, sir, but what of you? This would be all very well and fine for me, but you'll still be trapped here.'

'I shall have madam's fury to enjoy. And I shall know that you are safe from her, for there is not a thing she can do about it. I've talked to my lawyers. Not a damned thing!'

'Then I accept with humble gratitude,' said Edward, 'on the understanding that once my house is finished, you'll pay long and frequent visits.'

'So I will, if I'm still here to pay any visits at all.' Sir Herbert's voice sharpened. 'Edward, if anything happens to me you'll look after Agnes, will you not? The lodge is hers right and tight and I've left her enough money to make her independent, but *that woman* could make her life a misery if she'd a mind to it.'

'I swear, sir, but nothing *will* happen to you.'

'Then all is well.' Sir Herbert heaved a sigh of relief. 'Have a word with Thomas before you go. You'll find the poor devil in the stables. Come again soon, lad. I'll let you know when the papers are drawn up. Not a word to anyone – except Agnes – until then. There are certain – responsibilities – that go with the abbey, but I can tell you about those another time. And if I'm not able to do it, Peter Acres knows all about it, better than I do . . .' His voice trailed away, his eyes closed.

Alarmed, Edward bent over him. 'Sir, sir . . .' but his father only smiled.

'Need to sleep,' he murmured. 'Lewis is well out of it, all those miles away. Good luck to you, my son.'

Shock and anger carried Edward faster than he usually moved these days so that he was out of breath by the time he reached the stable yard and heard his brother's voice.

'The frog is infected – badly. I'll look at it again tomorrow.'

No matter what the state of affairs indoors, here Thomas exercised absolute authority. He showed no outward signs of being dominated by a most unpleasant woman, as he undoubtedly was.

'Thomas! Where are you?'

'Edward, at last! I'm coming.' All the old pleasure was in the lazy voice. He dismissed the groom, came through the door with both arms outstretched as if to embrace his brother then checked, surprising Edward by the vehemence of his exclamation.

'Dear God! I – I never imagined . . .'

Edward, with only one thing on his mind, was impatient. 'Oh come, Thomas! You heard that I had come back minus a leg. Whatever did you think I would look like? Father never even mentioned it. What have you been doing to turn him into an old man?'

Thomas, still eyeing his young brother in some horror, ignored both tone and question and Edward, seeing his genuinely troubled look, regretted his anger, and said more kindly, 'Come now! I was the fool. You didn't make me run off. You didn't bring down the mast in a gale. What blame attaches to you?' and held out a hand. Just as he had been unable to beat Thomas in physical fight, he was unable to sting him with words. As well hit a cushion stuffed with feathers, he thought ruefully.

Thomas took Edward's hand in both his own, wrung it hard, said, 'It's been a hard year, what with you and Agnes and – and everything.'

Edward took matters slowly, as he saw he must. If he plunged in belligerently he might never get to the truth. 'Doesn't Agnes still provide ointment? You seem to be in some need of it.' He gestured over the half-door towards the horse that stood in its stall, obviously favouring a painful hoof.

Thomas's eyes slid away from his. 'Er, no, she does not. That is to say, I don't like to ask her at present. Joe can make up what we need. It works well enough.'

'Your son prospers. You must visit him.'

'No! Eleanor says – that is, no, no!'

So confused did he seem that Edward regretted his taunt. If Agnes bore no malice it was not for him to fight what he saw as her battle, unasked.

Thomas made a great effort. 'You've been to the house. You met Eleanor, of course.'

Edward snorted. 'I wish you luck of her, Thomas!'

His brother remained unruffled by the rudeness. 'I wish I'd been there. She – she said something about telling you that I was in charge here, and she does sometimes have a way with her that seems hard, that is all.'

Edward tried again. 'Now you've attempted to excuse your wife's lack of manners, you can answer my question about Father. What has happened to him? He's become an old man.'

Like an echo of his wife, Thomas said, 'The blame is yours – and Agnes's, in large part,' so that Edward snapped, 'But not altogether. This is his own house, yet he has the air of someone living here on sufferance. *That* is not my doing.'

'You'll be moving back here now you're well again.' Thomas sounded comfortable, untroubled. 'He's not got over last winter's fever yet. You can keep an eye on him yourself.'

'Perhaps. For the present I'm staying with Agnes – and your son. Now where have they put Doll? You can give me a hand up.' He was getting nowhere and could stay no longer.

With a hand on the old mare's neck Thomas said, 'You can't ride this bag of bones. We must find you something more in keeping. You won't want Saracen any longer. Eleanor's sister, Edith, has been after him for months. Might as well sell him, don't you agree?'

'Just as well. Too much for me to handle now.' Edward's voice betrayed nothing of the hurt his brother's thoughtless words caused him.

A hand on Doll's rein, holding him back, Thomas said suddenly, unexpectedly, 'You've been in London. Were – were you there for the coronation? What was it like? Did you see the Queen?'

He coloured at Edward's surprise, tried to laugh the matter off. 'I wondered, that was all.'

Drily, Edward said, 'I wasn't there, and if I had been I doubt if Her Majesty would have seen fit to invite me.

Goodbye, brother.' Then, as something in Thomas's face – disappointment, embarrassment, he could not put a name to it – moved him, he looked back over his shoulder, called, 'The people cheer her wherever she goes. They say that she is like King Henry come again.'

Edward, at the end of his account, made a gesture of despair towards his sister. 'What am I to do, Agnes? Father has offered me the one thing above all others I want – land of my own, and such land! But the cost to him is too high. We cannot leave him sitting there, doing nothing. I tried to talk to Thomas – but he was only interested in finding me a horse more in keeping with my position in life than old Doll!'

Agnes had listened intently. 'If I had told you before how Father really was, what good would it have done? You would have gone storming over there before you were fit. I promise you, Edward, that I see him often and do what I can. With you back and working the abbey he may recover his interest in life. We can do no more.' She paused. 'So you will marry Benedicta Williams after all?'

Even in the dim light she knew he stiffened and glared at her; then he was standing, supporting himself by the back of the settle on which they had both sat and she could hear his breath, hard and angry. He bowed as low as he could without losing his balance and said, in savage mockery, 'Mistress Williams, good day. It cannot have escaped your notice that in the past I have been extremely reluctant to ask for your hand in marriage, even though the arrangement suited both our families. You are fat, and very boring, not at all what I look for in a life's partner. Now, however, I am – as you see – somewhat damaged, and I can find a very good use for the money that would form your dowry. This being so, I am willing to marry you.'

His voice broke on a hard sob. 'In heaven's name, Taggy, I may not like the girl, but I have no wish to humiliate her. It sounded so easy when Father filled my head with thoughts of the land, but it is not. You cannot tell me that she has heard nothing of why I ran off. I cannot face her, I cannot!'

He dropped back on to the settle beside her, and the next moment her arms were about him, enveloping, motherly.

'What shall I do? What shall I do, Agnes?'

'She has heard nothing, my dear, that I promise you. Father is not so stupid as you appear to imagine, and Thomas has held his counsel. The countryside knows for a fact that you went away because you were upset at being separated from Lewis, and for no other reason.' She laughed. 'I do not know what the hold is that you have over that girl, Edward, but she loves you more than anyone in the world.'

He pulled himself back, looked up incredulously into Agnes's face, and she continued, half-mocking, 'When you first came here and – explanations – were called for, I remember quite clearly our agreeing that twelve months was a long time. You may find that has been so with Mistress Williams. Meet her at least: give her a chance. I know her. She will make you a good wife, just as you will make her a good husband.'

'It would serve me right if she refused to see me, or saw me only to tell me exactly what she thought of me! Truth to tell,' he buried his face in her lap and his next words were muffled, 'there were times this past year when I would have given the world for one sight of her fat body and placid face. The Rosamund Emorys of this world are not for men like me. A pity it took so much of hurt to others to teach me that lesson, is it not?'

'It is indeed! And however am I to cure you of this self-pity, I wonder? Now, hark! Another young man demands my attention, and somewhat more noisily than you. If you will excuse me . . .'

Long after Edward left him, Thomas had stood in the stable yard, poking at weeds between the cobblestones, scuffing his boots on the patches of frost that still lay where the sun had not reached, unaware of the cold, forgetting his promise to Eleanor to return to the house as soon as he could. Inwardly he was so relieved that his legs felt weak beneath him. Agnes, in all the weeks they had been together, had told Edward nothing about the despicable part he had played in her rape. If she had, Edward would hardly have stopped short at attacking him with words. Through Thomas's mind flashed a picture of himself sprawled full length on the cobblestones in a fashion most certainly not becoming the dignity of a man who was lord of the manor in all but name, whilst his young brother endeavoured to batter his brains out with a crutch!

'And your son.' The child was often in his mind; he had more than once been tempted to visit him. Soon, despite Eleanor's strictures, he would do so. The difficulty would be in facing Agnes. Into his head flooded the excuses with which he had grown accustomed to smooth over a twingeing conscience. He had been drunk at his wedding feast, and who could blame him? Else he would never have given the key to Gilbert. He had told Agnes so and she must have understood for she had fostered his son most willingly. As for Rosamund Emory, his passion for her had lasted one flaring, fateful day, completely at her instigation, if he recalled aright.

'Beg pardon, sir.' Ben's voice was servile. 'Mistress Woodfall be asking if you will join her soon?'

Thomas started. 'At once, at once!' By the time he had entered the house, pulled off his muddy boots and made himself respectable enough for his wife's fastidious company he had persuaded himself, as he had so many times, that he had done nothing amiss. Had he not gone looking for young Edward when he ran off? Every young man had his affairs: Gilbert would have reached Agnes with or without his aid had he been so minded. He missed Gilbert; he had lost a friend. Even his mocking remarks concerning Eleanor's strong will were forgiven. If they met again he would tell him that he had been mistaken; she was a good wife. Just as his mother had been to his father. She saw straight to the heart of every problem, knew immediately what was best to do and advised him, so that his life was easier than it had ever been. He entered her room smiling. He had done nothing to reproach himself for, nothing at all.

CHAPTER VI

1

Roads and tracks had already dried out in great measure when Agnes drove her brother, in her small wagon with its padded seats and the canvas covering that kept at bay cold winds and blustery showers alike, to his meeting with Benedicta Williams and her family.

Seemingly intent on the way they must follow, Agnes, deputizing yet again for her father, smiled to herself at sight of her brother's face. That the past few weeks had brought back some of the flesh to her own face she had not stopped to consider, but she did observe that Edward looked far more like his old self than once she had thought possible. The neat beard that had turned out to be somewhat fairer than his brown hair suited him. Many a woman would have been pleased to welcome so upstanding a suitor, despite his disability, and she knew well that he had no need to worry about the affections of the lady concerned. Had it been Thomas with his flair – so like his father's – for persuading himself that an easy, if distasteful, course of action was the one he had always intended to take, how different the day would have been! But it was not Thomas, it was Edward with his imagination and sensitivity, and he looked as if he were being dragged on a hurdle to Tyburn, in spite of arrangements made and settlements arrived at over past weeks between Sir Herbert and Master Williams.

Since that first visit to his father, Edward and old Doll, whom he had refused to relinquish, had made the difficult wintry journey to Highwoods almost every day and Sir Herbert, rousing from his lethargy, had rejoiced mightily in Eleanor's reaction when she learned of his decision concerning the abbey lands. Spluttering with borrowed rage, Thomas had, at her behest, tried to overturn the decision, had found it legally binding, had bowed before its inevitability and his wife's fury alike. And when Sir Herbert followed up his initial victory by giving Thomas certain direct orders concerning the estate, Edward began to be more optimistic about his eventual recovery.

The Williamses' large, prosperous, sprawling house came into sight far too soon for Edward's present peace of mind. Master Williams and his wife greeted their visitors warmly and took them indoors to receive refreshments; of Benedicta there was no sign.

Thirst quenched, Mistress Williams said to Agnes, 'Perhaps you would care to see my stillroom again, my dear. I know my husband has much to occupy him today,' and Edward realized, with a jolt of horror, that they were leaving him alone to meet the woman he had agreed to marry for her money. The speed with which his host excused himself, the knowing, amused looks exchanged by the women, did nothing to reassure him; his brain seemed entirely to have ceased to function. Not one word of what he might say came to him. It was not until long afterwards that it occurred to him that, knowing the lady as they did, her parents and his sister had handled the matter in the right, albeit unorthodox, way.

He stood watching the door to the room as if when it opened it might admit a wild beast intent on his destruction. On the whole, he thought miserably, he would prefer it! Then the latch clicked and she was on the threshold. Had it been anyone else he might have suspected that she paused for effect, but not Benedicta. She, he knew, and felt the more guilty because of it, stopped because first sight of him made her pleased and happy and it took her a moment to control her beaming smile.

Quite what he had been expecting he no longer knew. Always he had allowed Lewis's dictum to colour his thoughts.

'She *bulges*, brother – in all the wrong places!' It had been that, combined with her quietness, his inability ever to extract more than ten words at a time from her, that had made Edward dislike her so much when his father had suggested her as a bride. Now she came towards him, small, still plump, but bulging no longer, and the nut-brown hair that hung beneath her neat white cap shone as if it had been polished, so that in relief and pleasure he relaxed a little, smiled, bowed and murmured a greeting.

She took no heed of his crutches, saw no fault in him. 'I am so glad you could come at last. Please sit down. Did you have a pleasant journey?'

As he took a seat beside her, Edward heard himself say, 'I – I don't know. I can't remember.' The truth of the matter was that he had been too terrified about arriving to think at all about the travelling.

Quite seriously she said, 'The catkins are full out down by the river, and everything is beginning to be so *green* again. Look when you go back; it would be a shame to miss it.'

He found himself being stupidly, uselessly obstinate. 'It will be dark.'

'Then next time you come, make certain you notice.'

There was a moment's startled silence, in which Edward realized that she was not merely making polite conversation nor teasing him; she really did think it a waste of time to come so far without appreciating the gentle, fertile beauty of the awakening land. Even her remark about his coming again held no guile; she was making things as easy for him as she could and putting her mentally beside Thomas's wife he knew, suddenly, that Benedicta's way was infinitely preferable.

'Have you heard from your brother again since his daughter was born?' Obviously she kept up with his family's affairs.

'No. Nothing. I dare say now the roads are opening up again . . . Benedicta, I must know . . .'

'Yes?' She faced him quite calmly, not helping him at all now.

'Will you marry me?' he asked bluntly. No 'I love you', not even a 'please'.

'Yes, if you please.'

For an instant he suspected that she was teasing him, or even, having heard of the escapade that still so weighed on his conscience, was taking malicious pleasure in putting him down, but a sideways glance showed that it was not so.

'Thank – thank you. You do not mind . . .?' He made an abrupt gesture downwards to his maimed leg. As well to get everything over at once.

She did not hesitate. 'We shall have no rushes on the floor.' Her voice was decided. 'There must be no danger of your falling.'

Touched at her solicitude, he reached out for her hand, found it warm and slightly trembling, raised it to his lips.

'I have something to show you.' He indicated a roll of parchment he had laid on a table by the door on entering, began to rise, but at once she fetched it, as matter-of-factly as if she had been fetching and carrying for him all their lives, in a way that gave him no feeling of dependence.

Expectantly, like a child, she asked, 'What is it? Will I like it?' and watched his face light up with enthusiasm.

'It is the plan for our house. Father has given me land, such land. A friend of mine has drawn it. He says it is the way all houses will look before long. It can stand at the east of the valley and face down to the river.'

The next moment, she holding one end of the plan, he the other, he had launched into details of architecture and building, unaware of quite how many times she stopped listening and raised her large brown eyes to his face, content to look at him, to savour the fact that the day for which she had waited so long had at last arrived, that he had asked her to marry him.

He stopped to draw breath, laughed a trifle shamefacedly

and said, 'That is it. If you like the idea, of course. Please say if you do not.'

'It is for you to say. But – but is it not rather, well, grand?' Almost he thought she would call him 'sir' or at best 'Master Woodfall' and his heart smote him.

'My name is Edward. Please say it.'

'Edward,' she whispered, and now her eyes were downcast to the plan that lay across their knees.

'Benedicta is a most unusual name.'

'My parents call me Bennitt. It suits me better.'

'It does.' Now had been his opportunity to redeem himself, to say something gallant, and he had not taken it! Letting go the parchment and grabbing his crutches he stood up, embarrassed, ashamed. But she appeared to notice nothing amiss, keeping her own grip on the plan most practically and re-rolling it.

'When – that is, before we are married I must give you – I had no ring to bring you today,' he found himself stammering. 'I am so sorry.'

Once again she looked him full in the eyes so that he wondered how much she knew of his past. 'Best to take my measurements with a piece of thread. Anything you bought on chance would have been too small.'

So matter-of-fact, presaging a whole lifetime of matter-of-factness. Would they ever laugh as he had seen Lewis and Anne laugh together?

'There is one thing I would like to ask you – Edward.'

'Yes, Bennitt?' And if at that moment she had asked him for the moon he would have promised it to her, so much did her kindness ease his guilty thoughts.

'May Agnes come to live with us when our house is ready?'

Much surprised, he said, 'If she wants to, of course.'

'Oh, she does.' By now they were crossing the room side by side and Edward was left to wonder just when the two of them had decided that; certainly not that day.

Edward looked entirely different as he and his half-sister drove home that evening.

'I gather you've been to the Williamses' house before?'

Agnes's stern face lightened. 'Often. They were most kind to me – last year. For your sake, of course. You noticed the elimination of the bulges, I take it?'

'So it was your doing!'

'I pointed out to her that she would never be thin, that to wear clothes that fitted properly instead of trying to squeeze into what she thought fashionable would make her look better.'

'And you told her you would live with us. Will you really? We would like it so much – both of us.'

'You speak as a couple already! No, no, forgive me for mocking – it was kindly meant. Yes, I will come to you, and gladly. The alternatives are not very appealing. I might return to Highwoods, which with Robert would be impossible, or I can go on living as I do now, with a succession of young girls to act as maid until village tales frighten them away, in which case I shall become a very strange old woman long before my time, waiting for – for those who know no better to come for me when something goes wrong and they have no-one else to blame!'

Edward put out a hand, touched her arm in silent under-standing and affection, and she smiled faintly.

'No need for any delay. You and Bennitt will live with me until your house is finished. She would never be comfortable with Eleanor.'

'Bless you for that, but we still have Father to consider. I cannot leave him indefinitely with those two. He is so unhappy.'

'He will not be there long, brother.'

Her face in the dusk was almost invisible, as always it seemed to be when she made these strange, confident predictions of hers.

'Not . . .? You mean . . .?'

'He will not be there long because he no longer wishes to be.' Agnes's whole concentration seemed given to the track ahead of them. 'The fever has left him, but it has taken his will to live with it. He longs to join your mother. Make him happy for the time he has left – by visiting him often – by giving him grandchildren – and neither you nor I have anything with which to reproach ourselves.'

Entering into her mood, Edward asked, 'Shall I ever truly love her? Bennitt, I mean. I felt so ashamed of myself today.'

'You will. She came out of that room with her face aglow! You will not be expected to sit staring at her each day, all day; remember that. You will both have your work to do, a life to live together.' She drew a deep, harsh breath. 'I tell you this, Edward, and it is between us two only. I find no pleasure in being able to foresee the future, as you know, but the future of the Woodfall family rests with you and your children, and with no-one else. You may take my word for that.'

And not another word could he get out of her until they reached home, where Robert's angry screams were stopped by his receiving what he obviously considered to be his first meal of the day. The cow's milk with which Abigail had tried to tempt him was no substitute, no substitute at all.

CHAPTER VII

1

As Agnes pointed out somewhat drily, they should be
grateful that Sir Richard Harrington had not sent Lewis
south on business twelve months earlier. Quite how five
adults and nine children would have fitted into the lodge,
she had no idea. But they would have had to try since Lewis
had roundly declared, after a brief visit to Highwoods, that
his entire family would camp out in the woods rather than
stay one night under the same roof as Thomas and his
wife, who was at least ten times worse than ever he
remembered her.

Leaving Anne and their children with Edward and
Bennitt in the house that now faced across the abbey
valley to the River Pen, Lewis completed his business in
London and was back within the week. The city was no
place to be in hot weather, he said. It appeared to their
womenfolk that he and his twin never stopped talking to
each other, and their laughter rose loud and long about
house and grounds. So far as behaviour went, Agnes and
Anne assured Bennitt, neither of them had aged by a single
day since their last meeting six years earlier.

Knowing of Bennitt only what she had learned from
infrequent, stilted letters and Lewis's highly coloured remi-
niscences, Anne, prepared to meet a sister-in-law with
whom the only thing she had in common was marriage
to a Woodfall twin and the regular bearing of children,
found waiting to greet her the mother of three small girls,

with whom it was so easy to be friendly that soon they were together almost as much as were their husbands. Bennitt was already rounding out to a fourth child – a boy this time for certain, she said.

It was from Bennitt that Anne learned in detail of the years' happenings on what were now two adjoining Woodfall estates. Since Thomas and Eleanor chose to consider themselves far superior to their farming brother and his wife, relations were cool, but once the rancour caused by the passing of the abbey land to Edward had faded the two branches of the family lived side by side with an outward show of friendliness.

Bennitt, in her turn, was amazed at the ease with which Anne had packed up six children, including boy twins less than three months old, and transported them the length of England.

'The only way, so far as I could tell,' replied Anne merrily, with a grimace at her husband, 'of meeting either you or Agnes before we were all old and grey!'

'Besides which,' added Lewis, 'now that old Tom has finally managed to start a family, how could we stay away? A national event, one feels. Who knows, Her Majesty may proclaim a holiday in honour of the occasion!'

'Bells will ring! Fountains the length and breadth of the realm will run wine! Largesse will be showered – but not by Thomas!' contributed Edward.

It was not until they tried to share their joke with Thomas and found that he did not appreciate it in the slightest that Edward remembered earlier questions regarding the coronation; remembered and carelessly wondered. Lewis merely took his eldest brother's rebuke at such light-hearted mention of the Queen as a further manifestation of his now excessively pompous manner that had obliterated whatever sense of humour he had once possessed.

Lewis had gone to the stables, to admire a new-born foal of which Thomas was inordinately proud, when Edward attempted to smooth the matter over. 'Cheer up, Tom! It was a joke, no more than that. Whatever ails you?'

Thomas's eyes slid away from his brother's face and he reddened. 'Nothing!'

'Ah! Eleanor has been giving you your orders again, has she?' It had taken Edward considerably less than five years to discover that one sure way of getting Thomas to talk was to disparage his wife.

'No, she has not!' said Thomas hotly. 'It – it – oh, damn it, Edward, William Fields was here yesterday. You remember him? We were at Oxford together. He came to ask if I knew where Gilbert Lovelace might have taken himself off to. No-one has seen him for a month at least.'

He saw Edward's mouth tighten and hurried to unburden himself of the remainder of his story. 'His lodgings are left as if he'd stepped out for an evening. No clothes missing, money where he always keeps it. No-one Fields has spoken to knows anything.'

Icily, Edward said, 'I thought Eleanor had forbidden you to meet him? I've a mind to tell her, then you really will have something to worry about!'

Thomas tried to work his way out of the trap into which he had fallen, muttered something about boyhood friendships, wondered if – er, that was to say, Edward didn't think Agnes – after all this time – might have . . .? No, no, of course not, but . . .

His voice trailed away as Edward did something he rarely did, since it seemed to him to be a waste of time – he swore fluently and long at his brother, grateful for the shipboard words of which he seldom had need. If Thomas breathed one word about Gilbert Lovelace in Agnes's hearing, or mentioned his vile suspicions to anyone at all, he – Edward – would see that he regretted the day! He ended by telling Thomas in no uncertain manner that the filthiest beggar in any gutter was cleaner by far than the man who had raped their sister and if the earth had opened and swallowed up Gilbert Lovelace, it was no more than he deserved. It was to be hoped he had dropped straight through into the flames of hell!

Appalled at the storm he had raised, Thomas begged

Edward to say nothing to Eleanor, swore not to mention Agnes and Lovelace in the same breath ever again and ended comfortably, 'He'll come back, he always has. Nothing to worry about, I dare say. Shall we go down to the stables?'

It was Bennitt, grateful that Agnes was not present when Thomas's family was mentioned, who explained to Anne, over-awed by the stern manner of her husband's half-sister, how the loss of her own small child had been followed by the taking from her of Robert Emory.

The boy had grown to a sturdy eighteen-month-old toddler when one day Thomas arrived at the lodge, patently ill-at-ease, with the message that his son was to go to the village for fostering by Parson Watson. It was, he said, not seemly that his sister should act as nurse to – ahem – to, well, that was to say . . .

Agnes's voice cut in upon his stumblings. 'He is to go because Eleanor would feel happier if he were not so readily identified with the family. Well for me, brother, that your mother did not react to my coming as Eleanor has to this child's.'

Thomas reddened. Marriage to Eleanor had already pointed out to him most clearly his way through life. If he took her often-given advice, things ran smoothly; oppose her and he was made to feel distinctly uncomfortable. He had almost reached the stage, towards which Eleanor was working, when she had only to suggest a thing for him to believe, instantly, that it was his own idea. Therefore he spluttered, 'Now, Agnes, come! I must do what I consider best for my son. Watson can tutor him until, well, until we decide what is best to do with him.'

Bennitt, not long delivered of her own first child and by now regarding the boy almost as Agnes's own, had heard in amazement her calm reply. 'Very well, brother. Tell your wife you have delivered her message. I take it that I am not forbidden to visit him?'

Relieved to escape so lightly from his sister's scathing tongue, Thomas had agreed. Of course, of course, and the child would join the Woodfalls for important family occasions; it was just that it was as well that he gain no false impression of his standing among them. Mopping his brow, he almost ran from the house. Had he stayed longer she might have enquired about Eleanor's health, as sometimes she did, forcing him to admit that she was not pregnant, showed no sign of becoming so. He swore bitterly beneath his breath as he rode home. There were things women knew about, especially Agnes, that could ensure his wife's fertility. And Agnes, of all people, he could never ask.

The next day, having refused Edward's offer to plead with his brother for a change of heart, Agnes loaded child and belongings into her small wagon and delivered them to Master Watson. What she said to his housekeeper Bennitt never discovered, but whenever she visited the child, which was often, she was deferred to on any matter she cared to raise.

'She seldom speaks of him, Anne, but her heart must bleed. Imagine losing two small children as she has done, and John Stratton, whom she should have married, lives nearby with his wife and family, as a constant reminder. Yet all the time, ever since Edward brought me home, she has been kindness itself. I dread to think what I would have done without her.'

2

Standing halfway along the still-rough road that led from a new bridge across the River Pen and rose slightly after a while to give an unobstructed view of his newly built house on the far side of the valley, Edward allowed his pride full rein for the benefit of their visitors. He waved a hand towards the wide expanse of trodden bare earth that still surrounded the building on all sides, the piles of surplus stone waiting to be carted away, and described it in glowing terms down to its large stable block and range of outhouses, Bennitt's walled garden behind the house and the sweep of gravel that would one day be laid before its main entrance.

'We need more trees for the parkland, I think, and time will mellow the edges. Next time you come it will be more beautiful than it is now.'

Lewis gazed obediently and dutifully admired the main door, deep set and wide, the diamond-paned windows set in a façade of black beams and white plasterwork, tall chimneys patterned in red and black brick, and tried to pull himself together. He narrowed his eyes to focus on the stonebuilt stable block, already partly hidden by half-grown trees and shrubs. It was a most substantial house, but no different to others, years old, he had seen dotted about developing countryside. It seemed to him that after the life he was used to the softer, warmer air of the south made him more tired than usual, for what he saw bore no relationship whatsoever to the building Edward was so grandly describing, where an archway led to a paved inner courtyard set about with buildings of fine red brick. It was, he said airily, such a building as was now favoured by wealthy gentlemen the country wide.

Quite how long Edward might have continued so no-one knew, but when, close by his side, Bennitt was unable to stifle a muffled giggle and he could feel Agnes's inward amusement reaching out to him, he found it impossible to maintain his own solemnity. He met his wife's eyes and both laughed out loud.

'Forgive me, Anne! Lewis, I – I . . .' Edward spluttered off into uncontrollable laughter again.

It was Agnes who said, 'Edward met a young architect in London who presented the plans for such a house as he has just described. He undertook to build it here – you may see the drawings before you leave, and drawings are all they will ever be, for Roger Welch had not the faintest notion, so far as any of us could see, of how to translate his plan into reality. The ground was cleared to his orders, wagonloads of stone were brought across from the old abbey buildings, and Master Welch disappeared one night with his advance fee, leaving Edward and Bennitt with no more than a pair of splendid pillars for the gateway – ' she gestured back towards the edge of the property, 'and the best maid I ever had carrying his unwanted brat!'

Sternly she looked at Edward. 'It is my belief that Master Welch carries those same plans about the countryside, selling them to the gullible. They are his pass to months of good lodging and all the entertainment he can find.'

By now Lewis had caught his twin's mood and grinned at his disapproving sister. 'So who undertook the building after all?'

'Master Jarvis from Downfelton.' Agnes was still severe. 'And a better job you couldn't wish for.'

Slowly they started on their way to the house, two by two, with Agnes bringing up the rear, and all the time Edward talked of the house that was nothing like his dream but which he and Bennitt would not change in any way. In the early months of his marriage he had been absent from the lodge every day, morning till night, purchasing and establishing the flock of sheep that must provide the estate's main source of income, rushing through his work so that he could ride over to his rising house, at first no more than an expanse of newly cleared ground and, presently, deep foundations, to offer unwanted assistance.

'Until,' put in Agnes, 'Master Jarvis told you the sheep had more need of you than he!'

Bennitt and I, Bennitt and I. The theme ran through all Edward said, so that Lewis, who from time to time over the years had wondered how his twin's enforced marriage was prospering and had had the wisdom to keep silent on the subject, realized that he had no need to worry further on that score. It was as Agnes had predicted: they had been so occupied in the work of setting up a home, arranging their livelihood and starting a family that before he had known where he was, Edward found himself lost without Bennitt to turn to and admitted to himself that she was the only wife for him, after all. She would never sparkle as did Anne, might never fight and make up, laugh and argue with him every day as Anne did with her Lewis, but they were happy together. She would gladly have died for him. To make him laugh was to her a pleasure so exquisite that it made her almost pretty.

Critically Lewis said, 'I never seem to remember the old village looking so – so bedraggled.'

'It lacks the shelter of the old abbey walls,' Edward agreed. 'Thomas has been badgering me for months now. He sees no reason for the cottages to stay where they are. He – or Eleanor, I suspect – wants to build a new village on his land, near to the church on the other side of the river.'

'And will you give in to him?'

Edward smiled. 'Oh, yes. It is sensible, after all, and I could use more free land. Perhaps we can call it a christening gift for his new daughter!'

'I like your new house very much,' said Anne, frankly envious. '*We* live in a fortress.'

'And have need to,' her husband reminded her. 'Not everywhere in the land is as peaceful as it is here.'

Edward nodded understandingly. Light-hearted though they seemed, he and his brother had had many a serious talk about life on the borders of Scotland and England. Lewis, it seemed, lived on a powder keg that might explode at any time; it was no wonder he was so thin and taut-looking. If only Mary Stuart had accepted her cousin Elizabeth's surprising offer of the previous year that Robert Dudley should become her husband, carrying with him succession to the English throne as his prize, it would have been different. As it was, the Queen of Scots showed a marked and – for Dudley – humiliating preference for the fair, beautiful Lord Darnley. And if it came to open conflict between north and south, Lewis had a shrewd idea which side his father-in-law's Catholic lord, Earl Percy, would take. The question then would be how far Lewis could support him.

But for the moment such worries lay hundreds of miles away, somewhere in an uncertain future, and Lewis brushed them aside, turning in all kindness to draw Agnes into their happy group. The next instant he would have given much not to have done so, for he found her watching Anne with so fierce an intensity that he had to prevent himself shouting at her, 'No, stop it! She is mine!' as all his old boyish fears reawakened. But almost at once the look of intensity turned to what in anyone but his strong, calm sister he would have called fear, and he shivered.

In their chamber that night he tried to put his feelings into words for Anne, but she had never had a half-sister whose mother was a known witch and who almost certainly had second sight. As she shook her bright hair loose about her bare shoulders and held her arms out to her troubled husband, Anne gave it as her opinion that he had too much imagination. Edward could count himself most fortunate: he had land any man might envy him, more that would pass to him on the death of Bennitt's parents, a pleasant way of life, and two women who in their different ways loved him totally. It must, she added reflectively, be something lacking in her that made her so glad, so very glad that she was the wife of a rough Border laird and nobody else.

3

After almost a week of happy companionship the junior Woodfall families, leaving only the small twins at Abbey House in care of Agnes, who refused to accompany them, were welcomed formally to dinner at Highwoods, following which the women were to be introduced to Elizabeth Rose Woodfall, the baby who would undoubtedly – Anne whispered to Bennitt as they escaped from Thomas's heavy-handed welcome – be the most amazing child that had ever drawn breath! Their menfolk would accompany Thomas in a tree-planting ceremony, one sapling to commemorate each Woodfall child of the new generation.

It was Edward's great sadness – and sight of his childhood home brought it to Lewis as delayed news of the event at the time had not – that Sir Herbert had lived only two years after Edward's homecoming. Bullied and badgered by her brother to do something to save a failing man who was not old, Agnes had done her best to make him understand that this was impossible when he did not want to be saved. Day after day, good weather or bad, refusing to admit defeat, Edward had fetched his father, at first on horseback, later by litter, to the skeleton of his new house, had urged him into giving advice, to planning the layout of the park and the walled garden he had promised Bennitt. All had been in vain; Sir Herbert faded away before the eyes of those who loved him for no reason that he ever gave voice to, dying in his sleep at the age of fifty-one, leaving Thomas head of the family and Eleanor to assume the status to which she had long looked forward.

It was hot in Eleanor's bedchamber, very hot indeed, since she would not have a window open for fear of draughts, and Bennitt and Anne found it unpleasant in the extreme, especially when the chief diversion offered was to admire a tightly swathed babe who screamed at the top of her voice, thereby proving that what she lacked in looks she more than made up for in lung power. At last Eleanor called the wet nurse to remove the child and allow them some peace and quiet; not before time, as her younger sister, Edith Stone, was delighted to point out to her.

It was well known to the countryside that nothing but good manners kept the Coulton sisters from each other's throats. What they said of and to each other could, when it was not too embarrassing, prove highly entertaining to bystanders. Today the obvious dislike between them did nothing to add to the enjoyment of their reluctant visitors. Eleanor was waiting for compliments; dutifully her sisters-in-law gave them. They were graciously accepted until Mistress Edith, watching her chance, leapt into a gap in the conversation.

'She is a healthy babe, sister, but I think my Matthew could give her weight at that age.' It was well known also that Edith's only child was the light of her life.

'So I should hope, sister.' Eleanor's voice was cold. 'Boys are always heavier than girls. It is a well known fact.' She turned to Bennitt, for whom she usually had but few words. 'Would you not agree, Benedicta? Your children are girls, are they not?'

Bennitt smiled. 'All of them so far, Eleanor.' She folded her hands complacently across her stomach.

She heard a murmur of approval from Anne and hastened to add, 'Your garden is progressing well, Eleanor. Do come and look, Anne.'

Firmly she dragged her sister-in-law to the window. The scenes Anne found so amusing filled her with disquiet. Anne would soon be gone north again; she and Edward had to live close to these easily offended relatives.

Thomas's men had worked hard on his wife's plans for a garden at the rear of the old house. Walled in rose-red brick, its formally spaced paths and beds took in part of what had been the moat and beyond, and today along the line of the end wall Sir Thomas was lifting saplings and placing them in holes earlier dug to receive them.

'And the tall skinny one in the middle is Rose, although it looks more like her mother!' Anne's irreverence was not to be suppressed.

But Bennitt was no longer worrying about her. Anne found her gazing, half-smiling, at her husband. How she loved him, Anne thought. However much their ways when they were together remained the same, the years had changed the twins. Lewis was strong as whipcord from his hard Border life, his brown face etched with thin lines at eye and mouth corners, whilst years of moving around on crutches had given Edward a decided stoop and there was often a frown between his brows; pain, if Anne were any judge. Now, as if linked in alliance against their brother, each man had an arm about the waist of the other and propped himself on one crutch. Anne saw Edward turn to Lewis and make a *sotto voce* remark that reduced the two of them to helpless laughter. It was undoubtedly at the expense of Thomas who, oblivious of their merriment, was placing another tree in another hole.

'They want him to make a speech,' she said and Bennitt wondered how she knew. Edward obviously said something of the sort out loud, was taken seriously, stood to be lectured by Thomas and in order to hide his mirth released himself from Lewis, took both crutches and swung away towards the small children who played on the grass like brightly coloured flowers amid their nursemaids.

Bennitt said, 'Look, Anne, I said Robert would be here,' and without reference to Eleanor opened a casement, took a small piece of stone from the sill outside and, aiming straight and true, dropped it at the feet of a boy of some five years old, drably dressed, who stood alone in a corner of the garden, his only movement towards joining his cousins being when he retrieved stray balls for them or set fallen little ones once more on their feet. Pityingly, Anne saw in him a child who had learned early and well the harsh lessons he had been taught. He would join in others' games when invited, not until. Then he looked up at the house and she felt a shock of surprise go through her body. There was nothing of Thomas about him; he was Rosamund Emory's son, and the image of her!

Softly Bennitt called, 'I'll be down to see you presently, little one,' and the child nodded eagerly, his expression lightening into happiness.

Anne wondered, and knew she must never ask, how much Edward's wife knew of Rosamund Emory, beyond the facts that she had borne Thomas this illegitimate son and that her bones lay in the family vault in the village church. What was obvious was that she loved the boy, and he her.

'Come down and meet him,' she urged Anne and thankfully they left Eleanor and Edith to their continuing squabble. That in their haste they did not close the window brought about the beginning of a tragedy, for scarcely were they gone than Eleanor said petulantly, 'They have no consideration. Close the window will you, sister?' and hunched her thin shoulders into her fur-trimmed shawl.

By the time Edith Stone reached the window, Thomas

and Edward were making their way back to the house, leaving Lewis to assist the men who were rapidly filling in the holes about the tree roots. Sir Thomas's voice rose quite clearly to her. 'Another girl, Edward. Can you and I father nothing but daughters?'

Edward was distracted from reply by his own two-year-old Ursula, lurching against him, holding up a chubby, daisy-filled fist.

'Steady, steady, little one, unless you want me on the ground beside you! What was that, Tom? Cheer up! Lewis has three boys already. The next one will be a son, mark my words.'

Glumly, Thomas said, 'There will be no more. The physician warned me.'

At that moment Robert, noticing Ursula's importunate craving for her father's attention, ran forward and pulled her firmly away. He was rewarded by a word of thanks and the cheerful grin that warmed his lonely small heart and as he led his small cousin away he did not hear the careless words that sealed his fate.

'Why worry, Thomas? What better son could you wish for than that one? Make him your legal heir, man, and your problems are solved.'

Neither man heard the casement above him click, could not have imagined with what malicious pleasure Edith Stone returned to her sister's bedside and imparted what she had overheard, adding, 'So much for your precious Rose, sister! Now if you would like me to help you out of your predicament . . .'

As soon as politeness permitted, the party from Abbey House made its farewells and left. Riding behind their husbands in a wagonload of children and nursemaids, Anne pulled a face at Bennitt.

'Agnes knew what she was about, refusing to go. That room! I can still feel it. I am so hot . . .'

Early the following morning young Robert Emory escaped to solitude, as he had become used to do on those days when Parson Watson was engaged with his pastoral duties. There was a Mistress Watson now, and a Watson child, but they were not encouraged to play together. Robert lived with them but he did not belong, as was made very clear to him by the words the parson chanted loudly over his head at family prayers. So often repeated, they remained in his mind and at a time when other, more fortunate, children were learning nursery rhymes, they came back. 'The sins of the fathers . . . visited on the children.'

What he had done to deserve the punishments so regularly handed out to him he had no idea. The only people who were kind to him, as he saw people being kind to other children, were a one-legged man and his small, plump wife whom he saw when occasionally, as had happened the day before, he was taken, dressed in clothes kept for such occasions, to the big, grey house where they had planted trees. There was a tall, stately woman who visited him regularly, enquired if he were happy and told Mistress Watson sharply when he needed new clothes. With her he walked hand in hand, listened as she talked, told him that if he did as he was told one day he would be a great man, but she did not smile. He thought her very beautiful but he could not understand much of what she said and was too afraid to say so.

Dearly he would have liked to stand beside those laughing men as they planted trees of varying heights, to watch the roots spread carefully out in the huge holes dug to take them, but the trees were nothing to do with him. When he was brought to the house he was sometimes greeted by a burly, fair man, but he did not belong there either. Such visits, despite the carelessly kind attention of this man, were not pleasant. There was a woman, straight-backed and thin, whose mouth was screwed up tightly and who never smiled. She gave orders, the child noticed, to the fair man, and the only words she ever spoke to Robert, bewildered and wondering why he had been brought to this splendid place, were unkind. Once she cuffed him hard about the ears, although he could remember no offence. He came early to the conclusion that he must be a very wicked person and he hoped that the lady and gentleman who smiled at him would never discover it.

Ever since he had been old enough to walk so far, Robert had been fascinated by the river that flowed past the village. He spent hours watching the miller's wheel turn and the water racing, churning and lashing out its white foam, but his happiest time was when he took a long stick with a piece of twine on the end and sat dangling it in the quieter waters upstream beneath the willow trees. He had no fishing hook but this in no way disturbed him. He watched the strong current that always, even when the river was low in summer, swirled about the roots of the trees, and enjoyed the way it carried his line out into the middle of the stream until, with a jerk as hard as his small arms could manage, he dragged it back and dropped it once more on to the water below the crumbling bank on which he sat and the whole process began again.

So engrossed was he in his game that his first intimation that he was not alone came when a hard, dirty hand clamped itself about his mouth and dragged him over backwards. Wildly he struggled, but he was unable to escape. Over him loomed filthy, bearded faces – two of the cut-throat beggars who roamed the countryside and about whom he had been warned. Fiercely they argued between themselves and the small boy lay, terrified, on the sun-warmed earth and heard them debate whether or not to knock him on the head and push him into the eddying waters about the willow-tree roots.

'Get a move on, Joe! The sooner it's done and we're gone the better.'

The man Joe laughed. 'How if I told you as I knows somebody, Bill, as would pay us all over again for a young 'un like this? No sense in losing good money, no sense at all!'

Robert blinked aside the tears that blinded his eyes just in time to see a large fist raised above his face. After that the river, the willow trees, all the life he had so far known, were swallowed up in darkness.

Later, there was pain in his head that made him feel very sick and he was being shaken so that he thought his head would drop off his shoulders. With a whimper he opened his eyes to daylight that seemed much brighter than usual, brighter and inclined, unless he squinted, to spin round and round. The shaking stopped and he heard one of his captors congratulating himself that the brat was not dead after all; not that he had believed he was. Children's heads were notoriously strong. If he had a gold piece for every time his father had clipped him round the ear, he would be a rich man by now, not forced to do this sort of thing for a living! His companion, Bill, who seemed slightly the less aggressive of the two, bent over the bemused child to hold a cup to his lips. Robert drank the brackish water it held and his sickness became reality. There on the grass he retched and heaved until there was nothing left in his stomach, and his head thereafter cleared surprisingly quickly, apart from the throbbing pain in his jaw where he had been hit.

The days that followed were a nightmare of hunger and unceasing travel, of sleep snatched wherever he and his kidnappers happened to be when night fell, until, after what seemed to the small child to be a lifetime, woods and fields gave way to something he had never seen before – a town. Any hope, however slight, he had entertained of escaping and making his way home was gone. He might have managed in the countryside if they had not watched him constantly and had not tied him to a tree each night, but here was row upon row of houses, bigger than any in the village, leaning crazily towards each other so that the sky was scarcely visible, every one like its neighbour. Alleyways led in all directions and there were more people than he had dreamed existed in the whole world, all of them seeming to shout at the tops of their voices. No-one took any notice of two men, dragging along a young boy.

They made their way through filth and noise, dodging in and out between wagons and handcarts and men and women laden with packs; always, it seemed to Robert, hurrying faster than his short legs could carry him.

He was given into the care of a woman, large, toothless and evil-smelling, who stripped him of his own clothes, replacing them with rags, before he was locked into a tiny room with a casement so high in the wall and so small that there was no hope of his reaching it, or of squeezing through it if he had.

The next morning they set out again, but not until the more vicious of his captors had given him warning. 'Behave yourself, do as I says and you'll live like a lord. Try to run off or tell people where you comes from and Bill 'ere and me'll know for sure, and one night when you aren't expectin' to see us, in we shall come through your window and . . .' He broke off to make an expressive gesture across the lad's throat with his dagger. 'Very nasty that 'ud be, no mistake, so you do as you're bid. Nobody wants you. They paid us to take you away, so where would you go, eh, where would you go?'

With these words of comfort and a final shake that rattled Robert's teeth in his head, they dragged him out into the streets again. Fear and lack of sleep brought an air of unreality to the whole scene but Robert still had enough of his senses about him to notice that the houses were becoming larger, the people no less noisy but better dressed, until eventually they stopped before a tall, dark house in a row of tall, dark houses. Three white stone steps led up to a heavy, iron-studded door.

Joe's confident knocking brought a maid servant who admitted them with little ceremony and no curiosity when he asked for the master of the house, and they were shown into a room that for a moment made the dazed child think he was back at Highwoods. Sweet-smelling rushes covered the floor and the furniture was so highly polished that had he been tall enough he would have been able to see his face reflected in the great table that filled the middle of the room. At this sat three men, and the maid respectfully addressed the youngest, plainly dressed, not unpleasant-looking. Robert, searching for someone he knew, thought that he had found Parson Watson in the second man. Although he wore doublet and ruff there was something about his bearing, even to the hands neatly folded before his stomach, that said 'church'. But it was at sight of the man at the head of the table, large, calm, with the longest beard Robert had ever seen, that with a muttered oath Joe went down on one knee, pulling the child down with him, and bowed his head. Bill, seemingly less well informed as to the man's identity, nevertheless thought it wise to follow suit and it was this gentleman, in a voice that sounded as if nothing ever surprised him, who asked, 'What have we here?'

Grovelling abjectly, Joe begged pardon for trespassing upon so great a gentleman, but he and his friend had come across this boy, unwanted as he was, thrown out by his family you might say, and had befriended him. Since it was obvious to anyone with half an eye that the lad was bright they had taken the liberty of bringing him to Master Jenkins, whom Joe had once had the high honour of meeting. It had seemed a better fate than that the lad should become a beggar, which is what would have happened if they had left him where they found him.

'And where exactly was that?' But Joe was overcome with loss of memory, and apart from mumbling something about several days' journey, fell silent.

Robert Emory, kneeling there with Joe's fingers biting into his arm, watched by three new pairs of appraising eyes, heard himself addressed in the kindest voice he had heard for some time. A finger was crooked in his direction.

'Come here, boy. No-one shall hurt you. What is your name?'

Slowly, on legs that threatened to give way beneath him, the terrified, worn-out five-year-old forced himself across unending floor until he stood close beside the man to whom all the others deferred, and all the time through his brain ran so many threatening things. He connected what Joe had just said with the sins of which he had been made aware all his life, remembered Lady Woodfall's unkind, pursed mouth and, more recently, Joe's threat of retribution if he did not do as he was told. For a moment he stood, swaying, by his questioner's knee, then bowed and replied, 'Robert, sir.'

His manner, the educated tone of his voice, obviously surprised his inquisitor, for he frowned and looked more closely at the boy.

'Sit down, Robert, or you will fall. Here, beside me.' He paused as the child obeyed, then said quietly, 'Jenkins!' and the next moment the beggar Joe found himself gripped from behind by the very strong hands of the young man to whom the maid had spoken. Slowly, inexorably, they forced his head backwards until he felt sure his neck would crack.

'The truth now,' said the young man crisply. 'Where did he come from? You know the penalty for abduction. Or perhaps I should arrange for your tongue and that of your friend – ' he cast a look towards the quaking Bill – 'to be loosened?'

But Joe, spluttering and choking, beating the air with his hands, intimated that there was no need to go to those lengths, sir. He was only too pleased to tell all he knew, and in the next few revealing minutes Robert learned that although his captors had no precise idea of where they had picked him up, they being travellers as a general rule and strangers to that part of the country, it had been somewhere in Leicestershire. They had been paid by a rich lady to take him away. He was unwanted, a bastard who was an embarrassment to his father's new wife. The pressure on Joe's windpipe slackened and a most uncomfortably sharp knee was removed from the middle of his spine.

The calm man turned again to the child. 'Whereabouts in Leicestershire is your home? Tell me quickly now, boy. It is possible that we may be able to return you there.'

Robert had never heard of Leicestershire and most certainly did not want to be taken there. He whispered, 'I do not know, sir, indeed I do not. I do not think I belong to anybody.' The next moment he was a small, pathetic heap on the floor, completely unconscious.

It was years later that he learned from Master Jerome, the priestly-looking man, what happened next. The two ruffians were dismissed with a warning that if ever they showed their faces there again it would be the worse for them. Then Amos Jenkins picked Robert up, placed him on a nearby settle and looked to Sir William Cecil for his orders.

'You start for Scotland immediately, as I said, Jenkins, but before you leave set someone to make enquiries; find out where the child comes from. You know what to do. Of course it may really be that no-one wants him – in which case I suggest you keep him.'

He turned to Jerome, who shrank before his level gaze. 'We may have more work for you, Jerome. If Jenkins is unable to trace the family, I look to you to educate the boy. He could serve us well. No family ties to take his mind off his work. The Lord knows we have enough of your ruffians, Jenkins – not,' he raised a white hand, 'not that I complain of them, but there are places where they cannot go. This boy might be very useful to us. Succeed with him and who knows? We may find others to join him. The concept interests me.'

He rose stiffly from his chair. 'I believe our earlier discussion was finished. The message is for Sir James Melville's ear alone, Jenkins.'

He bowed slightly to Jenkins and nodded, as to one barely tolerated, towards Jerome, saying coldly, 'Work on those papers tonight and get them back to me with your comments first thing in the morning.'

As the door closed behind him Jenkins spat into the rushes at his feet. 'Make enquiries! How much time does he think my lads have? A name for Robert. A name, a name . . .' He sauntered over to the window, looked down at the passing traffic and at sight of a creaking cart laden with barrels said, much amused by his own wit, 'Why not? To be sure, Cooper has a fine ring to it. Take him, Jerome. Christen him if it makes you feel better. Then – you heard your orders – educate the brat!'

5

It was very late on the day of his kidnapping before anyone had time to notice that Robert Emory was missing and even then it had none of the effect it would normally have had, for Highwoods and its surrounding district had more to think about than a lost child. It was Peter Acres, on his way to tend his flock in the abbey ruins who, almost at the very time that Joe turned Robert into a sack-wrapped bundle slung over his shoulder, came across Peg Morris in hysterical flight through the huddled hovels of the village. He stopped her progress and noise most effectively by tripping her with his shepherd's crook and slapping her sharply with the palm of one hand with far more violence than anyone would have supposed him capable of using, and listened to her panic-filled words. Holding the distraught woman firmly by one arm, he fought down the fear she raised in him and forced himself to go into her evil-smelling cottage, where he stood for a moment over the tossing, pain-racked bodies of two of her children. Bending closer, he inspected the dirty, red-blotched stomachs, the swellings that were rising hard and dark beneath each small armpit. The woman was right: it was plague.

Within the day several families in the tightly packed village had at least one member sickening of the dread, swift-spreading disease and those not smitten shut themselves away behind closed doors and shutters in hope that the contagion would thus pass them by.

Peter Acres hurried to Highwoods and informed Sir Thomas, who as Justice of the Peace must issue plague orders, ensure that all infected houses were marked and post notices on all roads leading into the parish. He did his best, but the sickness ran before him and a mass grave was barely opened in the churchyard before the first bodies were brought for burial. Whether they had died of plague or not no-one enquired; they were tipped into the pit with great haste and scant ceremony.

Thomas returned home to an hysterical wife who refused to allow him across his own threshold. All doors were bolted, and from a high window, holding a cloth soaked in vinegar to her face, she told him to find some other place of refuge until all risk to her and her child was past. At any other time, for any other reason, the servants would have enjoyed the sight of the pompous lord of the manor publicly discomforted, his wife so panic-stricken, but not now.

'The contagion must have come with the players who passed by last week,' he called up to her. 'It is too late for your precautions. Let me in! If we're to have it, we shall have it, you know that well enough.'

'Or your precious brother brought it from London. And he was here only yesterday!' she shrieked. 'Take refuge with him!' and she slammed closed the window.

Stunned by the sights he had seen, too sore at heart to blame her or to point out that if Lewis had indeed carried the infection it must now be locked in with her and Rose, Thomas obeyed her orders as he always did, remounted his horse and made his way to Abbey House.

Before the door Edward met him, white-faced, listened to what he had to say although he already knew it all. With calmness born of unbelief and grief he said through dry lips, 'Come in and welcome, Thomas, but the sickness is here before you. Anne – Lewis's Anne, she – this morning . . . and Lewis . . . he will not leave her . . .' His voice failed and he turned away, back into the house.

Not knowing what else to do, Thomas followed him. What he had shouted to his wife he believed to be true; there was no escape if the disease had man or woman marked down. He might as well be here with his family as anywhere. Besides, the thought flashed through his mind, Agnes was here; Agnes who knew so much about medicine. She would help them all. Even he whom she had cause enough to hate. He was not in the least surprised to find that she had taken charge of the household, segregating children and nursemaids in their own rooms in what all the time she knew to be a vain attempt to prevent the disease spreading.

Four weeks passed and as if it were some hideous creature that had left in the night, the plague was gone as suddenly as it had come. For most of that time Agnes, Bennitt and servant women worked continuously, pounding roots, preparing potions, brewing cordials, despatching them through Master Acres, who came daily to the door, to villagers who took them in gratitude. The poor souls, he thought, would have bowed the knee before anyone who offered them the slightest degree of hope or protection. There was no question of witchcraft now. And all the while Thomas worked as he had never worked in his life before, assisting Edward and workers whose numbers dwindled daily with essential work about the two estates.

But not all medicines went to the village or to farmers in the surrounding countryside, and nursing was as much needed in Abbey House as elsewhere, for despite all precautions the disease reached the children, reached and killed them in its frighteningly haphazard way. Two babies lay side by side in one bed; one sickened, the other remained healthy for so long that for some of them at least the exhausted, grieving adults maintained hope. But by the time Thomas was at liberty to order the taking down of warning notices, he found that although his wife and daughter were untouched, a goodly proportion of the rest of his family had perished.

Into the mass grave, alongside and atop each other, were tumbled poor and well-to-do alike; among them Lewis and his wife, their children Anne, Richard, Elizabeth and William, and Bennitt and Edward's entire family of little ones, Ursula, Mary and Isabel, together with serving maids and men.

When finally the shocked and grief-stricken survivors were free of stench and pain and fear and the rooms were cleansed, the fine new house held only Thomas, Agnes,

Edward and Bennitt, with Lewis and Anne's baby twins, Walter and Martin.

'Why? Why? *Why?*' Edward demanded of his brother in agony. 'There is no sense in it. No rhyme or reason!'

Thomas, in dumb misery, was shaking his head when Agnes, using words from the Bible in which she professed not to believe, said, 'One shall be taken and the other left. Go to Bennitt, brother, she needs you. Remember that she carries hope within her.'

Wearily Edward made his way to the light airy room, wood-panelled and spacious, with its large oriel window, that had been designed to contain so much of family happiness. How Bennitt had been able to work unceasingly without miscarrying the child she expected in the autumn he did not know, but she had. She had watched day and night over her beloved ones, had found strength to do things that turned Edward's stomach, and despite all her endeavours had lost them. Now she was huddled on the floor in one corner, bowed beneath the weight of her loss, untouched even by her husband's voice, unable to consider his pain. He could get no response from her; only she crouched lower, shrank away from him as from a stranger so that in exasperation he left her, set off as quickly as crutches and aching arms could propel him, to the small room where his brother's orphaned sons lay in their cradles, watched over by their wet nurses.

'Follow me!' he said. 'Bring *them!*' and was gone. By the time he reached his wife's room again the two girls, who had come south to face so much of fear and horror, were close behind him, the babes held tightly in their arms.

Straight to Bennitt Edward went, and all the grief, all the pain that filled him for his own lost children, for his twin and the family that had come visiting never to leave, broke out of him in a tremendous rage that set the nursemaids trembling and brought his wife to her feet as if he had grabbed her by her unbrushed hair.

'Stand up for the sake of our unborn child, woman.' Never in all their life together before or after did Edward speak as he spoke then. 'And now you must rear these mites for Lewis and Anne. *Do you hear me?*'

Half-turning, he indicated the maids with their swaddled bundles. 'Well?'

Bennitt took a faltering step forward, just as one of the babes gave a cry of protest against the arms that crushed him so tightly. At the sound, her face changed, came back to life. Tears streamed down her cheeks, ran unheeded on to the crumpled linen she had not changed for days, and she raised her eyes to her husband.

'Yes, Edward,' she said.

All danger over, Thomas returned to his home to find his wife unrepentant for her behaviour by which, she averred, she had saved their daughter and those servants who had stayed with her instead of running off panic-stricken to join their families. That the disease was strangely selective Thomas owned. Peg Morris, whose family had first been stricken, had lost her husband and all her children save two, and they the two, now half-grown, who lay all day on their piles of rags and looked into an invisible world of their own.

It was Agnes who brusquely pointed out to her brother that admirable as his idea of fostering the twins might appear, they must be returned to their grandfather in Barndale should he wish it, he being their closest relative. Accordingly Edward wrote to him, wrote and awaited a reply which was delayed by no-one knew what – impassable roads, Sir Richard's period of mourning – every possibility he and Bennitt considered, and for once Agnes failed them. She, who had always been so confident in her predictions, this time had none to make and she was absent when at last a letter arrived from the north.

Sir Richard wasted few words on his family's burial: he was man of his time enough to accept what happened to the bodies of plague victims. It was the last paragraph of his letter that surprised Edward and made his heart sing, for his wife as for himself.

'You and your wife will, I know, do what is best for my

grandsons. Keep them, educate them as is fitting and make sure that they are brought up always in the fear of the Lord our God. All the property I own will one day be theirs. If you will from time to time inform me of their progress and, when they are older, send them to visit me, I shall be content. Jessie and Maggie must stay with them until they are weaned, but send them home as soon as may be; they have families of their own who need them.'

Edward, even as he rejoiced with Bennitt, found himself wondering if Sir Richard had information he could not trust to a letter, whether the trouble with Scotland of which Lewis had talked was nearer than any of them had guessed.

That same night Agnes let herself out of the house, as she made a habit of doing each evening, and walked down to the river, to the place where Robert Emory had disappeared. In the weeks since that black day life had consisted of work, the sleep of exhaustion and work again, on and on. Drowned, said those few who had searched for the boy, for how many times had he been warned about playing there? Since his body had not been found downstream in the millrace it must have been sucked into a whirlpool; it would be trapped under some rocky ledge, never to be seen again. The boy's disappearance was never mentioned by his father. At least, thought Agnes bitterly, he had had the decency not to refer to him as 'a problem solved'. It had been left to Edward and Bennitt to add prayers for the soul of one small unwanted boy to those they offered for so many members of their family.

A piece of twine was wrapped about a willow twig and trailed, snatching and jerking, in the water. Leaning forward she pulled at it, detached it, very carefully wrapped it about her fingers. For a moment she stood there, head tilted back, as if she listened for something in the evening stillness, before she turned to go.

A man taller than she, swarthy-faced, dark-eyed, grizzled of hair, stood beneath a nearby tree, intently watching her, and as if they had last met only the day before instead of in her childhood, she said calmly, 'Good evening, Obadiah Hill.'

He stepped towards her, smiling. 'Deborah's daughter, Aglaia Samuel, and her image,' he said. 'It is good to see you again.'

'Agnes Woodfall,' she corrected. 'I took my father's name when he came for me.'

Obadiah looked at the white locks in her dark hair, the hollow eyes that spoke of more than recent tiredness. 'And it has brought you much sorrow. This is where the boy drowned?'

'This is where he – disappeared.' Calmly she faced him, her mother's youngest brother, the only one of his family not to condemn her mother when, having borne a daughter to a stranger from another culture, she had been cast out by her husband, forbidden to see her other children. From time to time, whenever his travels brought him near, Obadiah had visited the small cottage past Downfelton that Sir Herbert had provided for Deborah and her child until the day when, the victim of superstitious gossip and fear, she had been taken as a witch. Since then Agnes had neither seen him nor heard from him.

'You bring me news,' she said, and it was a statement, not a question. 'The sooner you tell me, the sooner you can go.' The smile that glinted in her eyes belied the seeming rudeness of her words. 'It is none so long since the plague. A culprit would still not come amiss.'

'We have been camped beyond Beddinglow,' he answered. 'The others have moved northwards and I must follow soon.'

He found himself reluctant, after all, to break the news that brought him to seek her, but Agnes did not hesitate.

'Lovelace,' she said, in certainty. 'What of him?' He started.

'Spoken like Deb. You have her powers as well as her queenly look. From time to time I have wondered, yet how could you not have? She was a seventh daughter and you in your turn her seventh. He is dead.'

Agnes put out a hand, drew him forward to the riverbank.

'Tell me why you – or yours – should care what happened to me, the daughter of an outcast? And how do you know that he was the cause of my – misfortune?'

As they sat side by side, Obadiah said, 'A handsome man, I hear tell, but with a large and ever-open mouth. One whose tastes ran in the same paths over the years. It is true news of your sorrow came to us, without our knowing its cause, but at a fair in London some two months past, Japhet Hill heard Lovelace in a tavern boasting that he had made an assignation with your young cousin, Rachael. A sweet girl, he said, a girl who reminded him of one he had known and enjoyed some years ago. He spoke your name.'

'Ah!' Agnes drew a deep breath. 'Cousin Rachael is still young and sweet, I trust?' Her tone was dry; the family had looked after its own and in so doing had taken from her the vengeance she had dreamed of.

'She is unsullied,' said Obadiah bluntly. 'That you were avenged at the same time pleased me, daughter of Deborah. No-one will ever find his body – nor if you look into my eyes – as you are doing now – from today until the end of time, will you discover what happened to him, for I had no hand in the deed. Only it seemed to me good that you should know.'

He rose to his feet as lithely as a man half his age. 'If I hurry I can be with my family before morning. You never knew them, or they you, but your brothers and sisters flourish. There are five more of them now since your mother's husband married again. A good woman. But I think he will never forget Deborah. As I shall never forget her – or you.'

Then, as if he had for a moment borrowed the gift Agnes had inherited from her mother and had tried so hard to lose, 'Go back to the fine new house you live in and let the past take care of itself.'

He went with no word of farewell, giving her no time to speak, fading into the dark background of the trees as suddenly as he had come.

Very slowly Agnes made her way across the meadows to the abbey ruins, stepping over fallen stones, catching her dragging feet in broken paving slabs half hidden in turf. For a moment, head bowed, she stood before the old altar, then moved to one side and knelt down by the small, grass-covered mound that was Angharad's grave. Very carefully she pulled from her fingers the twine she had found by the riverside and laid the coil of it on her baby's grave with as much care as if it had been a posy of flowers before, falling forward on to her face, she broke into a storm of weeping.

CHAPTER VIII

1

'Grass covers many things. It hides the scars of things we find hard to face, even to the work of men's hands that destroy the House of God. A gentle mantle.'

Even as Edward turned – startled, for his thoughts had been wandering – he smiled. Who else could comfort and rebuke at the same time? Long since, grass had lined the rough furnace pit dug in what had been the middle aisle of the small abbey church by King Henry's men. There they had used its timbers to stoke fires that had melted down the leaden roofing and re-formed it into shot to be carted away to armouries in London. And in five years grass had well nigh obliterated the unmarked mass grave in the nearby village churchyard. Since then other illnesses had come, taken their victims and departed, although none so totally devastating as plague; they were part of existence.

'Peter.' Edward disengaged a hand from his cloak, held it out to Master Acres and ruefully surveyed the few remaining stones of the old buildings. He found he was on the defensive; responded like the boy he had been.

'The stones were already disappearing one by one, who knows where, before I took them. Each time someone needed a grindstone or a gatepost. At least now they are still all together and form part of a dwelling.'

'Aye. And the altar stone is untouched.' Together they looked at the carved block under its cloth of faded golden lichen, beautiful still despite the erosion of wind and rain, raised their eyes to the high empty arches of the east window that rose so steeply behind it, and in the mind of one of them was the thought of a tiny mound beneath it on which flowers were no longer placed regularly, as once they had been. Agnes Woodfall and her lost babe still greatly exercised Peter Acres's mind, and still she stood out against him with a strength he could not combat.

It was quiet with the quietness of things past at the abbey now, the only noise that of the sheep that cropped the grass within and about it. The village that had stood hard by for two hundred years was gone, razed to the ground in the aftermath of the plague when Thomas, prompted by Eleanor, had renewed his demand and Edward had been too sore at heart to fight him. Looking back, he acknowledged that it had been a good move. Land had been cleared around the church and there the new village of Highwoods had come into being; neat huts with small strips of land for each man to till as his own. Still they came to the old site to grow the corn that was needed in abundance, the mill remained, and, be they never so deferential to the lord of the manor and his lady, still many thought of Edward as their master.

Peter Acres roused, patted the hand of the man he too acknowledged as master, although neither gave a thought to the distinction.

'I do not complain, Edward. Worse things could indeed have happened.' His tone became brisk. 'I sought you to tell you that the poor fleeces we held back are bundled ready for market. Unless you have other orders Jed will set off with them tomorrow.'

'Let them go; their quality is not as high as I had hoped but we need the money, however small the amount. One day soon you and I and Ben must talk about introducing a sturdier strain into our stock. The boys arrive home this afternoon. Will you come to the house to see them?'

'You sent them too early to school, Edward. Scarcely out of swaddling clothes!'

Edward laughed. 'Hardly that, but I shall tell Bennitt you agree with her! But what else could I do? You refused to tutor them and Parson Watson has little enough to teach anyone. It is my duty to make sure they grow up a credit to their parents.'

'I cannot switch from teacher to shepherd and back every five minutes, my son. The life here suits my ageing bones. Off you go now, your family will be waiting.'

As if to make up for the tragedy that had overwhelmed the family, life had been good in recent years. Before the end of the plague year, Bennitt had given birth, not to the boy she longed for, but to small Mary, who had been joined eleven months later by Cecily and in the following year by Anne. More girls, as Thomas had so glumly remarked, but Edward, able to observe Lewis's twins more closely than his brother, was of the opinion that that was no bad thing. Love them as Bennitt did, the boys led her a merry dance. Agnes had kept them in order, had administered summary justice until both had gone to Downfelton Grammar School in the autumn. And now they were returning for Christmastide.

As being the easier to deal with, Edward called Wat to his study first, acknowledging the child's polite bow and reading to him that part of his tutor's letter that spoke of his excellent scholastic achievements. The less satisfactory mention of the conscious charm that at so early an age was beginning to show in the boy's dealings with those with whom he came into contact, he omitted. Time enough to deal with that before the boy returned to school. There was nothing of Lewis in this elder of his two sons; to look at he was all his mother, from shining red hair and clear pale complexion to deep brown eyes. Tall for his age, he stood before his uncle's table, courteous and smiling, accepting praise as his due.

Martin was at the foot of the wide, shallow staircase, huddled on the bottom tread, arms about knees, when his turn came, with his small cousin Cecily pushed up against him like an affectionate puppy. 'Best get it over quickly,' said Wat as he passed, and Martin flushed at the implied taunt.

Edward Woodfall had once mentioned to Agnes an idea of his regarding these boys. It seemed to him that Wat had come into the world lusty and strong, high-coloured and always, even' from babyhood, sure of himself, so that there had been no colour, no charm left for Martin, who twenty minutes later had struggled forth like some shadow of his brother.

He had been laughed to scorn. 'Such superstition, Edward! You make me ashamed. What we have is another fair Woodfall. Give him twenty years and he will be the living image of Thomas.' She had turned to leave, although not before her brother's heartfelt 'Heaven forbid!' had brought a malicious grin to her face.

Martin stood now before his uncle, shorter by a head than Wat, light brown of hair, freckle-faced and, as was apparent when Edward Woodfall looked up from his papers to receive his bow, very, very worried.

'The work was harder than you expected, young man?'

'Yes, sir.' Head up, Martin stood his ground, attempting to avoid nothing.

'Wat did not find it so.'

'No, sir.'

'You do not enjoy your lessons?'

Martin shuffled his feet along the bare wooden floor, frowning, then burst out, 'He always has the answers but I never see him working. I wish I knew how he does it!'

For a moment his uncle waited for the childish 'It's not fair', but it did not come. Neither was there mention of his lively brother's escapades of which their tutor complained, and because of this loyalty Edward was preparing to let him off more lightly than he had intended when he was suddenly aware that he no longer had Martin's attention, that the lad's gaze was directed over his shoulder and that his distress had given way to a grin he was making a not altogether successful attempt to smother. Edward turned in his chair. There, at the small, many paned window, Cecily's lively face was peering in, framed in a rabbit's-fur hood. She was standing on something, with young Mary holding her steady. Although he could not see her, he had no doubt that beside her on the ground Anne was jumping up and down, angry at her own inability to take part in what was going on. At any other time he would have returned his daughter's smile; now, because serious matters were on hand, he half-rose to rebuke her, forgetting his crippled leg, as from time to time he still did even after all these years. He dropped clumsily back into his chair.

'Shout for one of the maids to take those children away!' he snapped and Martin ran to do his bidding, returning immediately to resume his former stance. Irritated with himself that he had taken his weakness out on small children, his uncle said, 'Sit down, my boy,' and easing himself back in his own chair, regarded the child as he obeyed. He could not postpone everything until after Christmastide; he must deal with the last part of Master Price's letter now. It confirmed something he had known ever since the boys began to toddle, something he had closed his eyes to, hoping it would go away. Wat would turn questions off with his bright, innocent smile, giving the impression that he had no idea what the tutor was talking about; Martin would not. How best to proceed? Warily, he decided, and in roundabout fashion.

'You have found it hard to settle to life away from this house?'

Again, 'Yes, sir.' Nothing more.

'Can you tell me why?'

For a second Martin's eyes dropped, then: 'I miss all of you and – and the animals, sir. It makes me hurt inside.'

'If Wat were not with you would it be easier? Master Price tells me he needs constantly to separate you.'

Martin flushed, yet he forced himself to meet his uncle's gaze again. Defensively he said, 'All the boys fight, sir. Did not you and my father . . .?'

Edward smiled. 'Often and hard, but throughout it all we loved each other, Martin. Our quarrels blew over like summer clouds. Yours do not, I think.'

Martin's eyes swam with tears of which he was bitterly ashamed, and he dashed a hand across his eyes.

'No, they do not,' he whispered. 'Master Price says it is sinful and I do my best to love Wat, but unless I do exactly

133

what he says . . .' He made a hopeless gesture. 'Tell me what to do, please.'

'Nothing for the present. Go out and enjoy your freedom. You have earned it. "Martin has tried hard",' he quoted (omitting the qualification 'although his achievements are but mediocre'); 'And I very much doubt that the sin – if sin it be – is all on your side. Away with you!'

Separate schools, he wondered, as the door closed behind his nephew? Should twins be kept apart? Agnes had not sneered when he mentioned this problem; she too had observed it. The dislike between the brothers went far deeper than sibling rivalry and whilst Martin fought against it and thought it sinful, Wat did not. In all things he took his own way and although many a time it was in jest, anyone and anything in his path suffered. It was Agnes's unspoken belief that the combined high spirits of his father and mother had become something warped and unpleasant in Wat.

Throughout that holiday the household saw little of Wat except at mealtimes and when he accompanied them to church. He was adept at slipping away; always he was vague as to his doings. And it was as Martin had said; his school holiday tasks were completed as if by magic.

Two days after their return it was as if Martin had never been away. Master Price's tasks done, he too spent time away from the house, but more often than not it was in company with his small cousins and many times Edward, on his daily tour of inspection, found him about the yards or pasture with the shepherds, intently regarding the animals, learning all he could, offering his own surprisingly mature observations, and always with three-year-old Cecily by his side as if she were his sheepdog.

'Are we to make a shepherd of you then, Martin?' he asked one day, coming upon the boy unseen.

The child treated the joke in all seriousness. 'One day, sir, when I've finished my schooling, can we drive some of your sheep up to Barndale?'

He and Wat had known of their northern inheritance all their lives, although they had met none of their mother's family.

'After school and university your ideas may have changed.'

And the problem of school and how to resolve the clash between two brothers so different in personality was with them again. In the event the problem solved itself in a way no-one could have foreseen or wished.

It was young Cecily who came running into the house, white-faced. 'Martin is all dead. He fell bang out of a tree.'

Her father grabbed his crutches and made his way into the hall, sending a maid to fetch Agnes and Bennitt, the one to go with him, the other to make ready with blankets, bandages and warm water the room kept for sickness and other such emergencies. He could not – would not – believe the boy dead, he told himself fiercely. Nevertheless, at first sight of the small body on the frozen ground, surrounded by a small knot of servants and farm workers, his heart turned over.

He let himself down beside the unconscious Martin, noting as he did so that the boy's left leg, just above the ankle, was bent at a sickeningly wrong angle; that splinters of bone showed yellow-white through broken skin. A hand on his chest confirmed that the boy still breathed and he smoothed back the hair from the serene, pale face.

'What happened, Wat?'

'He fell out of the big apple tree, sir.' For once his voice was small and frightened, its usual jauntiness missing. 'He – he was all right until I tried to help him up, then he fainted.'

'You did *what?*' Agnes Woodfall was kneeling beside her brother. 'Where is whatever sense you were born with, Walter?' He shrank away; she was the one person in his world who had never succumbed to his childish charm, and now her condemnation was scathing. Without pausing, she said, 'Bring a hurdle, Ben, and you, Gideon, find Jed for me. I shall need him to help me set this bone. He'll know what to bring. Walter –' her tone grew sharp again. 'Tell Aunt Bennitt we are coming. Run, boy, run.'

And trailed by Cecily, who had stood on the edge of the

small crowd with one fist stuffed into her mouth to stifle her sobs, Wat ran to do as he was bidden.

Once in the house, with Martin carried carefully upstairs and into the room made ready to receive him, Agnes ran skilled hands over his other limbs, over his body, felt the lump on his temple that had risen like an egg and was rapidly turning black, lifted one eyelid and peered at a dilated eye. Across the boy's body she faced her brother, who had come as best he might up the stairs and stood there, panting.

'You could have saved yourself the trouble.' Her mouth twitched into a faint smile. 'You've only to go down again. There's nothing for you to do here. With fortune on our side he'll stay unconscious whilst Jed and I do what needs to be done, but just in case – you and Bennitt take all the children as far away as you can.'

As he turned to obey, Jed arrived, bearing the strips of wood that would be used to splint the boy's leg once they had straightened it. No words passed between groom and mistress. They had worked together many times, on humans, on animals, sometimes successfully, sometimes to no avail, and he saw the knife in her hand with no sense of surprise; cut she must if she were to ease the bone back through the skin, to straighten the leg, to give them any chance at all of saving the boy's limb, if not his very life. Without waiting for command, he leaned heavily across the unconscious body, put large hands on the boy's leg just above the wound.

Edward and Bennitt had marshalled their little ones out of the house and were halfway across the orchard, with Cecily clinging to her father and he comforting her that her cousin was not dead, only – as he put it – sleeping because he had bumped his head, when the first sound reached them that told that Martin Woodfall had regained his senses all too soon. Scream after shrill scream of pain rang through the frosty air, sharp and hideous. For once in her husband's presence, Bennitt took the initiative and found voice enough to call, 'Follow me, children. Run now, run!'

Scooping up the toddler Anne under one arm and taking Mary by a hand, commanding Cecily and Wat with a look, she ran on and on, trying to turn matters into a game for them, all the while aware that her husband, when the first scream sounded, had fallen to the ground and crouched huddled, head buried in his hands. Then it was she realized that Cecily was not with her and, turning, saw that the child had gone back to her father, that an arm was about his bowed shoulders, one chubby hand patting his head. From that distance her mother saw her lips moving but could distinguish no words, saw Edward cling to her, rocking her backwards and forwards, put his hands over her ears that she might be spared the noise that was presently cut off as suddenly as it had begun.

Slowly, draggingly, Bennitt made her way back. She had given her first thought to the children, as was proper; it was Cecily, her father's favourite, who had stayed to comfort him, to be beside him when he was stricken by sounds that could not but remind him of his own ordeal at the hands of a surgeon. Bitterly Bennitt castigated herself for the feeling within her; she could not be jealous of a three-year-old girl, she could not!

Agnes Woodfall, who seemed never to be put out of her stride by anything, appeared at table as usual that evening. Bessie sat by the boy, she said; he was quiet and needed nothing at present.

Abstractedly, as he peeled an apple, her brother said, 'We must send to Downfelton for the surgeon first thing in the morning.'

'There is no need. He can do no more than Jed and I have done. The time to send will be if the worst comes to the worst.'

Anxiously Bennitt glanced at the children about the table, but the cryptic sentence meant nothing to any of them, although it struck fear into the adults who heard it. If infection set in, as it almost certainly would, the boy would die or must be crippled for life by amputation.

It was with that thought heavy upon him that Edward Woodfall, accompanied by his wife, made his way late that night, when all were abed, to the small sickroom beneath the eaves. They entered silently upon a place where the only light, apart from one pale candle, was that of the moon, riding full and clear in the frosty sky beyond the window put together by Master Jarvis's glazier from oddly shaped pieces of coloured glass salvaged long ago from the old abbey church. Everything was muted, dim, and by the bed where Martin lay motionless, his eyes tight closed, stood Agnes.

Whether it was because of the way her hands were lifted before her or whether it was the fact that as she leaned forward slightly she was speaking – well nigh chanting – and that her shadow ran huge, black and deformed up the wall and across the ceiling, Edward did not stop to consider. Through his head rang words once spoken, never forgotten: 'The future of the Woodfall family rests with you and your children . . .' and a wave of superstitious fear took him. For the first time in many years he remembered whence this sister of his had come, how she was regarded by the villagers, and in that fear he spoke one word in a tone of command that made Bennitt, close behind him, catch her breath. Agnes straightened and without a word of reply rounded the foot of the bed and moved towards the door.

They gave way as she passed; once more Edward said sharply, 'Aglaia!' and followed her out into the passage-way.

Her heart thumping against her ribs, Bennitt, as she looked at the closing door, crossed herself in the way Parson Watson told his congregation was sinful. This situation, the night, the strangeness of her sister-in-law's behaviour and her husband's reaction to it, made it a most comforting sin. Casting a hasty glance towards the boy on the bed, who appeared to be breathing normally, she ran back across the room and pressed her ear to the ill-fitting door panels. Voices came to her clearly.

'Agnes, the boy *must* live, do you hear me?'

'That, brother, is in the hands of God.' Agnes's calm was unruffled.

'And through the gift of healing He has given you, you are His agent. *There is no need for more.*'

After a short silence Agnes replied, 'Yes, Edward,' in a tone that held submission.

'You know these things, Taggy. *Will* he live?'

'Aye, he will live.' It was years since her brother had called her by the diminutive of her name, the diminutive or – the other. That she had not heard used since they dragged her mother away to kill her.

Edward, all severity abated, sounded more like his everyday self. 'The boy and his brother were left to us in trust. One day they will go to take up their northern inheritance. Until then we must keep them safe. Their branch of the family is the one likely to carry the Woodfall name into another generation, for neither Thomas nor I seem able to father a son.'

Agnes's voice softened, giving ease of mind to a much-loved brother. 'There will be a Woodfall in this house to carry on your name, I promise you, Edward.'

Pressed against the door, Bennitt almost cried out loud. She would give Edward a son after all these years, after so many girls! It never occurred to her to doubt Agnes's confident tones. Silently she crept back to the bed, put a hand over one of the sleeping boy's and gave herself up to dreaming.

2

On his hard bed in the small, cold room high in the roof of Master Jerome's house in Trinity Street, Robert Cooper opened his eyes to consciousness for the first time in many days and shut them again as quickly. He had been ill; somewhere a long way in the past he seemed to have heard the dull voice of Joan, the housekeeper, saying that he had a fever, that it would soon pass. But it was not Joan who watched him now. Master Jerome leaned over the end of the bed, thin and dark, glittering eyes intent; Jerome who taught him day after long, weary day, with whom he ate his evening meal before he climbed to this room to read more books, as the light permitted, until he fell into bed exhausted.

This room, that way of life, had been his without break for two years from the day Master Jenkins assumed responsibility for him, when he had been conducted the short distance to Jerome's house and the crashing of its front door behind him rendered it his prison. Had he been a child used to being loved and kindly treated he might not have survived, for although he was well clothed and given adequate food, there was no-one to speak him a word in friendship. But Parson Watson had done him a better turn than he knew with his harsh treatment; life in Trinity Street was in many respects the same as life at Highwoods. The work expected of him was hard, discipline was strict, rewards non-existent.

Where it differed was that now he was the pupil of a learned man who not only loved classical and modern languages alike but delighted in passing his knowledge on to a child he soon discovered to be an apt pupil.

Shortly after his arrival, standing before Master Jerome to be examined, Robert had had no hesitation in repeating the small Latin vocabulary that Parson Watson had beaten into him, carefully reproducing the pronunciation and inflexion of verbs and nouns as he remembered them. So intent was he on his task that it was some time before he became aware that he was being watched in disbelief. He stopped, awaiting the punishment he was sure must follow, wondering where he had erred, what he had forgotten. Then Jerome, with one of the few touches of humour Robert ever encountered in him, asked, 'I wonder if you will find it as easy to forget as to remember that rubbish you are mouthing, Cooper? For forget it you must if you are ever to speak and read Latin correctly, and I will accept nothing less. You have been taught by a fool, a complete – no, no, I am not trying to trap you into telling me whence you come! We have a hard enough task ahead of us, you and I, without wasting time on such matters as that. Here – take this book . . .'

Robert said no more than 'Yes, sir,' to this astounding statement but inwardly he smiled a small, surprised smile. He had thought Parson Watson to be so clever, and he knew the parson himself thought so too.

Before long, Robert had decided that Master Jerome was in fact two men. As a teacher his enthusiasm was boundless. Latin, Greek, several modern European languages, history and geography, mathematics, were presented to Robert as exciting things to be treasured and used, so that the boy quickly caught his enthusiasm and worked hard. Jerome could even read upside down and without appearing to look, as Robert discovered when they sat opposite each other, he working at some task assigned, Master Jerome reading through the piles of documents of all shapes and sizes that came regularly to him, annotating them, refolding them. He raised his eyes only if appealed to directly, yet would often provide a word or tense Robert needed at just the right moment. The boy's admiration was excited by this skill; he would have liked his master had there been any encouragement to do so, although Jerome's enthusiasm ran in harness with extreme impatience and many was the time that the thin cane he carried hissed down across Robert's fingers with all his force behind it. But once lessons were over, it was as if someone had snuffed a candle behind Jerome's eyes. He became unspeaking and brooding, withdrawing into a world of his own in which there was no place for Robert. Yet the boy felt himself to be trusted, for when Master Jerome was absent, be it only for an hour or for a whole day at a time, no more constraint was placed upon him than an offhand 'Carry on as far as you can with what we were studying yesterday, Cooper. We will talk about it when I return.'

Only when Amos Jenkins visited the house, which he did frequently, did Robert mark a change in his teacher. Then Jerome became well nigh tongue-tied and once, as he held out a paper towards the visitor, Robert saw his hand tremble uncontrollably. Perhaps, the child thought, Master Jenkins's lack of trust upset him, for how else could he interpret the fact that, unwilling to accept Jerome's word on his pupil's excellent progress, Jenkins brought lists of questions, stood over Robert whilst he answered them and took them away, no-one knew where, like some schoolmaster at an examination.

The pattern of Robert's life changed on a day, at the end of two years, when Jerome, shorter of temper than ever, criticized, corrected and tapped with his cane until the boy, whose own inborn hot temper was developing as he grew, could stand no more. He watched his tutor's bony fingers tear his hard-written essay across and across, throw the pieces at him with an instruction to do all again that night before he ate, and goaded to rebellion said, 'No, I will not!'

For a moment there was silence in the room, except that to Robert his words seemed to echo round and round the walls. A strange excitement filled him. He could not believe, as he stood there, eyes blazing, that it was so easy. He was going to get away with it! Jerome faced him unmoving, gripping the edge of the table between them, staring at the boy as if he had never seen him before, and in his eyes Robert read not the anger he had expected, not even surprise, but something approaching horror.

How long they stood there the child did not know; he braced himself to withstand punishment that for a time seemed as if it would not come. Then, as if he shook himself free from some spell, Jerome crossed himself and almost ran from the room. When he returned he held a light whip, the thin lash of which he ran through his fingers time and again.

Then it was that Robert Cooper learned that the cuffs he had taken all his life, the sting of the cane, were but mild punishment compared to what a man in a white-hot rage and armed with a whip could do to a child's back naked save for a thin shirt. He had taken three strokes, the first of which had driven him writhing to the floor, when Master Jenkins, delivering a bundle of papers for Jerome, heard his agonized screams and burst into the room.

One buffet from Jenkins's fist sent Jerome spinning into a corner and Robert, crouching between the two men, lifted a shocked white face towards two grown-ups who appeared to be fighting over him, or rather – as he soon realized – to be using him as an excuse to continue what was obviously a running battle.

'And who gave you authority to treat the child so? You might well have killed him.' The voice that Robert had always considered monotonous now had a cutting edge to it that made Master Jerome shrink away. The whip he had used so diligently and with such seeming pleasure dropped from nerveless fingers; he muttered confused and garbled words about discipline being good for a child and only carrying out orders.

'Whose orders?' demanded his visitor. 'You realize that if a word about this reached – a certain quarter – you would find yourself taken – what does it say in that book you professed to live by? – "whither thou wouldst not"?'

Jerome's face seemed to the watching boy to grow small and very pinched. His fingers made strange, vague gestures of abject apology and he spoke of bathing the boy's back himself.

'Get to that hellhole you call your room,' said Jenkins harshly, 'and pray for all you are worth to whatever God will listen to you. I will see you later.'

Jerome scuttled away like a mouse pursued by a cat, his feet pounded up the stairs, the door of his room crashed shut. Only then did Jenkins move. He poured wine into a goblet and knelt beside Robert, holding it to his lips, waiting for its warmth to revive the shaking child, before he called for Joan to bring rags and hot water and, telling Robert to bend over the nearest chair, bathed his back until the seeping blood stopped. There was no kindness in his action, nothing to make the child offer thanks, and presently the two stood regarding each other until Jenkins said, 'So I came at a propitious moment for you, young man. It will not happen again, I promise you.' His voice was once more flat and monotonous. 'One day I will tell you about Master Jerome. His is an amusing story, although Sir William would not thank me for saying so.'

Still the boy made no move; he stood as steadily as he could, stifling sobs that now threatened to overwhelm him, staring straight ahead, his lacerated back throbbing in time to the heart that pounded against his ribs. They were going to send him away. These people, to whom he had grown accustomed, cared for him no more than anyone else ever had. He wondered, with a dull pain in the pit of his stomach, whether, without knowing it, he had done something so wicked that nobody could love him, nobody could even spare a kind word for him. Then Master Jenkins's voice broke in upon his thoughts.

'It must seem an eternity since you arrived here. It is time to get you out for a while.' His laugh was dry, mirthless. 'Don't tremble so, lad; you have done no wrong as far as I know, unless you count displeasing Jerome a sin! You are large enough now for work other than this . . .' Contemptuously he indicated the books piled on the table. 'In future you will spend your afternoons either with me or someone of my choosing, learning a very different sort of lesson. Be ready to go out at noon in, say, three days' time. That mess he has made of your back will be healing by then.' And so saying he too pounded up the stairs and crashed, without knocking, into Master Jerome's room.

Whatever he said there took little time and when the tutor came downstairs he had regained his composure. He and Robert worked together on the Latin translation that had been the cause of the beating and it dawned upon Robert for the first time that in some way this priestly man – for so he still thought of him – lived in fear. Certainly for the rest of that day he was most subdued, and his manner towards his pupil at times verged on the conciliatory.

In the three years since that day Robert's afternoons had been much more to the taste of a growing boy. He rode mile after horseback mile, or practised fencing and wrestling with men all of whom, by their talk, owed loyalty and admiration to Amos Jenkins, until a day when Jenkins himself said, 'And there are other things you must know, young Cooper. You may not always have a blade handy when you need it, in which case bare hands must serve.' The next moment Robert found himself on his back on the grass, his teacher's arm pressing on his windpipe, the usually expressionless eyes actually showing amusement.

'I have you now, Cooper,' he said, only to feel, in the

same instant, his own dagger, snatched from his belt by the lad beneath him, pricking him in the stomach.

'And I have you, sir,' gasped Robert, at which the arm was removed from his throat and for the first time in all the years he had known him, Master Jenkins threw back his head and gave a great guffaw of laughter, exposing yellow-green teeth.

'God's wounds, boy!' he shouted. 'You'll do! I shall make something of you yet.'

And after that, lessons in self-defence progressed apace until Robert, in the isolation that was his lot once the day's work was over, often wondered how many boys of his age could creep up undetected, as he could, on a man and stab him from behind or even, if he threw his as yet light weight correctly, bring him down unarmed. The lessons disturbed him. He could see no reason why so many men should think of him as an enemy. He was aware, vaguely, that when he grew old enough he would like to teach Latin and Greek like Master Jerome, but he knew better than to question his teacher or Jenkins who, for all he had forbidden Jerome use of the whip, was quick enough with a blow himself when displeased.

Now, as once more his eyes flickered open, Robert thought that whilst he felt drowsy and warm it might be a good time to ask Master Jerome about teaching. Some long-suppressed desire to reach out in friendship to another human being, born of a dream he had had in delirium when a small, plump woman had smiled at him, put her arms about him and called him 'little one', made him want to tell Jerome that in spite of his strictness he really liked him far better than Amos Jenkins and his friends who said and laughed at things Robert did not think were funny in the slightest. He had actually moved his mouth in what he hoped was a smile, although being so weak he could not be certain, when his tutor said coldly, 'At last! Have you any idea how far behind you are with your work?'

Tears he could not control brimmed out of the child's eyes, ran down his white cheeks. Master Jerome had moved now; was standing by his side, peering at him with no sign of gladness at his recovery.

'Time makes all things clear, Cooper. All things.'

'Sir?' The tears choked Robert's voice and he turned his head sideways so that they might run away into his pillow.

'Robert Emory. "My name is Robert Emory", you said, time and again, in your fever. Fortunate that no-one but I heard you.'

For a moment the name meant nothing to him after all these years, then memory came flooding back: the name, the threats of what would happen to him if ever he told anyone who he was. Terror started within him and weakly he retched, whimpering, 'No, no . . .'

'Your secret is safe with me, Cooper, safer than you know. Hold your face still.' Taking a cloth from the stand beside the bed Jerome dabbed awkwardly at the boy's tears so that Robert, overcome by gratitude, turned his face against the cold, dry hand and tried to thank him, only to have the hand snatched away.

3

To the relief and delight of his family, Martin took no infection. Within days, the effects of the blow to his head had passed and the problem that exercised them all was how to keep an active small boy still and his mind occupied whilst the bones of his leg knit. There were times when he grew fractious, refused food, cried not so much from pain as at the boredom of life, and it was his Aunt Bennitt who sustained him. Hour after hour she sat beside him, talking of her own childhood, telling stories she had learned from her mother, bringing such work as she could to the child's bedside and even, when he was propped on pillows, putting a piece of wood across the bed and bullying him into sorting herbs, stringing dried vegetables and untangling the rough wool with which she and Agnes embroidered wall hanging after wall hanging, not only for decoration but to keep the draughts out of a house that was still new enough to suffer the effects of shrinking wood. He shared the tasks with Mary, and young Cecily was forever running in and out of his room, chattering and laughing, until at times he wanted to throw things at her. Then, later, he joined in lessons with the sisters, helping them with their early reading and writing.

Wat had long since returned to school when the time came for Agnes to free Martin from the splints that had anchored him to his bed through long, weary weeks. She showed Bessie how his leg must be massaged to bring back strength and use to it and thereafter scarcely visited the lad at all, but his Uncle Edward brought an old crutch along and bestowed it upon him, the twinkle in his eyes belying his frown.

'Ben has cut this down to the right size. Ruined it, to my eyes. But understand this, nephew – it is yours for a short time only. I can always find a use for it, even if only to poke a fire!'

A week later, once more sleeping in the bed he had always before shared with Wat, Martin was a full member of the family circle again, to the delight of everyone, especially Cecily, who leaped about him until she had to be warned to be careful that she did not knock her cousin off his feet again.

Then his uncle said to him, 'We must talk about your schooling, Martin. Master Price cannot take you back until the autumn. You will have fallen sadly behind Wat, I fear.'

Martin held his breath. Relief from Wat's constant company had been one of the few bright spots in his illness. 'Sir, sir, must I go back? Could I not stay here? I will help with the sheep – with anything you name?'

'So that when you go back to Barndale they will wonder why your father's son can barely read and write – and ask what I have been thinking of to let such a state of affairs come about!'

'I will walk to Parson Watson's every day, sir. He can teach me.'

His uncle made a grimace of distaste. 'Aye, if you want lessons in not smiling, especially on the Sabbath, and to be taught that joy in life is sinful, he is your man. But for nothing else.'

Martin's face fell. 'Yes, sir. I know it is not – not . . .'

'Sensible?' his uncle supplied, smiling. 'Nor is it, but I have not called you in here without giving the matter some thought. I'm loath to send you back to Downfelton. So, young Martin, when your leg is strong enough to bear you so far, you will come with me to visit a certain person who may hold the key to your problem.'

Master Acres, said the old woman who cooked for him, was out tending his flock 'thataways' and Edward Woodfall did not seem surprised that the helpful, pointing finger indicated the ruins of the old abbey. When they came upon him, sitting on a stone that had once been the base of a great, round pillar, and facing the gaunt skeleton of the east window, it seemed to Martin that he was praying, even though sheep grazed about his feet and he was quick enough to fetch them back when they strayed. He rose to his feet and awaited them in silence. There was no tugging of the forelock such as Martin had seen from other villagers. Equal awaited equal, and so Edward Woodfall addressed him.

'I bring you a problem, Peter, a sore problem. My nephew's schooling is all a-sea after his accident and he is anxious to stay here. Can I look to you for help, do you think?'

'So, after the merry dance you and Lewis led me you think I would go through the whole thing again?' It was the voice of a gentleman, not the country burr Martin was used to hear from such men, and which he had heard Master Acres himself use time and again about the village.

'Strange how you always won in the end!' said Edward, smiling.

The priest nodded in his gentle way, indicating the block of stone, inviting them to join him.

'And suppose I have forgotten all I ever knew?'

'Despite the fact that you come regularly to borrow my poor few books! How say you?'

'What exactly do you need?'

'A tutor for the boy. Someone who will live at the house as one of the family, and have the boy ready for Oxford when that time shall come.'

Peter turned to Martin. 'And you? You are willing to be taught by a shepherd?'

For a moment there had been hesitation in his quiet voice. Almost Martin expected him to add 'my son', and much that had puzzled his young mind became suddenly clear. This man tended sheep, knew much about them, but he was no more a shepherd than Martin himself. He came as often as he might to the abbey, sat in what had been its nave in an attitude of prayer, because this had – once – been his home, at a time when the Church was different and there were men called monks. Master Price had told him about them.

'You are no shepherd, sir,' he said bluntly, and coloured at his own forwardness. 'That is – I ask your pardon – but before – before the King changed the Church – you were here, were you not?'

'So I was. When this was the House of God and I . . .'

'Besides,' added Martin, dismissing Master Price's strictly Protestant lesson and coming to the thing that meant far more to him than any change in religion, 'if you won't tutor me I shall have to go back to school, and I'd do anything to get out of that!'

Both men laughed. 'Good manners and honesty together,' said Master Acres. 'I like that in a boy.' He turned back to Edward. 'You took enough of the stones from here to make me feel at home in your grand house! Young Sim will take over quite easily with the sheep. When do you wish me to come?'

'Within the week, if you please.'

'And, sir –' The words surprised Martin himself even as he spoke them; he had given the matter no thought, yet it seemed sensible and right. 'Have you any objection to teaching a girl at the same time?'

'Cecily?' The exclamation was his uncle's; although Mary was older, she did not occur to him. 'Why not? She is bright enough. The two of them might go well in harness together once she has mastered her letters.'

The idea did not seem in the least strange to Master Acres, and when Cecily herself heard that once she knew her letters she was to sit alongside her cousin and read Latin and Greek as did the Queen herself in London, she squeaked in delight. Quickly, confidingly, she put her hand into Martin's, looking up at him very seriously.

'I'll be good,' she said, then added, 'if Wat says anything about one of your legs being thinner than the other I'll hit him – hard. He won't hit me back because I'm a girl.'

Martin was not too sure about that, but her father was unable to hold back a guffaw of laughter. 'Minx! By the time Wat is with us again there will be no difference for him to notice. Just be sure your head is not thin, that is all. I want to find it so bulging with learning that you put Cousin Rose to shame!'

CHAPTER IX

1

It was a year since a clerk from the offices of the recently created Baron of Burghley, previously Sir William Cecil, had arrived in Trinity Street. His lordship had required Master Cooper's presence immediately.

Dressed in the doublet and hose he usually wore only on the Sabbath, eleven-year-old Robert rose from his bow before the great man to find a somewhat dog-eared and blotted letter being held out to him in not unkindly fashion, with an order that he correct its grammar and spelling, after which he was to translate it first into French, then into Latin. 'From my son, Thomas.' His lordship's tone was wry. To Robert it was more like the letter of a young child than a man of almost thirty, so badly written and misspelt was it.

Since that time, this first task being satisfactorily completed, he had gone to the offices in Whitehall on three days of each week and at the behest of one clerk or another had copied or translated documents and letters, reports, plans, accounts, all the time learning, increasing his understanding of the importance of the vast organization controlled by the quiet man who was the Queen's right hand and who had once decreed the life to be lived by a small, unwanted child.

For years, as he went about his work unpraised, unrewarded, there remained in the back of Robert's mind, fed by occasional dreams of happy times far away, the hope that one day he would give and receive friendship. He fought it, but it persisted, although he had no idea where to search for it. Most certainly not in the cold, bare house where Jerome taught him and regularly, ever since discovering his real name, used him in a way that sickened the boy and destroyed much of the enjoyment he had once taken in his lessons; not from other boys who had over the years come to the house for teaching, to be weighed in the balance of Jerome's high standards, found wanting and disappeared within weeks, if not days; not from Amos Jenkins and his fellows, who mocked even whilst they taught, nor – although here he had for a time thought that it might happen – from anyone with whom he came into contact at Whitehall. By his fellow clerks, all older than he by some years, he was, he knew, regarded with suspicion. Had he not been brought into their ranks by Lord Burghley himself and did not the great man from time to time fetch him away for a whole afternoon, no-one knew where? Behind ink-stained hands it was whispered that he was his lordship's bastard, being trained to follow in his work, although why, when he had sons of his two marriages, the spinners of tales could not tell. They solved their problem by ignoring the boy; saying nothing to him or in his presence unless it concerned work. That way nothing could be reported to the man they all served.

It was the afternoons when a servant came to announce, so that everyone from senior clerk downwards might hear, that Lord Burghley awaited Robert Cooper, that the lad came to hate more than any other times. For those outings, begun by his lordship in curiosity to see how the boy he remembered had shaped, and continued in careless kindness as his isolation from others of his own age became apparent, killed all hope Robert ever had of friendship. To great houses along the river he was taken, Lord Burghley's or those of his friends, made his bow to the grown-ups of the party and was turned out to join their children in gardens such as he had never dreamed of. It was there he discovered just how different he was. They were not as a general rule unkind to him – one child more or less made no difference to their pastimes and he was as well-mannered, as well-spoken as they – but their laughter meant nothing to him. He thought throwing a ball from one to another a waste of time, nor could he see any point in hiding in ridiculous places – so obvious to him – and waiting to be found by a shrieking boy or girl who pretended the task was difficult. At twelve years old the wellspring of childhood within him had dried up. He made belief, for politeness's sake, but make-believe was all it was; he neither gave nor received enjoyment.

So, one afternoon, he was standing in Lord Burghley's garden, one of a group taking turns to throw a ball high in the air for the person next to him or her to catch, when his mind had returned to a matter his work had disclosed to him only that morning. It had taken the thump of a misthrown ball against his chest to arouse him from his introspection.

A girl's light voice called, 'You'll have to fetch it yourself, Philip; he's day-dreaming,' and up to Robert ran a youth he had never seen before. He was some years older than the rest of the party but appeared not to find the game childish, and his presence was regarded as a high honour by the smaller children. He was handsome, would-be friendly and obviously well used to being liked.

'I am Philip Sidney. Who are you?'

Stiffly Robert faced him. 'Robert Cooper. His lordship brought me here. I work for him.'

'Good Lord!' Sidney was surprised. 'Well, please yourself, Cooper. Join us and welcome,' and he snatched up the ball and ran back to his admirers.

All would have been well had not the girl waiting for him said mischievously and clearly when he spoke to her, 'I don't care who he is, Philip. He's very much better looking than you!'

The next moment, although this time he saw it coming and tried unsuccessfully to avoid it, the ball, thrown with all the force Philip Sidney could muster, hit Robert again, hard, on the side of his face. This time there was no easy pleasantry. Sidney's voice was indifferent; he spoke as to a servant.

'Throw it back!'

For a moment Robert stood motionless, hands clenched

at his side, face stinging from the blow, before he retrieved the brightly coloured ball from a flowerbed and returned it as viciously as he could. The fact that it went astray, causing a shout of laughter, did nothing to calm him. He took to his heels and ran along a path down to the river, with the laughter of the other children ringing in his ears.

He would sit on the bank and watch the river traffic until he had control of himself once more, until it was time to leave; that would be safe. Then, at the very edge of the water, he saw a small man-made cave, intended, he supposed, for the shelter of boatmen awaiting their passengers. He flung himself into it like a rabbit into the safety of its burrow, dropped down and was sitting with burning face on updrawn knees before he realized that he was not alone. Almost beside him sat another boy, a book between his hands.

Robert sniffed, wiped away tell-tale tears of anger with the back of one hand and made to rise, wondering if there was nowhere he could be alone, when a thin, sharp voice said, 'Stay!' Despite its curtness the word was an invitation rather than a command.

His eyes now clear, Robert saw that his companion was younger than he. His face was as thin and sharp as his voice and studying the cast of his features Robert was not surprised, when the other moved, to find that he was hunchbacked and twisted of spine. Voice and manner were those of a gentleman born and bred, and he was much, much older than his age.

'My name is Cecil,' he said, 'Robert Cecil.'

'Robert Cooper. Your father brought me here. I work in his office.'

The explanation evoked none of the surprise it had caused Philip Sidney. 'I have seen you before. My father thinks well of you.'

Impulsively Robert said, 'I came in here to get away,' and found Master Cecil watching him understandingly, so that he knew that the book was an excuse for solitude.

'It doesn't pay to let Sidney upset you. He's only showing off.' There was quiet contempt in the sharp voice and with the words he returned to his reading, leaving Robert to his knees-up, head-down, thinking.

What, he wondered, would Lord Burghley's young son say if he told him the truth, that he had run away not to avoid the gibes but to overcome his own instinctive reaction to them. There had been an instant when he had seen Philip Sidney's face through a red haze. He could say, 'I almost killed him. He is bigger than I am and older, but if I put my knee in his back and my hands round his throat I could break his neck quite easily.' The realization horrified him; all that Amos Jenkins had taught him – coupled with a hot temper so long kept under strict control – had brought him to this. Unless he kept himself on a tight rein, one day he might kill a man – perhaps even a woman – for no better reason than that he was offended and off his guard.

How long he remained crouched there he never knew. But he made up his mind, drew a deep breath and rose to his feet, facing Master Cecil.

'I shall never cry again!' he said, and bowed slightly. 'Goodbye.'

2

Working methodically, rhythmically, Martin Woodfall gathered the watercress his Aunt Agnes had sent him to collect. He stood in the sparkling, shallow waters of the swift-running brook that a short distance away emptied into the deep waters of the River Pen, plunged an arm, dragged stalks taut, broke them, and threw the bunch into the basket on the bank, so that sparkling droplets fell from it in flight like a miniature rain shower. As he worked he whistled, happily, tunelessly. Somewhere nearby Cecily was gathering grasses to make a posy for her mother and all about him the trees were turning to red and gold. The gaily painted small boats of their leaves dropped into the water around him and sped on their way to the river. It might be the last truly warm day of the year and he was enjoying it, glad that Master Acres had allowed him an unexpected holiday. That was one of the delights being educated at home had brought him; there were treats such as a day in which to run free, something of which poor Walter, tight in school in Downfelton, knew nothing.

He was roused sharply from his happiness by the sight of green leaves among the red and gold that passed him – the leaves of the very watercress he had already picked, and as he straightened his back he shouted, 'Cec! Little fool! Stop wasting my time. Aunt Agnes will . . .'

He broke off, standing ankle-deep in the water, staring open-mouthed, for above him on the bank, taking watercress from the basket by handfuls and tossing it carelessly into the tiny current, sat not his cousin Cecily but his twin, neatly dressed, handsome as ever, his cap pushed on to the back of his shining red head. It was as if by the very act of pitying him he had conjured him out of thin air.

'Wat! I might have known it was you!' He gave no thought to the how or why of his brother's sudden appearance, being far more concerned to scoop up the greenery as it sailed past him. 'There's little enough of it as it is, and it's important Aunt Agnes has it.'

Wat sat back, watching his brother's vain efforts in some appreciation. 'What magic potion is the old woman brewing now? At dead of night and full of moon?'

Martin took no notice either of rudeness or absurdity, splashed out of the water and dropped back into the basket what stalks he had managed to retrieve.

'Don't you know anything?' he asked scornfully. 'Anne has a rash and watercress juice will make it itch less in the night so that the poor little thing can sleep without scratching.'

Wat rose to the challenge. 'Or ground ivy or burdock leaves,' he chanted. 'Just as good if you can stand the smell when you boil 'em! I know just as much as you about Aunt Agnes's remedies.'

As he spoke he stood up, proving himself still a head taller than his twin. Taking care to wait until Martin was drying his feet on the grass and pulling on his thick shoes, he took up the basket and hurled it and its contents into the middle of the stream. It landed in a deep channel and was carried at speed downstream between two streaks of dark green, water-flattened weed.

For a moment Wat regarded his handiwork with some complacency, and to his cost ignored his brother, then a well-aimed push took him in the small of his back and he found himself spluttering, face downwards, in the water. Struggling to his knees, to his feet, he looked at Martin consideringly, saw that beneath its freckles his square face had gone white, and prepared himself for battle.

'You can come out when you've fetched the basket *and* refilled it,' said Martin, and suddenly Wat was no longer laughing. His lips drew back in a snarl over his beautiful white teeth.

'Not without your help,' he said, and lunged at Martin's legs, throwing him off-balance, so that he too slithered into the water. Once their hands were upon each other they fought wildly, punching, scratching and kicking, even as they spat out the water that rose about them and choked them. The basket, the state of the watercress bed upon which they wrestled, were alike forgotten as each strove for mastery, and neither of them saw Cecily, attracted by the sound of shouting, running as fast as her short legs would carry her along the bank, squealing as she went, 'Aunt Agnes's basket! Get it back! Martin, help me!'

So intent was she on the fast-sinking wickerwork that she did not see how near she had come to the place where the stream ran into the Pen until the soft, dry banking crumbled beneath her feet and with a piercing scream she fell into deep water. The boys, by that time tiring, had dragged themselves up on to the bank of the stream and were lying there, gasping for breath, when they heard her cry for help. It was Martin she called, but Wat reached her first, saw in dismay the depth of water in which she struggled, rapidly being dragged under by the weight of her long, heavy gown, and held out a broken branch, urging the distraught child to hold on to it so that he could pull her

157

out. He was still standing there when Martin arrived, pushed him aside, and not waiting to remove his shoes, jumped in. In utter panic Cecily's flailing arms grabbed him about the neck and would have pulled them both under, for she took no notice of instructions to let him go, he would save her. At last, in desperation, his already depleted strength ebbing, he did the only thing he could do; he hit her hard beneath the chin, caught hold of her body as it slackened and fell away from him, turned on to his back and towed her to land where Wat, white-faced, hauled them both ashore.

It took some time to empty Cecily's lungs of water and even longer for her to recover from the effects of Martin's blow. He sat on the sun-warmed grass and held her tight to him, rocking her backwards and forwards, smoothing streaks of hair off her face, the only acknowledgement he made of his brother's presence being to look up once and say, in a quiet, emotionless voice, 'If she doesn't get better, I'll kill you.'

Wat, shaken by the whole incident, recalling mention of a cousin who had drowned in much the same place, made a stammered attempt at explanation; Martin knew he could not swim. After that he left the two alone. All the same he watched them keenly, noticed how when Cecily stirred, her first coughing word was for Martin, and that they looked at each other as if each must be reassured that the other was safe before anything else mattered. Feeling himself left out and not much caring for the sensation, Wat tried to take command.

'We must get her home before she catches cold. Can you walk, Cecily?'

'Wat! My head hurts and my legs are all wobbly.'

They wrung as much water as they could out of her sodden skirts and, with a cousin on each side to support her, she made the slow journey back to the house, at which time occurred to Martin the question he had not asked of his brother until then – 'Why are you here? You should be at school.'

Edward Woodfall asked the same question once he had made certain the children were not seriously hurt and had turned Cecily over to her Aunt Agnes.

Wrapped in a blanket, his hair drying richly red about his face, Wat smiled easily, charmingly. 'I ran away, sir. I needed to come home to see you all.'

His uncle frowned. 'In the middle of term? Do you know what you are saying? Heaven give me strength, boy; I shall never understand you!'

After which, sentence by sentence, he tore apart the tale the brothers had forced upon Cecily on the walk home, that she had fallen into the water and they had both jumped in to save her. He cut through the excuses that came so plausibly to Wat's tongue.

'We all know that you are as likely to work in the stables without being ordered as you are to jump into deep water! To make a young child lie to save your hide is despicable, Walter!'

'Martin agreed to it.' Wat was eager to apportion blame.

'And shall be punished equally, but if you had stayed at school, where you belong, the whole thing would never have happened.'

In the ten minutes that followed Wat saw no reason for his uncle to pray for strength. It seemed to the boy that the arm that wielded the leather strap across his back had more than enough power as it was.

Gasping a little, Edward said, 'You may go to your room for tonight, Walter. Tomorrow it's back to Downfelton and whatever punishment Master Price sees fit to administer. Send Martin to me, please.'

Now was not the time, Wat acknowledged to himself as he left the room, sniffing loudly, to broach the matter that had truly brought him home. He had long before realized that the discipline under which he lived was considerably sterner than anything Master Acres was likely to impose. The old fool had taught his father and uncle together, why not him and Martin? An escapade that involved climbing on to the school roof one moonlit night – for which Master Price had promised dire consequence – had made him decide to wait no longer. That he had miscalculated he now admitted; perhaps if he had managed to control his urge to taunt Martin all would have been well. He would, he decided with a martyred air, have to return to Downfelton after all and postpone his request until the end of term.

Having bathed Cecily, soothed her bruised jaw with salve and delivered her to her mother for comforting, Agnes turned her attention to the blanket-swathed Martin who, punishment over, sat silently by the fire in the kitchen awaiting her.

'Now, young man!' Before he could protest she had stripped away his wrappings, was paying close attention to numerous scratches on face and neck and a deep bite mark that disfigured one shoulder.

'It would appear that Cecily fought bravely! No wonder you hit her!' She had not heard the official version of the afternoon's happenings, for Cecily had been too upset to tell it; past experience of her nephews told her the truth.

Martin raised an anxious, tear-stained face. 'She will be all right? I have not hurt her much, have I?' He would have said more, but his aunt's ministrations made him fall silent, biting his lower lip.

'You saved her life, we both know that,' she said gently, and laid a hand on his head with more kindness than she was wont to show. 'Now, let me look at that ankle of yours. You told no-one you'd wrenched it, did you, you young fool?'

Martin held out for inspection the leg he had once broken, but he said nothing. His aunt applied a poultice of herbs and butter, bound into place by strips of linen. A wrench indeed! It bore all the hallmarks of having been repeatedly kicked, as if someone knew of a weak place and had concentrated on it. Seriously she considered whether to return to school with a most uncomfortably upset stomach might not serve Master Walter Woodfall right!

As he limped from the room, bound supperless for his bed, Martin said, 'The watercress – poor Anne . . .' and his aunt smiled.

'I'll fetch it myself. Rest well, nephew.'

Robert Cooper rose from his chair in Master Jerome's study, received his tutor's cold, silent nod of dismissal, gathered up his books and turned to leave, wondering if he would be able to find strength to undress before he fell asleep. He was at the door, the handle turned under his hand, when, 'Cooper!'

'Sir?' Obedient as always in word and manner, he returned to stand straight-backed before the thin figure hunched on its hard chair by the table. The numbers he had copied without interruption for five hours that afternoon seemed still to dance in their long black columns before his eyes and his body cried out for rest. No more work, not this evening. And not a summons to Jerome's room; above all, not that!

To his surprise Jerome picked up the candlestick by his elbow, held it so that its pale light fell on his pupil's young face.

'Your day was hard?'

The boy did not answer; every day was hard and the work expected of him increased.

'You find the work not to your liking?'

'I enjoy it, sir, thank you. And I will finish your essay tomorrow, that I promise.'

'The essay can wait. Pour yourself some wine, Cooper, and sit down.'

Robert did as he was bidden, taking his time. Why, after all these years, was Jerome making what seemed almost like an overture of friendship? Whatever his reason he was three days too late. Robert drank a silent toast to two young noblemen who had most certainly by now forgotten all about him but who between them had shown him the way he must take in life. A close watch on himself at all times; no friends, no relationships. Work, and progress through work, must satisfy him. That way lay no hurt, no danger. He set down his goblet, touched his books, and said, 'May I be excused, sir?'

His clumsy offer of friendship having met with the failure it deserved, Jerome nodded. As locked into solitude as the boy, he could think of no other way of putting into effect the instruction he had received from Lord Burghley that morning: 'By the way, Jerome, I'm pleased with young Cooper. An intelligent lad. But my son tells me he could well be at the end of his tether. I have no doubt he stands in awe of his teacher! A word or two of kindness would not, I think, come amiss.' Instead: 'Come to my room in one hour,' he said.

The breath that Robert Cooper drew was audible the length of the room. Books forgotten, tiredness for the moment overcome, he rose to his feet, facing his tutor. When he replied it was with the formal courtesy that had been expected of him ever since he could remember. There was no insolence in his voice, none was intended; its steadiness surprised him.

'With respect, sir, I shall not come to your room tonight or any night in the future.'

Not long after he rescued him from the beating that had never been repeated, Amos Jenkins had entertained Robert, during an afternoon's ride, with the story of Jerome's life as he knew it.

'We got hold of him about a year before you arrived in our midst, Cooper. He's a priest, sent from Rome. Came back here full of zeal. There is a brother involved somewhere too. Perhaps one day we'll lay our hands on him too. For one who professed to believe that helping to restore England to the Roman Church was a glorious mission and martyrdom something to be desired, he broke surprisingly easily. I've never seen another quite like him, in fact. Four of them altogether, there were, told off to do their work in different parts of the country. Jerome was taken as soon as he stepped ashore and the sight of the rack was enough to make him tell us all he knew, almost before we asked.' Jenkins's voice had grown yet more sneering. 'The reality against the dream, you see. It was not as pretty and easy as it looked in the pictures. Life is sweet! He betrayed his companions so quickly it was obscene. We caught every one, Cooper, every single one.' He licked his lips over the memory. 'Jerome was granted his life by Sir William on condition that he worked for us, which he has done ever since. I shall never forget it. But I trust our worthy turncoat as far as I could throw him. Which is why, my lad, if ever I ask you for information concerning him – whether strangers call at the house or so on – you will not be surprised, and will tell me immediately.'

It had made clear to Robert many things that had vaguely puzzled him but, strangely, the revelation intended by Jenkins to bring his opinion of the priest down to the level of his own had done nothing of the sort. It had taken Jerome himself to do that in some measure. Ever since, recovered from the fever during which he had revealed his true name, Robert had been summoned to Jerome's chamber from time to time, he had hated what he was made to do there. In his mind's eye he saw the priest's scrawny body prostrate upon the floor, naked but for a piece of material about his loins, arms outstretched as if he were nailed face downwards on a cross, and himself standing over him holding the whip that once long ago had scarred his own back. At first, as he obeyed orders and struck, he doubted if he had hurt his victim at all, but as he grew and his strength increased he had seen red stripes spring out on the bare flesh, had listened to babbled prayers of remorse, pleas for forgiveness, that became more and more incoherent until they died away into sobs of pain and he himself stumbled back to his own room . . .

He jerked himself back to the present, watched Jerome's thin, dark brows rise in assumed surprise. 'I cannot, I think, have heard you correctly, Cooper. Do you refuse to obey me?'

'In this, sir, but only in this.'

It was a warm evening and to the usual smells of the house were added the stench of the river that ran by the end of the street. Robert felt his knees shake, knew he must stand but could not. He collapsed into his chair, drew up his legs beneath him and clasped his arms about them in an attempt to control the outward expression of fear that churned within him. It was an attitude Jerome would normally never have tolerated; now it went unremarked.

'May I enquire when Master Jenkins gave himself the pleasure of telling you my history?'

Robert hesitated. 'I think, yes, about five years ago.'

'And you believed him?'

'Yes, sir.'

'Yet you appear not to have despised a renegade priest as others do – until now.'

Straightly Robert regarded him, finding no difficulty in giving an answer that might have sounded fawning, yet was not; it rang with sincerity.

'Master Jenkins is not – not always a nice man. No-one has threatened him as they did you. How does he know how he would behave?'

Jerome rose to his feet, pulling about himself the long robe he wore in the house, and stood over the huddled boy.

'Most perspicacious of you, Cooper. You will stand!'

Robert obeyed, holding on to the arm of his chair until circulation came back into cramped legs. Then he let go, put his hands by his side and faced his tutor unflinchingly. For one surprised moment he registered what he had never noticed before – that they were now of well nigh the same height. Glittering dark eyes held his, were fixed upon him as if he were a stranger new come to the house instead of having lived and worked there for seven years. He was thin still and childish of body, with none of the lean strength that would later be his, but the lines of his face were already austere and unyielding. He had conquered his trembling; he awaited inevitable punishment with no outward sign of fear.

Unhurriedly Jerome reached out both hands, held him hard just above the elbows. 'This is your final chance, Cooper. You will come to my room.'

The temper so easily aroused by Philip Sidney lay dormant. It never occurred to Robert to try on Jerome any of the tricks Jenkins had so carefully taught him. Perhaps he was too tired, perhaps he did not want to, or perhaps he was aware that Jerome had tricks of his own when it came to hurting people, for the grip of his fingers increased until burning waves of pain tingled down into the boy's finger ends and up into his shoulders.

'I will not!' and his voice that had scarcely yet begun to break wobbled, rose in a squeak.

The words were the same as before, yet now Jerome let him go with a gesture of revulsion as if somewhere behind them he heard something that shocked him. Thus released, Robert lurched backwards and sideways, coming up hard against the edge of the heavy table beside which he had earlier been sitting, and as if the pain of hitting his body against the unyielding surface strengthened him, he stood upright, unsupported, one hand pressed to his bruised side. His voice steadied, grew cold with the calmness of his later years, although his first words at least were of childish defiance.

'Tomorrow I will tell Amos Jenkins my real name. I will tell Lord Burghley and swear that I have always known it. What difference can it make to me? And then you will be unable to make me beat you any more!'

He fell silent, and whatever anger there had been between them died away. He held out his hands in a gesture of appeal.

'Whatever they do to me cannot be as bad as what happens inside me when you make me beat you. I am doing my best, sir, with the work that is set me here and at Whitehall, and I have dreamed of teaching as you do, but the day is coming when I shall not be able to stop myself hating you! That will not matter to you, because you have never liked me, but it matters to me!'

He looked down at his thin, outstretched hands, brought them together as if he were rubbing away something visible only to himself. 'Sir – when you have obtained relief for a sin most men would consider too great for forgiveness and are sleeping, I – who do not know what I have done to deserve it – spend my night washing my hands in the water Joan has left in my room, trying to cleanse them because of what you have made me do. I cannot stop myself. I wash and dry, wash and dry until sometimes sleep comes, although often it does not and the whole of the next day I must keep my eyes open and please you or some clerk with my work when all I want to do is to sleep. And I grow more and more afraid that I shall make some mistake that will – will be *important* in the copying or in the translations I do for his lordship, something that will cause trouble for an innocent person, who knows nothing of you or me or – or why . . .'

He stopped and Jerome watched him in silence.

Robert's hands dropped to his sides; wearily he said, 'Why me? Why me? There are ways of expressing penitence that involve the sinner alone, even I know that. But perhaps you enjoy being whipped – and that is a sin in itself. If you must continue with your beatings, find someone who gets pleasure from it also. Who did it before me?'

As he spoke he realized that his overwrought brain had betrayed him; he had not intended to make those last rambling remarks. He braced himself for the blow that must surely fell him where he stood, but Jerome did not move. Into his face had come a look of horror.

'Who told you about such things as that?' he asked. 'Where did you come by such information?'

'Where do you suppose, sir? Amos Jenkins and his friends have contributed greatly to my education. They tell me of things far worse than that, and they laugh.'

Quickly Jerome asked, 'They have not touched you?'

'Oh, no. Lord Burghley's protection counts for something.'

Was there a touch of irony in the boy's exhausted voice? Abruptly Jerome half-turned from him, stood with bowed head. 'I will trouble you no more, Cooper. It is past time you were abed. Away with you.'

Robert did not remember leaving the room; vaguely he was aware when he came to the stairs that he was too exhausted to go up other than on hands and knees. The last of his childhood, such as it had been, left him that night as he braced himself afresh to face what he feared lay within him, and silently he cried out, 'What of me, who has been taught how easy it is to kill, so that one day my temper must betray me? Who will have mercy on me?'

CHAPTER X

1

'Good morning, Cooper! I had begun to wonder whether we would ever meet again! I missed our outing yesterday. Where were you?'

There was anger underlying the sarcasm in Amos Jenkins's voice. Increasingly often these days young Cooper had good reason for missing what Jenkins considered to be a most valuable part of his training. And yet, he thought savagely, he was still required to present regular reports to Lord Burghley on the boy's progress.

'Well?' he snapped.

Robert, his arms full of papers it had taken him an hour or more to place in correct order, faced him squarely in the narrow passageway, and said in the quiet way Jenkins detested because it seemed always to put him at a disadvantage, 'His lordship detained me. I am sorry I inconvenienced you, sir. I saw Nick Rider; he said he would tell you.'

'And what of tomorrow? Am I to have the pleasure of your company then, or shall I be wasting my time waiting for you yet again?'

Robert ignored the sarcasm. 'Tomorrow I work at Trinity Street with Master Jerome. I shall keep our appointment, sir.'

Jenkins's discoloured teeth showed in a grin. 'Not altogether correct, Cooper. You will indeed work at Trinity Street, but *not* with Jerome. He will not be there. Come here and pay attention.'

He caught hold of Robert by one arm to pull him out of the way of passers-by. The carefully sorted papers, lightly held, slipped through his hands and fell about their feet in a disordered drift. Jenkins waited as Robert retrieved them. He showed no sign of irritation that what must have constituted a good deal of work would need to be done once more, and Jenkins's dislike of him increased. It made what he had to say all the more pleasurable.

'You cannot have forgotten what I once told you about Jerome's past? Yet in all the time since then you appear never once to have noticed anything worth reporting to me.'

Expressionlessly, Robert agreed that that was so.

'No matter, Cooper. Eyes far sharper than yours are kept upon him – in case after all these years he is tempted to return to his first allegiance, you understand. There is, however, something you can do for me. Tomorrow, as I say, he will be away. You will search his room, thoroughly, carefully, looking for anything that might indicate that he is in touch with his – shall we say – friends of former days. This is a serious job. Do it well.'

It took all Robert's resolution to enter Jerome's room next day; it looked as pathetic as it always had. The man, as part of his penance, slept on the floor. A rough blanket laid on wooden boards was all the comfort he allowed himself.

Carefully Robert tapped panelled walls that indicated no hollow space, thrust an arm up the long-unused chimney and was rewarded with nothing but quantities of dust, inspected the floor and found no evidence of even one loose board. He passed on to the only item of furniture the room held, a plain wooden chest, unlocked, which at first sight contained nothing but clothes, and precious few of those. There lay some pieces of worn white linen and the old greenish-black doublet his tutor had worn all the years he had known him; he had donned his only decent one to go visiting. Then his questing hands found, at the bottom of the chest, a small carved box. Lifting it out, he carried it to the window and, perched on the wide ledge, opened it to the light of day. What he saw filled him with such revulsion for his task that he had to sit without moving, commanding himself, before he could continue. He held in his hands the pitiful evidence of a man's failure to live up to a high ideal, be it never so misguided. There was a rolled letter, old and faded, from someone who said how proud his family was of Jerome and that he was always in their prayers; a tarnished crucifix on a silver chain; a Roman Catholic missal, surprisingly unused-looking; a rose, pressed, faded and brittle; and a picture of the Blessed Virgin Mary. All these lay upon a scrap of material, rich brocade in green and gold, fraying around the edges. Very carefully, consumed by an acute dislike of Master Jenkins and all his works, Robert was replacing the box in the chest when it knocked against something unyielding and, reaching down, he pulled out the last thing the chest contained: the whip, neatly coiled, which had been – and for all he knew might yet continue to be – Jerome's main means of penance.

As he stood there for a moment irresolute, with the cruel thing in his hands, he became aware that he was not alone and swinging round came face to face with Master Jerome who stood in the doorway, silently watching him. There was in his face no anger that his few belongings should be rifled, only a great wearinesss, and Robert, unable to speak, waited as he pushed himself upright off the door jamb and came across the room with dragging feet. He took the whip from his pupil's hands and stood looking at it as if it were a strange thing of great and extraordinary interest.

'Jenkins sent you. Over the years he has used my room as an exercise for many young men.'

Robert, prompted by something in Jerome's voice, asked, 'Could you not at least get rid of – of that thing?'

The other drew a deep, sighing breath. 'A scourge of small cords,' he said to himself, almost musingly. 'My soul is damned here and for eternity. You may tell your masters that I am still not strong enough to defy them.'

'I ask your pardon for what I have done, sir.'

Robert was at the door when his tutor said, 'I am grateful to you for being so careful. Not all the searchers have been.'

Robert reported to Amos Jenkins exactly what he had

found, knowing that his list would be compared with those of other, previous, intruders. Only, almost without thought, he omitted mention of the whip and thus was Jenkins prompted to take what he was pleased to think of as another step in the boy's training. Not, however, until he had himself referred to the whip and asked whether 'the old devil' had finally got rid of it. His face expressionless, refusing to give way to the anger that rose within him at the other's coarseness, Robert said, 'With respect, sir, that is a personal matter, surely? Nothing to do with – us.'

His hesitation was not lost on Jenkins. 'So you still find it difficult to count yourself one of us! You have been too softly treated, lad!' His voice hardened, abruptly, unpleasantly. 'I think it is time, Master Cooper, that I took you to the Tower. Today is a good day for it.'

The streets of London had years before lost their terrors for Robert Cooper; he had lived among their teeming, crowded smelliness for so long that he barely gave it a thought. But the Tower was a different matter. A royal residence it might be, an armoury, the Royal Mint, a menagerie, but in his mind, as in the minds of so many others, it was above all a prison from which so many accused people never emerged. As he walked beside Master Jenkins he knew that whatever lay ahead of him would be extremely unpleasant. That was the object of the visit; it was punishment for his failure to humiliate Master Jerome.

He was right. The sight he was to see stayed with him for the rest of his life. As they entered the Tower buildings, across the moat, through a huge gateway and into the courtyards, the boy kept his eyes on the stones beneath his feet. His heart pounded, his hands were clenched at his sides and their palms were cold with sweat. In his imagination he saw a dungeon, flambeau-lit, with instruments of torture all round it, such as he had seen in certain books. It came as a surprise, and he was not as prepared as he might have been, therefore, when Master Jenkins stopped outside a door on the ground floor of one of the inner towers. Jenkins looked at the boy beside him, a calculating look; then he opened the door and Robert, propelled by a push between the shoulders, entered hell, a hell where bright sunlight streamed in glory through slit windows and fell on a man's death agonies.

The room contained a desk, at which a clerkly man sat writing as if this were any office, and, with a huge man standing by the lever that operated it, the instrument of torture known as the rack. On it, his arms at full stretch above his head, legs taut, lay a youth whose head was turned to one side and who from time to time moaned slightly through foam-flecked lips. He was naked, save for the remnants of linen drawers, and had been beaten by someone who had enjoyed his work, not minding where the lash had fallen. His chest heaved convulsively, his eyes were closed and the blood that trickled slowly from his bitten tongue was bright against a sweat-streaked face that was the colour of undyed sheep's wool.

As Robert stood there, with Jenkins close behind him to block any attempt at escape, the clerk rose, crossed to the rack and said softly, 'Master James, Master James, can you hear me?' There was no reply, and the man by the gears picked up a bucket of water and dashed it in the tortured man's face. Master James groaned and between swollen lips muttered, 'I know nothing, I know nothing, I know nothing . . .' on and on, monotonously, as if it were something he had been saying for a very long time.

The clerk sighed. 'I have reason to believe that you lie.' His voice was quiet, level, and with mounting horror Robert looked into his face as he turned back to the desk. He might speak like a human being, he might walk, and write, but there was nothing, least of all regret, behind his eyes: they were empty. He was as much a machine as the instrument of torture he controlled.

At the threat of further agony the youth was struggling as best he might, pleading for mercy, swearing that he knew nothing. It did not avail him; at a sign the man by the lever gave a half-turn to his wheel. Master James's limbs stiffened, strained for a moment against the leather bonds that held them, before his body was raised clear of the wooden slats on which he lay and his eyes opened in a look that seemed almost to be one of surprise. Then, with a choking, wailing cry, his head fell backwards between his taut arms and the clerk, sighing his gentle sigh, made his sign once again. There came a cracking, tearing sound and with it a scream more dreadful than anything Robert Cooper had ever imagined could proceed from the mouth of a human being. Dimly he felt Jenkins behind him, gripping him with one dirty hand on either side his face, so that he might not turn his head, compelling him to watch the tortured man's chest rise and fall in a gasping quest for breath, to face the sight and sound of limbs being torn from their sockets, whilst all the time scream after scream of agony bounced off the walls of the bright sunlit room. Then, as suddenly as it had begun, the noise stopped. From James's throat came a gurgling sound, he made one last gasping effort for breath and his body went limp in its bonds. The clerk, rising in a fashion no less leisurely than before, said to his assistant, 'Take him away.'

Robert stood, dazed, with the sound of the dead man's screams still echoing in his ears, uncertain that he himself had not added to them, and watched as the man undid the bindings and, throwing Master James's limp body over one huge shoulder, left the room. Without its human sacrifice the rack was only a simple, slatted wooden table with a roller and straps at each end.

The clerk placed his quill pen in the ink stand and gathered up the papers on which he had been writing. As he turned to the door he shook his head and for the first time acknowledged Jenkins's presence.

'A pity, a great pity. It happens so, sometimes, even with the strongest of them. He had the information we need, I am convinced of that. Now I must begin all over again tomorrow with his father,' and with those words, mild and regretful still, with never a look at Robert, he was gone.

Robert found himself kneeling over the empty bucket being violently sick. Above him he heard Jenkins laugh and, shivering, fought for composure until he felt a hand on his shoulder, heard a voice, with a certain rough kindness in it now, bidding him come outside. In the open air, Robert's legs gave way beneath him altogether and he sat with his back to the base of the building, feeling sweat prickling cold all over his body. He was twelve years old and he had just watched at close quarters as a youth not much older than himself was torn limb from limb on the orders of a quiet little man who rated it no higher than 'a great pity'.

Turning his head against the cold stone he moaned, and Jenkins said, 'So now you will understand, young Cooper, that there are worse things in life than searching a man's room and reporting in detail when you are ordered.'

Robert's pallid face looked up at him. 'Dear God, no, not *that!*' he whispered. 'I cannot. I – I – you do not expect me to do *that?*'

Jenkins's voice became reassuring; enough was enough, the boy was still young. 'You could go through the whole of your working life and never see such a thing again, but you must understand that it happens. No-one racks a man for pleasure, not in England, but sometimes, when information is vital, it is the only way. Unpleasant jobs have to be done. Remember only that that man – the one you appear to feel so much pity for – would have slit your throat for a groat. Do you understand that? He was a foreign agent!'

2

Jerome took one look at his young lodger's face, led him into the study and sat him down.

'I gather you held back certain information from Jenkins. Never, *never* do that; he will always triumph in the end. Drink!' And Robert found a glass of wine pressed against his rigidly clenched teeth. He forced himself to swallow and the liquid burned fiery-hot into his violently emptied stomach so that after a moment or two he began to feel better. He put out a groping hand towards the priest and it was held strongly, reassuringly; the first time he had ever received any gesture of understanding from him.

'It was the Tower! Why did you not warn me? Why? You must have known what would happen!'

The boy's voice was almost a cry, and Jerome withdrew his hand. Calmly he said, 'What good would it have done? Life will bring you into contact with worse things than that, as you know if you are honest. It would have been wrong to lighten the blow.'

It was the first time for years that Robert had remembered that, in this at least, Jerome and Jenkins were on the same side, were engaged in training him to Lord Burghley's instructions.

'I must go out,' he said. 'I shall come back, do not worry about that, but I must walk until I am tired and – and this smell leaves my nostrils. I think it may take a long time.'

CHAPTER XI

1

'Will you knock him over the head, or do you want me to do it?' Amos Jenkins spoke as carelessly as he would have to any of the men with whom he spent so much of his life, and the words were out before he remembered that here, by the young man he faced across the narrow bed, they would not be appreciated at all. He heard himself say defensively, as cold, grey eyes met and challenged his, 'A jest, Cooper, only a jest! All the same, I can't see him being much help to us again and Sir Francis won't carry dead wood, you know that. Money is short enough as it is.'

Robert looked down at Jerome's deeply unconscious body. The only sign of life was the breath that whistled, harsh and laboured, through the loosely open mouth. Since the night seven years before when he had challenged his tutor, he had sat opposite this man through so many evenings: he carrying on his studies far beyond an age when he would have been justified in stopping them, or writing out reports on his daily work in an attempt to give himself time in hand; Jerome, if he had no written work of his own, bent over his beloved classics. If they talked it was always about Robert's Latin or Greek; otherwise they greeted each other on meeting, bade each other good night, and that was all, but there had come to be between them some distant kind of companionship.

Amos Jenkins, whose dreams of late had too often for his comfort been concerned with his own slowing reflexes and the fatal mistake he feared he must make before long, wondered whether his judgement of men was slipping also. He had expected an angry reaction but all Robert said, and that easily, was, 'Let Martha nurse him for a few days. He may recover. Time enough then to decide what to do.'

And it was with a relieved feeling of having struggled back on to firm ground again that Jenkins replied, 'Aye. Why not? He's been of use to us, after all. I doubt if you could have pulled off your masquerade as a priest last year without his tuition.'

'We both know I could not!' Robert's tone was grim. 'And it's worth a few days' grace for the information we gained then, I think.'

It was only rarely, as on the occasion to which he had just referred, that Lord Burghley released Robert to do the work for which Jenkins had spent so much time training him. The beginning of his own gradual downward slide Jenkins attributed not to increasing drink over the years but to the day when Burghley had heard about Robert's visit to the Tower and what had happened there. Jenkins had never forgotten the ensuing interview. If such visits were necessary they would take place under the auspices of a man of his lordship's choosing, not in company with Jenkins or one of his bully boys!

He grinned suddenly. 'I'd have given much to see you in action!' he said, surveying the thin, handsome face before him, its straight-lipped mouth, the cold grey eyes that made it look so much older than its years. Who would have imagined that that terrified child would grow up into this? He wondered vaguely who Cooper's parents had been, what his real name was, whether he remembered it himself? Jenkins found himself loath to ask. He took his leave, glad as always to get away from the young man's presence.

Left alone, Robert leaned over the bed, touched one of Jerome's cold hands, squeezing it hard in hope of eliciting some response. There was none; and the tutor was so deeply unconscious that despite his confident words to Jenkins, Robert doubted he would recover.

'Went down like a log, sir,' said Martha, who had replaced

the sullen, slovenly Joan some years before. 'Talking he was, one minute, the next . . .'

A seizure, the physician said. Serious enough. How old was Master Jerome? In his early fifties? Indeed, he would have guessed older than that. Oh yes, he had seen cases like this recover. Not completely, Master Cooper must understand, but sufficiently to allow the patient to move and talk again in some measure.

Robert, who had carried the companion of his childhood to his own room, stripped him of his shabby clothing and put him into bed, found that he minded the thought of his dying more than he would have suspected. He found also that although there were no longer whipmarks on the bony body, Jerome had inflicted upon himself another form of penance. Gagging at the smell, Robert cut away a hair shirt that stretched from neck to thighs next to his skin. Even as he removed it, dropping it to one side for later burning, revealing a body covered in an angry red rash and, in places, open sores, Robert shuddered at the thought of how constant must have been the torment, the irritation. To one as sensitive to dirt as he himself, it was far worse than any whipping, and very carefully he had washed the grimy body as best he might before the physician arrived.

He was often away for weeks, sometimes months at a time about his own work, but when he was in London Jerome's presence beside the fireplace in the evenings had become part of his life. The thought of the dark study – less cold in winter since he had grown old enough to insist on a fire when it was needed – with no-one in it but himself was not pleasant. He shook himself angrily, and went downstairs to make arrangements with Martha for bedding to be placed in Jerome's room for himself. Tonight he would lie on the floor, but tomorrow she must find a bedstead, he minded not where from.

Little Martha curtseyed, smiling up at her young master, and he smiled back as he left her preparing his meal. Long since he had discovered that he had the power to make women do for him whatever he wanted. He had only to smile, as he did now, and they were lost, not seeming to notice that there was nothing behind the expression, that he turned it on and off at will to suit his purpose.

The dismissal of Joan, her replacement by the younger, more conscientious Martha, had been one of the first of Robert's small triumphs over Amos Jenkins.

'Keep your spy in the house if you must,' he had said, 'although why you should think it necessary any longer I have no idea, but be it man or woman, let it be someone who at least does an honest day's work besides!'

Jenkins had laughed, but agreed. Robert Cooper's obsession with cleanliness in an age in no way renowned for it he found peculiar, but Martha had replaced Joan and ever since the house had been kept to Robert's high standards, whether or not he was there.

It was fortunate, he thought later that evening, sitting beside Jerome in case he should stir, that this had not happened a week, even three days ago. Then he would have been out of the country, part of a mission to France, sitting in at interminable meetings, making notes, providing information for senior delegates, so quiet that he was hardly noticed and doing much of his real work in other places, about palaces, in slums, with the high-born and the low alike; encouraging talk with sympathetic prompting, taking note of small things that very often the speakers did not realize they had disclosed, that he might compile a comprehensive report for Burghley and Sir Francis Walsingham on his return to England. Had Jerome fallen ill during his absence, Robert was sure that Jenkins's remark would not have been in jest; the knock on the head might have been simple, brutal fact.

He stared into the guttering flame of the candle, almost deciding that he would go to bed. It was obvious that the unconscious man would not stir that night, if ever again. Yet still he sat there, thinking. He had intended to visit Jenny that night, had looked forward to her face when she saw the gifts he had brought for her and Sim . . .

Whether he would have found it possible to keep his early decision to go through life entirely alone, he did not know, for he had not been required to put it to the test. The day, so long ago now, when he had paid his first visit to the Tower and had told Jerome that he must walk until he was tired had brought him some degree of comfort. Which way he went he could not at the time have said. With his mind in turmoil he had blundered, unseeing, along alley after filthy narrow alley, splashing through evil-smelling puddles, scattering piles of rotting garbage, barked after by dogs, called after by women, looked over by hard-eyed men who decided, his youth notwithstanding, not to tangle with him, twisting his ankles on ill-laid cobblestones and slipping in mud until, as dusk fell, he found himself in a narrow street that differed from the rest only in a certain smell, rising above all other smells, that made him realize how hungry he was. And in that instant a man's heavy hand took hold of his arm. He wheeled round, clutching instinctively at his dagger, and then as suddenly stopped. It was a man's hand that had touched him, a man's figure stood beside him in the gathering dusk, a head taller than he, but the broad shoulders stooped and the face atop them was that of a child, an idiot child, with a happy grin stretching a huge mouth to disclose broken brown teeth. As Robert relaxed a dirty hand, soft and fleshy, took hold of his, confidingly, trustingly.

'Nice man, nice man,' said the creature's slurred voice. Grateful for a kindly human contact, and somewhere at the back of his stunned mind amused to be thought a man, Robert asked, 'Who are you?'

The child-man grinned even wider but it seemed that such information was beyond his powers for he merely repeated, 'Nice man,' holding on to Robert's hand with surprising strength. Then a woman's voice shouted, a voice the idiot obviously recognized, for he giggled and waved. The next moment she reached them, a harassed, hot-looking, plump woman of about thirty years. Briskly she slapped the idiot's free hand.

'Sim! How many times must I tell you not to bother people?'

Sim's hand fell away from Robert's and his face crumpled in distress as the woman turned to the young stranger and curtseyed.

179

'I beg your pardon, young sir. He means no harm.' Her voice, with a not unpleasant foreign accent, was as worried as her face, and Robert hastened to say, 'I was startled for a moment, that was all.'

But the woman's face did not clear; by now she had had time to take in the bearing and clothes of the boy to whom she was speaking. He was obviously a gentleman and she wanted no trouble.

'Come, Sim,' she said sharply, 'time to go home.' Once again she curtseyed to Robert and would have hurried away with her charge in tow but that she was stopped by Robert saying, 'Before you go, mistress, perhaps you can help me. I have lost my way and I smell new-baked bread. Can I buy a loaf hereabouts?'

'Oh, indeed, sir. I keep the bakery myself. Only a few doors along, if you'd be pleased to step this way.'

Robert held out a hand. 'Sim,' he said quietly, and the gigantic childlike creature came to him instantly and took his hand once more.

Together the three of them walked through the alley and at the last house in the row the woman stepped through an open doorway into a passage which gave on to a small bakery. Beyond the house was a small fenced-in space and half-consciously Robert noted that this building, with its attendant risk of fire, must only be tolerated because its large chimney was on the side away from other dwellings. In case of accident, fire would be easier to control there than anywhere.

One end of the room was occupied entirely by a vast oven, beneath which a wood fire glowed red, and on a large table stood trays and lumps of brown dough. Other lumps, smaller and ready shaped, stood rising on their trays in the heat from the oven.

'If you'll be pleased to wait a moment, sir, I think you'll find my bread good eating.' Bustling forward the woman took a wooden platter from a shelf, put on to it a crusty brown loaf and held it out somewhat tentatively towards her visitor.

Standing there, still holding Sim's hand, Robert smiled

for the first time that day. The atmosphere in the small bakery was friendly, so homely that despite all resolutions he felt himself responding.

'Thank you, Mistress – Mistress . . .?'

Her lips lifted in a smile. 'They call me Baker, sir. Jenny Baker, because they cannot pronounce my real name!'

'Robert Cooper, mistress.' He bowed gravely in return. 'Would it inconvenience you if I ate here. I am very hungry.'

A boyish note sounded suddenly in his voice and Mistress Baker looked at him more closely by the light from the fire. He was gentry, sure enough, but he was little more than a child, and exhausted at that. It showed in his white face and the black bruise-like marks below his eyes.

'Sit down, if you please,' and taking a knife she carved the loaf into pieces and spread them with strong, bright yellow butter. She watched with a smile about her lips as he ate hungrily, with Sim crouching at his feet like some great dog waiting for crumbs.

Robert bent towards the creature, proffering a piece of his bread. 'Here, Sim, it is very good,' he said, in the same gentle tone he had used before, and Jenny Baker looked at him with renewed interest. So few people bothered with Sim. Either he disgusted them or he frightened them. Always they thought he should have been put down at birth like some unwanted kitten. Yet this boy with the unhappy face and strained eyes was kind, seemed even to like him.

Robert ate until he could eat no more. The events of the day receded slightly and he looked across at the yellow-haired, plump woman in the plain brown woollen dress, grateful for her kindness, feeling that some politeness on his part was called for.

'Is Sim your brother?' he asked, and she laughed.

'He is my son, my only child, sir. We came here from the Netherlands and my husband died just afore he was born. The midwife did say that that is why he is – is . . .'

'Still a child,' supplied Robert. 'And you have run a bakery single-handed all these years?' There was admiration in his tone as he looked about him at evidence of work well and efficiently done.

'Nigh on fifteen years. I must live, sir, and I do bake good bread, even if I says it myself.'

They smiled at each other. Here was a woman, thought Robert, old enough to be his mother, who talked to him with true feeling in her voice. He pulled himself together, asked if she could direct him to Trinity Street, but Jenny had never heard of such a place. With some diffidence she suggested that the young gentleman sleep at the bakery and no doubt in the morning someone would see him home. Sim would be glad to give up his garret for one night.

Robert received the suggestion with more gratitude than he was able to express. It must have been the heat in the bakery, he decided; he had thought he would never sleep again, and suddenly he was so tired that he doubted his ability to walk more than a dozen steps. Those steps took him up a ladder into a tiny room beneath the eaves, and he slept dreamlessly all night beneath a rough, woollen blanket, with his head on a pillow that smelled sweet and clean.

The Robert Cooper who descended into the bakery next morning was a very different person to the tired boy who had accepted her hospitality the night before; Jenny saw that at once. A night's sleep had restored him and the happenings of the day before had fallen into their place in a life that was seldom pleasant. At sight of his face, haughty and unsmiling, Jenny Baker felt a twinge of fear and pulled Sim sharply to her side. She would be glad when he was gone; she wanted no trouble. The thanks he gave her when he paid – as he insisted he must – for his night's lodging and food were courteous enough but remote and only at Sim, who came to him like some great friendly animal, did he smile.

'Goodbye, Sim.' He pressed a penny into the huge hand, to be rewarded yet again by the chant of 'nice man, nice man'.

With one of Mistress Baker's first customers to guide him to streets he recognized, Robert Cooper was soon back in Master Jerome's house and before long the bakery and the kindness he had met there was forgotten as he slipped back into the disciplined, emotionless world he had grown up in.

Three months later he found that Amos Jenkins had not told him the truth, for once more he went to the Tower, alone this time, with a message for the inhuman clerk, and again he witnessed the extraction of information under torture. This time the victim was a woman and afterwards, without giving his destination a conscious thought, he made his way unerringly through narrow ways to the bakery. Entering, he bowed briefly in response to Jenny's curtsey and found himself trembling, totally unable to speak.

Silently he collapsed on to a pile of rags in the warm corner where Sim rested from time to time and sat staring down at the dusty stone floor. Jenny went about her day's work and when Sim returned from his ramblings she kept him sternly at the other side of the room. Robert stayed there in the midst of honest work and warmth until he was able to command himself. He left without a word spoken on either side; only the hand he half-stretched out in Jenny's direction indicated his gratitude for her forbearance, and she grieved for the trouble she saw in the young visitor's eyes.

After that, Robert came to the bakery perhaps six times in a year. Sometimes he spoke no word at all, only sat and stared before him, but often he was ready to play with Sim. Jenny taught them both – or tried to teach them, for it was beyond Sim's powers – how to play 'cat's cradle' with a piece of string and marvelled that Robert seemed to have no idea of children's games, found them pleasing, was soothed by them. If Sim were absent she sat beside Robert and they made intricate string patterns together until the strain that had brought him there lessened and he departed. Never once did he give her any clue as to who he was, nor ask questions of her. He came, took peace from place and company, and returned silently to his other world.

In the schoolroom at Abbey House, Cecily Woodfall sat before the sheets of paper Master Acres expected to find covered with her Latin translation when he returned, and kicked viciously at the legs of her chair, as if it were the fault of the furniture that she was imprisoned there whilst Martin had ridden over to the manor with a message for Aunt Eleanor. She could have gone with him but for this hateful work, on her own pony or, and that she would have liked even better, riding pillion behind him, both of them laughing when the wind took her cap and tangled her hair. Her father would have let her go, in fact he had been upon the point of agreeing to her request when Aunt Agnes captured her and brought her back. Hot tears dropped on to the precious book before her. She did not want to be learned like the Queen, whom her mother constantly held up before her as a shining example for all women. She did not, she did *not!* What she wanted to do was to ride long and hard with Martin, even when at the end of their journey Aunt Eleanor and Cousin Rose – so neat and precise in their clothing and their ways – would stare at her dishevelled state and call her hobbledehoy behind her back. Not that she cared for that, for was not Rose to marry Matthew Stone when they were older? That had been settled for years, and serve Rose right, to be forced to live for ever with such a fat, spotty person!

Loudly Cecily sniffed, wiped her hot face with the back of her hand and sighed. Perhaps if she climbed out through the window, so that no-one saw her, she could lie in wait on the road for Martin and ask his help. He never got into such a tangle with his Latin. It might not always be right – 'Not quite what Virgil had in mind, my boy,' she had heard Master Acres say to him in his quiet way – but at least he would tell her something to put down and anything was better than this expanse of empty paper and a brain that refused to work.

'Cecily! Sweet Cecily!' The whisper came from the

doorway and she swung round to see dancing brown eyes in a smiling face.

She forgot her troubles, forgot her tears. 'Oh, Wat! You are early! Do be quiet, I'm supposed to be working.'

At fourteen he was grown up, that was her first thought: grown up and handsome, that was her second. Not a bit like Martin for all they were twins. Wat had the look about him of the handsome stranger she knew would one day come to claim her hand in marriage.

He removed his hat, flung it on to the table and saluted her, not by kissing the hot face she raised so innocently to him, but by taking her hand and elegantly putting it to his lips, as no-one ever had before. And all the time his laughing eyes were scrutinizing her closely.

'I have it!' he said. 'It could be nothing less to make sweet Cecily weep. The world is coming to an end, and she mourns!'

Cecily giggled. 'Wat! How awful to say such things. Suppose they came true!'

'Then it must be that my wicked brother has beaten you and locked you in here to await his further pleasure.'

'Martin? Of course not!' Cecily was recovering fast. 'Martin would never do anything like that. It – it's this Latin translation I must finish this afternoon or . . .'

'Or *then* Martin will beat you! Of course.' Wat cast a careless eye over her books.

'Master Acres will tell Aunt Agnes, and she will. I cannot make it come right. Will you look at it, Wat? You are so clever at this sort of thing.'

'Brilliant,' agreed her cousin complacently, and sighed. 'What it is to be set to work the instant I return from school, before I have even made my bow to Aunt Bennitt! No, come, I was only teasing. Sit down and take my dictation . . .'

Ten minutes later Cecily, with awe in her voice, said, 'You make it so easy. Thank you, thank you. But, but if it's all correct Master Acres will know that I didn't do it!'

Wat snatched up his hat, made her a low bow. 'Fear not, fair maiden! There are in that translation mistakes I would never make in a million years! Martin might, but not I.'

It was not right, Cecily thought, that he should always be so disparaging about Martin, with whom she studied and played and lived as closely as any brother and sister. She wrinkled her brows, suddenly feeling much older than twelve and a half years. Wat had never seemed like her brother; it must be because she saw so much less of him.

'You had better find Aunt Agnes,' she advised him. 'Mother is still abed. I have a new baby sister – Philippa, she is to be named.'

'Yet another sister!' Wat's tone was flippant. 'The dreaded aunt it shall be!'

Cecily was still puzzling over the question of her feelings for Wat when Martin returned from the manor, full of Rose's behaviour, wishing Cecily had been there to laugh with him at her airs and graces instead of being stuck indoors over her schoolwork. Had she finished it? Could he help?

Cecily smiled. 'No, thank you. Wat is home. He did it for me almost faster than I could write.' She had answered without thinking, was unprepared for his reaction.

'You let him do it all? Not just look at what you'd done and make suggestions?' His fair brows drew together. 'You'll never learn anything that way.'

'There's no need to sound so pompous, Martin Woodfall! Your help has not turned out to be so valuable in the past. And if it weren't for you being stupid and having to have lessons at home I wouldn't have to do it at all. Mother could have taught me to read and write just as she has the others and I need never have bothered my head with all this – this *boys'* stuff. Mother doesn't understand a word of Latin and she runs this house like – like clockwork. It's not necessary. I have to do it because you're here. And why me? None of the others ever have. It's not fair!'

It was true; Mary, her elder sister, to be married next summer, could do no more than read and write, and the girls who had come after, Anne and Katharine, had never joined lessons with Martin.

Cecily had always been proud at being singled out for special treatment, glad to think that she pleased her father in this way. She pulled up her angry thoughts. She had never

186

shouted at Martin like this before. She was behaving very strangely, and all because a boy she seldom saw had kissed her hand, had teased her so that she felt grown up. Miserably she opened her mouth to apologize, but was given no chance. Red to his hair roots, Martin looked crosser than she had ever seen him.

'I'll go and find Wat. I must say "hello",' he said, in a tone which plainly meant 'best get it over with'.

Wat, invited by his uncle to sit, leaned back, completely at his ease, and got ready to begin the speech he had been preparing for days. He looked at the man who had ruled his life since babyhood and saw no reason why this time he should not stand up to him and win. True, when he had pleaded to stay at home and share Martin's lessons he had been firmly turned down, but this time there could be no reason whatsoever for his uncle to insist on his continuing at Downfelton, then going on to university. Life was an adventure, and so he would treat it. His uncle looked older now, with his brown hair receding from his temples and deep lines on his face. The trouble was that he was like Martin, or rather Martin was like him – not that Wat minded; they were so unsophisticated, could understand nothing of the social success that was his.

Edward Woodfall smiled and age fell away from him. 'Well, Wat! How many years now that you've been coming home with glowing reports? Ten, or thereabouts? Give Master Price another year and then on to Oxford, which is where you'll leave me behind, for neither your father nor I did half so well.'

Wat, through his boredom, smiled courteously. Let him finish speaking, then . . .

'I can't go with you, but I thought that this summer you might like to visit Barndale. It will be yours, after all, yours and Martin's, and it's time you got to know it properly. What do you say to a month there? You and Martin together?'

'Thank you, sir.' Wat's answer was easy; he saw no reason to wait longer. 'It sounds pleasant but I don't believe my future lies in Barndale. I want to go to sea, as you did. Oh

. . .' as his uncle began to interrupt, 'if I could get a berth with Sir Francis Drake I might make my fortune in a couple of years. Two voyages to the Americas and with luck I can pour diamonds into Aunt Bennitt's lap! Please say yes, sir, please.'

His uncle's voice was stern. 'The answer is "no", Walter, as you very well knew it would be. You are a gentleman, educated to take your place as a landowner, not to risk life and limb on slender hopes of Spanish gold. Let me hear no more of these wild ideas.'

And Walter, who knew better than to oppose Edward Woodfall when he spoke thus, rose and made his bow. 'No, sir,' he said, obediently, but the look in his eyes was defiant. It was all very well for Martin. It was plain as a pikestaff what his uncle intended in that direction; no son of his own, so marry favourite nephew off to favourite daughter. Wat's expression, as he went to the room he shared with his twin, was not pleasant. Cecily was so young; still a child in her ways. She had not the faintest idea of the plans that were being hatched for her: it might be amusing to tell her.

But he had several weeks now in which to make Martin's life a misery. Sharing a bed, as they had since babyhood, it was impossible for Martin to follow his peaceable instincts by avoiding his brother. Never once, so far as he could remember, had a holiday passed without their coming to blows. And never once, he thought ruefully, had he won! Wat had learned to be affable enough in company; no-one heard the malicious verbal darts he planted when they were alone together, or saw the vicious blows that often accompanied them.

Wat, as adept as ever at avoiding the manual work his brother undertook as a matter of course when lessons were over or Master Acres granted a holiday, came upon Martin one hot August afternoon, wielding a pitchfork in a meadow near to Abbey House, sweating and sticky, supremely happy. The small estate had been home all his life and he loved it dearly, would have done anything for his aunt and uncle.

Behind him were piled haycocks, shapely and rounded; soon it would be time to go back to the house, but not before he had cooled himself with a dip in the river. As always when he was happy he began to whistle in a tuneless way that had been his father's, and thus did not hear his twin approach, ready for battle.

Wat crept to a place where his brother could not fail to see him, put one hand on his heart, raised his face to the sky and declaimed loudly, dramatically:

> 'And thus did Martin,
> Lowly swain,
> Pursue his work the long day through . . .'

As an opening ploy it was disappointing, for Martin only laughed. 'Pick up a fork and help,' he suggested without stopping, but Wat was not to be deterred.

'My dear Martin, how you can expect me to be so very – very *rustic* passes my comprehension. Has the old priest taught you that word, brother? *Com-pre-hen-sion?* It means . . .'

'It means you're an idiot, Wat,' said Martin good-naturedly, 'it's too hot to fight if that's what you're looking for, and this hay needs stacking before the storm breaks. Help me, there's a good fellow.'

But his brother merely made a gesture of deep despair, sank down against the side of a haycock and closed his eyes. His lips moved but no sound came and Martin, intent on his work, took no further notice of him until he sprang up, resumed his former dramatic stance, and began:

> 'The gentle lady
> Love of mine
> Is Cec'ly named,
> Quoth Martin, swain;
> But humble clod like I
> She ne'er will wed . . .'

The rest of his masterpiece was lost in Martin's rush, in his shout of 'Wat, that is *enough!*'

Fists raised, Wat's eyes had narrowed in delighted anticipation of the coming fight, when a voice said crisply, 'It is indeed enough. And more than enough! You will stop this nonsense at once, both of you!' and down between them, as if it had been a swordblade, flashed a carved, silver-headed staff their Aunt Agnes had of late taken to carrying. So close together were they, so swift was she, that in its descent it hit both boys, causing them to spring apart nursing stinging knuckles.

Martin stood speechless, head down, but Wat, recovering from first surprise, faced his aunt defiantly, the laugh that was never far away from him flickering in his eyes.

'Madam, your pardon. But when the Muse visits . . .'

'Back to the house, Walter! At once! Your uncle wishes to see you.'

Faced by the woman who had never yielded to his charms and never would, Wat swept her a low graceful bow and ran off as she had bidden him. Martin, red-faced and silent, once more set about his work, not noticing, in need to hide his embarrassment, how very slowly Aunt Agnes made her way back to the house and the remainder of the day's work.

Peter Acres excused himself early from table that evening. How could it be that he alone, of all who loved her, could see the agony of spirit that tormented Agnes Woodfall? Her family noticed no more than the abstracted silence in which she so often wrapped herself. Over the years all had become accustomed to his daily greeting, 'Is it well with thy soul, Agnes?' and her unvarying, uncompromising answer, 'It is well.' Only the two of them knew that the exchange had begun in earnest, an offer of help to be taken up when needed. To Peter Acres the words had become little more than a form of greeting but now, on this sultry evening twenty years on, she would come to him. What had made her decide to unburden her soul after all this time he had no idea but he doubted his ability to provide what she needed. His had become an undemanding faith, comfortable as a featherbed. She needed someone stronger than he.

He knew her well enough to be certain that she would complete the day's tasks, make certain that the household was ready for the night, prepared for next day, before she took heed for herself. The thunderstorm against which Martin had been working came and went, leaving behind it a sharp, cool breeze and a late evening sky dotted with small pink-edged white clouds, but Master Acres saw none of its beauty. He knelt at the *prie-dieu* in his room and stared into the pale light of the candles before him until his old eyes watered and stung.

'Ah, but I am too old,' he pleaded inwardly, his gaze intent on the tiny crucified figure on the wall between the candles, 'old and a most sinful man.' Panic welled within him. 'Oh most merciful Father, grant that she may not come!'

And to him, who had so often of late years failed in common observance of his priestly duties, always with the excuse that he had other important work to fill his time, came an answer. Father Bernard's hand, that had perished in the flames so many years before, lighted on his shoulder and the loved voice said, with the laughter in it that had so often been there when he had found the young Peter in trouble, 'Still after all these years you think only of yourself, my son? Will you never learn? One only is perfect. For bodily ills men visit a physician; for sickness of the soul they seek a priest. What doctor would ever admit that he can offer no cure? Even so the priest. You will say the words the Church prescribes which, because God is good, will bring solace to His troubled daughter. You are but His mouthpiece. How many times must I tell you, my son: speak as your soul bids you, admitting of no doubt, and you will do your Father's will because He will have it so . . .'

The voice faded; a knock on the door awakened Peter as from a dream and he pulled himself slowly to his feet, surprised to find himself alone. He waited a moment for his stiff legs to answer his bidding. What would Father Bernard have said if he had told him that many a time of late he had considered saying his prayers sitting down because of the pains in his legs? He shuffled across the room to admit the tall, gaunt woman who stood on the threshold, trembling as no-one but he had ever seen her tremble.

Quietly, as one who had no doubt, he said, 'Welcome, my child.'

She was barely in the room and the door closed behind her before she broke out, 'It is so dreadful for the boy. It is no fault of his. To be used so when the fault is mine, all mine . . .'

The sentences that poured from her lips were disjointed, almost hysterical, but as firmly as once he had dealt with Peg Morris in the village, although not so roughly, Father Peter put himself out of mind and thought only of Agnes Woodfall. Leading her to sit on the wide windowsill, so that the kind evening breeze blew into her face, he waited patiently. At last she gasped, 'Gilbert Lovelace has come back. They are the same, exactly the same.' It was the first time in all the years she had mentioned the man who raped her, and there was horror in her voice.

'Who is the same?'

'Wat! You do not think . . . You do not think a man's spirit can move into a child's body, do you, Father?'

This was not at all what he had expected and he frowned. 'From what little I heard of him, I cannot imagine Lovelace giving up his spirit to anyone. No doubt he is still making good – or bad – use of it himself.'

'He died just after the twins were born,' said Agnes soberly, and there was silence until she added, 'My mother's people – avenged me, so you see his spirit was set free.'

'Agnes, Agnes, you have no need to fear. What your people did was wrong, but when Lovelace died his soul went to the judgement it deserved. To each newborn child, a new and spotless soul. That is the truth: you must believe me.'

'I want to, I want to so much, but when I see him – Wat, that is – goading Martin, and staring at Cecily, I am sure that what I fear must be true. He is like no other Woodfall

192

I ever saw, and when he smiled at me this afternoon, it took me back . . .'

'He has more than a full share of his mother's high spirits, that is all.' The old man's voice grew stern. 'If you have conjured up this fear, it feeds and thrives on something deep within your soul. Once I told you that when you were ready to come to me on your own account I should be waiting. That is still true.'

Agnes stiffened. 'You know, do you not? You have always known.'

'I *suspect*, my child; only you can know.'

'And you will hear the confession of one who – who for most of her life has been a non-believer? One who can no longer struggle on alone?'

'Your parents had you baptized into the Christian Church. To come to full belief has taken you longer than some. It may be that you are the better for having fought your fight – and lost.'

Slowly the old man made his way across the room, pressed on the carved panelling beside the fireplace and disclosed a small, concealed cupboard. Within it, over his shoulder, Agnes saw the dull gleam of gold, the flash of candlelight on jewels – the responsibilities Sir Herbert had told Edward went with the abbey lands – ornaments saved and hidden before the old building was plundered. But Father Peter returned carrying nothing more than a long ribbon of dark red silk, which he placed about the shoulders of his everyday clothes.

He who, once firm guidance was withdrawn from him, had turned from full-time practice of his faith to take up the secular life, braced himself to listen to the story he must hear. Within his heart still he prayed, 'Oh God, our Heavenly Father, grant that through me this woman may be helped . . .'

Slowly Agnes went down on her knees before the old man, bowed her head over clasped hands.

'Forgive me, Father, for I have sinned . . .'

Five days after Jerome was first taken ill, Robert Cooper returned from his day's work to be greeted by Martha with the news that the old master was awake, so she had been told. The days of illness had raised Master Jerome's standing in the eyes of the servant girl. Expecting that when Master Cooper was away the full burden of tending the sick man would fall on her, she had found that all she was required to do, in addition to her usual work, was to fetch and carry upstairs and down from time to time. Always she was met at the door to the sickroom by a man who arrived before Master Cooper left and stayed until he returned. Gregory, her regular caller, had often sneeringly told her that his master said Jerome was of no use to man nor beast. Now he was moved to admit that Jenkins was astounded that Sir Francis Walsingham should provide an attendant, even if he were only old Henry, who was past active work. He must be intent on extracting every last pennyworth of information before Jerome died. It pleased Gregory to say thus much and no more to the girl; she listened open-mouthed, thought him great in his own right, a man entrusted with secrets.

Robert, passing his colleague on the stair, looked a question, was told that the sick man had not spoken but appeared agitated. Henry left with a brief smile and easy words to the effect that no doubt Cooper could calm him.

It took very little to set Jerome's mind at rest. As Robert leaned over the bed the dark eyes opened; they were slightly unfocused and a frown line stood between his brows.

'No delirium?' Lips that scarcely moved asked the question.

'None. All is well, sir.'

Being answered to his satisfaction, Jerome closed his eyes and appeared at once to sleep. Before many days were out he was physically as well as he would ever be. But he was sadly changed from the self-contained man who had been Robert's mentor for so long. One side of his face remained dragged down and immobile, whilst the left side of his body would, the physician said, be of little use to him; otherwise there was no reason why he should not regain strength.

But to Robert, under orders received from Walsingham, it was the recovery or otherwise of Jerome's brain that mattered. Each evening he visited the sickroom and talked, but what little speech Jerome managed was painfully slow; impaired memory left him groping for words, sentences trailed away half-finished, and several times when Robert mentioned mutual acquaintances he appeared not to remember them. All this Robert reported to Walsingham until, at the end of a month, just as Jerome seemed to him to be beginning to improve, he was told that no matter what methods he used he was to find out that same evening how much of his work Jerome remembered.

Robert found Martha, promoted now to nurse, carefully spooning food into Jerome's dribbling mouth and brusquely dismissed her to her kitchen. Taking her place at the bedside he held out a spoonful of broth, but Jerome turned his head away on the pillows like some recalcitrant child. 'No!' he mumbled. 'No more.'

'Then we will talk,' said Robert crisply. 'You will keep your eyes open until I give you leave to close them.' He raised his voice. 'Do you hear me?'

Quite what he would have done if the other had disobeyed him he did not know, but the sharp tones reached Jerome as earlier kindness had not. A harsh sound that might have been a laugh rattled in his throat and the twisted mouth said, more clearly than Robert had heard it speak since the seizure, 'Walsingham grows impatient?'

Robert leaned over and held water to the older man's lips. Bluntly he said, 'I must have information for him tonight. Take your time, but for both our sakes tell me as much as you can.'

Jerome frowned. 'Tell him – tell him I left no important work undone.'

'The Oxford matter is what concerns him. He received another letter this morning. He must know how far Master Renwick is to be trusted. If you have no recollection he must

195

send someone else to talk with him, but he would prefer your assessment.'

'Fetch paper and ink. I will dictate what I know.'

Half an hour later Robert held a report as lucid as any he might have written himself. Dark eyes, half-closed now in tiredness, watched him intently, and he was aware that he smiled in relief.

'I will leave you to sleep now,' he said, 'unless you would like me to read to you?'

It was an offer he had made many times before; always it had been met with obstinately closed eyes and ears that appeared not to hear, but now Jerome said, 'Tomorrow, if you will, Cooper.'

'Then I will say good night, sir.' Robert was about to turn away when Jerome said, almost casually, 'Did Walsingham mention Cremona?'

Robert's voice, when he answered, was gentler than its wont. 'Cremona and Mantua, sir. He confirmed certain things I had suspected for some time.'

'Old passwords,' said the voice from the bed. 'I am pleased he told you, Cooper, although it is not a matter I wish to discuss.' The twisted lips smiled but the sunken eyes were closed and although Robert waited, Jerome said no more. There was nothing to do but to accept dismissal with good grace. He was at the door when, as if against its will, the slurred voice said, 'I do not suppose – you have never heard anything concerning my brother, James?'

'No, sir; nothing.' Robert looked back.

Jerome's eyes were still tight shut; he lay as he had been left, looking as if he might never move again. His voice took on a savage note. 'There was a time when I was afraid I might come face to face with him in my work, but he was far too sensible for that. He must have remained in Rome. Who knows, we may yet see a cardinal's hat in the family!'

Robert crossed the narrow passageway to the room that until recently had been Jerome's, sat down on the bed Martha had obtained. 'You are closer to the man than anyone,' Walsingham had said, 'who better than you if he wishes to talk of the past as one day he surely must?'

Unwillingly, pity stirred within Robert. From the beginning, perhaps before he went to Rome, Jerome had been in Burghley's pay. He had not betrayed fellow priests, but helped bring to justice men he believed were about to do a great wrong to his country. All these years he had lived a lie, letting men call him traitor, accepting sneers instead of thanks, so that he might continue his work. Even the pathetic box of mementos in his room had been put there purposely to mislead Jenkins, so that he might never know what Jerome really did.

He was not, Robert told himself, naive enough to have expected Jerome to fall upon his neck. He must be grateful that he had sounded pleased at Walsingham's disclosure. Except in their lessons together when had they ever had anything in common, despite what he had been tempted to think? And why did he still feel the need to try to make a friend of a man who seemed much of the time not to like him?

The next day Robert informed Jerome that he was well enough to return to his own room, put his arms about the wasted body and as gently as he could carried him there and deposited him on the bed that had been installed where for so long had been no comfort of any sort. He looked down, prepared for some protest at such luxury, and found Jerome's eyes fixed intently on him, as he was aware they had been throughout the short journey. Then they closed in the familiar manner and Robert was once again shut out.

Deciding that it was weakness, compounded with the humiliation of being almost totally dependent upon others, that caused such dislike, Robert ignored it, making to draw the thick blanket over a body that all too soon these days felt the cold. But he was held off by Jerome's one service-able hand, which gripped him around a wrist, compelling attention. Once more the glittering eyes were upon him; the twisted mouth hissed, 'Whore! Did not James warn you? Dogs shall eat your carcass as they did that of Jezebel; it shall be as dung upon the face of the field.'

As he finished speaking his grasp loosened; he had

fainted. James again – and a woman! Robert, deciding that he had received his first – doubtless his only – glimpse into the past and inner life of Master Jerome, had turned to leave as quietly as he could when, as if he had not previously spoken at all, Jerome said, quite collectedly and in a much more friendly way than Robert was used to, 'The bed?'

'It will remain. No more sleeping hard, no more hair shirt. Your body will provide its own penance in future!' Robert came back to the bed, lightly, cruelly flicked Jerome's lifeless hand, his paralyzed face, taking petty revenge for the worries of the past weeks, for the exclusion from his work. Then, ashamed of his action, from the chest in the corner of the room he fetched the small book that until his illness had been constantly about Jerome's person and slid it beneath his tutor's good hand.

'Martha will come in later. I am going out. Unless you require anything immediately?'

The voice that answered him was so different from that of a few moments ago that it might have come from the mouth of a different person.

'Let him that is taught in the word minister unto him that teacheth, in all good things!'

With the packages he had brought from France safely beneath his cloak, Robert made his way through now-familiar streets to the bakery, his step the lighter for Jerome's parting words. That he should attempt what with him must pass for a joke – Robert recognized the quotation from Galatians – was as good as an apology. And now he was free to go to Jenny.

When work detained him late at night, or took him away from London, weeks passed between visits, yet always on his return Jenny and Sim were unquestioningly glad to see him. It had never occurred to Robert to ask if his unannounced visits were convenient, if Jenny had a lover who might object to his presence. He came and went as necessity dictated until one evening, some four years after his first visit, he had arrived to find Jenny alone, standing by the great oven with curling wisps of damp yellow hair sticking to her hot face and her dress clinging to the plump outlines of her body from the heat of her exertions. As he entered she smiled, the welcoming friendly smile that always calmed and warmed him. This time, however, he stopped in the doorway in mid-stride, as if he saw her for the first time; then, before she had time to move, as some self-protective instinct bade her do, he was across the room and, seizing her, had twisted one arm up hard behind her back. She cried out in fear and pain as he pulled her roughly, closely to him and his lips came down on hers in blind, ungovernable need for the use of a woman's body. Down her throat and breast his mouth moved, hungrily, clumsily – demanding, seeking, biting – whilst, still holding her in a vice-like grip, he tore with one unsteady hand at the lacing of her dress.

She did not – could not – struggle and made no further sound as he dragged her, with no word or show of kindness whatever, towards the garret ladder. On her bed he vented on her all his anger and loneliness, every feeling within him that might have become the first stirrings of love but which the years and manner of his upbringing had twisted and warped into nothing more than lust. Later he lay there exhausted and Jenny stroked the damp, dark head that rested so peacefully for the moment on her bruised breast. She drifted into sleep and when she awoke he was gone; only a gold coin on the windowsill and her battered body marked his being there.

The relationship thus cruelly begun was desperately one-sided. He demanded, he took, with few words, little kindness save the money he left each time, and no love. And Jenny gave gladly, as she came alive after long years of widowhood. The ribald remarks of her observant neighbours troubled her not at all. Never once did he question her regarding her life when he was not there and she was glad, although since her husband's death it had been blameless. The piety of her upbringing had, until now, developed in her a conscience that forbade her taking a lover, and her refusal to part with Sim kept away would-be suitors.

Now she found herself in a relationship in which her feelings veered between pride, love and fear. Pride came from the fact that a young gentleman should seek her out as instinct told her he sought out no other woman; love grew in a strange mixture of the passionate love of a woman for her man and the joy she would have felt in Sim had he been a normal son. But fear had by far the greatest part of her feelings. Everything about Robert Cooper spoke of a world of which she knew nothing, and one night when he was with her her suspicions were confirmed. There came feet on the garret ladder, the door burst open unceremoniously and two men entered. It was the usual method employed by those of Her Majesty's agents who made random searches through houses in all areas from time to time. In an instant Robert had swung his legs over the side of the bed, had faced the intruders, dagger in hand and mother-naked.

Had Jenny not been so afraid she might have seen comedy in the situation, for the two men obviously recognized him and the efforts of each to be first back down the ladder resulted only in their impeding one another. As they tumbled downwards one said, 'Sorry, sir. Didn't know you were here. It won't happen again.' Thus news of Robert's association reached Amos Jenkins, as most things did, and he found untold amusement at the thought of the fastidious Master Cooper, a woman old enough to be his mother, and a halfwit. He kept it to himself, partly from caution, but mainly because he had sense enough to realize that all men needed an outlet of their own choosing: his own was drink.

After that one of Jenny's neighbours followed Robert when he left and reported that he had gone straightway to Whitehall Palace, had entered between the guards with no more trouble than if it were his own home. Jenny was never sure whether she would be glad or sorry when, as must inevitably happen, he found a lady of his own age and class.

Now, when he stepped into the warmth of the bakery, Jenny was sitting on the bench before the huge ovens; a man had his arm about her, and her head was on his shoulder. Of Sim there was no sign.

At Robert's entrance they turned, rose hurriedly to face him and he saw the light of happiness die out of Jenny's face. She stepped in front of the man as if to shield him but he pulled her gently backward, faced the visitor with no sign of fear. He was a workman, stocky, ill-dressed and honest-looking, of about Jenny's own age, and his protective gesture was one that at any other time, with any other person, Robert might have honoured, but not here, not now.

He ignored the man, tossed his cloak back over one shoulder and threw his packages on to the table in a small cloud of flour.

'Sim?' he asked briefly and Jenny's eyes swam with tears; the man's arm once again went about her shoulders.

'Dead,' she said, and her voice broke in pain there was no mistaking. 'Two days after you were here the last time.'

'How?'

The man answered. 'A gang of young bullies in the alley, sir. Always taunting him, they were, as you may know. He fell and hit his head. Never woke up.'

'And you are?'

'John Smith, sir. Jenny and me were married two days ago.'

'You were so long away. I thought you would never come back this time and I was lonely. John will help me with the baking. He won't go away. He brought Sim home and looked after him until – until . . .' Jenny was gabbling, the fear in her voice very apparent.

'Of course.' Was that his own voice, Robert wondered, so calm and disinterested? Not only would John Smith not go away, life with him would be comfortable; Jenny would know what would happen from one day to the next. He did not sleep with a dagger under his pillow. The thoughts flashed briefly through his mind and were overtaken by a turmoil of grief for Sim who had loved him and whom he had loved.

He pushed one package towards the couple, picked up the other, put it under his arm.

'A bridal gift, Mistress – Smith,' he said, bowed and turned on his heel.

The next morning, amid squeals of delight, a gang of children, who might have been those who killed Sim, came upon something that blocked the kennel running down the middle of the alleyway, backing up the filthy water, causing it to spill out on to the garbage-strewn ground on either side. It was a wrapping containing a wooden horse and cart, carefully carved and painted. Either a wagon had gone over it or a man's heel had ground it into the mud. They did not care; battered and broken as it was, it was still a greater treasure than they had ever seen and they fought over it for days.

Part II

October 1584 – January 1585

CHAPTER I

1

'Thank you, gentlemen!'

The day's meeting, lengthened by the presence of their mistress in one of her most assertive moods, was over at last. Twelve members of the Queen's Council rose thankfully from their seats and waited as she stalked past them towards the door. She looked neither to left nor right, only one royal hand was raised as she said, 'Sir John, you will attend me!' and was gone.

Lord Burghley, handing papers to the clerk who met him in the passageway, heard the gasp of relief from the man by his side and bent his head to hide a smile in his long, silky beard. He admitted honestly to himself that today, with Her Majesty in one of her worst tempers, ranting, chivvying, correcting and overriding, he was thankful not to be called to bear her company. Before he returned to his work he would allow himself the pleasure of a walk through the gardens of Whitehall Palace. An aching tooth that had kept him wakeful over many nights was still today, its throbbing eased. Silently he thanked the apothecary whose skill had worked the effect, delaying the evil day when he must have it drawn.

William Davison, called into the meeting to clarify some obscure point of Scottish politics, interrupted his thoughts: 'If you will excuse me, my lord . . .?' Watching him scurry away Burghley longed to say to him, 'Have faith in yourself, man. She will not eat you. You would not be here unless she valued your judgement.' But it would have been of no use; a man well into his forties, talented and accomplished, respected for the work he had done on his country's behalf, Davison remained terrified of the Queen. That by no means made him unique, but with Davison it showed, thought Burghley wryly, and the royal eyes missed nothing. When she felt unkind, as today she had, she took pleasure in baiting him as a sadistic schoolmaster might some small and trembling pupil. There were times when Burghley had seen him blink rapidly as if to keep back tears although, to do him credit, he stood his ground. If ever there was a man designed by nature to live a quiet life on his estates with a wife and numerous children, that man was William Davison. But somewhere deep within him burned ambition that forced him, against his own better judgement, to spend his life in public service.

Burghley emerged into the October sunshine. The air was not yet unpleasantly cold and the smell of fallen leaves and damp ground was thankfully stronger than that of the nearby river. How he would enjoy the management of these gardens! He fell into an old, pleasurable habit, dreaming of redesigning, planting, sowing; was mentally telling off under-gardeners to watch more carefully the way they allowed weeds to grow in the broad, shrub-lined gravel walks when behind him, and as if its owner had read his earlier thoughts, a precise voice said, 'He's a capable man. If only she would stop jabbing at him like a child picking at a sore! He'll make a good assistant secretary.'

Much the same age as Davison, Sir Francis Walsingham looked old and, beneath the sallow darkness of his skin, was haggard and worn. Here was another whom the Queen tongue-lashed regularly, cruelly, but with him she was up against stronger stuff than Davison. Unwaveringly this man did his duty as he saw it, spoke his mind, remained unflinching before language that condemned him and his ideas in words he would have taken from no man, let alone any other woman, and returned to the fray like some small, persistent terrier until his ideas were finally accepted or, increasingly often, rejected out of hand. Yet it was Burghley's well-founded opinion that Elizabeth, although she did not like him, respected Walsingham's views more than those of most men.

'I grant you the brain is there, but do you think him strong enough to withstand what he must? Or even that she will be persuaded to offer him the post?'

'She will.' Walsingham's voice was confident; the shrewd face beneath the skull cap he affected gave away nothing. 'He is needed – or will be in the future.'

Burghley felt a shiver run down his back. They had worked together, these two, ever since Walsingham had returned from France eleven years earlier, and Burghley was well versed in extracting truth from diplomatic language. What Walsingham meant, although it remained unspoken, was '*I* need him.' It was not unknown for him to mark down someone he suspected of subversion or to pick out someone for whom he could see a use, years before his dark, inescapable web ever closed about them. What had he in mind for the conscientious, timid Davison?

Comfortably, as if nothing untoward had occurred to him, Burghley said, 'The sooner Hatton is back, the better for all of us.'

The Vice-Chamberlain was a man without fear of Majesty. Tall and handsome, blessed with a brain that made him the equal of most men, Christopher Hatton found no difficulty in dealing with his queen, even in her most crotchety moods. Honeyed words, the extravagant praise she so relished rose readily to his lips, flowed from his pen, and she lapped them up, the more so since Leicester, formerly Robert Dudley, after so many years of paying lip service to her whilst he philandered elsewhere, had finally married Lettice Knollys. After all their efforts to keep the news from Elizabeth's ears for as long as might be, it had given the French ambassador exquisite delight to inform her of her favourite's behaviour, and it had seemed for a time as if things could never be the same again. But Leicester – minus wife – was back at court, although something was gone from the relationship that had lasted since childhood. Only Hatton remained unmarried, completely faithful, and Her Majesty turned a blind eye to whatever shortcomings brought that about and, for all anyone knew, accepted his apparent worship at face value.

'Thank heavens, Frank, that you and I have never been favourites, nor ever will be. A perilous path to tread, or so it has always seemed to me. Not to mention . . .' Burghley lowered his voice against the ears of passers-by, 'extremely boring!'

Primly Sir Francis smiled. 'We were born to work, we and our kind, William, and as well some of us are.'

He broke off, catching his breath in a way his companion recognized from of old, so that he said, 'Here, man, sit for a moment; the sun is bright enough to give some warmth, you'll not catch cold,' and taking Sir Francis's arm, guided him to a stone bench beside the path, sitting silently with him until the spasm should pass. Beside the stomach pains Walsingham suffered his own toothache paled into insignificance. How much of it was due to actual bodily sickness, how much to overwork and how much to personal worries was something he found it hard to decide. Walsingham's daughter, Frances, new-married to the gallant Sir Philip Sidney, had made no demur when her father had agreed to stand surety for her husband's not inconsiderable debts. Yet she was a sensible enough girl and even in the midst of euphoria must have known, for it was common knowledge, the straits in which her father would find himself if anything went amiss. More of his personal wealth than was wise was committed to the upkeep of the intelligence network, at home and overseas, that was Walsingham's overriding passion and pride. The situation had gone on for years; it was only lately that Her Majesty had been persuaded to authorize some small official payment towards it, and that most grudgingly.

Now, with work, as ever, uppermost in his mind, Walsingham recovered himself, rose to his feet, drawing black, fur-lined robe about thin body, and made to go. In answer to Burghley's kindly question, he said, 'I shall do well enough. The pain comes and goes. Walk further with me, William, if you have the time.'

They set off side by side but not for long, for presently,

beside a shallow, ornamental pond where fish rose constantly to the surface and the ripples they made ringed wider and wider until they hit the stone edge and shattered, they halted once more and as if the words were torn from him, Walsingham said, 'If only we could know for sure that we never endanger the innocent we seek to protect.'

This from a man whose philosophy Burghley had more than once heard summed up in the phrase, 'Knowledge is never too dearly bought'! Quietly he, whose own methods had been known to be questionable when he felt occasion merited it, said, 'It must always be so, I fear. What troubles you?'

'Mary Stuart,' said Walsingham simply, as Burghley could have wagered he would. Her Majesty of Scotland, fast in Elizabeth Tudor's keeping these sixteen years, was never, it seemed to those who knew him, far from his thoughts. His correspondents regularly brought to his attention and his agents investigated plot after plot said to be designed to free her from her imprisonment, to bring her to the English throne in Elizabeth's stead and restore England to Roman Catholicism.

'Of course.' Burghley's tone was perhaps drier than he intended. The need to keep Mary on a leash was as plain to him as to any man, but he was not so zealously puritanical as Walsingham, whose mistrust of the lady, it seemed to many, verged on personal hatred.

'You may laugh at me – many do,' said Walsingham fiercely, 'but one day you – all of you – will come to realize just how great a danger she represents. We cannot afford to underestimate her. Remember past plots! Already I hear whispers of larger and better planned risings. But I am talking now of things overheard and misconstrued or even downright malicious in intent, every one of which must be investigated in case . . . Such as this . . .'

From inside his robe Walsingham drew a sheet of paper, grubby, dog-eared, and handed it to Burghley with a grimace of distaste. The writing was crabbed and difficult to read, obviously disguised; the words, however, were plain enough. If Sir Francis investigated the affairs of Sir Thomas

Woodfall and his family, who had close Catholic connections, he would find proof positive of a plot to murder the Queen and put Mary Stuart in her place.

Burghley peered closely at the ill-written paper. 'You know this Woodfall?'

'A very minor family and never a breath of anything against him. He must have a rabid enemy somewhere. If I knew who wrote this, I'd have his motive out of him quicker than it takes to read his letter, and . . .'

Behind him a woman's sharp voice said, 'Most commendable, Sir Francis,' and a beringed and bony hand, reaching over his shoulder, plucked the document from his surprise-loosened grasp.

The two men, turning, bowed low before their queen, waited as she read, met the piercing grey eyes that glared at them from the painted mask that represented her desperate attempts to cling to youth.

Once more she looked down at the paper and Burghley and Walsingham exchanged glances. Her face wore an expression they had seen at times over the years when it came to close personal relationships. Whoever this Woodfall was, wherever she had met him, he had in some way hurt her. Now she was engaged in the process of deciding what she wished to recall and what – because it was painful – forget. They saw her decide for happiness.

'Thomas Woodfall of all men!' She relaxed and a happy smile momentarily lifted the corners of the bright red royal mouth before her tone sharpened once more. 'I have no more dependable subject, gentlemen. You will burn this, Frank, do you hear me? Burn it and forget it.'

She did not wait for any response; she had given her order, it would be obeyed without question. Having shed Sir John somewhere on the way, today's quirk being to be unaccompanied by her ladies, she continued her walk, limping a little, despite all her efforts, from the sore hip that these days shortened the never very equable Tudor temper. Silently the two men watched her disappear through an archway into a farther, more private garden. Her impossibly orange wig was held high over the dark green, emerald-slashed gown she had worn to meet her Council. In efforts to maintain an even stride her hands jerked out from her sides like those of some puppet. Any other woman would have looked ridiculous; she did not.

'We can do no more, Frank! Wherever did she meet him, do you suppose? I'd swear no-one of that name has ever been to court, yet to judge from her expression he is not a man chance-met on some progress. He must go further back than that – much further. If only Kat Ashley were alive, she'd know for sure. All the same, best to bear in mind that it's the quiet ones that often spring the surprises.'

Grumbling, Walsingham stuffed the document back inside his robe. 'Do nothing and before long she'll want to know whether I've made sure it was some sort of hoax; go crashing in to search the man's home and she hears of it, and I'll be called to task for exceeding my duty, for disobeying a direct order. You know what she's like when it comes to men she's thought herself into love with when she was young. And especially since . . . Damn Leicester! Why couldn't he be satisfied with what he had, instead of wanting both sun *and* moon, so that we poor devils must take all the blame!'

The paper put away, not carelessly – that was not his way – but neatly, with other documents that might one day prove useful, Walsingham turned to matters of more urgency.

Early evening darkness fell, candles were brought and he worked on, reading between lines, making notes on actions others must take, writing to people who merited his personal attention. Engrossed in his work, he forgot the discomfort of his body, overlooked hunger, had lost all track of time when he was startled by a small contrived cough and a boy's shrill voice, would-be muted, piping, 'If you please, sir, I did knock but you did not hear. Her Majesty requests your presence immediately.'

It took a moment for Sir Francis's eyes to focus on the cause of the interruption: two bright eyes in a round, apprehensive face peered over his desk. The boy had come through anterooms empty of clerks at this late hour, had interrupted the Secretary of State because he was sent by one he feared far more, but his body was braced to leap smartly backwards should his reception be less than favourable. His attitude brought a smile flickering to Walsingham's drawn face; he and Burghley were not the only ones to suffer at Her Majesty's hands this day.

'Hurry back ahead of me, child. I'll come as fast as my legs will carry me.'

What had she thought of now that could not wait until morning? Something, obviously, that might disturb her rest, and for that she would disturb his, and send a child who should have been abed running along corridors and across courtyards, half-asleep.

The rooms leading to the Queen's apartments were quiet. The guards at the door came smartly to attention as he entered the audience chamber; he felt their eyes slide sideways to watch him as he passed. She was alone, as she had been that morning, although muted voices behind a tapestry-covered door bespoke ladies ready to come at her first call. By the window of her too-warm chamber she stood, tracing the outlines of the glass panes against the darkness with one ring-laden finger that from time to time she licked so that the pattern she drew gleamed wet.

His heart sank; once, long ago, when he had begun to be regularly at court, Burghley had warned him to beware these occasions when she reverted to childhood habits. Treat her gently, he had said. Mistress Ashley once told me there is no other way; it will pass with the night.

Walsingham was no ladies' man, but had she been his wife, or almost any other woman in the kingdom, he would have known what to do. He would have sagged at the knees, let his shoulders droop ever so slightly, so that they noticed and hurried to offer comfort to a weary man. But not with Elizabeth Tudor. Because he could see in them the ultimate good of England he had carried out her orders, no matter how counter to his personal views they ran, had negotiated prospective marriages the very idea of which made him shudder, being all the time certain, despite what she said and did publicly, that his work was no more than a ploy by a woman who had no intention of ever taking a husband, yet who saw the virtue of keeping the world guessing on the subject. And when he had been summoned to make his reports after being sleepless for days at a time, she had kept him standing all the time they talked.

It came, therefore, as a profound shock when, seeing him as a reflection in the glass, she turned and smiled so kindly at him. This was not the woman who that morning had peremptorily issued her orders. The severely cut gown she had worn then was replaced by the black and white she favoured of late, pearl-roped, diamond-sprinkled. In the flattering candlelight and with the softening of her expression, sharp, fleshless forty-five was once again a young girl.

'Sit down, Frank. Here, before the fire. Sit down before you fall! Do you never stop work?' Even her voice was gentle, and with her own hands she poured him wine, motioned him to drink.

Never once taking cautious eyes from her, he murmured grateful thanks and obeyed, all the time trying to work out what she was about to ask of him. Something that she knew would come better as a request than an order, so much was certain; her usual autocratic manner was quite in abeyance.

She took a seat opposite him, smoothed out the elaborately beaded embroideries of her skirt and her fingers traced a pattern, as they had on the window panes, as almost nonchalantly she asked, 'The letter you were showing to Burghley this morning – regarding Thomas Woodfall – what have you done with it?'

'Nothing, as Your Majesty ordered.'

She looked up then, stared him in the face half in defiance, half seeking assurance. 'It is not possible that he, he of all people, could be so changed as to want my life.' Her hands gripped together and twisted, a note of anguish cracked her voice. 'Dear God, Frank! There must be someone in this world I can trust!'

He came to his feet. 'I am Your Majesty's humble servant.'

'No, no, that is not what I meant, man. Sit down, do! You – and Burghley – and – and others, I do not doubt. I speak of people who offer friendship, at no price, and leave a warm thought that lingers, despite what the years bring of intrigue and treachery and disappointment.'

Walsingham sank back into his chair. 'There are such people, madam. You are loved, you need not doubt it.'

Her laugh was that of a girl, so different to the noise, sharp as a whiplash, that these days signalled her amusement. 'Thomas never loved me. As I recall, he was too afraid of his bride-to-be to do any such thing! We met and parted as friends and although I have not seen him for over twenty years, I still believe him to be so.'

He was silent, his heart sinking. She had some hare-brained scheme in mind, of that he was sure, something she hoped would bring back her girlhood, or at least make certain that her memories were true. Useless to point out that men changed with the passing years, as much as did women. Hoping to prevent he knew not what, he suggested, 'To my knowledge no shred of anything untoward has ever attached to Sir Thomas. Why not invite him to court, madam? Once here I can meet him and so doubtless reassure you.'

'No! I have thought the matter over, and my mind is made up. I shall go to him.' In the firelight Elizabeth's eyes glittered and she laughed aloud at the consternation her minister was powerless to keep from his face. He put forward the only argument she might permit.

'But it is so late in the year, madam. By the time arrangements have been made the winter will have set in; the roads . . .'

'*Arrangements*? I talk of a visit to an old friend, Frank, not a progress! Two days' travelling at most, lightly laden. Say two of my ladies, one of the young men who kick their heels out yonder to squire me and perhaps an escort of twelve.'

Her face was alight with mischief. As if there were suddenly no such thing in life as a sore hip she pirouetted before him on her toes, a thin pillar of sparkling jewels in the light of fire and candles.

'Now you may pour cold water on my plan, Frank! I will hear you out.'

As she spoke her chin lifted; she clasped her hands behind her back in the way men said was so reminiscent of her father. The girl vanished, swallowed up in the woman who for twenty-five years had given orders that were obeyed instantly and to the letter.

Sir Francis, having risen to his feet when his queen did, deliberately placed his goblet on a table, playing for time. One glance showed pencilled brows drawn together over her nose, thin lips held tight as she waited, no doubt wondering whether even he, who had told her so many unpalatable truths over the years, would dare to voice what he was really thinking. Almost he spoke the words on the tip of his tongue. He would have gone down prostrate before her to be allowed to point out the danger of what must happen to England if its queen died unmarried and having consistently refused to name her successor. But he drew back from the brink, contenting himself, even as his mind revolved possible ways of ensuring her safety on this crazy enterprise, by saying, 'But consider, Majesty, if – if perchance there *is* substance in the accusation. It would be . . .'

'Straight into the lion's den!' Her eyes narrowed, pleased at her victory over such an opponent; she knew very well what remained unspoken. 'Early tomorrow a messenger will be despatched to say that within three days at most I shall visit Sir Thomas. That, even if he is up to no good – *which he is not* – will give my Thomas no time to arrange anything.'

'Who knows what manner of men he has about him, Majesty? A dagger in the back takes little arranging. He may well, if he does mean you evil, consider his life well lost for such an act.'

'My mind is made up, Sir Francis. And should you for one moment think of attempting to forbid me, you will leave this room under armed guard – speaking to no-one – and will not be released until I please. The Tower is cold for a sick man at this time of year, you will find!'

At the deliberate cruelty of her tone, Walsingham raised his hands, let them fall in a gesture of hopelessness. Among the ways of averting possible danger to her he had certainly considered some method of preventing her departure; it was as if she read his thoughts. Not for one moment did he doubt that she would carry out her threat. She would soon repent, but in the meantime he would have spent an uncomfortable few days.

Wryly he admitted, 'There is nothing I can do, if you are determined. But if Your Majesty will at least consider . . . allow me, if go you must, to include a man of my own choosing in your train, someone who knows what to beware of and the steps to take if they become necessary.'

'I will not have my footsteps dogged by one of your villains, Frank!'

'No such thought crossed my mind, madam. There is on Burghley's staff a young man – a gentleman – who would perform the duty to perfection.'

Unexpectedly, gracefully, she gave in. 'Very well, very well. You may make your arrangements.'

With the words she turned away, as if unwilling to face him as she said, 'From what you said this morning I gather you know something of the Woodfalls. Sir Thomas has a wife, so much I remember. What of children?'

'A daughter only, madam, who is twenty years old.'

'No others, older than she?'

'Not to my knowledge, madam.' Walsingham frowned at her back. This was to do with her behaviour of the morning. She was setting her mind at ease with these innocent-seeming questions, he could tell, although none of them made any sense to him.

'Thank you, Frank. Away with you.' He had reached the door when her voice, dulcet sweet, stopped him. 'If it would ease your mind, my friend, I will leave in writing word that if aught happens, you are to be held blameless.'

Quietly he faced her, spoke in the forthright manner she accepted even if at most times she withstood it. 'My life is of little moment. Your Majesty is irreplaceable.'

He bowed low and left without awaiting a response. 'If anything happens to me . . .' She was acting like an irresponsible woman, not a queen, giving no thought to what her sudden death might mean to the country for which she and many others had worked so long. For an instant he thought her drunk, even mad. And there he was, back again to thoughts of Mary Stuart . . . One day, one day soon, something must be done about that enemy, but in the meantime he wished very much that he were at home, at rest from all responsibilities, with his wife to comfort and look after his miserably aching body.

And in the room behind him, Elizabeth Tudor laughed aloud as she summoned her ladies. Where Rosamund Emory had gone and what had become of her was of no consequence; she dismissed her from the reckoning as she had the many women Robert Dudley had known over the years. But for the sake of those innocent, happy meetings in the Hatfield meadows she was glad that Thomas had not reared Rosamund's child.

2

Amos Jenkins seldom met Robert Cooper these days; if their paths crossed at all it was usually in connection with Master Jerome's work. On this particular day it was only the chance of his being in Sir Francis's office when a messenger was required that brought it about.

'A moment before you go, Jenkins. Master Cooper will be at home, I think. Kindly deliver this to him.' The letter, folded and sealed before Jenkins's eyes, was yet another needle prick among the many that came his way these days. Walsingham barely looked at him as he spoke, made no enquiry as to whether he had time to act as errand boy, certainly had no thought of divulging the contents of the note. The clerk, Henry Loader, who would presently clear his master's desk of papers, would know more than Jenkins!

Cooper was indeed at home and as haughty-looking as ever, but Jenkins allowed none of his feelings to show. At the moment he could ill-afford to ignore even a syllable of

Sir Francis's orders or offend anyone who had his ear. A fiasco a week earlier had brought him nearer to dismissal from his job than was comfortable, and who should know better than he that in the case of a man with as much secret information in his head as he had gathered over the years, and a growing inability to control his tongue, such dismissal would doubtless mean his being found in some alley with a knife in his back. Cooper was bound to have heard about it. It seemed to Jenkins, desperately trying to keep sober and suffering agonies from past excesses, that the whole world knew. Yet Cooper was not impolite. He invited Jenkins to step indoors; but it was so far and no further. He stood in the hall like some junior clerk whilst the young man opened his letter, nodded in understanding, all with the distant courtesy that Jenkins hated.

'Thank you, Master Jenkins.' As he spoke part of his mind registered the shiny redness of the other's rapidly coarsening features, the trembling of hands he was powerless to keep still, and he recalled Jerome's growing reservations regarding this man.

Behind him came a sound Robert had been expecting since the day before and he stepped to one side. The purpose of the movement was two-fold; it took him away from the full force of Jenkins's foul breath, at the same time making way for Jerome who, coming in through the back of the house, dragged himself past them and into the study without so much as an upward glance.

The days of tutor and pupil were long over; no other boys came to be taught and drilled. Money was scarce and Sir Francis had added other work to the analysis of papers and the interrogations Jerome had always undertaken. The house in Trinity Street was said to have been Robert Cooper's for several years now, but he and Jerome still shared it. Shared what else? Jenkins wondered coarsely. It was the only explanation he had ever been able to arrive at for Jerome not long since having been thrown out. It was as simple as that and Jenkins was not overly surprised. Everyone knew the way priests behaved given a chance, and Cooper was an extremely handsome young man. Sneeringly

Jenkins laughed, said loudly so that Jerome could not fail to hear, 'How are the mighty fallen, eh? I remember the day when he was too proud to soil his fingers!'

Robert wasted no time on the taunt. Quietly he said, 'I will speak to Sir Francis,' more as if he were conferring a favour than accepting an order, and Jenkins found the door to the street held open for him. He was being dismissed by a jumped-up young so-and-so to whom he had taught much of what he knew and there was only one thing he could do about it. With great pleasure he coughed, raking into his throat all the phlegm he could muster, then spat fully and with accuracy, so that it ran in a thick shining trail across Robert's boot and slithered on to the floorboards.

The heavy front door slammed on the unwelcome visitor and Robert called, 'Martha, food and Master Jerome's robe at once, please,' and would have ignored the mess on the floor until later but that the maid noticed it herself, bunched up a cloth in her hand, knelt down and carefully wiped first Robert's boot, then the boards. As she did so she made the comment he had not, even to himself, concerning some people's disgusting habits!

'Thank you,' he said, and putting down a hand, caressed her head. It was as careless a gesture as if he had fondled a dog but it, and the gentle note in his voice, made her heart beat faster than ever it had for the long-departed Gregory.

In the study Jerome was leaning over the paper-strewn table, gripping its edge with his one serviceable hand to save himself from falling. He was cold through and through; only determination that his arch-enemy should not see him collapse had carried him thus far, and now he lacked even the strength to reach his chair. For two days and two nights he had been squatting, a bundle of filthy rags, at the corner of a certain lane, waiting for men who had not come, in the hope of overhearing information Jenkins had said was to pass. All that had happened was that the watch had four times moved him on and he had provided a constant target for urchins of the neighbourhood who had pelted him with the mud and filth that still clung about his person and stank out the room.

'More wasted time!' His speech had recovered somewhat since the days of his illness, but still it was slightly slurred, its old sharpness gone for ever. A note of dry amusement crept in. 'I could swear Jenkins does it on purpose and that he pays those louts to throw their muck at me!'

There came a tap at the door; Martha delivered what she knew from experience was needed and left without looking at the two men who employed her. There were long periods when both of them looked as neat as new pins, spent their time writing or in discussion with other men who came and went, or Master Cooper might be absent for weeks at a time, but occasionally one or other took it into his head to play beggar, as Master Jerome had done for these two days past.

Every time Robert touched Jerome's body it felt lighter, had become nothing but skin and bone. Limbs rendered useless by the seizure had withered and shrunk; each winter brought its outbreak of sores that now seemed scarcely to heal before more were added to them. But with the suffering that had turned his thinning hair grey and sunk his eyes deep into their sockets, there had slowly come to him a tranquillity of spirit that he had never expected to find. He dragged himself out and about, using his disability as an asset; posed as a beggar, collecting information as well as the few small coins that dropped into his filthy outstretched hand, watched people who had no idea that they were being watched. Robert would have wondered how he managed had it not been for the fire that still burned in the dark eyes. The brain that had made him so good a teacher was alive and flourishing inside its crippled shell and so long as spirit could prevail over flesh this man would keep on working.

Robert helped him over to the fireside and as he balanced there, one hand on the back of a chair, deftly stripped away his clothing. His impulse was to burn the whole ragged, soaking, evil-smelling lot, but they were part of Jerome's stock-in-trade – occasionally of his own – and must be taken away by Martha for drying against next use. Briskly, yet gently, he rubbed down the emaciated, ice-cold body, pulled clean warmed shirt and rough woollen robe over the head and helped Jerome to sit, kneeling before him to chafe his feet warm before he pushed them into fur-lined slippers. As he did so he looked up to receive the half-smile the action brought to the older man's face. The slippers he had brought from Italy as a gift; the acceptance had been dispassionate, almost offhand, but Robert knew Jerome to be pleased by them.

With a sigh Jerome leaned back, and took the tankard of mulled ale Robert held out to him. 'Jenkins will not trouble us much longer,' he said, and there was satisfaction in his voice. 'Walsingham was – to put it mildly – not at all pleased that he let Lawrence and his friends slip through his fingers.'

Jenkins's failing powers troubled Robert little. 'I have to go away tomorrow. Some friend of Her Majesty whom she has taken it into her head to visit. Walsingham doubts him, will feel happier, it seems, if I am in her retinue. At the rate she travels I cannot hope to be back in less than a week. Shall I ask Henry to come and stay with you?'

'Walsingham doubts everyone! And I'll stay by myself, thank you.' Jerome was thawing out now, relaxing in the warmth. 'Unless it means Lawrence is found again?'

'I think not. The name is Woodfall.'

As he spoke Robert was scooping up the rags, putting them and the bowl of filthy water outside the door for Martha to collect, and so did not see the effect his words had on his companion.

In his turn he sat down by the hearth, stretching out long legs to the heat. His own day, until the advent of Jenkins, had been uneventful, and now he must go away for as long as suited Her Majesty's whim. Efficiently he thought over work half-finished, deciding how to dispose of it to best advantage. He grew engrossed, as he always did, was composing the final paragraph for a report when Martha brought in food, which she put down on the one clear corner of the table.

As if the clatter she made were a signal that loosened his tongue, Jerome said, 'Cooper!'

'Sir?' Despite the closeness brought about by the many

personal services Robert had rendered Jerome since his illness, despite the fact that to the outside world their ranks seemed reversed by the work each now did, it suited both men to maintain the distance of the old master–pupil relationship. In the one place where he ever came near to relaxing, and with his mind still more than half-occupied by his own affairs, Robert answered automatically. It was some moments before he became aware that Jerome had not continued what he had begun to say, was sitting as still as if paralysis had again stricken him.

'Sir? There is something you wish to discuss before we eat?'

'Woodfall, you said? Of Sussex – Highwoods? Thomas Woodfall?'

'He is.'

'You cannot go!'

He had Robert's full attention now. 'The order came directly from Walsingham. I can hardly ask to be replaced for no good reason.'

'You can – can fall ill. A fever – we all get them. That girl in the kitchen looks downright sickly these days; say you've caught something from her, or from me and my filthy alley!' Faster and faster came the words, tumbling one over the other from Jerome's lame tongue. Then the stern self-discipline of years came to his aid. Using the carved staff that rested against it, he lifted himself up from his chair, held himself as straight as he could and stood silently awaiting the younger man's reaction.

Robert sat back easily, rested his arms along those of his chair. The hands that so short a time before had dealt competently with his companion's bodily needs now caressed carved leaves with a regular motion that was almost hypnotic. For an instant he was reminded with grim clarity of a prisoner, broken in body and terrified to the depths of his soul, who had once faced him in the same way, had babbled on and on for hours and had died without saying anything of value.

He said, 'Please explain,' and his voice remained as care-fully modulated as ever, yet in face of those two words every excuse, every mitigating reason Jerome had laid up against such a time as this vanished. He heard himself croak out the bald fact: 'Sir Thomas Woodfall is your father.'

Slightly Robert inclined his head and when it came his answer related only to the effect Jerome's statement might have on the work he must undertake.

'Your fear is that I am so like him that it will be remarked?'

'You are not in the least like him.' Jerome's words rang with certainty. The hands he watched so carefully ceased their movements and their very stillness increased his unease. Others interrogated by torture; it was before Robert Cooper that many a prisoner obdurate under pain broke without a finger being laid upon him. An air about him said that he already knew the answers to questions others had asked in vain, that there was no point in attempting to withstand him; fear did the rest. More than one man had sworn that a figure with white-grey eyes had appeared in his cell late at night, had leaned over him and read his thoughts. Jerome, for the first time, understood how such tales had arisen.

'There cannot be the slightest danger or Her Majesty would not go. It is, as you say, some start of Walsingham's. Your priestly conscience may be tranquil.'

Jerome winced. 'Honour thy father . . .? No, it is not that, although I deserve that you should think it.'

'Then we must consider the name "Emory", must we not?' The change in direction came like a sword thrust, without warning, and the flicker of a smile crossed Jerome's face. He should have known that the boy would go straight to the heart of the matter. The secret he had hoped to carry unspoken to the grave was no longer his to keep.

'Before – before I took the name "Jerome", I too was Robert Emory. Your mother was my sister. What I know of the matter is at second or even third hand, but I will tell you all I know.'

In effect he had said, 'You are my sister's bastard son,' but Robert did not stir in his chair, made no mention of all the years they had lived together with the truth untold between them. The questions he asked were disinterested in tone, polite in their phrasing.

'My mother is no longer alive?'

'She – she died at your birth.'

'At Highwoods?'

'Yes. She made her way there, although she knew that by then Sir Thomas was already married.'

'From your family home? She was thrown out?'

'No. She was a maid-in-waiting to Queen Elizabeth. She – she is buried in the Woodfall grave. They – Woodfall – offered to send you to my father, but he would not hear of it.'

'Your home is where?'

'Near to Barndale on the Scottish Border – or it was. My father and eldest brother, Henry, were "out" with Northumberland in '69 in the Northern Rising against the Queen. Everything was sequestered. There is not one of us alive there now.'

'And no-one anywhere else, except you and a certain cardinal?' A note of mockery sounded suddenly. Jerome's brother, James, had achieved the high rank of his own and his father's ambition a year earlier.

'No-one.'

'So I was raised by the Woodfalls, who did not see fit to give me their name, until somehow I came here?'

'It must be so. I was in Rome at the time. I know no more of the early part of your life. As – as you know, I found out your name when you were in delirium, and I was not surprised. From the beginning the resemblance was there and that day when you defied me and Jenkins rescued you, I saw – Rosamund – as she had been when a child – wilful, stubborn, come back to torment me. Dear God, I might have killed you . . .'

He swayed where he stood, exerted the last of his strength to remain upright as, quite indifferently, Robert said, 'So my mother was Rosamund Emory and your name was Robert. How many other people know of this?'

'No-one. Burghley knew my name in the old days, but not even he . . . James is out of the reckoning; it is between the two of us. But anyone who – who was – interested in Rosamund, no matter how many years ago, would know you. You are her image. It is the eyes.'

'Then I must disguise myself, must I not? How fortunate that you came home when you did.'

The room tilted suddenly before Jerome's eyes and at last Robert moved, sprang forward in time to catch his new-found uncle's sagging body and lay him in his chair.

As Jerome recovered, struggled to sit upright, Robert said, 'It has occasionally occurred to me to wonder how old I am. You can tell me that.'

'As near as I can tell, you must be twenty-five years old.'

'Thank you.' Was the boy grateful for that answer or was it a mocking acknowledgement of the whole discussion? Jerome could not tell. Tight in his fist he still held the carved staff. Even when he felt himself falling he had not let go of that; it was another memento from Robert's travels. Now, as if compelled, he held it out to the younger man, a treasured possession to which he had no right, since it had been given in friendship. He could find no words with which to ask pardon, not only for withholding news that had now been forced from him by circumstance, but for other, darker, things to which he had acquiesced and which he recognized full well had helped make Robert Cooper what he was.

He was not surprised when Robert spurned the gesture. 'You need that, not I. You may rest assured that what you have said will make no difference to the work I must do. I shall hardly go seeking revenge!'

He gave no quarter, showed no mercy, and Jerome closed his eyes. If he could have gone to sleep and never awakened he would have been glad, yet deep within him, alongside the relief of getting the truth into the open at last, lay a kernel of thankfulness. Over the years he had waited for Robert to display his mother's flaring, vicious temper, had been the harder so that if it lived within him it might be made manifest and reported before it was provoked by his work, which would have endangered others. Never had he seen a sign of it; ordinary hot temper, yes, once or twice, but even that now was throttled down inside a young man who showed little of what he was thinking. The Woodfall blood must be stronger than the Emory, he thought, and could only be grateful. That gibe regarding his priestly conscience was the only sign of personal stress. There had been one other occasion when he had said much the same thing. Jerome's mind escaped back to the day when, with as much relish as once he had told a child of Father Jerome's supposed defection from Rome, Jenkins had been unable to resist saying, 'Who would have thought it of that precious *protégé* of yours, Jerome! Eighteen years old and keeps a mistress old enough to be his mother. There's an idiot son, too. Very fond of him, he is. No accounting for taste!' And his tone had implied that present company was not excepted.

Thus had Jerome learned of the existence of a woman whose name he never knew, and of her son. The boy's name, too, would have remained unknown had all gone well, but late one night as he lay in the state of semi-sleep that was all that was possible to one who in the slough of illness spent long days and even longer nights without movement to tire him, there had come the click of a candlestick being set down on the wide windowsill, followed by creaking as the lid of the chest containing his personal belongings was thrown roughly open. Beneath his eyelids he had watched Robert, still booted and cloaked from the street, toss to one side whatever he did not need, remove something small from the box in which it lay with other fragments of the past. He had come to the bed, leafing through Jerome's missal until, with an exclamation of extreme impatience, he snapped it shut, caught its owner urgently by a shoulder and shook him fully awake. His voice when he spoke was hard and strange. 'The prayers for the dead! Which page? You are a priest of sorts and I cannot say them. Prayers – for a dead child . . .'

As well as he was able, lying supine, Jerome had obeyed; when asked the name to be remembered before God, Robert had said 'Sim', had stood there rigid and silent in the dim light until all was finished, had left with no word of thanks.

That was as much of Robert's personal life away from Trinity Street as Jerome knew. There had been no more visits to the mistress of whom Jenkins had spoken; so much was apparent, for after that night Robert had taken his pleasures much nearer home. Twenty-four hours later, Martha made the first of her visits to his room and Gregory came to the house no more.

Jerome was brought back to the present by pressure of a hand on his shoulder, opened his eyes to find Robert standing over him holding a wooden platter containing bread, with meat carefully broken into small pieces, an apple neatly sliced.

'Eat! You will need your strength for your begging tomorrow.' It was the kind of remark that occasionally passed between them as a joke, but today it made Jerome wince. He might not be sent literally to live in the gutter, if only because Robert appreciated the worth of the work he did, but he could not expect the relationship between them to be as it had; he had destroyed that for ever. His mouth was dry and the food so difficult to swallow that more than once he would have given up, save that he dared not. Sidelong he looked at his nephew, wondered what thoughts lay hidden behind the dispassionate face.

Had he possessed the power to read minds he would have been amazed. Robert, as he also ate, carefully laid to one side the many questions the past hour had raised for him. It was a habit long since developed, like a man sorting papers, placing at the bottom of a pile those that were not urgent. But one thing he could not leave. The idea that Jerome, who had for so many years lived a life few men would care to brave, should be afraid of him, caught at him and chafed like an ill-tended wound. He felt no surge of sentiment towards a newly discovered relation, any more than he felt anger that his ancestry had been kept from him. What he wanted – what he needed – was that things should go on as they had of late years, that the two of them continue to be comfortable together. Then, from out of the past, the way he could take came to him.

The meal over, he gathered together the papers he had

left scattered across the table and went to the chest beneath the window where Jerome kept his books. From it he took an old, much-used copy of Virgil's *Aeneid*. For a moment he stood with its familiar battered shape between his hands before he carried it across to the tired and hunched man by the hearth. Jerome dragged his dreary gaze away from the fire, ready to submit to whatever strictures the other should put upon their future living. But it was the voice of his pupil that he heard, deferential, respectful as in childhood, and on Robert's lips was the half-smile that had long signalled companionship one to the other.

'I have half an hour to spare, sir. If you are not too tired will you hear me translate, please?'

Robert's strong fingers closed briefly, warmly, about Jerome's one usable hand, conveying the message for which he had no words, carrying immediate understanding. So many times had they been through the book that Robert could have translated it without thinking, but that did not matter. For a moment Jerome could not speak, then he swallowed convulsively, braced his shoulders and said, as he had so many times over the years, 'From the beginning of the First Book, if you please, Cooper. "*Arma virumque cano . . .*"'

Long after Robert was gone, Jerome remained seated beside the fire, remembering.

'Henry is my heir; my other sons I give to Mother Church. James and Peter and you, Robert. It is arranged. Put the idea of any other life from your head once and for all.' His father had been inexorable and he had gone obediently off to his seminary when he would have given the world to be a scholar with a wife and family. Fortunate Peter to have died before the snares of the godly closed about him!

Rosamund, young as she was, had laughed on that day of departure as if she saw some subtle joke, and when he returned home, a priest ordained, to bid his father farewell before he journeyed to Rome, still she had laughed, but oh, so differently. In all her years of growing up nothing had been denied this only daughter and she had taken whatever she wanted, whenever she wanted it, not seeing any wrong.

The pleasure she found in teasing this brother who had been denied the life he wanted was infinite, until the afternoon she had come upon him solitary and sat so close beside him that he could feel the warmth of her body through their clothes, could smell her hair and skin, saw the tip of her tongue caress her lips as she turned towards him. Then a hand stroked his neck, her fingers walked softly around one earlobe, her breath on his cheek made him shiver, and he was lost. Afterwards he remembered little of what had happened, only that she said, 'Well now, brother – *Father* – who would have believed it of you! Remember me!' and still she laughed.

He fled headlong from his home, hating his sister, loathing the life to which he was condemned, believing himself eternally damned. It was on his way through London that he fell in with one of William Cecil's clerks who had taken him in and given him a bed for the night. Little talk passed between them; Emory's calling was evident enough to one who worked on the edge of espionage, as did Henry Richards, and the man's touch had been of the lightest, nicely tempered by the experience of years. 'If at any time you need a friend . . . if at any time you find your way of life no longer to your liking . . .' Truth to tell, once Emory was gone on his way, Richards had given him not another thought. There was small likelihood of his swerving from his first allegiance, whatever trouble now beset him.

Had the young priest's confessor been as perceptive of his charge's needs as Richards, Sir William might never have heard of Emory, but he was not and thereafter, through the following years, anonymous messages arrived from Rome from time to time, occasionally useful, more often worthless, until the time came when, about to return to England, Emory offered his services to his country in any capacity whatsoever.

And the life he had at first looked upon as revenge against everything that had led him only to torment and unhappiness he had come to believe was of far greater use to his fellow men and women than the path in which he had been raised. Even now, though, from time to time he saw Rosamund still. She stood in shadows, called to him through dreams, turned street corners a little ahead of him, smiling, tossing her beautiful head as she had when she had tempted him to his fall. But after all the years of self-torment he had forgiven her. How she would have mocked had he been able to tell her that he had at last faced the fact that the sin had been his as much as hers; he could imagine her laughter at the thought that it was her chance-born son who had played a great part in his finding his present degree of peace.

If Robert ever did ask questions he was prepared to lie, lie right royally, that he might never discover what his mother had been. He owed him that and it was a small sin to add to all the others. 'Thou shalt not take the Name of the Lord thy God in vain,' but he had done that and there was no undoing the past. Strange that he, who had made a mockery of the priesthood, should now find comfort in the book he had so long spurned.

As he pulled himself to his feet, made his slow way across the room, he bowed slightly to the shade of the woman who for more than quarter of a century had lain in the Woodfall family vault, and he thought of the constant service her son had rendered him, without being asked, through the humiliating years of his illness.

'Your son he undoubtedly is, Rosamund. His upbringing – for which I am in large part guilty – has warped him, and how could it not? But he is kind, as you never were!'

CHAPTER II

The very vehemence of the sound Agnes made, halfway
between oath and snort, startled Bennitt. In the comfortable room that had been known to the family as Mother's
parlour ever since the first children were born in Abbey
House, she looked across the sewing-strewn table at the
miserable, crumpled piece of material held out to her
between long brown finger and thumb and smiled, which
was perhaps Agnes's objective, although the mingled disgust
and annoyance in her voice was real enough.

'It was white when I began! Look at it now! There's
blood on it – and you must surely have cut it too small.
What baby will ever get its head into this? I should have
carried on with tapestries!'

Bennitt's own small, capable hands found no difficulty
whatsoever in setting stitches so fine that they could hardly
be seen. 'Take your time. You're pulling your thread too
tight. And the stitches are . . .'

'Hedge stakes!' Agnes heaved an exaggerated sigh. 'I'll
undo it and begin again. I hope young Mary will appreciate
all my trouble.'

'She'll be highly honoured, as well you know. You've
never been noted for your skill with a needle that I
recall.'

Agnes bowed her head in stately acknowledgement of the
family joke. 'True, but I have, I think, taught her one or
two things that must make her useful to her mother-in-law!'

She took up her small silver scissors and began to pick at stitches that for their very size she would find so much easier to undo than they had been to make.

And as she worked she marvelled that either of them could even talk as if all were well, let alone smile. It was six weeks since the family physician, John Lane, had told Edward that the pains that cramped his stomach and at times bent him double were caused by no passing illness. He might with care see out the winter; there would be no more summers for him. What was said between husband and wife when he told her the news Agnes never knew, but shortly afterwards, when they were side by side on their knees in the walled garden, picking at weeds that sprouted from even the smallest crack, Bennitt had reached out one soil-dusty hand to her. 'Is it well with you, my dear?' she had asked softly, in a paraphrase of Father Peter's long-discontinued greeting, and seeing Agnes's face crumple, had put out her arms and drawn Edward's sister gently towards her. Only after Agnes had sobbed herself into calm had Bennitt's small, plump face turned into the thin shoulder next her own, convulsed in pain. Why, oh why, she demanded heartbrokenly, could she not go with him as Anne had gone with her Lewis? Thereafter the matter had never been mentioned between them; all grieving was done in private. Agnes provided the herbal mixtures that to some extent dulled her brother's pain and Bennitt went about her duties, outwardly as serene as she always had been, that in accordance with Edward's wish, the girls might know nothing of his illness for the present. No stranger, seeing her, would have guessed that her world had been tied up as neatly, completely, as one of the bales of fleeces Edward sent regularly to market, and as finally; that when her husband died, although she might still move and talk, her life too would be ended.

In the twenty years that had passed since the outbreak of plague, Edward and Bennitt had reared five children of their own, all of them girls. Abbey House was a home in a way Highwoods, where Eleanor ruled supreme, never had been, and Bennitt knew the cause to be those very girls. In and out they had run from babyhood, through its passages, up and down its wide, shallow stairs, filling it with a life and happiness that, even now the older ones were grown and leaving, seemed still to linger in the air like the subtle fragrance of dried flowers.

The son Agnes had predicted so many years before had never been born: two girls had died in young childhood, not even one of several stillborn children had been a boy, and Philippa was the last, as Edward had said very firmly six years earlier when he stood by his exhausted wife soon after the birth. The future would take care of itself. Privately Bennitt doubted that he would have been as complacent had Martin not been so much to his liking. Dowries for Mary, Anne, Katharine and Philippa must come from the lands that had belonged to the Williams family, but Cecily, although she did not know it, carried with her the abbey lands entire, which would belong to her and Martin when they married. Thus the lands his father had given him would still belong to a Woodfall of Edward's line.

When Edward had first proudly told Bennitt of his plan, and she had laughed, Cecily was a child of eleven, Martin only eighteen months older. They were inseparable as they had been all through their childhood, but who was to say that they would make husband and wife? Edward had been supremely confident, nor did he give any weight to Bennitt's mention of Wat, who might well feel squeezed out by his twin's preferment.

It was impossible for anyone who had been present to forget Edward Woodfall's rage, two years later, when Master Price had sent word to Abbey House that Wat, following failure to obtain his uncle's agreement to his grand plans for a seafaring life that should make him rich, had taken matters into his own hands and disappeared, leaving behind only the briefest note of explanation. Never, Edward had sworn, should the boy cross this threshold again; furthermore, word of his irresponsible behaviour must be sent to his grandfather.

'He is Lewis's son, Edward. For your brother's sake you cannot cast him off.' Bennitt, still sure in her own mind that it was high spirits rather than thoughtlessness that led her elder nephew to behave as he did, had faced her husband with more courage than she had dreamed she possessed, and his reaction had been what she had hoped for. Holding her closely to him he had thanked her, with tears in his eyes, for reminding him of his duty, had – and he had laughed for the first time in days – admitted that it ill behoved him to speak of punishing anyone for running away to sea! When Walter returned, as he undoubtedly would, he should be received as a member of the family still.

Emboldened, Bennitt had prompted, 'And you will forgive him, Edward?'

But here she had met with less success. He would do his best in that direction, said her husband drily, but the boy's irresponsible behaviour absolved him from any feelings of guilt for preferring Martin. If ever he settled to the life for which he had been raised, the elder grandson's share of the Barndale estate must content Walter.

That Edward had chosen his second-born daughter to marry Martin came as no surprise to his wife or Agnes. Two girls had the Woodfall fairness, to three Bennitt had given her family's brown skin and hair, and all save Cecily had her gentle brown eyes. From Cecily's small round face, that was in all else so like her mother's, the Woodfall eyes blazed blue as in the sky of early summer, just as they did in her father and Aunt Agnes, and in Martin. Bennitt, who would have given her life for her husband, had watched with pleasure the growing of a girl who had the sense of humour of her father and the uncle who had been dead before she was born. As she grew, Edward often turned to her with his not always reverent observations on people they met. Cecily's eyes would dance in delighted answer. Sometimes they did not even have to speak; the idiocy of a thing struck them at the same time and they burst into peals of simultaneous laughter, yet always Edward, loving his wife, respecting her less agile turn of mind, took care to pull her into the heart of these occasions. There was room for all in his happy world. She never realized, perhaps because she never looked for it, how much Cecily had inherited from her too. Bennitt's was the determination she showed

234

when set upon a course of action, the kindness one and all met in her.

In and out of the canvas she held so firmly darted Bennitt's needle, with its tail of dull green wool, adding depth and shade to the pattern of leaves that would, when finished, make yet another cushion for her husband's chair, as if the very act of making meant that he *must* be there to use it, and her thoughts turned to her sister-in-law sitting so patiently sewing in a way that a few years earlier would have been unthinkable.

As with Abbey House, it seemed to Bennitt, so with Agnes. The outbuildings and gardens Edward had once word-painted for Lewis now stood in very fact beside and behind the house. Mud-trampled waste had become young parkland; all was well established, had weathered to blend into its surroundings. Just so had Agnes mellowed. Quite when the change had come about was impossible to say, but the taut, rigid look of her youth was gone, so was the – to others – frightening way she had of predicting the future. She had passed into tranquil middle age as one born again. The set of her mouth had gentled, her eyes had lost the wild, intense look that had made so many fear her as a witch. Now the villagers accepted as wisdom the remedies she took them in their illnesses and were glad to receive the food she carried at all times. Even young Mary's marriage to Geoffrey Stratton, a younger son of the man she had herself once loved and hoped to marry, had not troubled her serenity.

Three times or more in a week she visited Peter Acres at his cottage and the old man, so frail now that each winter Bennitt feared for his very life, resumed his role of priest, and together they prayed. That was the source of Agnes's inward happiness, Bennitt felt sure; she looked forward one day to being reunited with her dead, with an infant daughter and Thomas's son whom she had fostered.

As if aware of the eyes upon her, Agnes stopped her work of destruction, looked down at frayed edges, picked at short lengths of hanging thread. 'At least,' she said resignedly, 'young Anne can be glad. By the time she begins her family I shall have had so much practice that my work will be perfect.' Only a few months earlier Anne, younger by a year than Cecily, had gone to be the wife of Cary Ashby in the neighbouring county, a man not far short of her father in age, and had gone happily.

Having thus led Bennitt to the opening she needed, Agnes said calmly, 'There will only be two of them left soon,' and waited.

The anxiety she sensed in Bennitt, her surface calm notwithstanding, relaxed. 'Oh, why need Edward be troubled with the matter? Martin surely could have spoken to the girl himself. There can be no formality between those two.' Then, anxiously, 'She will accept him, will she not?'

Agnes, by now smoothing out her ill-treated sewing with some ferocity and little success, said soothingly, 'Did you ever know Cecily refuse her father anything?' and wished she could drive from her mind memory of the occasion three years earlier when seventeen-year-old Wat, returned home from a voyage that had not, after all, made his fortune, professing penitence for his actions and forgiven, if not trusted, had broken out of the woods ahead of her in the dusk, towing a laughing Cecily by the hand. Neither had seen their aunt and when they reached the main path the youth had put his arm about the girl's waist, bent his tall, handsome head over her and whispered something that sent her off into peals of laughter, but at the same time caused her to reach up a hand to touch his cheek in a way that made her aunt's heart leap, so womanlike was it. He had gone away again shortly afterwards and Cecily seldom mentioned him. Agnes had kept a watchful eye on her until all fear of trouble was passed but it would have done no good to worry the child's mother with what was, after all, only suspicion born of distrust of a nephew she had never liked. Martin was in no way as superficially attractive as his brother and he had always been there; Cecily was too used to him to see his worth.

Bennitt, relieved because she wished to be, said, 'Yes, of course. But sometimes, in spite of what Edward says, I think we should have prepared her.'

236

*

A little over an hour later Cecily was running, stumbling over her own feet in her haste, back to the house to seek refuge from shock, from the knowledge also that for the first time in her life she had lied to the person in the world she loved above all others.

And in the ruins of the old abbey church where she had found him, Edward Woodfall still sat, head in hands, no less shocked. His own life was finished as surely as that of the leaves that whipped round fallen blocks of stone and gathered in rustling piles in sheltered corners as if hiding from the wind that would move them on, and the dream he had for those he must leave behind him was shattered. From all their talk and argument two sentences remained with him, as if their echoes were trapped in the decaying stones and must resound there for ever: Cecily's cry of horror, 'But Martin is my *brother*, I cannot marry my brother!' and his own implacable, 'You will come to me within fourteen days at most to tell me you accept him!' He had limited her time even as his own was limited.

Martin had been sixteen years old when he had come to his uncle with words of stilted formality; the dream that had been Edward Woodfall's for several years was his also. 'Sir, I am come to ask for Cecily's hand in marriage – in due time.'

From that day his uncle's estate was as good as his; his younger grandson's portion in far northern Barndale mattered not at all.

Edward had felt it only proper for Martin, Wat being away, to spend part of each year in Barndale and the boy dutifully rode off there each spring, returning before autumn rains could make the road impassable. And when he was at home little seemed to have changed, except that having received formal permission to court Cecily, his attitude towards her became different. Still he pulled Katharine's hair, tickled Philippa until she squealed for mercy, but Cecily he treated with a deference that was new, new and somehow disturbing, until she came to the conclusion that he had grown up ahead of her and was

237

practising the manners he would one day extend to the lady he chose to be his wife.

But now Edward Woodfall, if he were to see the pair married, as he had every intention of doing, could wait upon tardy lovers no longer. His nephew's wooing had been quiet, forbearing, and in impatience and pain Edward had taken it upon himself to tell Cecily of the future that should make her secure and glad.

Fourteen days! So short a time and Cecily could see no way to escape what was decreed for her. She had lived alongside Martin her life long, played with him, studied with him, and even fought him on occasion, and together they had stood shoulder to shoulder when Cousin Rose and her mother sneered at the farming Woodfalls. And now the boy was become a stranger, a man who wanted to marry her. Wildly she thought, If I tell him I cannot marry him and he truly loves me, he will let me go, and, even more wildly, Fourteen days is a long time. Wat may be home before then.

She saw Martin before she had time to put her thoughts into order, and love and marriage were the last things on his mind. As she ran through the gathering gloom into the stable yard, the door to one of the loose boxes broke open and he stood there, holding high a lantern. It revealed him covered in muck, blood and wisps of straw, naked to the waist, his chest gleaming with sweat. He came towards her exultantly, eyes bright in his square, freckled face.

'Twins, Cec! Bessie has calved at last. Two of the finest heifers you have ever seen. Come and look, do come and look!'

She brushed past him without slowing down and all unsuspecting he let her go. She would come to look and admire in her own time.

It was Aunt Agnes who fetched her from the room that had been hers alone since Anne left home, dragged her bodily off the bed where she lay face down and in a voice she seldom used to any of Edward's children, said, 'You are awaited downstairs, mistress! Brush your hair at once and come with me.' It was evident that her father had returned, that he had told the others what had happened.

Sitting opposite Martin as they ate, Cecily studied him as she never had before. He kept his eyes on his food, quiet now, tired after his hard day's work. Before he came in someone had thrown cold water over him and his skin glowed beneath damp, curling fair hair that needed the attention of Aunt Agnes's scissors. She watched his capable hands tearing bread into pieces, listened as he replied gravely to some question put to him by her mother and wondered when he would speak to her himself, as he surely must.

Then her attention was drawn from him by the sound of her father's voice, tetchy, even petulant, as she had never heard it, 'In God's name, woman, leave be! I am not hungry! *Not hungry!* Can you understand that?' And as her mother shrank back Cecily, whose own food was sticking in her throat, looked along the table and felt tears sting her eyes. For the first time she noticed how drawn had become his thin face, how lank the brown hair receding from his broad brow. This man whom she loved more than anyone on earth no longer laughed as often or as spontaneously as he had, and there were new lines on his face, drawing his brows together and pulling his mouth tight shut when he thought he was not observed. Weeks ago Aunt Agnes had told her that he had a low fever he was finding it difficult to shake off – his father had been liable to much the same thing – and now it seemed to Cecily that by her behaviour that afternoon she had made bad worse. Seeing him each day the gradual change had made no impact until now, when guilt stirred within her.

Never had she been so glad when a meal ended, but she was to be allowed no respite. As her parents and aunt settled quietly down for an hour of ease before bedtime and she wondered if she might be permitted to go back to her room, Martin was at her side, her warm cloak over one arm.

'Come and see Bessie's calves now,' he said, so firmly that she was unable to refuse.

Many a clear night they had gone out so, in all innocence, and Martin had shown her how to find the various stars Peter Acres had identified for him from a chart of the heavens. How often the expeditions had ended in helpless laughter as Cecily became dizzy from much staring into the skies and they put their arms about each other for support! But tonight they walked sedately side by side in silence. Inside the stables they passed lines of stalls whose occupants snuffled, occasionally whickered at the coming of human beings they knew until, at the building's end, they came to the stall where, amid sweet-smelling hay carefully piled, black Bessie stood in utter contentment whilst her newborn calves nuzzled her flanks. She turned large brown eyes upon them, knew them harmless and forgot them, so that despite the turmoil of her feelings, Cecily laughed.

'Well done, girl, well done,' she said softly, and Bessie blew through her nostrils breath that lingered for a moment on the night air and was gone.

Cecily stood there, her eyes on the contented mother, turning over and over in her mind the things she must remember, and even now she was more intent on avoiding hurt to her ailing father than considering Martin's feelings. She had no inkling of the depth of them; surely they might be put aside if she were determined.

When Martin turned from the stall's half-door, putting a hand on her arm, the strain in his voice told her that things were not as simple as she had hoped.

'I had no idea that your father would speak to you this afternoon.'

She kept her gaze averted. 'What did he tell you?'

'He said you were surprised – shocked. He suggested I spoke to you myself, but I do not know what to say. I – I am sorry you are upset.' He was holding himself in check, forcing calmness into his voice.

Earnestly she clasped her hands together. 'I – do not – I cannot feel towards you as a wife should feel for her husband. I love you, Martin, I always have, but not in that way. Surely you do not desire a wife who can give you nothing more than obedience?'

240

Slowly, deliberately, he hung his lantern on a nail in the wall, then turned back, covered her hands with his, looking down at them so that she saw only the top of his fair, curly head.

'I love you with all my heart, Cecily. Please become my wife. I will be good to you, you know that. You will never regret it. Please.' It was the stilted speech of a man unversed in the arts of love; every word was truth, but in her mind it stood alongside the flowery, smooth-honed compliments his brother had paid her, and went for nothing.

She made no attempt to loosen herself from his grip. Only, standing so, her face pale and drawn in the dim light, she repeated, 'You must marry someone who can give you her whole heart, not someone who thinks of you as a brother.'

Still he pleaded. 'But it is you, and only you, I want. It is the suddenness of it, and I blame myself for that. Let me love you, Cecily.'

Gently, insistently he drew her towards him. She did not resist as he raised her face to his and kissed her; merely she turned her head to one side so that his kiss fell on her cheek instead of on her lips as he had intended.

'Martin, no!'

'Let me give you this, at least. I had it made for you.' From his pouch he drew something small, cloth-wrapped. Overcome by curiosity she took it, unfolded the material and found, shining steadily up at her in the dim light, a ring of thick gold, twisted and plaited in workmanship of great skill and exquisite beauty.

'Put it on.' But although she drew a quick breath at sight of it, she shook her head, desperately searching for an excuse. 'I doubt it will fit.'

'But it will, it will,' said Martin in triumph. 'I asked Aunt Bennitt and she said her rings fitted you, so I measured one, and here you are!'

He sounded so pleased with his forethought, but anger prickled sharply through Cecily, anger that she had been blind to what must have been apparent to so many other people.

'Am I the only one in the family not to be aware of your intention?' she cried childishly, pushing the ring back into his reluctant hands. 'Don't tell me you forgot to consult my sisters!'

The next moment scalding tears spilled over and trickled down her cheeks and she hid her face in her hands. She barely felt Martin's arm come about her shoulder, nor realized, until she was sitting there, that he had guided her to a pile of straw and knelt before her, one hand upon her knee.

'Cecily, listen to me; please listen to me, little one.' His voice was gentle, loving, and it was the term of endearment he had so often used in the past when comforting her in the small misfortunes of childhood that gave her strength to pull herself together and face him.

Martin looked at the tear-wet face and trembling mouth before him and smiled, a little grimly. 'Would marriage with me be so bad?' He almost added, 'It is your father's wish and he has so little time left,' but that secret was not his to share, and such pressure would have been unfair. He was himself trapped as firmly as Cecily. 'At least give me permission to hope, to ask again when you have had more time to become accustomed to the idea.'

His continued kindness and consideration were Cecily's undoing. To allow him to go on hoping would be cruelty unrefined. By the dim light of the lantern she looked smaller and more childlike than Martin had seen her for many a long year, yet when she spoke her voice, gentle yet determined, was that of the woman she had so rapidly been forced to become.

'There can be no hope, Martin, no hope at all.'

He peered down at her, narrowing eyes so like her own, and what he saw in her face made him ask sternly, 'Why not, Cecily?'

She had faced her father and lied when he asked her if she loved anyone else, and it had run so counter to her whole way of life that she marvelled at herself and was bitterly ashamed, so that when something in Martin's voice reminded her so much of her father, she gave way before him, laid bare the dream that had kept her in thrall and faithfully silent for two long years.

'Why not?' he repeated relentlessly.

With fumbling fingers she reached into the purse that hung from her waist, took from it a ring that she held out on the palm of one trembling hand. It was much less ornate than the one Martin had offered, smaller, thinner, and he recognized it immediately. 'Margery Moore gave it back to me last night,' said a laughing voice from the none-too-distant past. Between his teeth Martin ground out, 'Wat!' Wat, who had not been home often enough or long enough to become a brother, as he himself was.

Cecily nodded. 'He gave it me the last time he was home.' Her voice was scarcely above a whisper. 'After this present voyage – he is going to ask Father for my hand, and I have promised to marry him. I am sorry, Martin.'

Sorry? Sorry that she and Wat between them had made a fool of him? How he did not shout aloud in his pain he never knew. Through his head ran the tales, bawdy, lewd, with which his twin had tormented him the last time he was at home. Wat had other fish in the frying, then and now, and the last words he had said took on a new meaning, when at the time they had seemed only so kind as to be totally out of character. 'Good luck with your wooing, young Martin. Cecily is a good girl.'

He was aware of the ring he himself had offered pressing uncomfortably into one clenched fist and sought for her sake to collect himself, stalling for time, wrapping the object he had offered in love most carefully in its soft covering before he put it away.

'Martin, I swore not to tell, I swore on a crucifix Wat had. And now I have broken my word, but I could not let you go on hoping. Please – please, you will not tell Father?'

No, he would not tell her father because he would not for the world have laid another burden upon him in the last weeks of his life. Nor would he tell Cecily that if she waited until she were white-haired and bent, Wat would never come to claim her, fortune or no fortune. He had command of himself now, and turned to face her again, and silently he made a promise. If it meant he had to meet him and kill him, so be it: Wat should never cause Cecily one single day's unhappiness. It was a vow foreign to his nature, which was kind and gentle, but at that moment he undoubtedly meant it, and marvelled at the steadiness with which he said, 'No need to speak to your father yet. He gave us fourteen days, did he not?'

Cecily heaved a great, shuddering sigh, put out a hand to touch his arm in a gesture of gratitude in place of words she could not find, so that he wondered if she built her hopes on Wat miraculously appearing in the short time they had left, but although he did not draw away from her, he spoke in a voice that was impersonal and cold.

'Come back to the house before you catch a chill from the night air.'

The next day, before ever Cecily, red-eyed and heavy-headed, was astir, Martin had left the house, determined to be somewhere – anywhere – where he need not see her, even inadvertently, until he had worked himself into such a state of tiredness that the anger within him should fade and give him respite and he might think more calmly of the best course of action to take for all their sakes. He cursed himself for the fool he saw himself to be. Whilst he had stood aside, waiting for the girl he loved to turn to him of her own will, his unscrupulous brother had extracted from her – when she had been little more than a child – a promise he knew she would regard as binding but that he had no intention of honouring. No wonder he had laughed as he rode away!

Hour after hour, on an autumn day that was as grey as his feelings, Martin worked, laying and splicing the ragged hedge that separated the long meadow where their most valuable sheep grazed from the stubble of the corn land cultivated by the villagers for their own use. Hard though his hands were they became blistered by axe and billhook, and thorns tore his flesh as he chopped halfway through the sturdiest boughs and bent them sideways, meshing them in

244

with others, that come spring the hedge should grow thick, neat, impenetrable.

At last, whenever his strong arms needed a rest, he pulled dead wood and unwanted branches, all the tangle that had lain about the ditch, well away from the hedge, piled them up, packed tufts of hay in the gaps and struck sparks from his tinder box until a fire was lit. Then, leaning on the long, three-pronged fork he had taken along for the raking, he stood with his eyes on flames that reached upwards like tongues, licking and curling about the dry wood. His ears were filled with the snapping and crackling of their attack, but he saw and heard none of it, his mind was so absorbed by the thought of fourteen days during which he had either to bring Cecily to agree to be his bride or persuade her father to allow them longer time – impossible tasks both! – that not until the heat threatened to scorch him did he step backwards.

His first reaction, throughout a night as sleepless as Cecily's, had been to gather up his belongings and ride for Barndale. The further away he was from Cecily, the easier he would find it to forget her. At the moment he felt so sore at heart that he did not think he would ever recover. Nevertheless, his practical nature told him that as time went by he would doubtless find some other woman to marry and be faithful to, just as long as she was not small and brown-skinned and her eyes did not dance as Cecily's did. But thought of his uncle pulled him up. He could not leave; at least in the foreseeable future. Edward Woodfall would not live much beyond winter's end if what the physician said were truth, and looking at his increasingly drawn face, Martin had no doubt that it was. He, Martin, was needed here. It was the least he could do to repay the love and kindness he had received since babyhood. Whatever it cost him in the way of personal hurt he must remain at Abbey House and work by his uncle's side until the end.

So through the long, dark hours Martin Woodfall argued with himself, until finally he won his battle. Whilst he remained near her he would do all he could to treat Cecily as kindly as might be, and because he loved her he would make it as easy as possible for her to be in the same house as he. He faced an uphill struggle, but he was determined to do his best.

His uncle's voice made him start, and he realized that whilst he stood there the fire had consumed the wood and, apart from the glowing embers that lay beneath fluttering paper-thin white ash, had burned itself out.

'You've done a good job, my boy!' The voice was almost as hearty and strong as it always had been and Martin, turning, smiled at the man who stood behind him, resting between his crutches, looking much as he remembered him all his life. Yet beneath summer's brown his face was grey and his hands gripped his supports until the knuckles showed yellow-white. He was in pain and suffering more than anyone should be asked to suffer. But the subject was forbidden, and Martin answered casually enough.

'And not before time, sir! I should have got round to it earlier. I stayed too long at Barndale this year. All the same, I think it will take.'

'So it should,' his uncle agreed. 'Old Billy taught you well! Kill those embers whilst I find somewhere dry to sit.'

Martin wiped his sweaty, smut-covered face on his shirt sleeve and a few minutes later took a seat beside his uncle on a hollow log in the lee of the mended hedge.

Sidelong Edward Woodfall watched the young man who was as dear to him as any son. Much less like his mother to look at than was Walter, and certainly more solemn, there was something about him that brought Lewis back to his brother's remembrance so strongly that often he talked to him as if they were of an age. And now he was determined to give the boy a rest from the high drama of yesterday.

'You left so early this morning that you missed the excitement. Thomas sent a groom over with the news. A messenger arrived from London last evening, from the Queen herself. In two days' time or thereabouts she will be visiting Highwoods.'

'Queen Elizabeth? Coming here? Surely not!'

'I promise you that she is. Your Aunt Bennitt almost fainted at the very thought.'

He waited for the news to sink in and saw to his delight not awe at the prospect, but a reflection of the unholy glee that had come to him on first hearing; almost he hugged himself.

'The Queen? I'd not be living there for a king's ransom! Imagine Aunt Eleanor! Such cleaning and polishing, such cooking and preparation as you never did see – and she will supervise all and chivvy and bully to her heart's content. Only two days' notice, you say?'

'And Her Gracious Majesty will not be at all impressed – having seen it all so many times and on a far, far grander scale!'

The two men laughed together. The years had done nothing to make either of them any fonder of Eleanor. There was a short, appreciative silence before Martin asked, 'Why should the Queen come here, do you think? So small a place, and . . .'

'Ah,' Edward sounded smugly content in his own perspicacity, 'there was a time long ago – although it hasn't happened lately to my knowledge – when your Uncle Thomas would question anyone he thought might have seen Her Majesty, and then pretend that it was only idle curiosity. It seems to me that somehow and somewhere their paths must have crossed – in his London days, no doubt. Before Eleanor took him under control! We shall doubtless find out. One thing is certain, dear Eleanor knew nothing of it, or she would have used it constantly to impress Tom's importance upon us. I'd like to hear him try to explain it to her now!'

'It's late in the year for a progress,' observed Martin. 'The household will hardly be pleased to sleep in tents in this weather, and it's certain they won't all fit into Highwoods. Are we to be honoured also?' The way he looked at his fence seemed to suggest that he was considering making it even stronger at the very thought.

'Apparently not,' said his uncle thankfully. 'An informal visit, friend to friend, the messenger said, for all he's to stay to make sure that everything will be to his mistress's liking. Accommodation needed for no more than fifteen people, and most of them men-at-arms who will be content with outhouses!'

Martin grinned again. 'She's heard of the money Aunt Eleanor has piled up over the years and wants to borrow for her ships and soldiers.' The honour to Sir Thomas and his lady would come highly priced if that were so. Her Majesty's memory when it came to repaying her own loans was notoriously poor, just as Lady Woodfall's parsimony was a local byword.

'Poor old Thomas!' said his brother unsympathetically. 'And poor us if we don't watch out. Bennitt has offered as many of her stores as Eleanor may need – she could do little else – and you may be sure that the offer will not be refused. In return we join the guests when Her Majesty dines, so the womenfolk will have little time to look to our comfort. At least they will be pleased to have fine London folk to stare at for once. It will be the talk of the year, whatever brings it about.'

Martin's face clouded; he frowned at a small pile of twigs he was pushing together with one foot.

'Sir . . .' His tone was hesitant. 'Sir, I would not like to think . . . That is to say . . .'

'You would not like to think,' supplied his uncle calmly, 'that because of her behaviour yesterday I shall lock Cecily in her room on a diet of bread and water and forbid her the feast!'

Martin flushed. 'Something of that sort,' he agreed. 'She is unhappy enough at having defied you, without that.'

His uncle reached out, patted his arm. 'And what of you? If it were me she had treated so, I should want to do far more than lock her in her room, I think!'

Martin rose abruptly to his feet, and paced swiftly to and fro as if unable any longer to keep still. 'I would not have her hurt for the world.'

Edward frowned up at his nephew's set face and, sorry as he was for him, the irritability that had come with illness and increasing pain took hold.

'You've left things a little late for such high-flown sentiments, young Martin! What have you been at all these years? The two of you have been together constantly, yet you appear to have made no more headway than . . .'

'I wanted her to come to me of her own free will, sir. The fact that I've misjudged and left it too late doesn't make it any easier to bear, I assure you!'

'If I'd known what a ham-fisted job you were making of it, I'd have taken it in hand long before this. That damned brother of yours would have known what to do, take my word for it. He would have had the girl wedded and bedded long since!'

To Martin's infinite credit he kept his temper, remembered the warning Aunt Agnes had given him when he returned from Barndale at the summer's end: 'Don't upset him, and if he says things you would never have expected to hear from him, remember that it's his illness talking. It changes mind along with body, I'm afraid.'

Martin pulled a boyishly rueful face. 'I'm not as quick as Wat, sir. Never was.'

He picked up his uncle's crutches, held out a hand to help him to rise. Edward Woodfall stood a moment, gasping, waited until the cramp in his stomach lessened enough for him to speak, then said in his old voice, 'But worth a thousand of him!' and his old grin passed fleetingly across his face. 'Today,' he observed conversationally, 'is the first day that I have been unable to walk this far without stopping at least three times.' It was to something unspoken that Martin responded bluntly, 'I shall stay here.'

He heard his uncle draw a sharp breath of relief, did not know that he was remembering his own long-ago reaction when a girl he loved had preferred somebody else, honouring Martin for being stronger than he.

'God bless you, my boy. I know that it will not be easy for you. She will marry you, never fear, and love will come after that – to my way of thinking it's there already; she just doesn't know her own mind. Perhaps after – after I am gone you will find she . . .'

And at the anguish in the older man's voice Martin stayed

the hot words that sprang to his tongue. Cecily must want him for his own sake, not turn to him in grief at the loss of her beloved father.

'Who knows?' he agreed expressionlessly, and kicked savagely at the ashes of his fire, so that the breeze caught white dust and whirled it in all directions. Fourteen days! What could he do in so short a time? Damn Wat, and damn his own stupidity!

CHAPTER III

When Robert reported to Sir Francis the following day he found him racked by stomach pains and fighting to maintain concentration on his work against the effects of the draughts his physician had given him. His instructions were vague: information received – not thought reliable – however, no chances to be taken – Cooper would understand. Irritably he added that Her Majesty was in most capricious mood.

It was Robert's opinion, which grew steadily stronger from the time the small retinue set out, that daylight had brought Majesty second thoughts. Could she have seen a way to accomplish it without loss of face, she would have called off what she must all along have known was a dangerous enterprise. With any other than Walsingham she might have done so; most of those about her took her mistakes upon themselves from time to time, if only to make life easier for all concerned, nor would she ever have felt conscious of any element of triumph in their attitude. With Sir Francis she found this impossible; he too would dissemble his true feelings, but behind the sunken eyes so discreetly lowered would have lived relief that she had backed down and she was not prepared to give him so much satisfaction. So, thought Robert, she continued on her way much like some child, knowing she was wrong but stubbornly refusing to apologize.

The feeling of the whole band was ill-tempered. Sir Thomas Heneage, called upon to act as Vice-Chamberlain in

Sir Christopher Hatton's continued absence, rode hunched into his cloak like some irritable bird, whilst Lady Cobham and Lady Patchett were not pleased at being required to undertake such a journey when the autumn weather might at any moment turn to chill in earnest. They had confidently expected to remain at Whitehall until after the Accession celebrations and proceed to Greenwich for Christmastide. The curiosity that burned within each was all that made the outing bearable. They understood – the truth not being available to them – that Her Majesty went to Sir Thomas at his invitation. The visit was sudden; if he were some new favourite they would not be sorry to get a good look at him.

Far less well attended than on many a day's hunting, Her Majesty set forth. Some distance behind her rode Andrew Stratton, chosen because he hailed from Sussex, and a somewhat effete young man Stratton could not recall having seen about the court before.

Robert Cooper had presented himself before Jerome in guise of Sir Edward Linton. False hair that might slip was of little use when it must remain in place for days; there was no time to grow a more luxuriant beard. Eccentricity he had aimed for and eccentricity he had achieved. The dark hair that was usually so neatly brushed straight back from his high forehead now clustered over it in tight curls and his trim beard – by whatever means Jerome could not imagine – had been parted in the centre so that it stuck out in two points, one either side his chin, and from the end of each depended a jewel that bore great resemblance to a lady's earring. His clothes were garish even by court standards. His shoulders stooped and he appeared nowhere near as tall as he in fact was – an effect achieved by bending his knees slightly as he walked. His remarkable eyes were little to be noticed since he was obviously short-sighted and screwed them up when focusing on things he would see. Jerome professed himself pleased; the Queen was not! Having, however, committed herself to a bodyguard of Walsingham's choosing she uncharacteristically accepted the so-called Sir Edward without comment. Robert doubted whether the Queen would recall his mother after so many years, but he could afford to take no chances; therefore not even for a moment did he drop his charade.

What time he could afford – or would allow himself to spend – considering the family disclosed to him by Jerome had passed none too pleasantly. Before he was brought to Trinity Street at five years old he recalled nothing, no matter how hard he tried, and doubtless that was to the good. Every scrap of concentration, all his attention, had been demanded by his present masters. There had been no time to lament whatever went before, good or bad; it had faded and disappeared altogether.

Having nothing to remember, he went to Highwoods expecting nothing. There was within him no well of sentimentality that might spring up when he saw the man he had now been told was his father, and no anger either. It was in the nature of man to take his pleasures where they were to be found, and his mother, that sister Jerome recalled so vividly over many years, could have been no innocent seduced by a man chance-met. He brought to mind Jerome's denunciation when his mind was astray in illness. 'Whore! Did not James warn you?' he had asked, and the words were too vehement to be forgotten. Since his mother had not returned to her home after his own birth, it could not have been that little escapade for which she had been brought to book; she had obviously been a young lady of few, if any, morals before that.

Regarding Jerome Robert refused to speculate, preferring, needing, to take him as he had found him over years of living in the same house. That he was embittered by the way his sister had turned out after a devout Roman Catholic upbringing might well have been sufficient to set him running, and somewhere along the way he had come within Cecil's persuasive ambience, had accepted service that once and for all disbarred him from home and family. Yet still he apparently had feelings of guilt, so that he had been pleased to make his sister's bastard flog him as a way of seeking personal relief. Rosamund Emory, her son decided, had much for which to answer;

let her sleep in the vault at Highwoods undisturbed by his thoughts.

After a night passed at Layton House, the royal party would arrive at Highwoods around noon. The day was dry and pleasant; not sunny, yet still not grey, and from beneath down-drawn eyebrows and the over-large feather that curled about his flat velvet hat, Robert took stock once again of his fellow and wondered if it came to a fight, as Walsingham was certain it would not, how much assistance he could expect from Stratton. A pleasant face, atop a gangling body; fair hair, blue eyes and hope. That must, Robert decided, have been what had brought him, a younger son, to become one among many dancing attendance upon his queen in hopes of receiving preferment. What Walsingham's files had not disclosed was that it was love of a lady, and she well above him in station, that kept Stratton lounging among the pack of hangers-on who frequented the ante-chambers of royalty, when he would much rather have had an outdoor life in Sussex.

Capricious, Walsingham had said of their mistress, and she was seemingly intent on proving him correct, for no sooner was she informed that they were now within sight of the boundaries of Sir Thomas's estates than she sent her ladies and escort on ahead, to announce that she and her squires would arrive in due course, when she had seen more of the countryside. She was not, after all, in any hurry to encounter her friend who must have ridden out to meet her.

Setting spur to flank, she turned her horse into a rutted track that was little wider than a footpath. Hoofprints, the marks of wheelrims on either side its grassy centre, showed it to be well used, but Andrew, following close behind their mistress with Robert, met his look of enquiry and shook his head. They would, he whispered, have to retrace their steps before long; beyond the village the track petered out at the riverbank. He was not going to be the one who pointed this out to Her Majesty whilst she was in her present mood.

Smartly, knee to knee, they followed the Queen who, once into the lane away from her attendants, slowed her pace.

Robert would have wagered that again she was wishing that she had not acted on impulse.

To their left a high, tangled hedge, beginning to brighten with berries and decorated with seed heads on trailing tendrils, hid meadowland that could only be glimpsed through occasional gaps in browning foliage. To the right a bank, high and weed-entangled, with a wide, deep ditch hacked out of its top, contained the sheep that grazed in numbers on pasture that despite the time of year still showed thick and green.

They saw no-one; doubtless every soul not kept to his or her work was waiting by the gateway to Highwoods to cheer Her Majesty past. All the same, Robert urged his horse nearer the Queen's, disregarding the frown Andrew gave him, which was intended to show that he knew his place, and so should Linton. If wanted, he would be called forward.

When trouble did come, it was without warning. One moment Her Majesty was half-turning in her saddle to observe to the young men behind her that Sir Thomas's land appeared to be in good heart, the next her horse, startled by a small animal that shot through a gap in the hedge beneath its hooves, had half-reared and, shying away from the cause of its fear, deposited his rider firmly on her back against the steep bank and made off along the lane.

Andrew Stratton had always prided himself on his agility, but before he was halfway out of his saddle the companion he had privately dismissed as useless was on his feet by the Queen's side, his long, surprisingly plain dagger unsheathed in his hand, and looking as if he knew how to use it. Her Majesty, no less startled than the horse which, having unseated her, went only some dozen yards along the lane before returning to stand head down, as if ashamed of its behaviour, had recovered her breath, was sitting at the foot of the bank, brown velvet hat rakishly over one eye, her mouth already open to emit her precise, very unladylike opinion of the whole incident when a girl's voice called, 'Floss, come back here at once!' and through the same hole in the hedge wriggled

Cecily Woodfall, pushing before her a small, cloth-covered wicker basket.

She came to her knees, obviously having heard the commotion in the lane, knelt at gaze for an instant, taking no notice of the men, seeing only a lady so inelegantly sprawled before her, with no idea of who she might be, worried only that she might be hurt, appalled that it was her fault. Still on her knees she looked the Queen in the eyes, gasped, 'Are you hurt, madam? Oh, please say you are not! My father will be so angry. He warned me about Floss and I took no notice.'

The flow of unwomanly language died on the Queen's lips at the novelty of being addressed as an equal by a young girl, albeit with the deference due an elder, and seeing Andrew start forward, mouth already open, to correct her, she said sharply, 'Stand aside, gentlemen, and be silent!'

Robert's dagger was back in its sheath; he had relaxed enough to turn in search of the cause of the disaster. A thin, half-grown runt of a sheepdog, feeling the urge of her blood, was streaking across the meadow behind him, intent on rounding up as many sheep as she could manage before someone put a stop to her game, whilst Andrew, red-faced with embarrassment and the anger he felt towards a friend of his childhood who had so thoughtlessly ruined his slim chance of making a triumphal return to his family home, stood motionless, as ordered, clenching and unclenching his fists.

On her feet now, Cecily bobbed a curtsey to a lady of high degree. 'May I help you up, madam. If you have got your breath back, that is.'

Elizabeth's mouth twitched in amusement as she moved from side to side, cautiously at first, testing her limbs. 'No damage,' she said decisively, 'at least, nothing but . . .' She scratched savagely at her ungloved left hand, leaving red marks along it, and Cecily looked more closely at the spot where Floss's victim had landed. Browning though the plants were, fresh summer greenness gone, they were still vicious in their effect.

'Nettles! Oh, please, let me help you to move. No, no, do

not put your hand down again! If you move here to your left the ground is clean and dry, and I will see what I can do.'

It pleased Majesty to slide sideways in somewhat ungainly fashion as she was bidden; once there to sit and wait for the next order this concerned girl should give. Cecily ran a few yards along the lane, pulled strongly at large, coarse-veined leaves, gathering them into a bunch, and returned.

'Aunt Agnes says it is fortunate that nettles always grow alongside the best remedy for their bite,' she confided. 'Dock leaves! If you will allow me to rub your hand . . .' Although she did not know it, she was talking after the way she had so often heard her aunt use, soothing, bringing back a shocked person kindly, slowly to her senses, and what she said did not matter; it was (as she understood it) essential to continue talking. Therefore, without thinking, she asked, 'Am I correct in calling you madam, or is it my lady?'

'Madam will do, child!' The royal face was quivering with laughter that went unregarded by the girl before her. Never since dear Kat Ashley had anyone spoken to her so.

Cecily took the Queen's hand and touched it gently where the small white bumps that so irritated stood proud of the tight skin, an action that, combined with her words, so shocked Andrew that he broke his mistress's prohibition, began to speak. This time it was Cecily, busily squeezing the juice of dock leaves on to her sovereign's hand, who silenced him.

'You'd be a lot more useful, Andrew, if you looked to your lady's horse instead of standing there like some stranded fish. Run your hands over that near foreleg, he's standing as if he's twisted it.'

Concentrating on her task, firmly massaging green juice from the broken leaves into the hand she held, Cecily was unaware of the delighted look Majesty directed at Andrew Stratton's discomfiture. Standing unregarded, holding Andrew's horse now as well as his own, Robert reflected that it was as well that the Queen chose to be entertained. Many a maid in her service had bruises inflicted by the same royal hand to show for far less offence. And Andrew, sulkily obeying Cecily's behest, had turned his back on

257

the scene altogether; the young madam would receive her comeuppance soon enough!

Cecily took a freshly laundered handkerchief from her purse, folded and bound it about the hand she held. With a breath of relief, she said, 'If you hold that in place for a while with your thumb, the stinging will be gone.'

She sat back on her heels, for the first time taking stock of the lady who until now had only been someone in need of help, recognizing in her one who was undoubtedly come with the Queen into this quiet corner of Sussex.

'Well, child?' The Queen's voice was interested. 'What now?'

Cecily flushed, said ingenuously, 'That is the most beautiful riding habit I have ever seen. What a good job the ground is dry and marks will not show. You have come with the Queen, have you not? You must have or Andrew would not be with you. You will forgive me, please, and – and not tell Her Majesty what I have done?'

Trembling, she waited. 'The Queen will do nothing to harm you,' said the Tudor voice that could be so sharp. 'All the same, I advise you to keep your dog under control. The next damage he does may not be so easily repaired. And you yourself, do you often scuttle through hedge bottoms like some little brown mouse?'

'No, madam. I was taking a short cut. I am very late because tonight we are bidden to Uncle Thomas's to dine with Her Majesty and I must help my mother and young sisters to dress. But Mistress Catchpole who lives at the forge must have her meat pie if the sky should fall.'

The Queen reached out her unwrapped hand to Robert who, bowing over it, helped her to her feet.

'Uncle Thomas? Then you are a Woodfall?'

'Sir Thomas's brother Edward's second-born daughter, madam. My name is Cecily.'

'And you know young Stratton here, that is obvious!'

Cecily grinned at the young man who was leading forward his mistress's horse. 'Since childhood, ma'am. His brother, Geoffrey, is married to my sister, Mary.'

258

Her eyes still twinkling, Elizabeth allowed herself to be assisted to the saddle.

'If she is like you, child, he has a good bargain! Now, if I retrace my way I should come to the road to Highwoods, I think?'

She had found her loophole; no need, after all, to acknowledge that her impulsive ride had led her nowhere. Andrew, still smarting under indignities heaped upon him by young Cecily, thought maliciously of the moment when the girl must discover the mistake she had made, but Robert, as he rode after the Queen he was here to guard, turned his head and stared at Cecily Woodfall as she gathered up her basket and ran into the field to capture her dog. His gaze was very intent.

To give Andrew Stratton his due, long before the day was out his irritation towards Cecily had given way to worry about her reaction once she discovered to whom she had spoken so easily and, even more, what might befall her had the Queen's mood towards her changed. He would not, after all, like to see a friend of his childhood made the butt of Her Majesty's often savage humour, little though there was he could do to prevent it if she so chose.

That evening, as he followed the Queen into the great hall at Highwoods along with the rest of her retinue and Sir Thomas, who gallantly escorted her to her seat, he had a full view of Cecily's face as for the first time, to her knowledge, she saw the Queen of England. Even at a distance he could see the girl's stricken expression, the way her head turned from side to side as if wondering whether to run and where to. No-one else, so far as he knew, noticed her trouble; all were too absorbed in gazing at the guest of honour, whose severe riding habit had been changed for a robe of silver tissue, closely embroidered with sworls of black beads. Behind an impossibly red wig her silver-beaded lace collar stood high and rope after rope of lustrous pearls hung from neck to waist. The hand she rested upon Sir Thomas's sleeve was no longer green-stained, nor were there blemishes to mar it; the dock leaves had done their work. From every knuckle diamonds gleamed.

It was unfortunate that Lady Woodfall had chosen to wear one of her more elaborate gowns, red brocade, gold-thread sewn. Beside the Queen and ladies who had long before learned to complement their mistress's clothes rather than vie with them, it looked hard and tasteless and made her thin, pale face washed out and old. She had had the sense to dress Rose in virginal white, pink-trimmed, but the visit had not gone well for Lady Woodfall since its beginning, and her daughter's looks were for once small consolation.

From the moment that Elizabeth, with her two attendants, dismounted before the door of Highwoods and held out her hand to Sir Thomas, who knelt to kiss it, Eleanor knew that for the time being she herself was of no account at all in her own house, unless it were to provide whatever Her Majesty might choose to call for. She had made her curtsey, which was coldly acknowledged, whilst the Queen's eyes raked her from head to toe and evidently disliked what they saw. Eleanor would have given much to learn the trick of thus conveying thoughts without once uttering an impolite word.

'You will excuse us, Lady Woodfall, will you not? We shall have time to talk later, you and I. Now, Thomas, what have you been doing all these years? For a moment there I doubted whether you'd make it back to your feet, man! You've put on weight since those days by the river!'

Elizabeth's voice was pitched deliberately so that Eleanor could not help but hear, and stupid Thomas went away with his sovereign on his arm, laughing like some besotted schoolboy. Another one who should receive his comeuppance at a later time!

Seated between Rose Woodfall on the one side and Edith Stone on the other, Andrew Stratton yet found his mind turning to Linton. The man puzzled him, his absence this evening even more so. From time to time the servant whose honour it was to serve the Queen appeared through a nearby door; her food came not from the ornate dishes from which other guests ate but was, as usual, specially prepared by her own cook. Andrew talked politely to the ladies and wondered where Linton hailed from. If he was under orders, as seemed likely, whose, and why? The feast was over before he noticed the stooping, over-dressed figure slip into the hall to take a seat at one end of the high table, where he had the main guests always in view.

A toast to Her Majesty having been drunk, the company sat back to listen to her response. The Queen's retinue, Sir Thomas, his wife and their daughter, together with Rose's betrothed in all his spottiness, graced the top table, whilst at the two set at right angles to it were neighbours, Strattons, Ashbys, the Mayor of Downfelton, fellow magistrates of Sir Thomas's, the headmaster of the grammar school and their ladies and, very humbly, Master Watson, still priest of the village at Sir Thomas's gates. In the years since Her Majesty's accession he too had acquired a wife, as he was legally entitled to do, but Mistress Watson, in deference to the Queen's well-known and outspoken views on married clergy, was not in the company. Edward Woodfall, his wife and family were seated well towards the end of one table. It was what they had expected and truth to tell, Edward thought, as he sat there braced by an extra-large draught of Agnes's painkilling cordial, he would give hearty thanks that night that his Bennitt, in her dress of deep gold brocade, did not look such a fool as did Eleanor! Complacently he looked along the line of his daughters, interspersed with the local youths Eleanor had thought appropriate to their station. They were playing their part in a way that made him proud. Even six-year-old Philippa – and it was well beyond her bedtime – sat without yawning and whispered to the young boy beside her. Whatever they were discussing might well lead to mischief on the morrow, but at least now it was quiet! Martin, his hair neatly trimmed by Agnes and wearing an outfit of dark blue, black-slashed, would have made anyone proud. Only Cecily sat mumchance, her face whey-coloured above the neat ruff about her throat, and fidgeted with her dress. As if, thought her father angrily, she could not leave her own problem at home for one night as he had! What else had the chit to worry her?

Eleanor Woodfall silently ground her teeth, hearing in every word the Queen spoke measured rejection of the feast she had had prepared, the elaborate preparations that had – considering the short notice allowed – made this evening as perfect as might be. What was the guest of honour saying? A visit between friends was always a pleasant thing, and this one was long overdue. Elizabeth, smiling sweetly at Thomas, whose florid face flushed even redder than was its wont, dropped acid slowly, with great accuracy and pleasure upon his wife's lacerated pride. She had not intended so much ceremony to be raised on her account, as she had told her good Sir Thomas, so staunch a friend when she had needed one. In those days he had refused her invitation to court, having chosen rather to return to the simple country life and marry the lady to whom he had long been betrothed.

Eleanor felt, rather than heard, the ripple of suppressed pleasure that echoed round the room at her discomfiture. So many of her neighbours had been condescended to over the years, few of them had no axe to grind, including her own sister, Edith.

The Queen had no difficulty in making her voice heard from end to end of the hall, and suddenly Eleanor held her breath.

'It is my hope, Sir Thomas, that twenty years will not elapse before next we meet. It would please me greatly to give you some gift by which to remember me, yet the one which comes most readily to mind is entirely selfish on my part. When I leave tomorrow it is my wish that your daughter, Rose, shall accompany me to serve as maid-of-honour about my person.'

Sir Thomas was honoured, deeply honoured, his wife was triumphant and Rose's eyes gleamed. The Queen's thin hand was held aloft in a flash of diamonds: the murmur of voices died instantly away.

'Come forward, Cecily Woodfall!'

All eyes turned to Edward Woodfall's amazed family, who knew nothing of the day's earlier events, and to the girl who took a deep breath, rose from her seat and with her chin high walked firmly towards the high table. Through her mind chased thoughts of what she might say when her sins were brought home; the punishment must fall upon her, not upon her family, anything but that.

She sank low before the Queen in a billowing of green brocade, bent her head as if retribution might fall upon her there and then, only to hear a voice say, 'Stand up, child. I have something for you.' The morning's mood held; Majesty chose still to be amused. Across the littered table between them she held out Cecily's handkerchief, laundered, folded, cleansed of stains.

Cecily ventured a quick upward glance as she took it, opened her mouth to utter the apologies that filled her, and was forestalled.

'Do not apologize, Cecily Woodfall! Mistress Rose here will find that the court can be a lonely place to come to unknown and unknowing. I propose, therefore, that she shall have a companion; a small brown mouse.'

'Majesty!' Cecily could scarcely get out the word, but already the Queen's gaze had passed beyond her, to where the girl's family sat as if turned to stone.

'Master Edward Woodfall, you have a kind and dutiful daughter who rendered me service this morning, not knowing who I was. You will permit me to take her from you for a while?'

With his hands pressing hard on the table before him, Edward made a supreme effort, hauled himself upright and bowed low towards the shimmering figure at the far end of the hall who had, by so careless a gesture, rendered his carefully laid plans for his family's future impossible of fulfilment, at least in his lifetime. He spoke no word, nor did the Queen expect any.

'We leave tomorrow afternoon,' she said, 'and sleep at Layton House. What you do not have time to get ready here will be provided for you in London.'

Dismissed by a wave of the hand, Cecily curtseyed, turned and almost ran back to her seat, oblivious of her father's drained face, or the anxious way her mother, Aunt Agnes and Martin were staring at him. Drumming through her head to the exclusion of all else was the thought that now the fourteen days she had been allowed did not matter, did not matter at all!

Her Majesty was pleased to call upon the boys from Downfelton Grammar School, whose hastily assembled pageant she declared to be greatly to her liking before, through lines of bowing, curtseying guests, she was escorted to her chamber. Once free of her stiff, uncomfortable gown, warmly wrapped in a soft robe, Elizabeth summoned Sir Edward Linton. Her ladies, at a sign, retired to the far end of the room, out of earshot.

'Sir Edward, you will inform Sir Francis that I hold two hostages against their fathers' good behaviour.' She gave a sharp crack of laughter. 'We must keep his mind easy on this matter!'

For a moment, although it was undoubtedly a trick of the firelight, she thought that eyes she had never before seen properly opened wide and transfixed her with a cold stare, and most certainly the voice that replied 'Majesty' was deeper than Sir Edward's customary effete, lisping tones. With a wave of her hand she dismissed him and found her amusement gone also. The figure bowing himself out of the room was as he had been throughout the journey. He had been quick to her protection that morning, now she remembered it, very quick indeed, but that was only as it should be. She shivered and shouted for candles, more candles!

In the open doorway to his room, Matthew Stone's mother held his elbow in vice-like grip.

'Pull yourself together!' she hissed at the miserable youth, and her voice was even sourer than her sister's. 'Bear in mind that whatever the girl does matters nothing to you now!'

With the words she turned, to collide with the stooping form of Sir Edward, who appeared covered in confusion, peered closely at her, most abjectly begged her pardon and tripped on his way still muttering at his own clumsiness.

CHAPTER IV

Young Philippa was sound asleep long before the Abbey House party reached home in the dense darkness of a night that was beginning to promise rain, and Cecily, who had cradled her all the way, relinquished the plump, childish body to her nursemaid without causing so much as a sigh. She guided Katharine, half-asleep in spite of her determination to stay awake as long as her elders, to the room the two youngest children shared, had unlaced the gown of which the child was so proud before the nurse was free to put her second charge into bed.

For a moment Cecily stood beside them, thinking numbly that this time tomorrow she would be far away from this house where she had spent all her life and wondering, despite her recent longing to escape, how long it must be before she would see it again. Slowly, feeling as if her legs would not obey her behest, she went back downstairs, why she could not have said except that she had been aware, even as she took the children upstairs, that somewhere behind her – and she unable to turn to look for fear of dropping her sister – her mother and Aunt Agnes were whispering urgently together. That what they said concerned her father she had no doubt; no sound of his voice came to her, which was strange, since her mother was always near to him, always deferred to his wishes.

In Aunt Agnes's comfortably padded wagon, old-fashioned and very shabby now, but still used when a

265

family party went out, the two women had sat one on either side of him, so close that in the dim light cast by the two lanterns that were for the driver's benefit they had seemed almost to be holding him upright. Certainly he had sat with closed eyes and had uttered not one word the whole time.

Cecily's immediate response to the Queen's announcement was, she knew, totally selfish. It presented the way of escape she had so desperately sought from her immediate problem, and as departing friends congratulated her, joked that they would expect her to remember them kindly when she was a great lady, the euphoria had held. Then, as swiftly as hanging smoke before a sudden puff of wind, it was gone, and sight of her father's face took its place. She had not understood quite how set he was on her marriage to Martin.

She took comfort from the idea that she would only be away until the Queen's sudden whim had outworn itself. She was level-headed enough to know that girls such as she, and even the self-regarding Rose, were not the stuff maids-of-honour were made from. A few weeks at most and doubtless, whatever Rose thought, they would find themselves back at home with stories of high life to retail, but very little else to show for the experience. And by then Wat must have returned to claim her.

No doubt the maids of Highwoods, already worked off their feet preparing for the Queen's visit, were even now packing the gowns, the linen, the shoes and cloaks Rose would need in London. Her Majesty's careless offer of 'things to be provided' applied to the less well-equipped Cecily rather than to her cousin, whose many outfits were, as she never tired of pointing out, of the latest fashion and richest material. But the trouble in Cecily's mind overrode even the quantity of work entailed in assembling her own few goods and packing them into the boxes that would carry them for her.

At the foot of the staircase she met Aunt Agnes who, in reply to her anxious, 'Father – what of Father?' cut her short.

'Too much wine on top of my cordial,' she said briskly.

'Martin carried him off to bed and your mother has gone to make certain that he is all right. A fine head he will have in the morning, and I shall be to blame!'

She took her niece by the shoulders, turned her firmly about and gave her a push towards the staircase. The sooner she was stripped of the gown she was wearing the better, she said, for that must be packed and, no! she needed no help. What were maids for if not for such things? Cecily's place was in bed, to rest if not to sleep, since the Queen was hardly likely to want her looking as tired as she did now! What was that? How many times must she repeat it in order to be believed? There was nothing amiss with Edward Woodfall that a few weeks' patient rest would not put right. As for herself, she would fall exhausted and sleep when all the excitement was over!

But her niece, reluctant to obey and turning backwards at almost every dragging step, saw an underlying grimness in her aunt's expression that made her want to cry out that she would not go. She would tell her about Wat and ask her help, as she should have done before. And Aunt Agnes had perhaps not entirely lost her gift of second sight, for she followed Cecily into her room, and once she was in bed, looked down at her and said, 'You will go to London as directed by your monarch, Cecily; you will make us all proud of you – no fear about that – and beforehand you will say nothing that may trouble your father. I will take your promise. Come!'

Promise given was promise accepted where those Agnes trusted was concerned, and at noonday, when Andrew Stratton, with a servant to lead a packhorse, rode up to escort Cecily and her belongings to Highwoods to join the main party, Agnes said nothing that was not brisk and matter-of-fact.

'You have three good gowns, child, and here is money to provide whatever else you need.' She lowered her voice. 'Look in the bottom of your boxes when you arrive.' A stately, serene smile bade her niece farewell.

Her eyes brimming with tears, Cecily turned to embrace her mother, was hugged wordlessly and passed on to her father, who stood as white-faced as his sister had predicted, found her tongue speechless and waited silently before him.

However he managed it he did not know, but somehow he conjured up the grin that all their lives had meant love and companionship between them. 'That I should beget a jewel for the Queen of England to covet! God bless you, my girl. This is for you,' and into her hand he placed the long pearl drop, set in silver, that was all he had to show for the short-lived seafaring days that had crippled him.

'To remember me by, my love,' he whispered and Cecily, hearing her mother choke back a sob, held out her arms and all three embraced until Martin's voice, grave and kind, said, 'Time to go, cousin,' and he stood by to mount her on the pony that had come to her following Anne's marriage.

Quietly he, who had spoken so few words to her since the evening in the stables, looked up at her and smiled a smile so like his old self that she blinked away her tears, leaned forward, would have taken his hand, but that suddenly he stepped close, bowed his head against her knee and stayed so for a moment before, as if fearing for his self-control should he speak, he wrenched himself away and strode off into the stable yard.

'No looking back! Chin up and ride out smiling,' said Aunt Agnes authoritatively as she took charge of the situation, and Cecily obeyed, albeit the smile wavered at the mouth corners. She fell in beside Andrew and rode off down the narrow road that led between parkland trees, over the River Pen and out through the gates of Abbey House.

Andrew, glad himself to be returning to London but sympathetic to the tightly held lips and tear-filled eyes of a girl he had known and liked since childhood, said, 'Cheer up! You'll be back again soon enough and he won't run away!'

'He?' she questioned unthinkingly.

'Martin, of course. From all Wat said last time he was home I expected you two to be married before now, I must say! Come, we cannot keep Her Majesty waiting any longer.' He spurred forward and there was nothing for Cecily to do but follow him.

*

The Palace of Whitehall, it had been observed, was more remarkable for its situation than for nobility of structure. Its assortment of buildings, of different times and in different styles, was so vast, with its hotchpotch of galleries, living quarters, presence chambers, chapels and all the work rooms and stores needed to support the army of people who lived there, that it seemed to Cecily that she had ridden into another world, one that revolved around one woman. Its sole purpose in being was to shelter and entertain her, to provide for her and those who served her, from the highest to the lowest.

Decorously the cousins had ridden side by side for two and a half days' journey, as Lady Cobham bade them, with Pullen, Rose's maid, amidst the baggage somewhere to the rear. They effaced themselves and must stay effaced until summoned, which would apparently not be until London was reached. It was at journey's end, as the cavalcade rode through the crowds who never failed to welcome the Queen they counted most particularly their own, and in at the ornate Italianate King Street Gate to the Palace, that the complacent smile Rose had worn slipped for the first time.

Sir Edward Linton it was who dismounted, waited for the servants to pass and barred the gateway to Pullen. Any assistance her two young mistresses needed would be provided, he informed her, and his voice was nowhere as soft as she remembered it at Highwoods, where along with other servants she had peeped often at these distinguished visitors. She should wait until she found someone reliable riding in the direction of Sussex and accompany them. He tossed a coin in her direction, made a careless gesture of his hand and the pikes of the guards on duty crossed before the woman's offended, terrified eyes, crossed and stayed unmoving until she turned away, troubled – to give her her due – as much for the sake of the spoiled girl who had been her charge through childhood as for herself, and became lost in the crowds.

A flicker of disquiet passed through Cecily at thought of

the woman, one who had never treated her kindly, thus turned adrift in the streets of a city of which she had no knowledge. It would have been so easy for someone to point out before the journey began that she would not be needed. Yet the expression that contorted Rose's face, that closed her thin lips upon a hastily stifled protest as Sir Edward wheeled suddenly towards her, showed less concern for her maid than for the fact that lack of her might be an inconvenience. From then dated Cecily's determination not to allow herself to be over-awed by this cousin who had managed to intimate over and over that *she* was the one the Queen had honoured; Cecily's status was, as always, far lower and entirely due to her uncle's high standing.

In Rose's pale face the Woodfall eyes somehow managed to appear slightly vacant, like a cow, as Martin had pointed out one day when she and Cecily had come to odds. Carelessly comforting, his arm had dropped about Cecily's shoulders and he had invited her to wager on the looks of any offspring produced by Rose and Matthew Stone, the only colour in whose puffy face came from the pustules that erupted, crusted, scabbed there in regular succession. There was no doubt, they had decided between them, that each child was in danger of resembling nothing so much as the pink-white worms to be found under stones at the riverside. Apprehensive about the future as she was, Cecily saw Martin's freckled face before her and suppressed the first giggle she had felt like uttering for three whole days.

The servant, Taylor, in favour of whom Sir Edward had turned off Pullen did what she must for the newcomers, but her disdain was evident and it was with something approaching pleasure that she showed them into a chamber at some distance from the coffer chamber shared by the other maids and saw both shiver with cold. There was a bed, large enough for two, a small table, a stool and a carved chest for each girl's wearing apparel. There she left them and Rose having sunk down on the bed on the verge of tears at such treatment, it was Cecily, with no intention of being more uncomfortable than needs be, who unpacked their boxes of belongings. Ignoring her cousin's tearfully

270

petulant orders to 'Be careful with *that*, do!' briskly she arranged all and to her infinite joy found, at the bottom of one of her own boxes, a note in Aunt Agnes's bold, round hand. 'You may have need of clothes like these, and no doubt of the herbs. Find the still rooms and remember what I have taught you.'

Beneath her hands lay a polished box which held pot after pot of salve, stoppered, sealed and labelled, each in its own compartment, and bags of dried herbs such as Cecily had often used at home. The whole had been wrapped in her old, brown woollen dress and cloak and at the very bottom lay the heavy shoes in which she had gone about at home on all except high days and the Sabbath. What use they might be to her here she could not imagine. They served only to feed her homesickness and she tried to cheer herself up by imagining the sensation she might cause if she dressed so when .called to the Queen's presence.

To everyone in residence, male and female, of high degree or low, the newcomers were a joke, to be stared at in high disdain, in pity, or with cruel laughter. Never before had Her Majesty chosen girls other than from high-born families to enter her personal service. So amusing, so obviously a quirk of middle age, and the laughter was directed also against the Queen, taking petty revenge for wrongs real or imagined. To Cecily's relief, dress was not a problem. Measuring both with a practised eye, Mistress Hyde, Mother of the Maids, produced dresses in green similar to those of the other six young ladies with whom they would share whatever duties the Queen found for them.

Accustomed to being employed the day long, or free to go her own way, Cecily found the routine she was expected to follow boring in the extreme. Day after day in over-hot rooms, she watched the brilliantly dressed men and women who thronged about the Queen, wondered who they were, and wished with all her heart that she could let her family know how much she missed them. She passed time composing a letter in her mind, a letter she could never send since she had no idea at all of how to get it to them. There was humour, to one brought up in so free an environment, in noting the jealously observed pecking order that flourished in the first household in the land. Servants of all sorts, grooms, ushers, maids, chamberers, as well as those of higher degree, each in turn gave orders to those below him, who passed them on yet again to others. Someone here, thought Cecily, and heard her father and Martin laugh and her mother give vent to exclamations at the waste of it all, someone must do the work, but it is difficult to discover who. Everyone is so *important* and busy making sure he or she is noticed. And would you believe that a public footpath runs right through the Palace grounds? Perhaps someone should tell Uncle Thomas next time he is severe on a poor soul caught taking a short cut through his park!

The ladies-in-waiting are very grand, ladies in their own right, and we maids must pay almost as much mind to them as to the Queen herself. They are what you would call her companions. She talks to them a great deal, they pay her many compliments and accompany her even into her private rooms, which we maids do not. On formal occasions we stand unmoving for hours, ready at the Queen's side in case she requires anything. At other times we must embroider or make music or sing for her. Rose comes into her own then, for Aunt Eleanor had her taught to play the lute and her voice is very sweet, which mine is not. I stand as far in the background as I can and hope the Queen will not notice me! One girl, who sang particularly well one day, was given a pair of embroidered slippers by the Queen. I think Rose hopes something of the sort will happen to her, although she would not have been pleased, later, to hear the girl say that they were only cast-offs and that she had better in her own wardrobe!

Expecting nothing, Cecily made her niche as Rose, expecting everything, did not, and – music apart – she was in far better case than Rose, since she had studied. Now it was needed she was amazed to find how much of Master Acres's teaching she remembered. Called unexpectedly by the Queen to advance and translate a Latin tag scribbled in the margin of a book, she acquitted herself most creditably, was commended, and earned Rose's sulks in consequence.

Rose's upbringing had ensured that she knew nothing of such things. The Queen's harsh, 'God's teeth, girl, you are barely literate!' earned the sniggers of all who heard it and deflated poor Rose's ego for ever in that company. It was Cecily's involuntary look of sympathy for her hapless cousin that brought the first tentative outreachings of friendship from a girl she had occasionally noticed watching her as they went about their duties together.

'The only thing to do,' said a sweet, high voice in Cecily's ear, 'is to make yourself as small as possible and pray she doesn't throw anything!'

The smile that accompanied the advice was mischievous. 'My name is Lettice Pemberton. I've been wanting to talk to you for days. You must be finding it very strange here.'

Cecily acknowledged the truth of the last observation with a rueful grimace. Lord Pemberton's daughter was at home in these surroundings as she herself could never hope to be, and from then on Cecily had someone to talk to. It did not occur to her that she had gradually become accepted by others, that it was Rose who was cold-shouldered.

'Not a very nice person, your cousin,' pronounced Lettice severely, and would not consider Cecily's excuse that they were both of them still homesick beyond belief.

'She could be here a hundred years and she would still understand nothing,' she said, then, suddenly, 'You know Andrew, don't you? Andrew Stratton.'

Cecily grinned. 'We're related by marriage. I've seen him looking at you as if – well, as if he could eat you!'

Lettice blushed hotly to the roots of her soft, dark brown hair. 'He only stays here because of me. What can come of it, I don't know.'

'You like him?' Cecily's question was whispered; the Queen was standing near enough to take swift action if she overheard chattering and chose to be displeased.

'I love him,' said Lettice simply, 'but my father will never allow me to marry him.' At which point their conversation was interrupted.

'Cecily Woodfall!' The Queen's voice was sharp. 'You will stay behind when the others retire this evening.'

273

*

Quite how Rose would manage to unlace her dress without assistance if Taylor were not awaiting her, Cecily did not know. The other girls, giggling and whispering together, were unlikely to offer the assistance of their servants, even if Rose could humiliate herself sufficiently to ask. They made their curtseys and left, but Cecily did not move as the Queen sent her ladies ahead of her into her bedchamber, stalked over to her writing table and pulled paper towards her. One and all went gladly, thankful for the end of a day when their mistress's mood had been brittle and unpleasant. Lettice passed her friend with a glance of compassion, a slight touch of arm against arm; then Cecily was alone with the Queen.

Quill was poised over inkpot like some dagger about to stab downwards when Her Majesty said, 'Don't stand, child. Sit by the fire until I have done.'

Cecily obeyed, but remained on the edge of the seat and bolt upright, ready to move at a word. And it seemed strange, in a room silent save for the scratching of pen upon paper and the occasional rustle of falling ash among the logs in the hearth, that she should suddenly feel cold when all day she had been drowsy from the oppressive, airless atmosphere.

The Queen laid down her quill, read through what she had written, tilted it slightly in the candlelight to make sure the ink was dry, then folded the note and sealed it, firmly and deliberately pressing into wax the impress of a ring she drew from one bony finger.

'Take this to Sir Francis Walsingham,' she said, 'Wait for a reply and return with it.'

Cecily curtseyed, was taking the letter held out to her when, 'Stay!' and she froze where she was. One thin hand reached out, took her by the chin and held her unmoving whilst the hazel-grey eyes that could be so hard and cold, or burn hot with temper, regarded her closely as if they sought the answer to some riddle. Then as abruptly she was released and the Queen asked, 'You know where Sir Francis is to be found?'

'I will enquire, Majesty.'

The bedizened face inclined slowly, almost approvingly. 'One way, to be sure. But I will save you such trouble.'

She ignored the bell standing to her hand and raised her voice in a shout that must have been audible three rooms away. And so promptly that Cecily knew he had been awaiting the summons, a page threw open the door, bowed low.

'You will take Mistress Woodfall to Sir Francis, John,' and Her Majesty turned back to her writing table; her head was bent over paper before the door closed behind them. Had they had cause unexpectedly to return, they would have seen her hands, rigid and trembling, come up to cover her mask-like face. But no-one came; her ladies did not interrupt her. No-one wished or dared to until called, and Elizabeth Tudor remained, shoulders bent, elbows on table, for a long time.

John's attitude to Cecily held none of the respect he had shown on the night he summoned Sir Francis to the Queen. She had almost to run to keep pace with him through galleries and corridors, turning left and right in a twisted maze she could not hope to remember. At last they came to a door giving into a large room containing rows of tables, deserted now; there he waited only long enough to point a finger towards another further door, saying blithely, 'In there!' and was gone before Cecily could thank him or ask if he would wait to escort her back.

A faint line of light showed beneath the panels, and guided by it she crossed the room in which the boy had left her, knocked, entered as bidden and waited until the man she had often seen in Her Majesty's presence chamber or hurrying from one place to another on business, looked up.

The only light in the room came from one candle on Sir Francis's desk; the pool of gold it cast was small and somehow as secretive as the man himself. Beyond its range the shadows gathered, made no impression upon the impenetrable darkness in the corners of the room. No fire fought the chill. The window was small, a mere patch of lighter darkness in the whole. The place was smaller than she had expected, far more spartan than others of nowhere near Sir Francis's standing considered their due.

Curtseying, she presented the letter. No need to say whence it came, only, 'I am to await your reply, sir, if you please,' in a voice that showed none of the awe she felt.

Sir Francis broke the seal, slowly smoothed out the paper - two sheets – one of which he laid aside, read and re-read the other. Its matter, although short, was obviously weighty, for he pulled the candlestick towards him and read yet a third time before he said, kindly enough, 'I shall keep you only a short time, Mistress Woodfall,' and sat back to ponder, finger to lip.

She was still in the grip of surprise that he should know her name when he startled her further by staring into the deep darkness beyond the edge of the candlelight.

'Cooper!' he said, and the tall figure of a man detached itself from shadows where he had stood unobserved. A long, thin hand reached into the pool of light, taking the note Sir Francis held out. No more of him was visible, strain her eyes as Cecily might.

'You for the present, I think,' Sir Francis was very matter-of-fact. 'Straightforward, would you say?'

The young man, unlike his master, read through the Queen's message but once, and that rapidly, said nothing but turned the paper over and wrote on its reverse side. His hands were disembodied in the ring of light and Cecily watched them, fascinated. It was much like watching the Queen write; both attacked the paper, quickly covered it with tall, spiky characters that from a distance were impossible to read at all. Finished, he slewed the paper round for Sir Francis to read, received a nod of the head and a brief, 'I see no reason why not. I will arrange it.

'You will present my most humble duty to Her Majesty and say that I will attend to the matter at once,' he continued. 'No need for me to put it on paper.' He was already bending his head back to his work when a thought seemed to occur to him.

'A moment, child! Do you know your way back to Her Majesty's apartments? Who brought you?'

'A page, sir, and I think he may not have waited. I shall find my way by myself.'

He tut-tutted in some irritation. 'No need for that. Allow me to present Master Robert Cooper. Cooper, Mistress Woodfall is newly come to join the Queen's maids and finds the Palace strange.'

The figure beside the desk bowed. 'To escort you will be an honour, mistress.' His voice was crisp and pleasant, so that Cecily involuntarily smiled her friendly smile into the gloom.

They had reached the door, he was holding it open for her to precede him when the thin, precise voice behind him said, 'I require the information we were discussing by nine o'clock tomorrow at the latest.'

'Yes, sir.' No more, and nothing in Master Cooper's voice to remark, yet Cecily felt him draw slightly away from her, as if suddenly he had been reminded of something unpleasant, but when she ventured to glance up at him, he was intent upon drawing a long dark cloak about himself and his face was still not visible.

'It would have been quicker to go across the courtyards,' he observed, 'but you are not dressed for the night air. We will stay indoors.'

Easily he accommodated his long strides to those of his much smaller companion. 'You are beginning to enjoy your new life, mistress?' He sounded interested, friendly, but Cecily was wary.

'Thank you, sir, yes.' She had no idea who this Master Cooper might be, but he appeared at home in the Secretary of State's office and must be of more importance, therefore, than Andrew Stratton or young sprigs like him who had little function other than to lounge about, to play and dance and generally endeavour to bring themselves to the Queen's notice. She was using what Martin teasingly called her 'visitors' manners'. Strange how often since she left Abbey House that Martin, his sayings and doings, recurred in her thoughts.

With Master Cooper talking easily, politely of the various places through which they passed the way back seemed to

Cecily to be shorter than it had with John trying to run her off her feet. He took her through the Great Hall and Watching Chamber that were the beginning of the Queen's apartments. The crowd that thronged it during the daytime was gone since the cause of their being there had retired, and servants were busily clearing away the rubbish so carelessly deposited on the floor. At the doors to the Privy Chamber, where stood Yeoman Guards, Robert Cooper halted and bowed, half-smiling, saying, without uttering a word aloud, that this was where she must be. Here in stronger light Cecily saw him properly for the first time and liked what she saw. He had given no sign of being irritated at being commanded to squire a young girl from one end to the other of the rabbit warren that was Whitehall Palace, although she knew from what she had overheard that he had work still to do elsewhere.

'I thank you, sir.' Cecily dropped him a low, respectful curtsey and hurried away.

One thing that had not yet ceased to surprise her was that never once had the formidable-looking guards ever denied her admittance; that they should remember who was allowed within the Privy Chamber and who was not amazed her. At first she had been inclined to smile at them in gratitude until Rose, who passed through with her nose in the air, well knowing that here were two more beings whose reason for living was to serve her and others like her, had pointed out to her cousin how stupid she was, and ordered her to stop making fools of them both. It was still all Cecily could do to keep her face solemn as she passed them, however, and she was so concentrating on the decorum required of her that she paid no further attention to Robert Cooper, who stood unmoving until the door closed behind her, before he drew a hood far over head and face, pulled his cloak tightly about him and set off resolutely to the work that awaited him.

CHAPTER V

The Queen would not leave her Privy Chamber for some time, but the throng that crowded the Great Hall and Watching Chamber had already begun to assemble; some with business for Her Majesty's attention and appointments that would carry them past less-favoured mortals and the guards at the doors, some who came in hope of gaining an audience on some matter important at least to them, those who had no greater call on Majesty's time than that she might take one of her erratic fancies and call a man forward because she liked the way he smiled or admired his height and breadth of shoulder. Very garishly dressed, some of these last, each and every one in the best he could afford for a day that might mean the beginning of his fortune.

Robert Cooper, standing in a window embrasure of an outer gallery, had a clear view of all who came that way, watched them with half an eye, envying none. He waited for one person, and he saw her long before she was anywhere near him. Little Cecily Woodfall, due to attend Her Majesty and behind time again! Wondering, from the look of her, which was the lesser of two evils. Run and she would arrive breathless and dishevelled; walk, and although presentably neat, she would be late. The one would bring the royal wrath upon her head as certainly as the other.

The girl had smiled at him when he led her through a labyrinth of corridors and left her safely at her destination. Wary she had been, sensibly so with a stranger in a strange place. She had never to her knowledge seen him before, would have been astounded to discover that he was the stooping effete Sir Edward Linton who had accompanied the Queen to Highwoods. Even young Stratton, with whom he had ridden shoulder to shoulder for two days there and two back had not recognized him when they later came face to face.

The visit to Sussex had been his because he fitted into the Queen's close entourage. Sir Francis had not even required a report on his return, being relieved that all had gone without mishap. The Queen's securing of hostages, as she termed it, was her petty revenge for what she considered to be over-zealous behaviour of a minister whose work she respected but whom she could not like. The two girls would remain at court until the day when it suited royal humour maliciously to ask Sir Francis if he was certain all danger was over; then they would be sent home.

Robert had been securely back in the routine of his everyday work for two weeks and more when he was summoned to Sir Francis's home to face a man trembling with more than the weakness of continuing illness. There was, after all, it seemed, treachery deep and dangerous at Highwoods. Action was being taken and Cooper must renew his acquaintance with Mistress Cecily to find out what, if anything, she knew. Thus he had been present to escort her when the Queen, by prior arrangement, sent her to Sir Francis.

From the moment she crawled through the hedge after that ridiculous dog brought down the Queen's horse, Cecily Woodfall had been often in Robert's mind. Physical reflexes had obeyed their training, had taken him instantly to stand by the Queen's fallen body, ready to give his life in her defence, but in the same instant the feeling had swept through him that the thick curtain that obscured his early life had been ruthlessly dragged aside. Part of his mind had seen again the plump, brown-skinned lady, dreams of whom had brought some comfort to a boyhood devoid of affection. Here she was, twenty years on, still as young, still concerned for others. The curtain had stayed open for a split second only, but it had been long enough. The girl on hands and knees must be some relation to the woman he remembered, daughter no doubt, and mirror image. Satisfied that she was no danger to his mistress he had stood aside, unable to look away, whilst unselfconsciously and with all the kindness in the world she rendered help to one she saw only as a lady in need.

He had watched too, later that same day, when becomingly gowned and in company with the rest of her family, including the mother his wandering mind recalled, the little brown girl had discovered exactly whom she had spoken to as an equal and in so maternal a fashion. Back with his court friends, Andrew Stratton had related the episode as a great joke, although he had omitted to mention that Cecily had ordered him to look to a horse's legs rather as if he had been some groom, and that he had obeyed. There had been laughter and general agreement that it was fortunate that Her Majesty had been in one of her better moods, but it was not unkind laughter; if anything it had raised Cecily's stock among the young men. Robert's own impression had been that the Queen, so surrounded as a general rule by flattery and sycophancy, had been touched by a young girl's simple kindness.

He had looked his father straight in his fleshy, ageing face and felt nothing, no pang, no desire to know him better. The sight of Sir Thomas and his lady wife preening themselves in the glory of a royal visit was not an attractive one. Robert had found the other branch of the Woodfall family far more interesting.

If he were any judge, all was not well in that little party. Flanked by wife and sister, who kept their attention almost solely upon him, Edward Woodfall had sat silent throughout the meal. The cousin, Martin, had done his duty when it came to entertaining his neighbours but at any lull in conversation always his gaze had sought Cecily and held, stern and unyielding, whilst she had most certainly avoided looking his way at all. Only the young children looked unreservedly happy.

His own job would have been easier if she were not so

kind. He remembered again the nearest thing to amazement he had ever seen on Sir Francis's face when, delivering information it had taken him all night to obtain, he was handed a pot of salve left 'for Master Cooper's hands, if you please, sir,' the morning after he had acted as her guide. That she had noticed – and it could only have been when he was writing at Sir Francis's desk – that the knuckles of his right hand were swollen and red, and had cared enough to try to do something about what she must suppose to be chilblains, had twitched the curtain of the past aside once more, adding to his distaste for this morning's task. How fortunate for Sir Francis that he was so parsimonious in his use of candles that his face had remained in shadow, thought Robert, grimly amused. Otherwise the girl would doubtless have been plying the Secretary of State with some remedy or other guaranteed to ease the pain of the stone that had kept him fast in bed for days.

Robert burned the paper Sir Francis had passed to him; he knew its contents by heart: 'The girl Rose is a fool,' it said succinctly in the Queen's emphatic script, 'Mistress Cecily, who carries this note, will bear further questioning. She is a pleasant child.'

In other words, Robert thought cynically, the kind approach until she betrayed herself and her family. 'You for the present, I think,' Sir Francis had said, but both had understood the unspoken, more honest, 'Better you than Jenkins.' Half an hour in the hands of one of his ruffians and the child would swear black into white to save what remained of her skin.

She was upon him now. Having reached a compromise between running and walking, and with her head bent as she smoothed her billowing skirts, she did not see him as quite deliberately he stepped in front of her. She came up against a man's hard body, caught a whiff of freshly washed flesh and found herself gripped firmly about her upper arms until she regained balance and composure both. That she recognized him instantly did nothing to lessen the tone of abject apology in which she spoke.

'Master Cooper! I am so sorry, but I am very late.'

No thought came to him of using the smile that turned Martha limp between his hands. Here was a child and as such instinctively he treated her. The half-smile that lifted the corners of his mouth was very like the one Jerome knew, companionable and real.

'A happy accident, mistress. It gives me an opportunity to thank you for sending me the salve.'

He had released her now, put one hand to his chest. 'Although if you go about always at such a rate many of us may well have to ask you for a cure for bruises!'

Patting her hair now, flustered at her lateness as she was, Cecily yet responded to the friendliness in his voice; so Martin might have spoken, and as to him she replied.

'I trust you may survive, sir, although I am truly sorry for my clumsiness.' Then, as he showed no sign of moving, 'Please let me pass. I am on duty this very minute and Her Majesty does not like to be kept waiting.'

'So I am told.' Still he did not move. 'You have nothing to fear, however. We are under orders from Her Majesty, you and I. She does not expect you to arrive with her other maids.'

He took her gently by one arm and propelled her to the side of the gallery, out of the way of the hurrying crowd, and they stood in the window alcove overlooking the gardens as if they were alone in the world.

Cecily stared up at him suspiciously, her blue eyes wide, so that he continued, with a mocking note in his voice, 'The Queen, ever solicitous for the well-being of those about her, has noticed that you are looking pale. It seems she puts this down to your sudden transition from country to town life. Sir Francis has charged me with an errand for Her Majesty that will take no more than an hour to despatch and she felt that you might benefit from accompanying me. We can then spend the rest of the day in whatever way you choose.'

She felt her face burn red and her eyes wavered and fell before his. Robert drew a deep breath and strove to maintain lightness of tone. 'Either we must tell Her Majesty that you refuse to obey her command, since I am obviously untrustworthy as a companion, or we will ask Mistress Rose . . .'

He stopped as Cecily's confusion vanished and her infectious laugh rang out. 'You would not ask Rose to come with us? On her day of rest? Oh, how she would hate that! And I should never hear the end of it.'

She curtseyed low, mocking in her turn. 'I obey Her Majesty's kind command. If you will be pleased to wait until I have changed my gown for something more suitable . . .' The friendly smile lit her face, made her blue eyes dance, and she was gone back the way she had so recently come. It did not occur to her, who was naturally kind, to doubt that the Queen had noticed her homesickness.

As she vanished, so did the lightness in Robert's manner. His mouth resumed its thin, tight line and as he waited he drummed his fingers impatiently against one leg. When she returned, more speedily than he had expected, she was carrying a thick cloak and wearing a plain moss-green riding habit that amazingly, it seemed to Robert's critical gaze, did nothing to detract from the startling blue of her eyes. Whoever had chosen the colour had known what she was about; it made the girl's skin glow. The little brown mother no doubt. She came back to him happily, trustingly. Still he stood where she had left him, stiff and straight. It crossed her mind that had he been Martin he would have been leaning against the wall; she doubted if Master Cooper ever relaxed to the extent of leaning against anything.

Her own pony, which she had not seen since the day she arrived in London, was saddled and awaiting her in the courtyard, next to a tall, bay mare that made her mount look, Cecily thought, almost like a toy. Side by side they threaded their way through the streets that led to the Strand and there Cecily waited, her horse's head held by a groom, whilst Robert disappeared inside a large, newly built house. They set off again in silence, she content to follow where she was led, knowing nothing of the ways through which she was taken. From time to time she glanced at her companion; he rode as she had seen him stand, straight-backed and graceful, a frown drawing his straight black brows together.

He was engrossed in the outcome of whatever business he had been about, she supposed, and did not interrupt him.

Soon true, unspoiled countryside claimed them and Cecily, feeling her heart lift, realized how much she had missed it. She was looking round so happily that when Robert spoke she was startled.

'I am at your command, Mistress Woodfall. What is your wish?'

Not even his seriousness could destroy her mood and she replied without thought, 'A stream to sit by and a field to run in . . .' Her voice died away as she heard her own words. This comparative stranger had been ordered to act as her escort and she was sure, without looking at him again, that it was the last way of spending his time that he would have chosen. The kind of carefree day she had so often enjoyed with Martin and her sisters had nothing to do with him.

Raising her chin, she said, more stiffly than she intended, for she did not wish him to think her ungrateful, 'I have enjoyed our ride, Master Cooper, and am ready to return now. Doubtless you have much work to do.'

But you are my work for today, mistress, you and your family, thought Robert grimly, wondering how long it must be before someone told her what had happened. That job at least would not be his! He reached for and found some degree of lightness; after all, he had learned over the years to act in whatever way most quickly attained the ends he sought, and he had never found it overly difficult before. He urged his horse to a faster pace.

'A stream and a field you shall have. This may be the last day this year when the sun has even a vestige of warmth in it. We must not waste it. Come!' and he led the way unhesitatingly along deserted tracks between hedges already bare of foliage, save for the occasional evergreen, past holly bushes decorated with their bunches of bright berries, through grass pressed into deep ruts by the passing of cartwheels after autumn rain, until at length before a gateway in a high, untrained, bramble-thick hedge, he drew rein and said over his shoulder, 'This field leads down to a ford. We can rest there in comfort.'

Tears were pricking Cecily's eyes and she blinked desperately to stop them spilling over on to her cheeks. Loudly she sniffed, in a manner Cousin Rose would certainly have deplored as unladylike, and drew a gloved hand across her face, but her efforts were in vain. 'It reminds me of home,' she whispered helplessly and looked down at two teardrops that had plopped into her lap. A large white linen square was pushed into her hands.

'Wipe your eyes.' Robert's voice was gentle. 'When we have eaten perhaps you will tell me about this home that is worth crying for.'

They were in a large meadow now, crossed by a rough track, deep-rutted and much used. The grass on either side was cropped short and browning, and as they rode over a tree-crowned ridge the land sloped steeply away before them to a ford across a shallow stream, where the water ran clear and sparkling over round, smooth stones.

Cecily's momentary sadness was gone; without waiting for help she dismounted and pulled the saddle from her pony, as she would have done had she been at home.

'Along there, I think,' said Robert, pointing to a large, half-ruined barn before he too turned his horse loose, throwing both saddles under a nearby tree.

All thoughts of propriety forgotten, Cecily removed her hat, gathered up her skirts and ran down to the water's edge. Closing her eyes, she listened to the sound of the water rippling over stones until it seemed to her that at any moment she might hear her sisters' laughter as they played beneath the trees and Martin's shrill whistle as he fished some deep pool. Then Robert Cooper broke her dream by bidding her come and eat. He had spread out his short, black cloak on the ground in one corner of the barn, sheltered from any wind, yet roofed over only by the pale blue, cloud-dotted sky. Resting on rough linen napkins were bread and lumps of crumbly cheese, two rather wizened apples and a flagon and two pewter tankards.

'A feast,' said Cecily contentedly, and sank down amid her spreading skirts. For a time they ate in silence until, his first hunger satisfied, Robert leaned back on his elbows. From the look on his companion's face he could tell that she was once more about to suggest returning to the Palace; he had much to find out and assess before that. Therefore, looking at nothing in particular, he began the task that had brought him there that day, so offhandedly that it seemed almost as if he were not interested in a reply.

'Cecily Woodfall! A month ago no-one at court had heard of your family, let alone you and your cousin, yet here you both are, as close to the Queen's Majesty as it is possible to be. How much of what they say about you is true, I wonder?'

Cecily blushed. 'What – what do people say, sir?'

'Let me see.' Robert raised one hand, fingers spread, and turned them down as he enumerated: 'One: that it is strange for the Queen to choose as maids girls of so staunchly Roman Catholic a leaning. Two: that long ago she was in love with Sir Thomas. Three: and this you must not repeat, that Rose is their child! Four: . . .'

He got no further, for Cecily was holding her sides, helpless with laughter. 'Rose? *Rose!*' she squeaked. 'She is the image of Lady Woodfall – no doubt about *her* parentage, you may be sure! *Rose!*'

For a moment he did not disturb her, then, 'But something of all this must be true! You are a Roman Catholic family?'

She had not even considered it seriously enough to reply, but now, as she sobered, she said, 'Of course not! We attend the village church, but Father says he'd as lief stay at home. Parson Watson's sermons are very long, and very, very boring. And we have no-one to interrupt him as the Queen does when she is tired!' Her eyes twinkled at him, wholly innocent, 'And you must promise not to repeat *that* to anyone.'

Robert looked puzzled. 'Then where did the tale spring from?'

For a moment Cecily considered. 'Oh, I dare say because Martin's mother was Catholic. But she's been dead since he was a baby. He goes to church with us. I doubt if he gives the matter a thought.'

Robert shrugged. 'So much for rumour! Your family means a great deal to you, does it not?'

Picking the last crumbs of bread and cheese from her skirt, Cecily had become entirely solemn. 'I did not realize quite how much until I had to leave them.'

The man beside her remained silent, waiting, and narrowing her eyes as she looked down at her interlaced fingers, Cecily went on in a small voice, 'Only the day before Her Majesty ordered me to court I was thinking that I would do anything to get away, anything at all.'

Her voice faltered, and there was silence again until Robert prompted her. 'Something had happened to make you unhappy?'

For a moment she hesitated, but his voice was sympathetic and it was so long since she had been able to talk to anyone. Not even Lettice knew about Wat.

'My father told me I must marry – marry Martin.' Even remembrance of the horror she had felt brought her up short, so that Robert said, 'Martin?' as if he had never seen the young man in question in his life.

'My cousin. I told you, he lives with us because his parents died. He has been like a brother to me. I – I never, never thought . . .' Her voice trailed away.

'Perhaps you care for someone else. What about the young man your cousin boasts of?'

'Matthew? Oh no, he and Rose have been promised since they were babes. She could have anyone she wanted you know, she is so rich, and all Uncle Thomas's estate will be hers one day.'

Even to Robert's ear, practised in detecting what was implied beneath what was actually said, there was no hint of jealousy in her voice. It was a fact of life that men preferred Rose, if only because she was an heiress, and Cecily saw no reason to grudge her her swains. She sighed suddenly.

'Everything is a question of land. I have no brothers of my own and Father thinks that if I marry Martin the estate will stay safely in the family after he dies and that I will bear Martin sons so that the line will go on unbroken. Matthew Stone's family has coveted our land for as long

288

as I can remember. Even if he gets Uncle Thomas's land by marrying Rose, Father doesn't intend him to get Abbey House as well.' Dreamily she added, 'There is – there is Wat, of course. He's Martin's twin, but Father doesn't like him. He's away at sea. It seems that everyone at court knows my Uncle Thomas.'

'Her Majesty's friend from long ago!' Robert's tone was dry.

Cecily giggled. 'Aunt Eleanor thinks they're very grand. But even she had no idea that he had ever met the Queen. Imagine keeping a secret like that!'

Idly Robert laughed. 'Most men would think it something to boast about, I agree. Perhaps he is better than most at keeping secrets?'

He received no answer; he doubted whether the girl beside him had even heard the question, so engrossed in her own thoughts had she become.

'And will you marry Martin – now that the shock has worn off? And, what is perhaps more to the point, does Martin want to marry you?' No need to ask the question; the boy's scowls on the night of the banquet were explained.

In a voice that showed all too clearly the innocence of her relationship with her cousin, Cecily replied, 'That is the surprising thing. It turns out to be Martin's dearest wish. Yet I had no idea of it at all.' Her mind went back to her parting from Martin the day she left home. 'Oh, yes. He does want to marry me,' she whispered, and her voice was troubled.

'It seems to me, if you do not mind my prying so, as if you care for someone else.'

Cecily felt hot colour rise in her cheeks. 'I – I . . .' she began, and stopped. She must ask Andrew Stratton exactly what Wat had said to him, something she had been putting off from day to day.

'I don't know,' she said lamely, and Robert, seeing no profit in pursuing the matter, rounded it off neatly. 'Andrew Stratton, perhaps?'

Cecily came back to life. 'He loves Lettice Pemberton. Everyone knows that. He wouldn't look at me if I were the last woman in the world.'

'Foolish Stratton!' said Robert quietly and poured more ale into Cecily's tankard. 'Your father would surely not force you to do anything against your will? You give me the impression that you love each other dearly.'

Out of the corner of his eye he saw Cecily's face light up; she drew her knees up beneath her chin and hugged them, childlike. Robert frowned at the fervour that came upon her, but he was here to make her talk and listened without interruption as proudly she told of an estate built up from nothing, of the fostering of orphaned nephews, and of the spiky relationship they enjoyed with the senior branch of the family, of how Wat had run away to sea, and Martin had justified all the faith placed in him, of sisters married, of sisters who were still children. How long she talked she did not know; once started on the subject of her father and home she could go on and on.

Her companion, propped against the stone wall, had his eyes closed. For a moment she thought he slept, but he was wide awake. What price Martin, or Wat for that matter – and from the way she smiled when she spoke his name he was the fly in the ointment! – what matter all the others, the sisters, the aunt she had mentioned in passing? The family, he thought suddenly – and was surprised by the bitterness the idea caused him – that had seen fit to disown him. He knew an overwhelming desire to hurt her for the joy remembrance of them brought to her voice, as well as for the worry he had seen in the face of her mother at the banquet, and said, 'He has done well, for a cripple!' and opened his eyes to gauge her reaction.

It was immediate and overwhelming: he had spoiled her memories, brought her back to earth. Unsteadily she said, 'He is *not* a cripple! At least I have never thought of him so, and I know Mother does not. You should see them together. When I marry I want my life to be like theirs.'

'I had no intention of hurting you; I was admiring only. What do you talk about, you and your father?'

'Almost anything.' Cecily was smiling again at her thoughts, completely unaware that she was answering what amounted to an inquisition. 'We make each other laugh a lot. He says I remind him of his brother, Lewis.'

'So you spend much time with him when you are at home?'

'Whenever I am not helping Mother or Aunt Agnes and he is free. Aunt Agnes taught me all I know about herbs.'

'So I owe my healing fingers to her!'

'Or to Mother's receipt book. I cannot quite remember which. I am glad the salve worked.'

'Thank you,' said Robert gravely and then, strangely as Cecily later thought, although at the time she was so relaxed that the oddness of the question did not strike her, 'Would you call your father an ambitious man? Or perhaps he leaves that to your Uncle Thomas?'

'If you knew our family, Master Cooper, you would never ask that. My father always says that he does not know what possessed him to run away to sea – he was born to lean on a gate and chew a straw. And Uncle Thomas cares for nothing but his hunting. "Idle to a man!" Father says our motto should be, except that he is not idle in things that concern the estate, you understand. He had a fever this past summer that will not leave him but Mother cannot get him to rest.'

'Something on his mind; something of importance perhaps?'

But he had lost Cecily's attention again; her small brown hands twisted and locked together. The fear she had mentioned to Aunt Agnes had been brought into the open by her talking.

'I came across him once when he was not expecting to see anyone and he had a hand pressed to his side as if he were in pain. He said that it was nothing but . . . Suppose he were not there when I got back? Before I left he spoke about a day when I would need someone else to look after me.'

Her voice was that of a desolate child and her face was pinched and afraid. Robert felt a pang of pity that he must drive her on to talk about what was obviously a source of unhappiness to her, but it did not show in his voice. 'Your mother would get word to you if anything were seriously amiss.'

'She loves Father so much that if – if anything happened to him I think she would die too.'

She shivered despite the comfort of their shelter, and Robert said casually, 'You can have nothing to fear. And you must find it interesting to meet as many people as you do at court. Although I imagine your family often receives visitors at – what do you call it? – Abbey House.'

Cecily shook her head, diverted for a moment. 'No, very few. I cannot remember when we last entertained a stranger. Laziness again! Uncle Thomas sees more people than we do, of course, being far more important!'

She shook her shoulders as if sloughing off a burden. 'You have let me chatter on and on. Father always says that once I begin I am like a magpie. I forget that not everyone is as interested in my family as I am.'

'I have enjoyed our talk. Which ship does your cousin Wat sail in?'

'The *Larkspur*.'

'So!' Robert sounded impressed. 'With Sir Francis Drake's fleet, and due home any day, I believe.'

Cecily's expressive face glowed. 'I *do* hope so. It is so long since I saw him.'

So it was brother Wat with whom Martin had to contend. Or would have if either of them survived this web of intrigue. Robert turned the topic, and the mocking note she had heard before returned to his voice.

'It seems to me that someone should tell Her Majesty that one day in the countryside is not sufficient. Keeping you at court is like imprisoning you!'

Unsure whether or not to take him seriously, Cecily said rather breathlessly, 'Indeed you must do nothing of the sort! Have you ever seen the Queen in a rage? She is terrifying! Besides, Cousin Rose might be sent home as well and she and Aunt Eleanor would never forgive me that.'

'You need not worry your head,' Robert assured her drily. 'I do not have the Queen's ear.'

'But you work for her.'

'As do we all,' he said smoothly. 'I go wherever I am sent, here or abroad.'

292

Cecily's interest was concentrated on him, her shyness diminished. So many questions he had asked her; surely she in her turn might show interest in his life.

'You can see little of your home. Do you live in London?'

'In Trinity Street. I was brought up by a foster father.' He hesitated, then said brusquely, 'I belong to no-one.'

'Not even to him?'

A corner of Robert's mouth twitched. 'He would not thank you for that idea, mistress. He did what he was paid to do, no more, no less.' However true the statement might once have been, it was not so now and he was ashamed of it.

But Cecily found nothing amiss. 'The wrong side of the blanket,' said her father's voice in her ear. 'No more questions, little one. Hold your tongue!' As if the words had been spoken aloud Robert looked at her, frowning, and she flushed. In the place where they sat, grass had spread over what had once been a barn floor, and close to her hand was a clump of daisies, still in this sheltered corner in flower, but dried out and crisp. To hide her confusion she reached down and picked as many as she could reach. Piling them into her lap she bent her head and set to work. Quickly and deftly making a slit in the stem of the first flower with her thumbnail, she threaded the next flower through, and so with another and another, until she had a chain long enough to make a circlet for her head. Then she fastened the ends together and crowned her hair with it. So intent did she become, and so many happy memories did it bring back of days when she had made similar garlands for the children, that she had recovered her composure until, looking up when her task was finished, she startled on her companion's face a look so bleak that she reached up a trembling hand and snatched the flowers from her head, feeling foolish in the extreme.

It was he who picked up the fragile flower chain that lay on the ground between them. 'Now it is broken. You must mend it. It is a pretty idea.' From the tone of his voice Cecily could tell that he had never come across the pastime before.

Seeing a way of apologizing for asking questions that she felt had caused pain, she said impulsively, 'Hold out your hand,' shortened the chain of flowers and fastened it about his wrist, just above the white cuff that showed beneath his doublet sleeve.

'A small payment for your kindness today, sir,' she said gently, inclining her head over his hand.

She reminded him of Sim; Sim, with whom he had been able to be completely natural because Sim could never betray or use him, and he smiled at the thought. Cecily Woodfall would certainly not be pleased if she knew that he was comparing her to a halfwit, yet what they shared, to Robert's mind, was innocence. If he were not careful he would find himself trusting this girl as he had vowed never to trust man or woman. For a moment he was so rigidly still that she thought she had angered him, then the half-smile that seemed his happiest expression came to his lips and he said, 'Thank you.'

The moment passed as quickly as it had come and he retreated once more behind the sternness habitual to him. 'Come,' he said sharply, 'it is time to go back.'

Whilst Cecily tidied up the remains of their meal, Robert fetched the grazing horses, and saddled them. When he came back she noticed, and was not surprised, that the daisy chain had gone from his wrist.

'I am glad you have enjoyed your day,' he said formally, as he assisted her into the saddle. For a moment he hesitated as if he would say more, then he jerked himself away, swung into his own saddle and urged his horse along the rising track from the ford as if some enemy pursued him. Although he waited for her in the lane and they rode back into London side by side, he never again looked at her, nor did he speak until, holding her pony's head whilst she dismounted, he bade her a courteous goodbye. His face remained impassive; if emotion had moved him in the meadow it was gone completely now.

She had almost crossed the courtyard when Andrew Stratton broke away from a group of young men returned from a day's hunting.

'Cecily!'

'Another note for Lettice?' she asked mischievously, but he frowned.

'Where have you been with . . .' He gestured towards Robert Cooper's retreating back.

Cecily looked blank. 'He has been kind to me, Andrew.'

He raised impatient eyes to heaven. 'Cec, you goose! There are some people one cannot afford to be seen with!'

Came a shout from his friends and he was gone.

Jerome, awaiting Robert's return, heard him come into the hallway and made what haste he could to the study door, catching him just as he reached the foot of the staircase.

'I need a word with you,' he said, having spent more time than he could well afford thinking of the best way to break what could only be regarded as bad news.

Robert stopped without turning; his usual courteous manner had entirely deserted him. 'Well?' he snapped, and Jerome drew back.

'We can speak in the morning,' he said.

Robert sat at the small table beneath his window and wrote a brief report on his day:

'I have spoken to Cecily Woodfall. If there is any conspiracy in her family I am convinced that she knows nothing of it. She is so open-natured, almost childlike, that I find it impossible to believe that she would have been able to dissemble had she known. There can be no danger in her remaining in attendance if it is Her Majesty's gracious wish.'

His part in the whole affair, he told himself, was over. Cecily had become his concern for this second time because the Queen wished her to be gently treated and he could be trusted to keep his hands off her, to obtain information without resorting to the methods so much enjoyed by Jenkins and his colleagues.

He took his report immediately to Sir Francis, returning by the most roundabout way he could think of, walking until he was tired enough to sleep from sheer exhaustion.

CHAPTER VI

'No!' Robert said the word harshly, for the third time, not even looking up from his food as he spoke, and Jerome felt the argument slipping away from him.

'The child will be yours. You cannot turn the girl out into the street.'

'Mine it may be, but she cannot stay. We must have a woman here whose mind is on her work, not half on some mewling infant!'

'Then you will tell her so yourself. I fancy she will not be surprised, since she was so loath to speak to you that she begged my intervention. In the name of God, had you noticed nothing? Could you not tell that she . . .?'

Robert cut incisively into the other's impassioned words. 'I'll speak to her,' and he pushed away his plate, wiped his hands free both of grease and the matter under discussion.

There was no more to be said. Jerome, who for reasons of his own had had a night of broken sleep, eyed with distaste the bread and meat for which he had no appetite.

'Mind you do!' he said, and grim amusement caught and held Robert. Spoken like an uncle, he thought, although never once had Jerome claimed the standing to which their blood relationship entitled him. Now Robert, watching him push his plate away, saw him wince at the movement.

'Suppose, before I leave, you tell me what ails you. Sores again?'

Jerome brought his serviceable arm across his chest, touched the other gingerly. 'Boils!'

'Let me see!' More purposefully than Jerome liked, Robert rose, strode round the table, took firm hold of the older man's robe and shirt together and stripped them down from his left shoulder. Lifting the shrunken, useless arm he surveyed the armpit before, much as if he spoke to a child who for fear had hidden something damaged in accident, he asked, 'How long has it been like this?'

'Three days. I thought they might go away.'

'When have they ever before? You mean thought of the knife frightened you.'

Through teeth clenched in his lower lip Jerome gave a gasping laugh. 'True,' he acknowledged. 'If you will ask Master Hammond to call I will get it over before my courage runs out altogether.'

Robert's grip on his arm gentled, his voice lost the hard note it had held all morning. 'I'll do it for you myself. I make no charge – and I hurt less!'

With the words he was gone to fetch his fine-bladed knife that had done like duty before, and Jerome sighed in relief. Whatever else that vicious blade had been used for in all the years since its owner had bought it in Florence he would not think; there was no doubt that in Robert's hands it would solve his problem more quickly and less painfully than could any physician.

Ten minutes later he was lying back in his chair by the hearth with the boils lanced, the pain receding and a pad of clean linen in place to prevent chafing. Robert helped pull his clothes straight, and tucked the useless arm into the front of his shirt.

'Keep that so for the present. I'll look at it again tonight. And,' he added drily, as he wiped his knife clean and gathered up blood-stained cloth and bowl of reddened water, 'I'll do the other thing tonight, too.'

Jerome's eyes closed. There were papers to see to, but they could wait. A short sleep would clear his head, would clear . . . He was asleep before Robert left the house.

*

At Whitehall Palace Cecily, chivvying Rose into action, was a good deal less considerate than Robert had been to Jerome. They were, she said roundly, due at the Queen's apartments in less time than it would take to walk there with the decorum her cousin insisted was proper to their station, and she had no intention of being late again. She would, she added airily, say to anyone who asked that Rose simply could not be troubled to get out of bed these chilly autumn mornings! She met Taylor's eyes and grinned and to her surprise the maid, dourest and most surly of creatures, stretched her mouth into an answering smile. Cecily's clothes would be folded and neat when she needed them; Rose's would have been less carefully handled.

It occurred to Taylor that Mistress Cecily had passed a bad night. There were dark rings beneath her eyes and she might, from the redness about them, have been crying. Despite the spirited manner in which she dealt with her cousin, she looked depressed; not that the other young madam would notice anything that did not pertain to her own comfort.

Not only had Cecily not slept, she had spent a goodly part of the night, naked save for her cloak, standing by the window that looked out over the huddled mixture of rooftops of the huge palace that was her present home. There was no moon, cloud hid the stars; all she could see against the blackness of the roof was a slightly lighter line that was the sky, and superimposed upon all, reflected in the glass, her own face, pale and hollow-eyed. Having at last summoned up sufficient courage, she had questioned Andrew Stratton concerning Wat's comment about her marrying Martin. It was a mistake, was it not? She had surely misheard him? Andrew not only confirmed it but had told her things about Wat's behaviour that made her put her hands over her ears and run for the shelter of her room.

It took so little time, five minutes to give a kiss and make a promise, less than that to discover that the man to whom she had given it regarded it as, at best, some game, but — more likely — a malicious barrier to prevent her belonging to his brother. She wondered how much of the whole sorry story Martin knew or suspected.

She called Martin to her, he who had been an ever-present part of her life, familiar, loving and as loved as parents or sisters. She had seen Wat only rarely when he came home from school, at first to tease her, later to say mockingly complimentary things for the pleasure of seeing her blush. Then he had run away, to return two years later, sure of welcome and forgiveness, a sophisticated stranger, dangerously attractive to a young girl who lived so secluded a life. His face even now easily displaced his brother's in her mind; she saw his laughing brown eyes, the handsome face tilted slightly to one side, heard his voice say caressingly, 'One more voyage, my Cecily. Then I shall be rich and you will be mine. Mine and no-one else's.'

So she had waited and treasured the token he gave her, whilst her imagination painted him more and more attractively and she had told herself that when the time came her father, who denied her nothing, would change his mind about Wat, would see that he was someone to be proud of. Like Martin, said the voice of her conscience, honest and forthright. Never until the night he told her of his love had it occurred to her to value the way in which he treated her as one set apart from her sisters. Now she weighed Wat's behaviour, his insistence on silence, against Martin's willingness to wait for her to make up her mind, and saw it as a thing tarnished, as surely as if the ring he had given her was base metal and had corroded in her hand.

She had crawled into bed, cold and aching, as dawn broke. Wat did not want her, never intended to claim her, and she had refused Martin, had hurt him so bitterly that surely he would turn elsewhere to seek a wife, no matter what her father's wishes.

When Lettice, just before noon, came to tell Cecily that she and Rose were to speak with Lady Patchett at once, Rose went head in air, ready to transfer on to her cousin whatever blame there was to be for such minor offences as might be laid at her door.

So short a time later that Cecily was never able to believe it, she stood numb and unseeing in the middle of Lady Patchett's room, unmoved from the spot on which she and Rose had made their curtseys on entering. At her feet crouched Rose in screaming hysterics, fists beating at the none-too-clean rushes on the floor, face red, eyes starting.

Without conscious effort, Cecily came out of the trance that held her; bent and slapped her cousin hard across the face much as she might have disciplined a troublesome dog, and Lady Patchett smiled inwardly. That was one action it would be a pleasure to report to Her Majesty.

Her cousin's shrieks reduced to gasping sobs, Cecily straightened, folded her hands before her and stood still. Inside her head a voice louder than ever Rose's had been was screaming that what she had heard was not true, could never be true, that some terrible mistake had been made.

She felt Lady Patchett's hand on her shoulder, more kindly than she had ever known from a lady well nigh as autocratic as her mistress. Ignoring the still-grovelling Rose, she said, 'Come, child, sit!' and placing Cecily in a chair, held wine to her lips.

The girl swallowed, made to speak, failed, tried again, and managed, 'Tell me again, please. What did you say, madam? I think I have forgotten.'

Her Majesty had been correct, thought Lady Patchett; Cecily Woodfall knew nothing of her family's treachery. There was no play-acting here.

She repeated, 'Sir Thomas Woodfall, your father and your cousin, Martin Woodfall, have been arrested and charged with high treason. Evidence against them is irrefutable, I fear.'

Still Cecily was held in ice-like calm. 'Not my father! Not Martin! Never, never! What are they said to have done?' Treason came in many shapes, albeit the ending was the same.

'Plotting to murder Her Majesty and bring Mary Stuart to the throne of England.'

A movement that was almost a smile came to Cecily's

white lips. 'Soon everybody will know how absurd the idea is.'

Moved by unexpected pity, Lady Patchett murmured, 'I hope so, child.'

Cecily shook herself. 'What of my mother and sisters? My aunts?'

'You need not fear for them. They remain untouched.' Except that soon they will be dispossessed of all they own, she added silently.

'And Rose and I may go to them?'

'No.'

One word, and before she had time to say more, Cecily asked, 'The Bridewell?' Her education had not been neglected during her short stay in the city.

'Most certainly not!' Lady Patchett was outraged. 'You have done nothing to deserve imprisonment. Now you will go to your room. Try to rest. It is Her Majesty's pleasure that if you can command yourself and go about your duties as you should, you continue in them for the time being at least. You will find it preferable to long hours alone.'

With the determination she had inherited from her mother Cecily made her curtsey to Lady Patchett, took Rose by an arm and hauled her to her feet.

'Walk!' she commanded fiercely. 'Walk, or I'll hit you again, and so hard that your ears will still be ringing tomorrow!'

There was high courage there, Lady Patchett told herself, surprised to find how much she liked and pitied the little Woodfall. Both girls would need all their spirit in the days to come, until the Queen finished whatever game it was she was playing with them and despatched them home.

To Cecily, on the long journey to the room they shared, it seemed that everyone they passed had somehow heard of what had befallen, that no-one spoke but concerning the downfall of the Woodfall family. Steadily she walked, chin in air, towing Rose as a teacher would some recalcitrant pupil until, their room reached at last, she gave her a push that in small part relieved her feelings. Rose landed face downwards on the bed, lay there moaning and hiccuping.

For the second time in twenty-four hours Cecily stood looking out over the rooftops, this time in daylight, and now her personal disappointment meant nothing at all to her. From a distance came the noise of workmen erecting stands for the tiltyard jousts that would mark the anniversary of the Queen's accession. Cecily's anger rose in time to the beat of their hammers. How dare the world go on so unconcernedly whilst innocent men fell victim to injustice! Father, Martin – and Uncle Thomas. Her mind turned to Wat, who was due to arrive home in the near future. Someone had told her that. Who? Of course, Robert Cooper, on a day that was a million years away. And all the time she had been telling him about her home and family, the menfolk of it were being dragged towards their prison, had perhaps even been there already.

She clenched her fists and pressed them to her mouth, determined not to give way but to do all she could to help her family. The tangle of her feelings for Wat no longer mattered; if she found out where his ship was to dock and was able to contact him, he must help.

Without a backwards glance at Rose, who still lay across the bed, Cecily set out. She found Andrew Stratton in the gardens, in an alcove clipped from a yew hedge, hand in hand with Lettice, with no thought for the outside world until it broke in upon him in the shape of a small, rather rumpled and desperately unhappy figure.

'Cecily! We have heard. What can I say? It cannot be true!' But even as he spoke he was peeping round the edges of his hiding place to make sure that he was not observed talking to the daughter of a traitor. It was an attitude the cousins would meet often in the coming days, and always it raised within Cecily the scorn she felt for the first time now.

Coldly she said, 'I will detain you no longer than needs be, Andrew Stratton. Tell me which port Wat is likely to return by. I must find him.'

From the blank look she received she knew that there was no answer to be had here. She barely waited for him to stammer out, 'I do not know. We talked only once or twice.'

'But being such a gallant and knowing London so well, you know where Trinity Street is?' Her voice rang with savage sarcasm.

'Er . . . Trinity Street?'

'Trinity Street. Master Cooper lives there. *He* will know about Wat.'

'My dear Cecily, you cannot go about the city streets alone to visit a man you hardly know. Besides, he . . .'

'I remember exactly what you said, Andrew. Not the sort of person I should know. But I'd speak to the devil himself if he would help me now. If you cannot tell me, I'll find it myself.'

Anger swung her on her heel, had set her off on a lone quest when Andrew shouted, 'Wait! Cec, come back!' and she heard his feet pounding along the walk after her.

He caught up with her, closely pursued by Lettice, who appeared to be urging him on.

'Don't go off at me like that, for pity's sake, Cec,' he said miserably. 'You can't go alone, you wouldn't get ten yards. Change into something less conspicuous and I'll meet you by the Western Watergate in half an hour. It's quicker by river and – and better not to have horses standing for people to wonder at.'

His voice was troubled and determined, and with the first offer of help she had received, Cecily felt her fragile self-control cracking. She thanked him with tears in her eyes; no need to point out what associating with her might mean to the future of an ambitious young man. And this was the attitude her mother and sisters must be meeting, alone and with no-one to defend them.

Deep red flooded upwards under Andrew's fair skin. 'I may not be much of an escort, but I'm better than none, and if you think I'll let a friend down because . . .' His voice trailed away and he patted clumsily at Lettice's arm that was suddenly clinging to his sleeve.

'Oh, Andrew!' she said in utter adoration, and for the tone in which she said it he would have taken Cecily to the ends of the earth if that had been her wish. She had tied her favour about his sleeve and he turned proudly to Cecily. 'We'll do what we can between us,' he said.

Although Andrew was suddenly no longer proud of it, certain midnight forays with his cronies had made London well known to him; he had no need to ask directions to Trinity Street. Strongly, directly, he rowed the small boat himself. It was the first time Cecily had been on the river, as crowded with traffic as any of the surrounding streets. And at any other time she would have enjoyed the experience, storing up sights and sounds – even the stench of it – ready to describe them to Katharine and Philippa. Now she sat and stared unseeingly at the water slopping between the boards at her feet and wished the journey over before it was begun.

Nor, once they had tied up at the watersteps at the bottom end of Trinity Street, was Master Cooper's house hard to find. The first urchin they asked, one of a gang playing happily in the mud, pointed it out with a grin on his grimy face, caught the penny Andrew tossed him and proffered the advice that they should beware of the old man if he was at home; very ready with his staff he was.

Even had Andrew not tried to hide as much as possible of his face by pulling down his hat to meet the upturned collar of his cloak, Cecily would have been well aware of what she had brought him into. The enormity of her behaviour struck her for the first time and she stopped short of the house they had come to visit so that he in his turn halted, turned to her in surprise and, to judge from his voice, no little hope.

'Changed your mind?'

'Not about coming,' replied Cecily firmly. 'Just about bringing you with me. Bless you for all you've done, Andrew, but I think you should wait for me, either back at the boat or somewhere hereabouts, where nobody will know we are together. Please.'

Secretly relieved to obey her, and ashamed at the relief, he watched her knock at the door of a tall, narrow house, saw her admitted, before he turned and sauntered back to the river. If she had not returned, he told himself, before the wavelets that were lapping the muddy foreshore touched the third step, he would go after her.

Master Cooper was not at home, said Martha, eyeing Cecily's plain brown woollen gown and cloak with interest, but she would speak to Master Jerome, if the young lady would be pleased to wait.

In all the time since Robert returned from Highwoods Jerome had asked no single question concerning the family there, with whom his sister had so briefly been connected. He had, he told himself, no right; if Robert wished to talk he would do so. Yet when he pulled himself to his feet, refreshed and with the throbbing beneath his arm quieted to a dull soreness thanks to Robert's ministrations, it somehow came as no surprise that the visitor curtseying before him introduced herself as Cecily Woodfall, and hoped he would forgive her for intruding upon him. He made as near to a bow as he could manage without use of his staff, needing all his strength to remain upright.

'Robert Jerome, mistress; and you are welcome. You must forgive me if I sit. Perhaps you will join me? You are seeking Master Cooper, I understand?'

He saw the visitor assessing his physical state, from part-paralyzed face and slurred voice, to the useless side of his body, not in pity but in understanding, as one to whom such things were part of a life she knew, then she was at his elbow, upholding, strengthening. At first sight she had supposed him old, this foster-father of whom Robert Cooper had spoken, but he was not. The white hair and lined, fleshless face resulted from the ill-health and suffering that today made it difficult for him to keep his feet.

It was long years since any woman had come near Jerome in anything save duty, and his reaction to this small, brown girl with her reddened eyes and determined, kindly manner startled him. If she could have passed to him some of her youth, have cured his withered limbs, she would have done so, that was obvious, and his rare smile twitched at his face.

'Now you can tell me why you are come.'

Cecily took the chair that was Robert's, and when she sat her shoes, thick-soled and useful, barely touched the floor. With hands folded in her lap, she poured out the whole story, ending, 'So you see, sir, I must find Wat and I am sure Master Cooper knows where his ship will dock, for he mentioned it. Please can you tell me when I may see him? I will come back then. If – if you do not mind, that is.'

So the girl had enjoyed her day in the country; for Robert – for a moment Jerome closed his eyes – it had been a job of work. It explained something he had noticed that morning. Watching Robert's hands as he prepared to deal with the tormenting boils he had been aware, even as he gathered up courage to face the bite of the knife, that the skin between the boy's scrupulously clean fingers was dark pink and soft. He, too, had been awake when he should have been sleeping. So long it had been since he complained of washing his hands time after time, unable to stop himself. A childhood habit outgrown, Jerome had hoped and believed. But it was not. How many times, unknown, had his work sent him back to it through the years, the last time following his outing of yesterday?

He was quiet for so long, staring at Cecily although his thoughts were elsewhere, that she said in a small voice, 'I should not have come, should I? But I am desperate. Do you know what it means to have nowhere to turn? There is no-one but Wat any more . . .'

She was rising to go when Jerome said, 'You are mistaken. I am not angry. I will pass on your message to Cooper. No need for you to come all this way again.'

He had no reassurance to offer, most certainly must not commit Robert. He held out a hand. 'Is there nothing else you would ask him?'

'I cannot involve others in my family's troubles, sir. Master Cooper was kind to me, that is all, and I – I am not sure what else to do.'

She had reached for and taken the outstretched hand when, forlorn as she was, her attention was diverted. From his skin, roughened by the sores cold weather always brought him, rose the odour, unmistakable and oh, so dear, of Aunt Agnes's elderflower salve. Involuntarily she smiled.

'Master Cooper gave you some of my salve, I can smell it.'

'Yes, child, he did, and very effective it has been too. It does not work so well on boils, however.'

She was shocked. 'Oh no, not boils! For them there is nothing like a bread poultice. Tell your servant to make one; it is not difficult.'

Jerome, who would have died rather than ask Martha for assistance with his bodily ailments, either directly or by way of Robert, thanked her.

'You are not to get up,' she told him, severely maternal, and released his hand. 'If you have boils, they will throb each time you move. Your servant will let me out. Good-bye, sir.'

Now that she had taken some action, however small, her colour, indeed some of her youthful vivacity, had returned, and she seemed to him a very different person from the one who had entered. So much so that as he obeyed her instructions and sat back in his chair, he frowned once more. He would give her message to Robert, but that must be the end of it. A hideous end, as far as her family was concerned, but an end nevertheless. She would not be the first innocent child of a guilty family.

He was still mulling over the news she had brought, hearing her voice that had been speaking to Martha growing fainter as they reached the street door, when there was a shout, shrill and horror-stricken that, feeble as he was, brought him to his feet, searching for his staff.

It was – there could be no mistaking it – the voice of Cecily Woodfall, but now, in contrast to her manner with him, it rose clear and piercing above a swell of children's voices close outside the window. In it he heard shouts of 'Andrew' and orders to 'leave him alone', demands to know how they could be so cruel.

The Andrew appealed to seemingly arrived, for a man's deep voice joined in the racket, sundry cries of pain arose and the street urchins, from whom Jerome himself had suffered in his time, were gone to resume their activities in some safer place. He reached the street door, still held open by Martha, who was peering out in a mixture of horror and delight, in time to be ordered to one side by a Cecily Woodfall he would not have imagined could exist. She was covered in mud and her bright blue eyes blazed from a face that bore evidence of battle. By the morrow she would have a black eye that would be hard to disguise! But had she been stripped naked, he thought, she would not have cared. Behind her came a tall, fair man, gasping for breath, who tried at every step to persuade her to give up to him the burden she carried. He passed by Jerome with a brief, 'Andrew Stratton at your service, sir,' his eyes barely leaving Cecily, but she ignored him, clinging fiercely to what she held.

In her arms, limbs dangling loosely, head bouncing up and down to her every step, was a child, and inwardly Jerome groaned. The street idiot! The gang had set on him, as they did whenever other pastimes palled, and she had dived in and rescued him. It was to Martha that Cecily, carried away still with anger, said, 'Where can I put him? Quickly, now!' and the servant, receiving Jerome's acquiescing nod, led her to the kitchen, indicating a bench that stood along one wall.

Carefully Cecily deposited her burden, who showed no sign of stirring. One arm and leg, stick-like, with disproportionately large joints, hung swinging over the side of the bench, a huge head lolled drunkenly and a mouth hung slackly open, as to Jerome's knowledge it always did.

Having provided water to Cecily's orders, a cloth to remove the mud in which the boy was caked and another to bathe his sores, Martha had run to fetch something soft to spread on her spotless floor for the child to lie on in more safety. Only when she had dealt with her patient as best she might, did Cecily look up at the two men in the doorway. She singled out Jerome.

'Do you know him? He must live hereabouts, poor little thing.'

'Martha?' Jerome passed the question on. He had seen

the child often enough but had no idea where he might live.

'His mother lives in an alley along the road, sir. A lot of them, there are.'

Not all like this one, Jerome hoped! For a moment he had a vision of what Robert would say if he returned to find his house invaded by the riff-raff of the neighbourhood. It was something he preferred not to dwell on. He said, 'It might be as well if Master Hammond looks him over before we alarm his mother. Fetch him, will you, Martha?'

'Poor little devil,' said Andrew. 'Catch!' and he threw a coin to Martha. 'That should pay the physician's fee.'

Cecily had come back to Jerome. 'You shouldn't be standing there, sir,' she said sternly. 'Let me help you back to your chair.' Her tone grew rueful. 'If I have exceeded my place I ask your pardon but "inasmuch as ye do it unto one of the least of these . . ." You understand?'

Jerome understood only too well. She had disrupted the household, causing him to move in a manner far more violent than any he had contemplated that day – he could feel the dressing Robert had applied slipping down inside his shirt and had a dreadful feeling that if she knew of it this girl, who had troubles enough of her own, would insist on replacing it! – and finally she disarmed him completely with a quotation from St Matthew.

Andrew, following them back into the study, attempted an apology. 'It's time I was getting you back to the Palace, Cec,' he said severely and Jerome startled even himself with his rusty laugh.

'Clean yourselves up before you go. How will you explain what has happened to your face, mistress?'

Aware of it for the first time, Cecily felt the bruising carefully, appreciated the situation and was silent.

'A bread poultice?' suggested Jerome, delicately malicious, and knew that she understood his dread of being doctored by a woman as well as if he had spoken it aloud.

The impish grin her father loved so well flashed across her face and was gone. 'Everyone will have a splendid time wondering who hit me!' she said.

*

Jerome awaited Robert's return that evening with feelings so mixed that he could not separate them. The unconscious child in the kitchen was the least of his worries. If he, who had avoided women for so many years, had been moved by the kindly innocence of Cecily Woodfall, what of Robert? He hoped, very much he hoped, that the boy had not been drawn to her strange mixture of the maternal and the childish. But in the course of a whole day spent alone together, how could he not have been? He had seen the way Martha eyed her when not running to her bidding and had the feeling that she recognized a rival.

'You had a visitor this afternoon, Cooper.'

Having pulled off his boots and unlaced his doublet, Robert sat relaxed, stretched out his legs towards the fire, his eyes closed. 'Nothing that need take me out again today, I trust.'

Deliberately Jerome said, 'Cecily Woodfall asks if you know at which port her cousin Wat will dock and when.'

'She came *here*?' The pale eyes were open again. 'So they have told her. She was not alone?'

'A lad called Stratton brought her.'

'Andrew Stratton? Who would have thought it!' Robert had regained his self-control; once more closed his eyes.

'No doubt,' he said drily, 'she proposes to storm off to Plymouth to bring her cousin riding here full tilt to right her wrongs.'

'Are they wrongs?' Jerome found that the memory of the indomitable small brown face made him want to know. 'I have heard nothing, one way or the other.'

Robert frowned. 'I would have said so, following the Highwoods jaunt. I would indeed. There was no – no *feeling* of intrigue about the place. You know what I mean. But Sir Francis has proof of guilt.' He paused. 'There is nothing I can do, nothing.'

'As to what she would have her cousin do,' said Jerome, 'after this afternoon I can believe she would try anything!'

Robert listened to Jerome's account of the fight in the street and was told of the idiot child who now lay in his

310

kitchen, the physician having said he should not be moved. Scarcely was the recital ended when Robert was on his feet, striding towards the rear of the house. Jerome, following as best he might, arrived to find him standing in the doorway, arrested by sight of Martha on her knees beside the boy Cecily had rescued, gently mopping his face with a damp cloth. She sat back on her heels, looked up at Robert, and for once was not over-awed.

'He's bad, sir. It's as if he isn't inside his body any more, like.'

Robert knelt beside the child, raised one limp eyelid to disclose a much-dilated pupil, let it fall. Then he stripped back the blanket that covered the pitiful naked body. Not all the bruises had been administered that afternoon. So many scars of different ages and sizes knotted and webbed the filthy, ill-nourished flesh from chin to ankle. But the bruise that stretched from below the ribs to deep into his abdomen, darkly red and grossly swollen, was, unless Robert was much mistaken, the result of feet applied recently, hard and repeatedly. As gently as he could he touched the swelling and the child stirred in his unconsciousness and moaned. Something, thought Robert, had burst inside him; there was nothing anybody could do. Carefully he replaced the cover.

'What did his mother say?'

'Nothing, sir. Truth to tell, she was glad to have him off her hands. There's a lot of them, very crowded.'

Robert stood up. 'He may stay but no-one, *no-one*, not even his mother, is to visit him. If she insists, she can take him away at once. You understand the rule about visitors, Martha?'

'Yes, sir.'

'Did you find out his name?'

'Hasn't got one!' Indignation sounded in Martha's voice. 'She said he couldn't answer so 'twasn't worth bothering.'

Jerome, watching intently, saw distaste contort Robert's face, but it was gone immediately and there was nothing in his voice to make Martha wonder as he said, 'Sim! You will call him Sim,' then added, changing the subject so swiftly and calmly that he might have been speaking of some other person's concern, 'Have you no relative to take your babe when it is born?' *Your* babe, not our babe, most certainly not *my* babe, Jerome noted.

But Martha was grateful that the matter was broached at all, and without the cold, hard look that frightened her even whilst she worshipped.

'My sister might. She's got four of her own, one more wouldn't matter.'

Slowly Robert nodded, spoke as if they might not see each other again in all the months before the child's birth. 'See to it. You are to take care of yourself. Ask for anything you need. All will be well.'

He put out a hand, touched her pale cheek in a light caress and had already turned to leave when she said, 'If you please, sir; the young lady said I was to make a bread poultice for Master Jerome's boils. I've put mustard in it, like she said. I hope it won't bite too much.'

CHAPTER VII

Edward Woodfall moaned. Beneath his back he could feel deck timbers rising and falling in the slow ocean swell and once, opening his eyes for an instant when it seemed to him that the creaking grew suddenly louder, he saw a lantern high above him, swinging from its hook in the roofbeams, a gleam of gold all blurred and rainbowed round the edges.

The ship's carpenter had cut off his crushed left leg above the knee; so much he remembered and was surprised that it did not hurt more. He thought of the humiliation, when he got back to England, of crawling to beg forgiveness of his father for running away from his responsibilities, of having to confess that his new life had ended after only one voyage, not in some great sea battle, not in some fight with a foreign privateer, but in the crashing down of a broken spar in a gale, and he too slow to avoid it.

He supposed that now he would go back to Highwoods and there wear out the rest of his days. Then before him, into the golden light, across it and away into darkness once more, with the half-running, half-skipping steps of childhood, moved a procession of girls, brown-skinned, brown-eyed and sturdy, ones who had never grown beyond babyhood, some children still, others already reaching young womanhood. He had run away to avoid being forced into marriage with Benedicta Williams, yet he had a bevy of daughters the image of her. One turned towards him and waved as she ran, her eyes gleaming just as Lewis's had when some mischief passed between them. Cecily! His dear, dear Cecily. He had a daughter with eyes of the Woodfall blue who was already a woman when he was no more than twenty years old himself, and he laughed at his cleverness.

The laugh was swallowed up in agonizing pain and Cecily vanished with the rest. Gasping for breath, he tried to move and could not. If only his leg was crushed why had they removed all his limbs? The deck was motionless now beneath him, motionless and very, very cold. Only overwhelming pain remained, burning in every joint; throbbing and pulsing, overriding even the spasms in his stomach that had plagued him for so long; pain and, as he opened his eyes again, the lantern. That still swung gently to and fro, shedding its soft golden light in a pool about him.

He was fully conscious now for the first time since his torturers had dropped him like some broken doll, limbs sprawling, joints swollen and black with the blood beneath the skin. His neck hurt too, but that was from bracing himself backwards against the other pain. If he were careful he could turn his head, and slightly he did so. He was no longer in the cell where he had spent the interminable waiting days since arriving at the Tower, where the accumulated coldness of years and lack of Agnes's cordial had locked him into agony he had thought could grow no worse – until certain devils in the shape of men and their contrivances had shown him the fallacy of that idea! This place was windowless, the vaulted ceiling so low that a tall man might find difficulty in standing upright, save in its centre. Not that that would concern him now. He was buried alive until the day when they took him forth to . . . His mind shied away from thought of the death he had deliberately brought upon himself, took refuge in his only consolation – that he had accomplished what he had set out to do, to save his family insofar as that were possible.

The plan had formed in his head almost immediately he had been arrested, and certainly before he had begun the jolting ride to London in the farm wagon commandeered by the band of men who had taken them up. Over the years, and increasingly of late, news of plans and rumours of plans to instal Mary Stuart in Elizabeth's place, and the ruthless putting down of all suspected plots, had reached even Sussex's secluded countryside. Edward did not believe that action would have been taken against the Woodfalls without some evidence, however wrong, having come to light, and equally he was sure that things would go easier for the others if one man confessed sole guilt.

Unable to speak either to Martin or to Thomas, who rode in the certainty that it was all some terrible mistake and that once they arrived in London he would be released by command of Her Majesty, who was his friend, Edward had prayed that this last gamble of his might pay off, that his illness might not carry him off too soon, that they would come for him before the others. The few painful, degrading weeks of life left him were small sacrifice if it meant that only he were convicted, that the others went home in safety.

Once alone and with time dragging slowly past, however, things had been by no means so easy. Unable to eat the scanty food provided, his body had grown weaker by the day until only fierce self-resolve kept him alive. At the same time his mind became the more active and he saw with increasing clarity what he intended to do to those he loved and who loved him. Bennitt, who had well nigh worshipped him even when, as a boy, he had been so appallingly rude to her and whose life since their marriage had been bound up in his comfort and ease; their daughters, conceived in love, reared in happiness; Agnes, who had cared enough to throw in her lot with his.

He would confess and they would hear that he had done so. Despite what love told them to believe, how would they support it when neighbours spurned them, when friends dropped away, as assuredly they would? His hopes rested wholly on Martin. Even if Thomas, released, declared innocent and unsullied, bowed to Eleanor's inevitable pressure to have nothing to do with the family of a traitor brother, he could rely on the boy doing his best for the well-being of Bennitt, Agnes and the children. Perhaps he would even take them to his grandfather in Barndale. Abbey House and

315

all his father had given him would be forfeit to the Crown. If Thomas made an offer for the land it might be taken back into the original Highwoods estate: not given to him and his descendants after all, for all his grand plans, but loaned so that he might learn the meaning of true happiness there, before he handed it back. Finally he had achieved a certain contentment, devoid of hope.

'Lord, now lettest Thou Thy servant depart in peace . . .' In peace, not in pieces, he and Lewis had often chanted as lads when they wanted to tease Father Peter, and the words recurred to him now as being most apposite. He asked forgiveness for blasphemy that was not intended, only a boyish prank recalled. He groaned again; no need now for unnecessary bravery, there was no-one to hear him. Then he found that there was. The lantern still swayed above him, but now he was not fooled. It hung not from any beam but from the hand of a man bending over him; the voyage on the *Heart of Mary* had been long ago.

A throb of fear jerked his agonized limbs; perhaps somewhere he had made a mistake. In the grip of agony that had had him screaming for mercy, pity at any price, that had ripped away his consciousness no matter how hard he fought against it, had he said something wrong?

If he had given them cause to doubt, tomorrow it would be all to go through again, the pains of death, the fires of hell. Question after repeated question, agony upon agony. Anxiety shook him. Whatever he had said, if brain and body betrayed him and he told a different story, they would turn their hands to Thomas and Martin after all. That they had not done that yet, he knew. Through the buzzing of a million bees in his ears had come a voice, just before he began to confess.

'We shall get nowhere with this one. I know the sort. Besides, he's half-dead already.'

And the reply: 'We have our orders. It is this one we work on.'

The altar ornaments were one thing; he knew about them. But letters, the letters, the letters . . . They had held them before him, bearing his name, incriminating, accusing. Before ever they left Abbey House they had flourished the artefacts that had for so many years lain hidden and unregarded; things, they said, that proved his Roman Catholic allegiance. (Peter, dear Peter, why did you keep them burnished so brightly!) But not, until today, the letters. Where had they come from? Where? He knew as little as his questioners.

He found himself praying harder than he had prayed for anything for years that he might not survive the night. He could not face that room, those quiet businesslike men of pain again. Yet if he were not there, they would set to work on Thomas – and on young Martin. For the boy's sake especially, he must find the strength to withstand whatever else might be done to him, must endeavour to retain sufficient clarity of mind to tell the same story, repeat the same lies, word for word, until he was certain they were believed.

Dear God, dear God, of Thine infinite mercy save my innocent family. Let my miserable life be sacrifice enough . . . But they could not wait until tomorrow, it seemed; they had come for him now, before he had time to gather what small reserves of strength were left. He passed his swollen tongue over cracked, dry lips.

'Who are you?' His voice came out as a croak.

The man knelt beside him and as he leaned forward, placing his lantern on the floor, showed himself shrouded from head to foot in a dark hooded cloak. Being the Angel of Death, if he put back the hood he would doubtless disclose a skull.

'My name is Robert Cooper.'

No need to see the face after all, the voice was distinctive, the words he had heard it speak only a short time before chillingly memorable.

'You were there.'

'Towards the end I was there,' agreed Robert.

'Then you heard me confess.' The whisper was infinitely weary. 'I told everything I know. The guilt is mine. My brother and nephew know nothing. There is no more to be gained by – by questioning me again.'

As if for him the matter ended there, his eyelids drooped. That afternoon, in light stronger than this, Robert had seen the greyness of approaching death in Edward Woodfall's face. Had he arrived to find him dead he would not have been surprised, yet the man's voice, although faint, was steady enough. He would, thought Robert calling on past experience, go out suddenly like some candle flame caught in a draught. How much time he had left there was no way of knowing and he said, 'I have a question. Not for them; for myself.'

Edward felt surprise, not only at the words, but at a tone of urgency in the other's voice, yet he was fearful and on guard. He considered this different line of approach; they sought to entrap his tongue whilst he lay half-conscious. If only he could clench his hands, dig his fingernails into his palms. Anything that would stop the cell swinging about him and prevent the dark shape of this new inquisitor growing and shrinking in so strange a way; but he could not. Silently he waited.

'Why did you lie?' For a moment Robert thought that his insistence had brought about the end he feared. Edward's eyes rolled up in their sockets and he put an arm beneath his head and moistened his lips with a rag dipped in water.

Edward felt the trickle of it run cold down his chin and neck, yet the last time he had heard this voice he had been on the rack and it had asked – not of him – 'How much longer must you take?' There had been no humanity in it then.

They had not believed him after all, and so they had sent this man who put questions in a voice that sounded strangely compassionate. He must be certain that he had succeeded in saving the others; he made a last effort at a bluff. Narrowing his eyes, he peered upwards, tried to see the face beyond the edge of the light and could not.

'I told the truth. Your colleagues – that repulsive little man who sat there writing – they believed me.' Even in the midst of his agony he had heard the satisfied sigh: what had gone amiss?

Sharply Robert said, 'They are not my colleagues. They might well believe you. You named known Papist agents.'

'Then my family – all of them – will be safe? The entire blame is mine. This – *this* will not happen to them? You swear?'

Small need for it to happen to Sir Thomas, thought Robert drily. As he and the jailer walked together towards Edward's cell the man had been talkative. 'Twice they tried the thumbscrews on this one and he told 'em nothing. Talk about stubborn! It was the rack this afternoon, and if you ask me he's finished. Came apart at the joints like some overcooked fowl as soon as they touched him. You'll get nothing more out of him, sir. Now that brother of his – he's mad, and likely to stay that way, if you asks me. Spends all his days yelling for somebody called "Eleanor" to come and save him. Seems at first he reckoned on the Queen herself appearing! You can hear him all along the passage when the fear's on him strong. Other times he crouches in a corner and whimpers something cruel.'

Very offhandedly, Robert had asked, 'And the boy, Martin Woodfall, who came with them?'

'Not worth bothering with, sir, so I'm told. He's being taken care of. Not one of mine, he's not.'

Edward was repeating his question more urgently now and Robert replied, 'Her Majesty would not care to think of your brother – as you are now. Royal affection is a powerful thing.'

The answer was evasive, but it seemed to content Edward. Suddenly, why he did not know, he believed that the man beside him was telling the truth. This Robert Cooper was not one of them after all. Hard though he sounded, the aura of inhumanity that clung to everyone else in that terrible place like the stench of a slaughter house was not present in the tall figure beside him. He had indeed come of his own accord to straighten out a point that puzzled him, and with that realization came trust also. For a moment Edward fought against the feeling, dreading that it was his weakening body that was refusing to fight further despite his will; then he gave in, relaxed as far as he was able. It no longer occurred to him to be wary in case this unseen young man was setting traps for his tongue. Somehow, deep within himself, he knew that he was not.

Robert repeated, 'Why did you lie?', watched bitten, blood-encrusted lips twist into the shadow of a boyish grin.

'What – what makes you think I did lie?' Edward asked, in a whisper that was little more than a breath.

'You named Sir Evelyn Talbot-Jones as the man who visited you at Christmastide. He died three years ago in Paris.'

'Why did you not tell them this afternoon? They will find out when they make enquiries.'

'Not unless they search the bottom of the Seine. Sir Evelyn died in a riverside fight,' and despite the impassive tone of the young man's voice, Edward had no need to ask who else had been involved in that fight. 'He was a man constantly on the move; when they find no trace of him they will think that he made France too hot for himself and moved on. But tell me what you know of him, and the letters that were found in your house.'

'Many years ago he visited me – and Thomas for that matter – knowing of our connection with the Catholic Harringtons – to draw us into some crazy plot against Her Majesty. Much the same as the present one. We sent him packing. I used his name because the letters were unsigned and your – your friends wanted a name. Where they came from I most truly do not know. I swear it on all I hold most dear. The man who arrested us – Jenkins, I think his name was – flourished papers as he came out of the house, but they could have been anything. All I saw clearly then were the altar ornaments given to my family for safe keeping when the abbey was dissolved. The letters I had never seen until they were shown to me this afternoon. The question that plagues me is "Why me?" It can only be that I have an enemy. After such a quiet life as mine has been that seems quite amusing in its way!'

'Jenkins? He came himself?'

Edward made no answer; under Robert's hand his fingers twitched convulsively. 'There is something – strange. It seemed to me – it seemed . . .' His voice stumbled as he groped for words and his greying brows drew together. 'Have you – have you seen them?' he asked.

'I have not.'

'They were old,' Edward assured him. 'Not recently written, I'd swear.'

Robert leaned forward. 'You are certain of that?'

'The paper was brownish towards the edges, even – *there* I noticed that. One of them cracked and broke across a crease – as they unfolded it.'

He stopped, laughing a little even as a stab of pain seized him. 'It did not occur to me until afterwards. I had other things on my mind at the time!'

But his visitor was not amused; when he answered Robert's voice was stern.

'I shall find out what is happening.' His voice softened. 'I doubt it will be in time to save your life.' Somehow, with this man who had delivered himself up to save the rest of his family, it was impossible to lie, on this point at least.

The ghost of a laugh shook Edward. 'Like this it would be no more than an existence at best! Besides, I have been dying these six months and more. I have a canker in my belly and very little time left. It made my decision to confess all the easier.'

Robert made an impatient gesture. 'But the stigma must be lifted. I shall report what I know. At least your estate will not be confiscated.'

'And to whom will you report it? Someone in authority must be involved. People are surely not arrested like this without someone's permission.' There was a mocking note in Edward's faint voice. 'Step carefully, lad; step very carefully.'

That he, who had done little else all his life, should be so warned brought ruefulness to Robert's voice. 'You are right. Who do I trust?'

'All I ask – all I – ask,' began the voice that was labouring now, 'is that you do your best to – safeguard my family.' The bitten lips twisted into a smile. Now that he was certain in his own mind that he had accomplished what he had set out to do, a serenity had come upon Edward, although whether it was the serenity that sometimes accompanied the approach of death or stemmed from happiness remembered, Robert was unable to judge. Even in the dim light Edward's eyes looked at something visible only to him and infinitely dear. 'My dearest Bennitt, a better wife than ever I deserved, and my girls and their Aunt Agnes,' he murmured.

Robert bowed his head, remaining silent until Edward found curiosity enough to whisper, 'So that is settled, but it does not explain why, if you do not belong here, you should choose to come to my – my exhibition this afternoon.'

They had come to the point Robert had hoped they would never reach. One thing only he knew; truth, half-truth or downright lie, he would make this man's dying as easy as he could. Picking his way carefully, he said, 'It seemed to me that the man your daughter Cecily loves and talks so much about would not – no, *could* not, do what you say you have done.'

Even so, Edward came out of his peace; his head jerked convulsively and there was entreaty in his voice: 'Dear God, the child has not been hurt! Tell me that it is not so – tell me!'

Robert compounded a mixture of fact and fiction. 'You need have no fear. She is safe at court. Her Majesty has a liking for her little brown mouse. We met and talked, that is all. Sir Francis Walsingham himself was present for much of the time, and a page the Queen sent with Cecily as her guide.'

Edward relaxed. 'My Cecily!' he whispered. 'And what did the girl say to make you so sure of my innocence?'

Across Robert's mind flashed the memory of a day beside a stream when a girl who had made a daisy chain for him talked so easily, so trustingly, of a beloved father.

'She told me of a man who loved his way of life, who was not ambitious and who would do no harm to anyone – if only because he was too lazy!'

Amazingly, there came that same weak splutter of laughter. 'As disrespectful as ever! The minx knows me well. Taken as a whole we are a lazy family. My Cecily is a daughter to be proud of, do you not think so?'

With one hand Robert made a quick gesture, as if he would brush aside something that troubled him. 'I scarcely know her. We met since it was necessary to establish her innocence or otherwise, as she is so close to the Queen – and to remain so, since it is Her Majesty's wish.'

Painfully Edward moved his head from side to side. 'The Queen I am accused of plotting to kill!' Almost he had exhausted his strength; his eyes closed and his mouth fell open. Once again water trickled into his throat and he was aware of a careful hand wiping his sweat-beaded forehead. He drifted back, found himself irritated beyond measure that he could see nothing of this man who knew so much of him and his family. Fretfully he said, 'Hold the light up. Why must you lurk there as if you are ashamed to be seen?'

Robert pushed back his hood and raised the lantern, holding it to one side so that its light fell full upon him, and the broken man on the floor caught a quick breath. The line between past and present shivered again and there, swimming in the golden glow, was a face he had not seen for nigh on thirty years.

'Rosamund – Rosamund Emory!' He waited for it to dissolve and pass, as had so many of his dreams, but it stayed, substantial yet different. Those distinctive eyes of black-rimmed light grey had not changed, but the features, although finely cut, were those of a man and there was about them a bleakness Rosamund Emory, with her zest for living, would never have owned.

'I do not understand,' he whispered beseechingly.

'A family likeness,' returned Robert drily. 'Rosamund Emory was my mother, and your brother my father.'

'But their son died . . . was drowned . . .'

'So that was the way of it.' Robert's voice grew harsh. 'Lost in some river and no body ever found, no doubt.'

'On the day you disappeared – plague struck the village. Dear God! The terror – the terror and the panic. So – so much confusion – so much pain – one small boy was not missed until evening time. You . . . you had always played by the river. It fascinated you.'

'Not missed even by his family, when they should have been worried about him then above all other days?'

Edward drew breath, carefully husbanding what strength he had left. 'You remember nothing? You did not live with – your father. The village priest fostered you.'

'Until a short time ago I had no idea who my parents were. My life, as far as I am concerned, began when I was five years old. That was when I was handed over – sold, if you will – to one of Lord Burghley's agents. The name I carry he gave me with as little care as if he were naming a hound.'

With the words he put down the lantern on the stone floor, retreating once more into his darkness.

'Abducted? Dear God!' Edward was horrified. It never occurred to him for a moment to doubt the young man's story. The evidence of his own eyes told him it was true and there had been the ring of absolute sincerity in Robert's voice.

'My wife, your Aunt Bennitt, loved you, Robert. We mourned you, lad, amongst the others we lost at that terrible time. And all these years – all these years . . .' His voice trailed away and there was no sound but his breathing, growing shallower now and more difficult, and, somewhere close at hand, the dripping of water.

'I was fortunate,' supplied Robert, because he found himself unable to bear the silence, pain-filled not only for the present but with sorrow long over. 'Burghley himself saw to that. I received a good education and work in his Department of State. You must believe me when I tell you that I seldom come here. This afternoon it was because – because of what Cecily told me.'

'You love her.' Faintly Edward smiled, as if the idea did not displease him.

Stiffly Robert said, 'She reminded me of someone who was once kind to me. She was kind herself.'

'If I could move,' said his uncle, 'I would take your hand,' and Robert, responding involuntarily to the kindness, found himself stretching out one of his own hard, dry hands towards the broken man by his side.

'Why sacrifice yourself for your brother Thomas?' he said angrily, remembering clearly the pompous, self-important, wife-ruled man he had seen at Highwoods.

'We have not always – seen eye to eye, it is true, but he is the head of the family and that means – a great deal – to me. Eleanor has not been a good influence upon him. Too full of her own importance! If ever you see her you will know how true that is!'

Somehow they both laughed. That Edward Woodfall should be attempting to comfort Robert Cooper whilst he himself lay so near to a most hideous death struck neither of them as strange.

'You – you will see Cecily again?'

Sharply Robert said, 'I doubt it!' but Edward smiled.

'If – *when* – you do, tell her I said that she must do as her heart tells her. I was wrong to plan out her life as I did without speaking to her first.'

'Even,' asked Robert, 'if her plans should include Wat instead of Martin?'

Once again he achieved more of a reaction than he had anticipated. 'She told you that!' The broken body made a great effort to move and the twisted mouth said with loathing, 'So that was at the back of it all. Never Wat! Never! I want the girl's happiness – that profligate could bring nothing but heartbreak.'

The outburst took the last of his strength and he lay silent, gasping, until, troubled still in his mind, he managed, 'You – you are sure that Thomas and my nephew will be released?'

'They must be. What cause to hold them after what you said this afternoon?' He hoped more than he had hoped anything for a long time that Edward Woodfall believed what he said. He was aware of his uncle's eyes, deep-sunken in his pallid, sweating face.

'So the questioning is over, but I am not a brave man, Robert. I doubt I shall make a good end on the scaffold.'

He believed all was over bar the dying, thought Robert, when it most certainly was not. Tomorrow they would come for him again, to repeat their torture, using well-tried, subtle

325

methods of questioning designed to trip up a man's tongue, to separate truth from falsehood manufactured in hope of relief. If he lived until the morning, and he was surprisingly strong considering all he had undergone. If he lived . . .

Briskly Robert pulled his hand free, rose to his feet and crossed the tiny cell, his head brushing the low ceiling, to where a bucket of brackish water stood with a cup beside it. For a moment he hesitated, then with his back to the prisoner filled the cup, added the contents of a phial he had taken from his pouch, and returned.

Touching his uncle gently on the shoulder to rouse him, he said, 'I must go now. Drink this water. It will ease your throat.'

'Ah, stay a little longer – just a little longer. Your presence brings comfort, my boy.'

'I cannot, sir.'

Edward sighed. 'You are a thoughtful person, Robert Cooper, who should have been Robert Woodfall. Will you come again before – before . . .?' His tongue refused the words, even as his mind dreaded the thought.

'If you wish it.' Robert's voice was steady now and unrevealing. He slid an arm beneath his uncle's head, raised it from the floor and held the cup to his lips.

'Drink deep. Who knows how long it may be before anyone else comes near you.'

With the words he tipped the cup so that Edward involuntarily took a large gulp. Then, as its bitter taste caught his throat, the rim was pressed hard against his teeth and Robert's arm tightened about his neck, giving him no chance to reject the poisoned liquid. A smile came into his eyes; he drained the draught without a struggle and for a few seconds lay back on Robert's arm with a contented sigh, like a child at the end of a tiring day.

'Blessed are the merciful,' he murmured, almost silently, and Robert flinched away from the gratitude in the words.

A blessed lassitude spread throughout Edward's tortured body; all pain had fled. The cell, Robert Cooper, the ring of light, were all fading.

'May God bless you, Robert. My family . . . tell them . . .'

His gaze passed over Robert's downbending shoulder as if suddenly he heard someone call him. His face was the face of an old man, but the voice that came from the twisted lips was that of a boy, strong, joyous and happy at sight of a loved one.

'Lewis! There you are!' So strong was the impression he gave that Robert turned, expecting to see someone standing behind him. When he looked back the diseased and tortured shell that had been Edward Woodfall was limp; his eyes, all life gone from them, stared sightlessly up into the darkness above him.

For what seemed to him a very long time, Robert stayed motionless by the body of the man who had given his life in a vain attempt to save the rest of his family. At length he put out a hand and placed it over the older man's heart; it was still.

Wearily he took hold of his lantern and stood up. He had murdered his uncle, an uncle who had cared enough in the final agonized moments of his own life to try to bring comfort to a nephew he hardly knew. Despite Edward Woodfall's absolution his soul lay heavy within him. So many lies and half-truths he had told a dying man, and he had come equipped to kill him, had intended to do it from the first, whether he were asked or no. The fact that it was an act of mercy in no way assuaged his guilt.

He drew a deep breath, composed his face once more into the bleak mask his world knew so well. If his story were to be believed, if he were to pursue the truth of what had happened to the Woodfall family, he could not even pay his uncle the respect of closing his eyes. For a moment longer he stood, then took up the pail of water and dashed its contents full over the face and chest of the dead man.

It was a small matter amongst all the rest, but running through and through his mind – and he unable to stop it – was the thought that in this place of agony and death he had been called by his Christian name by a member of his father's family for the first time that he could clearly remember. And it had been used in love and forgiveness: 'May God bless you, Robert.'

He opened the cell door and when he shouted there was no tremor in his voice. Amos Jenkins would have been proud of him, he thought dully.

'Jailer! Look to your prisoner! His heart has failed. And I did not get the answers to my questions after all!'

CHAPTER VIII

'There is nothing I can do, nothing,' Robert had said when Cecily sought his help, might in truth have amended it to 'nothing anyone can do', and Jerome had no cause to doubt that there the matter rested. The routine that was always his when in London Robert followed unaltered. When they were together at their ease he never lapsed into the brooding silence that had occasionally overtaken him in the past when matters troubled him deeply and beyond his dealing. And Jerome had allowed himself to be lulled into his sense of security until Martha broke the strict rule that stated her place was to do her work without comment, to venture an opinion only when asked.

Jerome had, in fact, viewed askance some change in her attitude since she had been nursing Sim; the maternal instinct was developing early in her, stemming from care of so helpless a creature no doubt, and once or twice it had spilled over, to his horror, into her dealings with him. He was, therefore, prepared to cut her short at the least opportunity. But this morning, because she was so obviously worried, he listened.

'If you please, sir.' She stood in his room screwing her apron into a crumpled mass between her hands in so agitated a fashion that for a moment Jerome thought that the child under her care must have died in the night. 'I think Master Cooper must be ill, indeed I do. He never stirred when I took his water, sir; sound asleep and not undressed neither.'

Horrified, she added, 'He's got his boots on still and him so fussy about that sort of thing. Covered in mud they are, and it's all over the bed.'

'Thank you, Martha. Change the sheets when Master Cooper has left the house. And put on a clean apron – and keep it straight, girl.' Jerome showed none of the worry the maid's words exploded within him and, curtseying, she went away.

Throughout his laborious dressing Jerome mulled over what she had said. At the head of the stairs he met Robert, wide awake and immaculate as ever, accepted the arm that was offered for his assistance. The boy ate well; Jerome could detect nothing amiss in his manner, though he was well aware that he was dealing with one as well trained as he to conceal emotion.

The only thing that made it different to any other of a hundred such mornings was that Robert, who had a habit of reading as he ate, did not once look at the papers he had brought downstairs with him. Jerome was not altogether surprised when, having wiped his hands, he sat back instead of rising, and said, 'Give me your opinion of Amos Jenkins, sir.'

Jerome had no need to think. 'The man is almost at the end. He has drunk far too much over the years and his body will accept no more. His brain is affected, I believe.'

'Enough to make him do something desperate for which he has no authority, in hope that he can bring himself back into favour, would you say?'

Jerome shrugged. 'What has he to lose? I can't see him caring for any damage he might do. One way or another, the end cannot be far off for him, and he knows it.'

'Thank you, sir.'

Jerome was left alone to bring his worries into perspective. Not for the first time of late he cursed himself for the ways he had helped drill into Robert, ways that rendered him unable to ask help if he had need of it, as Jerome was certain he had now.

Unmoving he sat at the table and Martha, peeping round the door to find out if it were time to clear away the remains of the meal, encountered a glare that had her still muttering apologies beneath her breath when she reached her kitchen. But it was not Martha's face that Jerome saw at all, it was that of a small, brown girl who had showed him kindness and had approached Robert for assistance in a way that was foreign to both of them. Angrily he told himself that for all he knew Robert might well have dismissed her plea – and the fate of her wretched family – as easily as he would have had everyone believe.

Challenged, Jerome could have put forward no acceptable reason to support his theory that it was the Woodfall family that was disturbing Robert. All he knew was that a light sleeper of fastidious habits had lain down still wearing muddy boots and had not stirred when someone stood over him. Putting this together with his own reaction to Cecily Woodfall he feared that Robert had at last found someone who had awakened in him emotions until now suppressed, and she in the midst of a family catastrophe. What right had he to interfere? Even as Martha knew her place, so he and Robert kept their lives separate. Jerome covered his face with his usable hand. He was old before his time, old and ailing, and ever since Robert had so generously accepted their blood relationship he had found himself unable to resist caring more and more about what affected him. In all the years since his return to England he had been most scrupulous in asking nothing for himself. Now, for Robert's sake, he must try to get word privately with Burghley before the day was out.

He told Martha that he might not be back until evening.

George Bailey wished very much that he had kept his head down on his chest and passed Amos Jenkins without so much as a word of greeting. But he had not. At sight of the coarse red face, looking happier than it had for many a long month, his talkative nature had got the better of him and he had stood directly in his path. As a result he was pinned against a rough wall, unable to breathe anywhere near as easily as he wished, and with a nasty feeling that his straining toes were not touching the muddy ground. His old woman was right – not that he would admit it in a thousand years – always telling him to keep his mouth shut, she was. Get you into trouble one day, she said; it looked to George as if that day had arrived.

And to make it worse, he could not for the life of him work out just what he had done to offend, just spoken to a man who often in the past had been glad to pay for snippets of gossip, small pieces of information. George, in his misery, became aware that he was being shaken; more than that, his head had bumped against the wall behind him in distinctly painful fashion.

'Now, George,' said the hoarse voice close to his ear, 'slowly now, tell me again what you just said, word for word.'

George, the grip on his doublet being slightly loosened, gulped in air, took a quick look to left and right for any possible way of escape, found none, and obeyed.

'I only said, "One Woodfall less to be hanged and gutted after last night," sir, that's all.'

Once again his teeth rattled in his head.

'The other bit, fool,' snarled his tormentor, 'the bit that came after that!'

'Can't remember what I said, sir, not exact. Let me go, please. I never meant no 'arm!'

The back of his head came into contact with the wall again, so hard that George heard the noise resound all along the alley in which they stood and was sure his skull had cracked.

'Cooper, you said,' prompted Jenkins, with such venom that George's memory returned on the spot.

'Oh, that, sir! One Woodfall less to be hanged and gutted after last night – like I said to Master Cooper when I let him out of the cell.'

Jenkins's grip relaxed completely and gratefully George stood on his own two feet once more.

'Well now, George, suppose you tell me what Master Cooper has to do with the Woodfalls, eh?'

'Dunno, honest I don't.'

332

'Neither do I, George. But he visited Edward Woodfall, you say. Begin by telling me how long he was there.'

'An hour or so, I reckon, give or take . . .'

'Hear what went on, did you?'

'No, no, sir, that I did not! More than my life's worth to be caught listening when that one's around, as well you must know. Besides, I had me rounds to do, same as always. Got his pass, he has; not for me to stop him.'

'Comes often to see prisoners, does he, George?' The hoarse voice had grown deceptively gentle.

'Not above once or twice that I recall. Not his job, sir, as I take it.'

'Then why last night, my lad, and why Woodfall?'

Unable to answer the question but afraid to remain silent, George supplied, 'Furious he was when I went to let him out. White with temper and yelling that he hadn't got the answers to his questions. Never saw anything like it! He'd thrown water all over the prisoner – no chance of rousing *him*, and so I told him. Gone for good, I says, and – and he swore and threw the bucket at the wall and stormed out. That's all, sir, every bit of it, honest it is.'

A small coin flipped into the air, to be caught in Bailey's eager palm, and he was off as fast as his legs would carry him. Keep out of that one's reach in future, he would. High time to be looking for some other person who would be suitably grateful for whatever he had to tell, without treating a body like a dog.

Jenkins stood where Bailey left him and the content that had filled him before the encounter was gone, as surely as if it had floated away in the runnels of muddy water about his feet. This way and that his brain whirled, without reaching any conclusion except that it was time Master High and Mighty Cooper was dealt with! Such a perfect plan it had been; every detail had fallen into place so easily, and people into his hands. It would have restored his reputation completely. What had taken Cooper to visit Edward Woodfall? His only connection with the affair had been to question the girl, and a waste of time that had been! Cooper never swore and Jenkins could not recall the last time he had seen him in a rage. He had pretended anger to fool the jailer or he had indeed lost control of himself. The implications of either alternative were not pleasant to Amos Jenkins.

There was nothing he could do. Robert knew it to be true, but that had not saved him a night pacing his room until mental as well as physical exhaustion felled him across his bed. One fact returned to him over and over: Jenkins himself had gone to make the Woodfall arrests and that in itself was unusual. Why? Because he could not trust anyone else to find evidence that wasn't there? And why the Woodfall family?

There was nothing he could do. Nothing he *wanted* to do! He began to compile the agenda for a meeting Burghley had called for the following week, at any other time so routine a matter that whilst he did it half his mind would have been on the next task to hand. But today he could not concentrate. Three starts he had already made when Burghley passed the open door, a clerk following him carrying Privy Council papers. Robert made a fourth start, spoiled paper and quill point alike and gave up. He left in his turn. No-one questioned; Master Cooper held a position the definition of which was blurred about the edges. He came and went as he chose.

Quite what he had in mind as he made his way towards Sir Francis Walsingham's office he was not sure. If Burghley were gone to a meeting of the Council, there too would be Walsingham and it was hardly likely that he would be allowed to examine papers in his absence. But he held on his way and the question did not arise, for he reached his destination just in time to see Sir Francis go back into his own room.

There had been a time when, with an eye to his successor as Chief Clerk, Henry Loader, who was getting near to retirement, had borne Robert Cooper in mind. As dedicated a man as himself, Loader thought, the only difficulty being whether Burghley would let him go. But the young man had made strides since those days. Loader smiled as the tall, spare figure stopped before his table, answered a polite enquiry regarding the health of the ailing Mistress Loader. He informed Robert that Her Majesty had been unable to attend a Council meeting today and as it concerned several matters on which she was determined to have her vehement say, it had been cancelled. He saw no reason, therefore, why he should not ask if Sir Francis could spare time to speak to Master Cooper.

Minutes later Robert was in the small office Sir Francis found suited him so well, interrupting what seemed to him to be an unusual flurry of movement. Without obviously doing so, he noted the stacks of paper on Walsingham's desk, the very way the man himself was seated, and knew that for some reason he would not have to explain what had brought him here.

As neat as ever the papers, any one ready to bring to hand at a moment's need, but in the middle of the desk were ones Robert knew immediately were those in which he was interested. Walsingham, who habitually sat back in his chair when talking, fingertips to fingertips, like some deliberating bishop, was leaning forward so that his hands shielded these particular papers from view rather in the way Robert had sometimes guarded his childhood lessons from Jerome's sharp eyes when he was afraid that they were not up to his tutor's high standards. In those days the hands had as often as not been helped to move by the swift, stinging tap of a cane. Since that course was hardly open to him here, he was about to say something he hoped would sound more respectful than the questions pounding through his head, when Sir Francis forestalled him.

'The Woodfall affair,' he said, and it was a statement, not a question. 'Sit down, Cooper, and read this.'

It was a report, signed by Jenkins, although not in his hand entirely, and it told Robert nothing he did not already know or suspect. Following information laid and evidence found at Highwoods Manor and Abbey House, Sussex, Sir Thomas Woodfall and his brother Edward had been arrested, taken to the Tower, and questioned. Attached were their confessions. Jenkins was of the opinion that Martin Woodfall, a nephew taken up at the same time, knew nothing that would be of value. No need to read Edward Woodfall's confession, Robert knew well enough what that contained, and a quick look at the sheet signed by Sir Thomas set him grimacing. A textbook confession, any one of a hundred Robert had read in his time. He doubted, very much he doubted, noting the shakiness of the name at the end, whether Sir Thomas had the faintest idea what he was being asked to sign. 'Just your name here, sir, and you can go home. All a mistake,' someone – probably Jenkins – had said reassuringly, and the poor fool, driven clean out of his wits by fear, had signed his own death warrant.

The torn letter Edward Woodfall had mentioned was missing from the accompanying packet but the remainder made his point well enough. Not only were they old; despite efforts to age the superscription by rubbing dust into the paper, the ink differed noticeably from that in the body of the letters. Robert, who could well remember a time when Jenkins would have beaten anyone producing such pathetic forgeries half to death, refolded them neatly and laid them back on the desk.

Rather as if he were commenting upon a junior clerk's untidiness, he said, 'Slipshod in the extreme, sir.'

'Fabricated from beginning to end,' said Walsingham grimly. 'Had I not been sick the matter could hardly have progressed so far without my knowledge. How do you find yourself implicated, Cooper?'

Quietly Robert said, 'Because of what Cecily Woodfall told me when I spoke to her – on your instructions – I went to her father's questioning. What he said then caused me to visit him in his cell last night. I was with him when he died. He was undoubtedly innocent.' He paused. 'With respect, sir, may I ask whether the family first came under suspicion through one of your regular informants?'

Sir Francis snorted. 'I received a miserable anonymous letter that looked like nothing so much as a malicious attempt to bring ill fortune on the Woodfalls. That was what made the Queen determined to visit Sir Thomas. Women treasure memories of youthful – er – romances. She forbade me to take action on it. Your being a member of her retinue was the only concession I could obtain from her.'

'Jenkins saw the letter, sir?'

Sir Francis looked him directly in the eyes. 'I gave it to Loader for safe keeping.'

'And is it possible that Jenkins . . .?'

'No need to beat about the bushes, Cooper. How else would he have fastened on to the Woodfalls?'

'Surely even he would not make a random search in hopes of finding something . . . He saw Loader with it, perhaps?'

'If you remember, Cooper, he brought you the message that you were to accompany the Queen. It was then he saw a letter which appeared to be important, just when he was casting about for some *tour de force* that would show me he was still up to his job after the Lawrence fiasco.'

'So in hopes of saving his drink-sodden neck he came back, read the letter and arrested the Woodfall men, using evidence he provided himself?'

'Except,' Sir Francis pointed out precisely, 'except the altar ornaments. Those I believe he did in fact find hidden at Edward Woodfall's house.'

'I would rather say "put away", sir. As many another family the length and breadth of the land keeps relics from the old days. Not for religious use but because of their beautiful workmanship.'

Sir Francis overcame his personal puritanical preferences sufficiently to agree that this might be so.

'You have faced Jenkins with this, sir?'

'I have not, nor shall I, but I cannot afford to employ people who are sinking so fast into untrustworthiness as he. No-one, we should all remember, is indispensable.'

Robert accepted the implied warning with bowed head. That Walsingham had known the nature of his errand before he arrived he put down to the fact that someone must have passed on details of his visit to Edward Woodfall the previous evening. What surprised him was that he had been allowed to question the Secretary of State as he had. That he owed such latitude to Burghley he could not know.

Leaving the Council side by side with his colleague Burghley had said, in considerable irritation, 'Some time, Frank, you must tell me exactly what you used Robert Cooper for in the Woodfall affair. You've cost me the services of one of my best men.'

Robert ventured one last question. 'And now, sir? Knowing that innocent men have been trapped into confession by a rogue?'

Sir Francis took control of the interview finally, firmly. 'Now, nothing. I cannot call one man back to life, nor restore the wits of another who appears to have become totally insane and cannot live long.'

'There is the young Woodfall arrested at the same time, sir. And what of the womenfolk left behind?'

Still Sir Francis was patient. 'Rare though cases of this kind are, Cooper, you know what must happen. For the good of the state I shall use the situation as it stands. Information begins to come to hand concerning a genuine widespread and well-organized plot to bring the Stuart woman to the throne within the next twelve-month or so. Anything that can be done to forestall it is legitimate in my eyes. Thomas Woodfall was a personal friend of the Queen: it may be – and I pray it will – that because she feels his defection so deeply she will agree to move against Mary Stuart now instead of later. Two confessions, two deaths. Neither will have been in vain. Upon us lies the onus of keeping this country at peace and Protestant, and it is not always a pleasant job. I have no need to tell you that.'

He had not indeed. It was what Robert had all along known must happen, what he had been fending off with the shield of his reiterated 'there is nothing I can do'. He was sufficiently well acquainted with the almost personal animosity Sir Francis bore the Scottish queen to know that he would use any weapon he could to bring her down, nor care overly whether it were tarnished or no. The fate of Martin Woodfall and a parcel of women was of small consequence. One was not even worthy a trial and execution, would die slowly of neglect in some cell – that, too, he had known to happen, nor had such things worried him on other occasions as it did now; the others had friends who would see them housed and fed.

Robert rose to his feet. 'Thank you for giving me so much of your time, Sir Francis, and for taking me into your confidence.'

He was bowing, ready to leave, when Sir Francis's thin voice said, 'No blame for what has happened rests upon you, Cooper. You must not think it.'

'Thank you, sir. May I ask one more question? Who is likely to get the Woodfall estates, do you think?'

Sir Francis permitted himself a smile. 'Since Her Majesty has no need of gifts to sweeten her favourites at present, they are to go to the highest bidder, and that being so are likely to remain in local hands. One Matthew Stone's offering price is hardly likely to be bettered.' He paused, frowning, and his tone became wry. 'Lord Burghley would say that I see plotters behind every tree, but it does seem to me that that young man has benefited greatly from the downfall of this family. Take it all in all it is an uninteresting property, fit only for a minor gentleman, and I have no time – or wish – to pursue an enquiry further.'

Once more Robert bowed. No time, no wish, because the evil has served your ends, he thought. His hand was reaching out towards the door latch when, as if something had just occurred to him, he stopped.

'May I see the report once more, sir?' He ran his eyes down it quickly, turned over the page and back again, searching for some particular point and failing to find it.

'Something is missing,' he said calmly. 'Martin Woodfall has a twin brother, Walter. He returns on the *Larkspur*, which I believe may already have docked at Plymouth. He could be troublesome.'

'Thank you, Cooper. The matter shall be attended to.' Even as Robert left, Walsingham was making a neat note to remind himself – and someone else – that immediate action was needed.

Slowly Robert walked back to his own office. What, he asked himself, and shied away from the answer, had made him betray Walter Woodfall? Having accepted Walsingham's dictat, had he made sure that a loose end was tied up? Or was it to make certain that Edward Woodfall's dying wish would be respected and Cecily not made unhappy by her cousin Wat? Walsingham had never for one instant doubted that he would connive at the destruction of an innocent family. He was trusted, and with cause. For the good of the kingdom use must be made of this opportunity lest worse befall, and the fact that it left a minor member of Lord Burghley's staff feeling filthy to the depths of his soul was a small price to pay. The matter, Robert told himself, was over. And so he believed for some four hours.

He completed the troublesome agenda with ease, worked steadily on until, in mid-afternoon, with the November light already beginning to fade, he was summoned into Lord Burghley's office. No reason was given but he took with him papers he thought would be required. But when he knocked at the door the voice that bade him enter, although it was familiar, was not the one he expected to hear.

In the large padded chair behind the desk, swallowed up by its size, sat a young man who had become part of the department of late. He was in his early twenties and Lord Burghley was his father. He appeared to be without official appointment but was always there, observing, noting. General talk said that when the time came for Burghley to step down his son would succeed him. Many were the malicious remarks made – by those with but a fraction of Robert Cecil's intellectual brilliance – concerning his dedication to work which, they sneered, was his substitute for the normal enjoyments of youth denied him by a twisted body. Great was the speculation as to whether Her Majesty, who was known to favour the handsome and physically perfect, would appoint to high office one whose attributes lay solely in the mind. Yet many people had decided that where Robert Cecil went power would follow, a fact that meant much to the hangers-on who these days constituted so large a part of the court. To his face at least he was increasingly treated with deference.

His thin, clever face was little changed in feature since the day when two boys had met briefly in a shelter by the river; he had looked much more than his years then. Now he seldom smiled. Already the burden of responsibility lay heavily upon him. Without preamble he came to what was for him a small matter among many.

'Master Cooper, I need a man, a confidential clerk by title, to be more than that when called upon. I have had my eye on you for some time and my father has today agreed to release you.' His voice quickened. 'There is much to do, Cooper, and I intend to do it, for this monarch and for the next. Come with me!'

Transfer your allegiance to me – one ambitious, ruthless young man working for another – rise with me to higher things, things that belong to the future, was what he was really saying.

'I accept, sir. Thank you.'

A smile flickered across Cecil's face and he sat back at his ease. 'Good! I leave for France tonight. Finish off what work you cannot pass on to others and join me as soon as you can. I expect to be away for upwards of a year. It should prove interesting.'

The interview was over; Robert bowed and was about to leave when the other's thin, cold voice asked, 'How long a leave of absence do you require to set right what little can be set right?'

If the sudden question were a test to discover how his new employee coped with the unexpected, Cecil could only have been gratified at Robert's reaction.

'With the roads in the state they are in at this time of year, not less than a week, sir,' he said calmly.

'Then you should be back here in, shall we say, eight days' time? Sir Francis is certain that you will do nothing to jeopardize what has been done in the affair. That must still stand.'

'Of course.'

Cecil leaned forward so low over his papers that nothing but the top of his auburn head was visible, but Robert stood his ground.

'Might I ask how you know, sir? Sir Francis does not, I believe.'

'That Sir Thomas is your father?' Cecil's mouth quirked at one corner. No need to admit that until that morning neither he nor his father had known any such thing. He could still hear the slurred voice that had issued from an ailing body, 'I ask your help for Cooper, my lord, although he would not thank me for doing so. Sir Thomas Woodfall is his father, and although he will do his duty unfailingly the matter has been hard on him. As for his mother, the boy's true name is Robert Emory, as once mine was. I owe this much to him at least.'

'You are correct, he does not, but my intelligence work is better than his!'

Robert murmured some sort of thanks and was once more turning away when Cecil said, as if the thought had just occurred to him, 'You may need to watch your back. You know where my house is? Go there and ask for Peters. He will supply two men to ride with you. One never knows: he – the worm, that is – may turn when he finds he is discovered. You may tell him – the worm – that he has what he wants!'

Robert Cooper walked down the narrow, wood-panelled passageway in as near a state of confusion as had ever been his. The Woodfall family, it seemed, would not leave him in peace. Not only did Master Cecil know of his relationship to Sir Thomas; he appeared to entertain much the same suspicion as to the original source of their troubles. Robert saw and appreciated what others feared in the hunchbacked youth. Not only had he a good intelligence service, he possessed the rare ability to make what might appear to be a leap into the dark and arrive at the correct destination. Cynically he supposed that this leave of absence, the offer of assistance, could be designed to place him securely in Cecil's power, under an obligation, but such consideration could wait. He had been given a chance to see that Matthew Stone came by some part at least of his deserts and might, at the same time, make secure the lives of the Woodfall womenfolk.

Obedient to the orders of the man who paid him, a youth

stood in the growing dusk, pressed close against the wall in the mouth of an alley close to Jerome's house. Trinity Street was deserted and Robert's footsteps rang firm and loud on the cobblestones of the narrow walkway as he approached. From beneath his doublet the youth drew his dagger and stood ready. The footsteps, unfaltering, were upon him and he had raised his hand when suddenly they quickened, there came the swirl of a heavy cloak about his face as victim twisted round to meet would-be assailant. The stroke intended for Robert's back caught him above the elbow of his left arm, tearing a gash, long but not deep. Then, faster than he could think, the youth found Cooper behind him and a strength he could not gainsay had him down on his knees. The knife clattered to the ground and he clawed with both hands at the arm about his throat that pulled him backwards over a knee pressed uncomfortably into the small of his back.

'Fool! Did no-one ever teach you to make certain you cast no shadow when you lay in wait?'

As he spoke, Robert, feeling blood trickling warm down his arm, reached sideways, scooped up his assailant's dagger, long and scalpel-sharp. For a moment he watched the flickering light from a nearby torch play up and down its length then, holding it against the youth's face, continued almost conversationally, 'Well now, Gregory, which phial did he dip this into?' and knew he had no cause to worry. Gregory showed no fear that the knife might touch him, not even fear of the man who had outwitted him. In the years when he had regularly visited Martha at Jerome's house he had seen Robert Cooper times enough with his head in a book, docilely learning, never answering back when sternly rebuked; his present performance notwithstanding he regarded him as rather soft.

A certain injured pride sounded in his voice: 'I'm good enough without that.'

'Not this time, lad. Tell Jenkins so when you meet again.' The quiet voice was almost soothing; there was nothing in it to warn Gregory to struggle. Yet as he spoke Robert dropped the dagger; both hands moved to the youth's neck, tightened,

343

twisted. There came a sharp crack and without a sound the body of his attacker went limp against him.

So much for one of Jenkins's young hopefuls who had lasted less than two weeks with Jerome. Not a brain in his head, Jenkins had agreed, laughing, as he kicked him out into the street. But poor scholars might make good assassins. Robert dragged the body into the alleyway out of sight, pulled his cloak tight about his wounded arm and walked on as if nothing untoward had happened.

CHAPTER IX

Martin might have warned Rose that Cecily was to be looked out for and avoided at all costs on the rare occasions when she lost her temper, but it had never occurred to him to do so and so she cowered into a corner of their bedchamber with her hands over her face whilst Cecily, like some belligerent boy, stood over her and fiercely urged her to get up so that she might have the pleasure of hitting her again. Her anger was the greater because what Rose had just said was precisely what family loyalty had had Cecily striving not to think ever since their world fell apart. That her father and Martin were innocent she had believed from the outset, with a faith nothing would ever shake, but she had been unable to still the small voice that whispered that all that had happened might have been the result of Sir Thomas, goaded on by his ambitious wife, doing something too wicked and foolish to contemplate.

She had done her best to push the idea down into her sub-conscious but now, when news had come that Sir Thomas was tried and condemned for confessed treason and Rose had collapsed in hysterics, wanting to know whatever would happen to her and – a poor second – to her mother, because of his actions, Cecily had rounded on her like a young fury. *Her* father's brother would not do such a thing and whatever happened to Rose and Lady Woodfall would be no more than they deserved. Gripping her shrieking cousin by her hair and shaking her back and forth like a rag doll, she had

345

left the wretched girl in no doubt that if she begged for her bread in the gutter no-one would turn aside to give her a farthing!

The fight was ended by the arrival of Taylor, bearing a pile of clean linen. Dourly she informed them that she could hear the noise at the foot of the stairs, that they should both be ashamed of themselves. At sound of the gruff voice Cecily came to herself and remorse flooded through her. She hastened to make amends in the only way she could, aware even whilst she offered that Rose would only think she was being accorded her due. Was it any surprise that her first thoughts should be for herself? She had been spoiled her life long, thought the world turned for her benefit alone.

'Come now, Rose. Sit down. Let me straighten your hair. Now!' Cecily's voice took on the ringing tones with which Aunt Agnes addressed erring maids. Cecily had lately found, to her surprise, that the method worked on Rose too.

Obediently Rose sat, allowed Cecily to find and remove the pins from her tousled hair, closed her eyes as the gentle combing began. In a moment of self-pity Cecily wished that someone nearby cared enough to do the same for her and that she might be so easily soothed. There had been no lack of people eager to tell her that she must expect the news that day had brought, even in respect of her own father and Martin, but some instinct of self-preservation prevented her from dwelling on the possibility. What of her father, she had asked, and received no reply. Worry for her mother no longer kept her wakeful; grief seemed a thing impossible. Somehow she gathered to herself strength to live one day at a time, conquering fear, forbidding hope. The part of her that loved and cared for other people was numb. Even now she could not entirely believe what she had been told.

To eager-eyed observers, and there were many, she showed no signs of the emotion that held Rose in her room day after day, red-eyed and sobbing. There were times when Cecily stood outside her body and watched it go its determined way as if it were a stranger. It took its appointed place in the Queen's chambers, was screamed at or praised or ignored, as were the other maids, and did its duty faithfully and well. The insults and calumnies heaped upon it by those who thought it wrong that they be asked to associate with the daughters of traitors it ignored with a strength born of sureness of its own absolute right. Only once had it gone down on its knees to Majesty and begged to be allowed to go home. And the reply had strengthened resolve as kindness would never have done. 'You have no home. Be grateful that I give you both a roof over your heads.' And all the time the piercing royal eyes watched for the first sign of a breakdown in the body that was Cecily Woodfall. They watched in vain; the round face remained outwardly calm, save for the occasional flicker of proud pity for anyone who could think ill of its family. Legs curtseyed and fingers worked on the everlasting embroidery demanded of them. Then, when the day was over, back to the cold room below the roof where Rose, unable to command herself, spent her days heaping up complaints to spring on her weary cousin. Cecily had borne moans, wails, had soothed the terrified girl, assuring her that of course Matthew Stone would still wish to marry her, laughing away her fears that soon they themselves would be taken off to prison, until today when she had heard another speak aloud what she herself dreaded might be true and she had flown at the cause, determined to silence it.

Hope of Wat had not outlasted the first shock of Lady Patchett's news. She had turned instinctively to him as the only free man in her immediate family; now she wished passionately that she had never visited Master Jerome, prayed that she had not brought the law down on another innocent head. With a heartache that saw him clearly for the first time, she admitted to herself that even if Master Cooper troubled to find Wat – and she had heard no word from him – it was unlikely that Wat would do anything to endanger his own neck on behalf of a family he had deserted. He would look after himself, as he had always done. For the first time Cecily, her long infatuation so cruelly killed, wondered how Martin had come to have so untrustworthy a twin.

From the blotched face between her soothing hands came

a low whimper, like that of a child. 'I want to go home. Take me home, Cecily. I don't like it here.'

It had constantly been instilled into her all her life that she was more to be regarded than her nearby cousins, but now Rose's overweening pride had vanished. She wanted attention and comfort in her unhappiness and believed, as young children believe, that it was easy to come by. She put up tear-wet hands to grasp her cousin's wrists and Cecily freed herself gently.

'We have to stay here, my dear,' she said, and might have been a nursemaid with a cosseted charge. 'At least for the time being. All will be well.'

'But you won't leave me tonight? I don't like it when you're not here and there's only one candle. The shadows come to fetch me . . . Stay with me . . .'

Determination notwithstanding, Cecily's irritation bade fair to come back. 'I cannot. I have to attend Her Majesty. Remember I told you that there is to be dancing. So many people arriving for the Accession Day games . . .' Tell a fairy tale to a child; anything, anything that might divert her.

'How can you? How can you, when you know what she's done to us?' Rose twisted round on her stool; swollen eyelids opened wide and eyes Martin dubbed vacant accused the cousin who when they stood side by side was a head shorter than she. Briskly Cecily stopped the lament that was about to begin.

'I have not the faintest idea what Her Majesty has done, but I do know that my father and Martin – and your father too – have done nothing wrong, and I will not shame them by giving way.'

Rose's mouth, ready to ask, 'Not even when you hear they have been condemned also?' snapped shut at the look on her cousin's face and Cecily went on, so offhandedly that she marvelled at herself, 'Besides, colour and warmth and food is much better than this miserable room. Come with me!'

She saw Rose's face quiver and added hastily, knowing it to be one of few things that might stir the girl into activity and disliking herself for the manipulation, 'It seems to me sad to waste that splendid pink gown of yours. At least put it on so that I may see what it looks like. But *not* until you have bathed your eyes in cold water. Hurry now!'

They went down to the Great Hall together, and if Cecily felt that she was leading a reluctant – albeit splendidly dressed – child by the hand, she gave no sign of it. So different they were in looks and build that no-one would have taken them for members of the same family, a fact that had always pleased Rose greatly. Fair and pretty in pink brocade, a ruff of silver lace high about her neck, she had overcome her tears, had hidden their traces beneath dabs of cosmetic that would do nothing at all for Cecily's complexion, which still showed brown against a hooped gown of pale green brocade, its bodice stiff with tiny white beads arranged in sprays of flowers. She had been so proud of the gown, made for her when they first arrived in London, had looked forward to taking it home to show off to her mother and sisters.

'Stay close to me,' she said firmly, 'and do remember that the Queen cannot abide to hear you sniff! Smile, all the time smile. You have no reason to hang your head.'

They took their appointed places behind the Queen's chair, near enough to respond immediately if she required anything, far enough away not to overhear the lavish compliments paid Her Majesty by guests honoured at being seated in close proximity to the royal person. The crowded hall was loud with music and voices; colours whirled and twisted before Cecily's eyes and she smiled as she had bidden Rose to smile. The Queen herself was not dancing tonight; therefore none of her young attendants moved. Then, suddenly, Andrew Stratton was bowing low before Her Majesty, was daringly seeking, had received, permission to ask Mistress Woodfall to join in the next dance.

This young man, fair and handsome, was beginning to be troublesome. Twice recently Lord Pemberton had approached the Queen requesting that he be sent away, that she thus end the most unsuitable courtship of his daughter Lettice who, when the time came, must marry someone of her own standing and her father's choosing. Bored for the moment by the conversation in her ear, Her Majesty took time for a small personal pleasure, said sweetly, maliciously, 'Most certainly, Master Stratton. If I were dancing tonight you should have the pleasure of *my* company for your gall, if for no other reason. *Rose*, come here, Master Stratton wishes to dance with you!'

The boy dissembled well; who would have guessed from his manner that he had been presented with the wrong Mistress Woodfall? He offered his arm to Rose as if she were the one person in all the world he wished to be with, led her to her place in the long row of ladies, took his place opposite her. They bowed, curtseyed, began the intricate patterns the music dictated, all without his smile slipping once. It was, Her Majesty thought, a pity he was not better born and that certain favours she might need to ask of Lord Pemberton in the near future made it inadvisable for her to antagonize him by saying that she saw no reason why Stratton should not make an excellent son-in-law.

So intent was she on watching the results of her unkind stratagem that she missed a sight that might have afforded her less amusement, if more interest. The guards at her back parted for a second, a black-clad arm came between them and drew Cecily Woodfall gently back through an arras that was barely disturbed by her passing. Lettice Pemberton stepped sideways to fill the gap, the guards stared ahead so woodenly that no-one would have guessed that all had been previously arranged, and the dance went on.

There was no element of force in the touch that urged Cecily backwards through a concealed door into a quiet, dimly lit gallery. She was there, face to face with Robert Cooper, almost before she realized anything was happening. He bowed, battling with a sudden impulse to abandon the whole crazy scheme that had brought him in search of her. Calm and self-possessed she stood before him; still, in spite of everything that had happened, so innocent, so trusting.

He said, 'If I ask you to accompany me unquestioning, will you believe me when I swear that you have nothing to fear?'

Unhesitatingly she agreed, as he could have wagered she would.

350

'Then put on a warm gown and cloak. I will wait for you here.'

The green brocade of which she had been so proud was suddenly an encumbrance. 'I cannot unlace myself and the maid will not be in my room. If you wait until this dance finishes, I will ask Rose to help me.'

He held her back, replying sternly, 'That you will not! The less that young woman knows of anything the better. Any help you need you must accept from me.'

It was free from any embarrassment. He accompanied her to her chamber and she stood in the passage with her back to him whilst his fingers moved downwards, untying, unlacing, efficient and impersonal. Then she closed the door on him and hastily put on the brown gown in which she had visited Trinity Street. It was the warmest thing she possessed and Taylor had cleansed it of the mud she had carried back that day. With the woollen cloak over it and her feet in the stout, buckled shoes she had so often worn at home she was ready.

Quietly they walked back through the Palace, past other revellers who had slipped away from the general throng, among servants scurrying hither and thither with food and great flagons of wine, between guards at the main door, across a courtyard and down to watersteps where a boat was waiting, an oarsman in attendance. From him Robert took his long cloak, wrapped it about himself, pulled the hood forward so that his face was hidden, then stood back as the boatman handed Cecily into the bobbing craft and she took her seat.

And so along London's river for the second time, but downstream now, through waters crowded even at this late hour, onward until they passed between the pillars of London Bridge where the water ran high, smooth and swift. Her companion sat beside her, leaning slightly to one side as if to avoid even casual contact, and his shrouded black form would not have encouraged questions even had they not been forbidden. She was just wondering whether she might ask how much further they had to travel when they began to thread their way to the side of the waterway, making

351

for steps that seemed to Cecily broader and better lighted than most they had passed, and she caught her breath.

Even had she tried to speak, her dry throat would have emitted no sound. A short time before she had been in a hall filled with gaily dressed ladies and gentlemen, in the presence of the Queen of England; now the Tower of London loomed over her. How many times in the past weeks had Rose babbled on this subject, swearing that the interrogators would come for them when they had finished with their parents? Stoutly Cecily had laughed the idea to scorn; now she could not, despite Master Cooper's assurance. What better way to get her here quietly, than by such a trick?

Robert rose to his feet and as if in answer to her unspoken thought repeated, 'I promise you that you have nothing to fear.'

Cecily stepped ashore. 'Nothing to fear' was meaningless in connection with such a place. For one moment she wondered if she were being taken to see her father. It took her all her time to keep up with Robert's long strides. All she could do was to accept his word. Side by side they crossed a drawbridge over a moat that was no more than a mass of shifting, sparkling stars in the light of flaring torches about the gateway. Challenged by a sentry, Robert put back his hood, said a brief word. There was no hindrance to their entrance, and as the heavy door crashed to behind them and was locked, Cecily darted one frightened glance over her shoulder. It sounded so very final, even though the light that streamed from the nearby guardhouse looked friendly and warm.

From the doorway George Bailey looked hopefully at the young man he had seen the night before. Would Master Cooper prove to be as generous in return for information as Jenkins had been? He essayed a smile, received a cold stare that gave him an uncomfortable feeling that his morning's dealings with Jenkins were no secret, and hastily retreated inside.

At an inner lodge Robert said, 'Woodfall. I'll take the keys, Joe. No need for you to stir,' and the warder nodded into the darkness, said, 'Thank you, sir. At the end on the left, it is.' He handed over a lighted lantern, returned gratefully to his brazier with scarcely a glance at the girl who huddled there in her cloak.

'Come!' Robert slowed his pace and it was as if an invisible hand were placed beneath Cecily's elbow so that she took heart. Across courtyards they went, between buildings, with never a pause, in quietness broken only by the noise of their feet, distant calls from the river outside the forbidding walls and once, so that Cecily gasped with shock, the roaring of a beast somewhere close at hand. She had forgotten that the Tower housed the royal menagerie!

Robert unlocked a heavy door set in a tower wall, waited for Cecily to join him and closed it behind them. The dim light of his lantern cast shadows up to vaulted ceilings and across stone walls; shadows like enormous birds, swooping above their heads. The coldness within the building struck even through Cecily's thick cloak and she shivered. Robert paused at the top of a flight of steps that plunged downwards into total darkness.

'Take my hand. The steps are narrow and the damp makes them treacherous. Stay as close to the wall as you can.' Cecily gripped a hard, gloved hand and, holding her skirts tight about her legs, followed as carefully as she could. Even with his support she felt unsafe and rubbed her shoulder along the rough stonework for steadiness.

There was a stagnant smell about the place such as she had smelled at home in hot, dry summers when the water in the millpond shrank and left bare wide, muddy banks, and she wondered briefly whether they could be under the river. Water dripped incessantly from the roof and where the lantern light caught the walls they gleamed smooth and wet like bright green silk. But stagnant water was not all there was to smell. As they came to the bottom of the staircase, the nauseating stench of animal waste and filth became mixed with that of dampness, and Cecily retched. In all that place the only sound was the shuffle of their footsteps and the dripping of water, yet on each side of the passageway in which they now stood – and so close together that she wondered how small must be the rooms to which they gave access – Cecily saw door after heavy wooden door, each with a small hole in it, iron-barred.

Robert raised his lantern and peered in through the grille of the last cell before, for one instant, he turned back to Cecily. Although his face was once more hidden by his hood she could feel him staring at her, as if he regretted his action and would immediately take her back. The moment passed; he took a pitch-headed torch from a bracket on the wall, lit it from the lantern, unlocked the cell door and put his shoulder to it. It opened slowly, protestingly, with a harsh grating of wood over stone, and the wave of foul air that rushed out made Cecily hide her face in her hands. Himself untroubled, Robert entered the cell, leaving her to follow. It was a small, windowless stone room, so narrow that standing in its centre it was possible with outstretched arms to touch opposite walls, and long enough only to allow a man to lie at full length. The floor was piled with straw and in that straw lay a huddled figure that made no movement at their coming.

Robert took one stride forward, would have stirred the body with the toe of his boot, but in that instant the flaring light showed Cecily all she needed to see and with a fierce, 'Do not dare touch him!' she had snatched the torch and was on her knees. The fair head was dirty, unkempt and stubble-bearded as she had never seen it, but unmistakable.

'Martin!' she breathed. 'Oh, Martin!'

He lay with his knees drawn up almost to his chin, shuddering uncontrollably, naked save for the rags of the working clothes he had worn when they dragged him away, in filthy straw through which something scuttled and was gone. Fetters about wrists and ankles had chafed his skin so that sores had formed and the flesh above and below them was red and swollen.

Above her, Robert's voice said, 'Give the torch to me. Do you want to set everything alight?' But although she obeyed all her attention was on her cousin. Without rising she stripped off her cloak and wrapped it around him, raising his head gently, carefully into her lap.

He was icy cold to her touch, cold as the damp, oozing stones on which he lay. She smoothed the lank hair back off his face, bent to kiss closed black-ringed eyes, and she picked stalks of wet straw off his chest. It seemed impossible that this half-starved, frozen man, whose very bones showed through his skin, could ever have been the sturdy, laughing boy by whose side she had worked and played so innocently.

Robert jammed the torch into a bracket on the wall and went out into the passage. Even the noise of the door closing meant nothing to Cecily; he doubted if she heard it. Why should he be surprised? Dock leaves for a lady nettle-stung, salve for the sore fingers of a man she had seen but once, a cloak she needed herself to cover a man dying of cold. The girl was a born comforter. The girl was a *fool*, he told himself bitterly and did not for an instant believe it; he was the fool! He leaned against the wall, never feeling its dampness, and closed his eyes, cradling left arm in right in an attempt to ease the throbbing wound, and waited.

Inside the cell Cecily shifted her position, drawing Martin higher into her lap, so that for a time at least the warmth of her body might come between him and the floor. Light from the torch flamed across his face and he roused, dragged his chained and shaking hands from beneath the cloak and over his eyes, with a moan of pain.

'Martin . . . speak to me, please, Martin . . .' Those who marvelled at her stoicism would not have recognized her now. Feeling had returned in full measure, and although it brought pain there was also a strange, never before experienced sense of joy. Her voice trembled, broke in a sob against which she fought with all her might, and the sound reached him, pierced his numbness so that for a moment he opened his shaded eyes, squinting to lessen the pain.

'Cec? Is it you?' Pale lips moved in the ghost of a smile. 'I knew you would come if I called long enough,' then, as consciousness returned fully, on a rising note of horror, 'Not you too! Please God, not you! They cannot! Not you!'

Cecily hastened to reassure him. 'No, no. Close your

355

eyes and be still. I was brought to see you by – a friend, that is all.'

Manacled hands reached out, felt the familiar woollen dress, found it dry, reached up to her downbent head, ran over hair still neatly held in the net of silver wire she had not troubled to remove, and were satisfied. His head turned on her lap and he said dreamily, 'He doesn't know much about fire, this friend of yours. Imagine thinking you'd get anything in here to burn!'

Suddenly he sounded so like the Martin of old, happy days that Cecily said, 'It would smoulder well. Like the reek of the stackyard fires Ben lights when Polly is hanging out the washing at home.'

'He only does it because she refuses to marry him.'

'Really?' She held him more closely. 'I didn't know he loved her.'

'He doesn't,' said Martin, 'but she can cook better than any other woman for miles around!'

Suddenly, unbelievably, the cold and stench, the torch-bitten darkness, no longer mattered. They were alone together in the world and Cecily felt an aching tenderness run through her, so that she bent over him, laying her head against his.

'I wish I could put my arms round you, Cec, but they don't move very well. I think . . . I'm afraid . . .' So securely did her affection enfold him that he had been about to speak his mind, to tell her that he was dying, slowly, that she must not mind because others needed her; but as if she knew what was in his mind and could not bear to hear it, she forestalled him.

'I have mine about you. As long as we're together, what matter which way about?'

Martin recovered himself as she gently rocked him to and fro like a baby. 'If I'd known it would have this effect on you, I would have got myself arrested years ago!'

Once more spluttering laughter took them until Martin was racked by a hard, dry cough and the tears Cecily had refused until now to shed sprang burning and hot to her

356

eyes. He had his eyes closed now against the flaring of the torch.

'Do they ever bring you a light?'

'Never. Sometimes the darkness seems lighter than others, and I hear – things – come and go, so there must be ways in and out for small creatures.' He did not tell her of the endless dark hours when he waited in terror for the rats to stop beside him instead of running when he moved. Then he would know for sure that the end had come, that they knew he was too weak to withstand attack, and he would be eaten alive.

Brokenly Cecily said, 'What has happened to all of us, Martin? It's like some nightmare and none of us will wake up, will we?'

Gently she stroked his hair back off his forehead and he said, 'They are treating you well, are they not? And the sainted Rose, of course?'

Now it was Cecily's turn to keep silent; he knew nothing of what had happened to Sir Thomas, and she would not tell him. 'Rose and I are still kept at court. I do not understand why, unless it is Her Majesty's form of revenge.'

'Everybody has gone mad, completely mad,' said Martin quietly. 'What other explanation can there be? Cecily, promise me something; never, never, try to run away, to get back home that way, will you?'

She knew what he meant. The idea had occurred to her often in the early days. 'No. They'd catch me before a day was out and it would do no good to anyone. I shall just have to wait until I'm allowed to go – when the Queen tires of keeping us. Besides,' her voice sank, 'I don't know what Rose would do if I were not there. I pulled her hair until she screamed this afternoon; she's as awful as ever, but I couldn't leave her.'

'Well done! Give it a tug for me next time, will you?' They were children again for a short space of time, until Cecily asked, 'Martin, what of Father? Do you know where he is?' She asked, but she had no need of an answer. If this were the treatment meted out to a cousin of her house, there could be no hope at all for its master.

Martin's head moved from side to side slowly, painfully. 'They parted us when we arrived.' He reached for consolation. 'You must not imagine him in a place like this. Some of the cells are – dry at least. It's so difficult to keep track of time in the dark. I seem to have been here for ever.' His voice cracked and he turned away, trying to keep his fear from her.

'Cec, my dearest little one, if we never meet again, remember that I love you. I – I am sorry I hurt you that night in the stables. Make Wat behave himself. If anyone can, it's you!'

He was saying goodbye and she could not bear it. She sniffed and said roundly, 'Damn Wat!'

'It's no good damning him, he always wins, always,' said Martin bitterly. 'I've never once beaten him at anything.'

'Well, you can forget him now,' said Cecily, 'because I have. Andrew Stratton told me about him – about why – why . . .'

Her voice trailed away but Martin, drifting back into his half-world of cold and stiffness, only murmured, 'Sweet Cecily, my one and only love. Give my love to Aunt Bennitt and the others . . .' And then, as if he were half-asleep, 'Talk about home, just for a little while until you have to go, so that I remember. Sometimes I lose it altogether.'

Cecily's voice grew firm. 'Remember the verses Father taught us of a winter's evening?

> In springtime we rear, we do sow and we plant,
> In summer get victuals, least after we want.'

Martin, recalled by past happiness, roused and whispered:

> 'In harvest we carry in corn and the fruit,
> In winter we spend as we need of each suit.'

And Cecily continued:

> 'The year I compare, as I find for a truth,
> the spring unto childhood, the summer to youth.

358

The harvest to manhood, the winter to age:
All quickly forgot as a play on a stage.

Time past is forgotten ere men be aware,
Time present is thought on with wonderful care,
Time coming is feared, and therefore we save,
Yet oft ere it come, we be gone to the grave.'

The meaning of the words sank into her mind and her voice
faltered. Robert shouldered open the door in time to see
Martin put up one trembling hand and caress his cousin's
wet cheek.

'You recite better than you sing!' he whispered, as if that
were comfort, and so they must have found it, for they both
laughed. Robert stood beside what to him, in that place, was
merriment unbelievable.

'We must go now,' he said, fully expecting her to refuse,
but she did not. Without a word she laid Martin gently down
on the straw and pulled her cloak high about his throat. Her
face was set and resolute. She never knew how she managed
it, but she smiled, and whether or not he saw it, he heard it
in her voice.

'We shall meet again, I promise you,' she said, and with
the words leaned down and kissed him, first on his forehead
then, lingeringly, full on his cold, pinched lips as she had
never kissed anyone, not even Wat. It came so naturally, so
sweetly to her that her whole being thrilled to it. 'I love you,'
she whispered.

'I know you do, sweet Cecily. Thank you for the poetry,'
and he turned his head away that she might not see the tears
that shamed him but which he could not control.

Cecily, rising to her feet, turned to Robert. 'May he
keep my cloak? He is so very cold,' and the man who
had brought her to this bitter-sweet meeting looked briefly
down at the half-starved and shivering man on the floor,
who now seemed unaware of their presence. 'You will need
it yourself,' he said. 'Besides, they will not allow him to
keep it.'

He extinguished the torch by thrusting it, hissing, into a

pail of water – Martin's drinking water, Cecily supposed, watching the thoughtless action – and the lantern's pale light was all that was left them. He stood aside to allow her to precede him from the cell and the clash of the door's closing reverberated along the black passageway, was flung back from the vaulted roof, so that she put her hands over her ears as the noise echoed through her head.

She waited then, as Robert had known she would, ready to join battle with him on Martin's behalf.

'You cannot leave him there, you cannot! He will die! What will they do to him?'

'I do not know,' he said, bracing himself to face the attack, but all she heard in his voice was utter indifference. 'Come!'

'Not until you answer me!' Tonight she had begun to perceive the truth of her feelings towards Martin and now there was another – evil – truth to be faced.

'I will not come!' she repeated and reached out to catch hold of him lest he start off without her. He stiffened as she touched his wounded arm and she mistook the reason. This one person she had hoped might help her – if only to find Wat, a broken reed at best – was part of the authority that had destroyed her family and rage shook her. Always kindly treated, she trusted everyone until she had sure reason to doubt them. In future she would doubt until they proved trustworthy, from the Queen down to her lowliest servant!

'Of course you know,' she hissed at him, not stopping to consider whether, if he were what now she thought him, it was wise to make an enemy of him. 'Even I – fresh from the country as I am – do not suppose that just anybody can walk into this – this place as easily as you did tonight by muttering a word in someone's ear. What a fool I was to trust you! How you must have laughed!' The tears she had shed for Martin were gone; she was fighting on his behalf as surely as if she wielded dagger or sword, and as long as she wounded this man, who was the only enemy with whom she had come face to face, she did not care.

'I wonder you can sleep at night when you think of the evil you do. How many men and women are there in this place, dying and in pain, because of you?' Her voice vibrated suddenly. 'Oh, what have you done? What have you done?'

Despite the lantern he held, her companion was almost totally in darkness, shaded by the hood that remained so far forward over his face, and suddenly her fevered mind saw him, dressed so, in a chamber her imagination conjured up, where men like Martin, tortured beyond bodily endurance, screamed for mercy that did not exist whilst he, in the quiet, cold voice habitual to him, repeated over and over again questions to which they did not know the answers.

'May God have mercy on you, and may He forgive you. I never will!'

Throughout her outburst he had stood unmoving before her, giving no sign that he so much as heard her words. Now he said, 'I am not responsible for what you saw in there.'

'But you or others of your kind delivered him and my father and Uncle Thomas to the men who are, did you not? Explain the difference between you. Make me understand!'

For a moment she thought he would not answer her until suddenly, swiftly, he well nigh dropped the lantern to the floor and with one hand caught her shoulder in a grip of iron. Roughly he forced her back against the wall and with his face only inches from hers hissed with an anger that matched her own, 'Everybody is innocent. No-one ever so much as thinks of breaking the laws of the realm! But *those of my kind*, as you call us, are the reason that you and your kind sleep peacefully in your beds at night!'

He stopped, aware that she had him backed into a corner, that for her he was attempting to justify the part of his work he had always hated. But Cecily ignored the burning waves of pain his twisting fingers were sending through her body. She had returned to the things that had been uppermost in her mind since Lady Patchett had sent for her, and anger drained from her; she would have gone down on her knees and begged for answers if that would have moved him.

'My father? My mother? What has happened to my sisters – they are only young children! No-one will tell me. And if them why not me?' She broke off, looking in horror at the doors about them that stretched back endlessly into the dank, evil-smelling darkness. 'Tell me where they are, please.'

Robert's cruel grip relaxed. The fury that had sounded in his voice was gone; only a great weariness was left, to match her piteous pleading. He had lost more blood than he supposed, that must be it, and it had taken with it the ability to fight even a young girl.

'Your mother and sisters are at home, unharmed. I can tell you nothing more. To have brought you here at all is more than I should have done.'

She felt him weaken and took new heart. Had he pushed her into a cell and left her in darkness she would have rejoiced as at a victory.

'So you have done something you should not have done! At least you have so much will of your own!' The scorn in her voice was biting. 'Tell me why you did it. Tell me!'

The temper Robert had fought to master brought up his right hand in a clenched and quivering fist, so that she screwed up her eyes and waited for the blow that must fell her. Then it dropped again to his side and he grated out, as if the words were being forced from him, 'Because I talked to your father, and I – I liked him.'

At the words Cecily raised clasped hands imploringly towards him. 'He is here? Let me see him, please. Oh, *please*.' But even as she spoke the quiet certainty that her father was dead came to her. There was no need to beg further on his behalf, nor for Master Cooper to confirm it; he was past the help of anyone on earth.

As from a great distance she heard her companion answer her unspoken thought. 'He died peacefully, not under questioning, that I swear to you. The fever of which you told me was too much for him.'

He watched her fight for self-control until at last she was able to draw herself up with a pathetically proud gesture of her head.

'Before or after you took me out into the country?' she asked, with such hardness that he raised a hand as if he,

362

in his turn, would fend off a blow, turning the gesture into the putting back of his hood from his face. Why should he fear this child? He had only done his duty.

'After. Some time after.'

'But he was in custody then. You took me out to question me, did you not?'

The truth was bearing in on Cecily now faster than she could deal with it, but she must go on, even though every question, every answer, ripped from her all hope, every last degree of the trust she had placed in this man. There was no help to be gained from him, from anyone.

'Under orders, mistress. You cannot suppose that I enjoyed what I had to do?' She had him in a corner now, like a cat with a mouse; instinctively she knew it and she tore onwards.

'So my father died – *peacefully* – in conditions such as Martin enjoys, no doubt. Why did you not tell me before? It is no kindness to keep the news from me. You – you were with him?'

'I was.'

'Why, if he were not under question?'

'Because of what you told me of him. I – I wished to see him for myself. He died speaking of your mother and someone called Lewis. And his cell was not like Martin's.'

'So you brought me here because you liked my father?'

'For that reason, yes, but also because of Sim.'

'Sim?' The name meant nothing to her.

Robert caught up the lantern and turned on his heel without looking at her further, and she stumbled after him, hearing his voice over his shoulder.

'The child you rescued in the street. Because of what you did for him.'

She had almost forgotten the incident. 'Has he recovered?'

'He died this evening. He was injured inside; there was nothing anyone could do.'

From the depths of her own sorrow Cecily remembered babes of her mother's, stillborn or dying young, yet always mourned, and was startled by the depth of feeling in Robert's voice.

'Oh, his poor mother. She will miss him. Sim, you said?'

'She is relieved. One useless mouth less to feed! Not once did she ask after him. He lay in my house from the time you found him until he died. *I* called him Sim; *she* had not even named him.'

He did not say that he had pressed Jerome into service late one night when Martha was abed so that the boy should not die unchristened. Jerome might not regard himself as a priest but he was, and so Robert had trenchantly reminded him, as for the third time that Jerome could recall he lashed him with his apostasy.

Not meaning to say more, he heard himself explain, 'I named him for my Sim, who was the – the same, and who died in much the same way, with no-one by to aid.'

He had stopped walking and for a moment there was silence. So little she knew of his life beyond his upbringing by a foster-father. Sim might be a son, chance-gotten almost certainly; she was unable to question.

'I am sorry,' she whispered, acknowledging to herself the inadequacy of the words even as she spoke, but her sincerity brought him swinging round to face her, needing to make her understand what he had never before revealed to anyone, and she saw his features contorted in pain.

'He did not care what I did for a living.' Raw, savage bitterness rang in his voice. 'His mother was afraid of me but he – he was glad whenever I went – home. He did not know that I am a person one cannot afford to be seen with!'

Cecily caught her breath. 'You did hear what Andrew said that day, after all. I hoped you had not.'

Roughly he said, 'I had no need to hear, mistress. *I* am not an idiot; I have always known what people say. It is true. But it – helped – to have someone – even someone like Sim – who was not afraid of me.'

She began to walk forward again, but when he saw her shiver he took off his long, black cloak and wrapped it about her shoulders, over her own that was wet and filthy.

'Try not to fall over it,' he said brusquely, and strode on ahead, up the steps and out into the night as if the last few revealing moments had never been.

She remembered little of their return to the Palace, save a vague feeling that her companion must be feeling the cold, for he sat with one arm cradling the other and his head half-turned against his left shoulder, but when she offered to return his cloak he refused it so curtly that she dared not speak to him again.

When the oarsman aided her from the boat, shocked reaction had set in. At the top of the steps to the Queen's watergate her legs refused to take her further. The walk back to her room stretched ahead like a day's journey, and as Robert came slowly after her she used the last of her strength to appeal for help.

For a moment he stood there, gazing down at her pinched, small face, drained of its youth by all she had gone through, all she had discovered that night.

'Put your arms about my neck.' Stooping, he gathered her, a cloak-wrapped bundle, and carried her through quiet galleries and corridors until they came once more to the doorway where earlier he had helped her undress. When he set her on her feet her legs buckled under her and he put out a hand to pin her against the wall. She leaned there, looking lifelessly up at him.

'My father is dead,' she whispered, through the high singing noise that filled her head, and it was as if she were imparting the information to a stranger who knew nothing. 'He died *there*, where Martin is, in that dreadful place, when he should have been at home . . .' Her voice rose hysterically. 'He should have been at home, with all of us to look after him.'

With an effort Robert raised his left arm, felt blood trickling down inside his sleeve. The weight of Cecily's body had caused the carefully bound gash to open and it hurt more than he would have expected. He took her by the shoulders, and this time his hands were very gentle.

365

'Your father no longer needs help, mistress, but I swear to you that if I can arrange for Martin to be moved to a drier place I will do so.'

He shook her slightly to make certain he had her attention and although the blue eyes she raised to him were dazed, he knew he could rely upon her common sense. 'Not a word to your cousin, not a word!'

He took his cloak from her, knocked loudly on the chamber door. There came a scuffling noise and it was opened by an obviously terrified Rose, naked beneath a blanket pulled hastily about her. As he put Cecily into her arms he heard the petulant voice say, 'Where did you *go*? I *needed* you. Who is that man? Cecily, Cecily . . . you smell *foul!*'

He swung the cloak about him, wound one end tightly about his injured arm and turned to go. Lie after lie he had told to a girl who, although she no longer trusted him, remained kind. At least she had not mentioned Wat again. How well it would have sounded, to be sure, 'Oh, *that* cousin, mistress. Let me see, I believe I arranged for him to be killed just after his ship docked.'

Robert let himself into his house as quietly as he could, expecting no-one to be astir, saw a line of light below the study door and paused. It was late for Jerome to be up. Stealthily he opened the door, saw that all was well and would have withdrawn without speaking but that Jerome put down his book and said, 'There you are. Come in for a moment,' in a way that could not be rebuffed this side of rudeness.

If he had deliberately delayed his bedtime on Robert's account he disguised it well, remarked that he had no idea that it was so late, asked if Robert had made all arrangements for next day's journey.

Robert answered curtly, still showed no sign of intending to linger. 'I shall see you before I go. Good night.'

Jerome lurched out of his chair more quickly than he had moved for years, his staff, flourished across the table in a wide arc, caught a fold of Robert's cloak, twisted, and held.

In a voice of authority such as Robert had not heard from him for years, he said, 'Not until you tell me why you are coddling that arm. Show me at once!'

Robert gave in and sat down by the side of the table, pulled off cloak and gloves to display cuff and sleeve saturated in blood. 'I can deal with it myself.'

'That you cannot! Martha will bring more linen. I warned you not to go out again. What on earth have you been doing?'

Robert left the question unanswered. Sharply he said, 'We have two good hands between us. Leave the girl to her rest. What needs to be done we'll do ourselves.'

He sat patiently, assisted as was required, until once more he was neatly bandaged.

'Thank you. Good night.' At the door he turned, aware of ingratitude, with no wish to hurt, and said in the oblique way usual between them regarding any matter that might easily become emotional, 'When I come home from these jaunts of Cecil's I shall need to find you just where you are now – by the fire with your nose in a book! Good night, sir.'

From the way Jerome looked at him he knew the older man had been worrying. But he responded in kind: 'No need for you to worry about Sim. I'll put arrangements in hand tomorrow for his decent burial.'

Because of what he had told Burghley, his nephew would spend most of his time in future away from Trinity Street and he himself would be lonely, but what did that matter, if the boy were happy?

Ten minutes later Robert was in bed and sinking into sleep. Tomorrow, well or ill, he must set out for Highwoods to bring to book the man who had caused the downfall of a family for the sake of land he coveted. Cecil had put that weapon into his hand for reasons of his own; Robert was under no illusion about that. Matthew Stone under obligation and fearful might be a useful tool in the future. Cecily Woodfall, whether she fully realized it or not, belonged to her cousin, Martin, and that same weapon, if only he could work out a way to use it – which at present he could not – should be used to ensure that the Woodfall family continued into the future through the two of them, as Edward Woodfall had hoped and planned.

CHAPTER X

Edith Stone's strident voice carried all too clearly to her son's ears from between the curtains of her litter.

'Wait there until I come for you. Make sure all is as it should be!'

Matthew pushed indoors past old Price, who remained alone at Highwoods as caretaker, muttering in a hangdog way that would not have pleased his autocratic mother that he had come to look over the house. It was as well for his peace of mind that he missed the expression with which Price regarded him. Looks might not kill, but they could well warn of lifelong enmity.

Minutes later, with a stout oaken door between him and a servant who would never forget allegiance to the Woodfalls, he felt as secure as ever he did these days. All his life his mother had ordered and he had obeyed. For as long as he could remember, humiliation had been piled upon humiliation. He knew full well that had she been able to read and write, she alone would have compiled the letter that had brought him the Woodfall estates. He would have known nothing of her bid for power had she not needed a clerk. He had written, and shortly afterwards the Woodfalls had been arrested. Yet his mother's plotting had stopped short at that one letter. She had been as surprised as he when agents, arriving from London, had produced incriminating documents. In her triumph she had not understood that since her hated sister's family was undoubtedly innocent – even Matthew believed that – someone else must be involved in what was happening, someone well placed enough to produce agents and documents to order. This knowledge, which his mother refused to accept, filled Matthew with horror; it was not until he received a communication informing him that his offer for the sequestered lands had been accepted that he had ceased to feel that he was living on the brink of some gulf into which at any moment he might slide to his doom. That was when inborn greed overcame fear, he stopped trying to understand what had happened and did his best to accept at its face value his mother's assertion that fate had been on their side; there really had been treasonable documents at Highwoods for the finding.

As to one thing Matthew Stone was determined. On the day he held in his hand papers confirming his title to Highwoods and all its lands he would be free. His mother would never again draw him into danger. She could take her high and mighty self to Abbey House whilst he, now that the land was his without need to marry Rose, would take his time in selecting a bride, someone biddable and timid who should acknowledge him master in his own splendid establishment.

Today the great hall was cold, its hearth ash-choked, but it filled him with pride. He pictured himself entertaining neighbours, strode the full length of the room, hands clasped behind his back, in a way he fondly believed showed his newly increased importance, gazed from the big, diamond-paned windows across parkland that was impressive even when, as now, it was drab with winter.

And so he saw the riders from the moment they turned the bend in the road, coming through the trees at a smart trot. Two brawny attendants, shoulder to shoulder, well matched, well mounted, dark-cloaked. The man they followed, who swayed so easily in his saddle, was no stranger. Here perhaps at last was the messenger he awaited, in all likelihood redirected from Stone Grange. The part of him that gloried in his new role as lord of this manor told him that such visits would soon be his due; the part, much smaller, that guarded his conscience suddenly wished that his mother were in the house.

'Sir Edward Linton, sir.' Price's mumbled announcement was almost inaudible but Matthew needed none. Such a man, once seen, would be hard to forget. His outrageous appearance at the time of the Queen's visit had precipitated a battle between mother and son which had drawn the lesser inhabitants of Stone Grange together in pure delight. What Edith Stone, at the top of her not inconsiderable lung power, had told Matthew concerning Sir Edward, his appearance, his undoubted lack of morals, when she found her son eager to imitate his style of dress, the way he forked his beard and embellished it with pearls, had offended the admiring Matthew, but it was as nothing to the discovery that his own sparse whiskers would neither part, nor support jewels, however small, that his hair would not remain in curl and that even had he been able to obtain them, the outrageously exaggerated clothes favoured by Sir Edward looked completely laughable on a figure less than perfect.

Today the beard was forked, to be sure, but it was unadorned. For travelling, it seemed, Sir Edward favoured clothes which although colourful were less ornate in style. Brown velvet, emerald-green slashed, showed beneath the serviceable cloak he threw back from his shoulders as, with his mincing walk, he passed Price to greet the man he had made an unpleasant journey expressly to see.

Rarely had Robert Cooper been ill; the need to struggle in order to concentrate was almost unknown to him. Yet today, apart from the deep anger he felt towards Matthew Stone, he was beset by minor irritations that normally he would have ignored. On his first visit he had curled his own dark hair; the present damper winter weather might not have supported this and the wig he had obtained itched more than he had imagined possible, whilst his skin felt sticky and cold.

Matthew Stone looked as he always did. The sallow face below thin, straw-coloured hair was spotty. Close-set eyes seemed almost to disappear when he smiled, and his full mouth was wet and loose-lipped. Robert was not surprised that Cecily did not begrudge him to Rose. But his thoughts were not evident from his manner. With a flourish he bowed. His lisping voice clearly intimated that he had never had reason to be unsure of his welcome anywhere.

'Good day, Master Stone. To meet you again makes this whole miserable journey worthwhile! So inclement the weather, do you not think?'

Trembling with excitement, Matthew hurried forward, his hands obsequiously waving. 'Welcome, Sir Edward. Will you sit down? The house is empty at the moment, as you will have gathered, but I dare say the servant can find a flagon of wine.'

Then, somehow, his visitor's hat, gloves and whip were in his hands as if he himself had been a servant and Sir Edward had passed Matthew to take not the seat to the left of the cavernous fireplace that his host had indicated but the carved, padded chair, higher than any other in the room, that faced it. As had been intended, the move disconcerted Matthew who presently found himself sitting on a low, hard chair facing an effete, slightly bored young man who flicked away mud splashes from his splendidly cut clothing, surveyed long hands, patted his black curls a trifle anxiously, conveyed by one glance his contempt for anyone who would allow a room to be fireless on such an afternoon and managed, at the same time, to look as if he had been born to Sir Thomas's own seat.

He refused the offer of refreshment, said, 'It is fortunate that I mentioned your name in the village and was told I might find you here, or I should have wasted much time. Such a journey! However, we have business to our mutual advantage to conclude and I may yet make shift to get to my next destination before nightfall.' Heavily, wearily he sighed. 'Such is the fate of we who must carry out Her Majesty's orders. Heigh ho!'

The affectation impressed Matthew. Eagerly, greedily he asked, 'Business, Sir Edward? What may I do for you?'

Robert put one elbow on a chair arm, cupped chin in hand, being most careful not to disturb his beard. 'Before we come to that, Master Stone, you would perhaps wish to invite your lady mother to join us?' The tone altered not one whit, it was the words that caused Matthew's stomach to jolt in most uncomfortable fashion. 'She, I believe, has some large say in your business dealings?'

'No!' Involuntarily Matthew came to his feet and cast a glance over one shoulder as if he expected Edith Stone to materialize from thin air behind him. 'No! I – I can deal myself with whatever brings you here, sir.' His eyes, which from the outset had been unable quite to meet Robert's veiled gaze, darted a glance at him, looked quickly away and he sank back further into his seat, heart pounding.

Robert smiled kindly, reassuringly. 'A most commendable sentiment on your part, my dear Stone. I like a man who sees it as his duty to keep ladies free from worry in times as dark as ours. There is much need for vigilance if we are to keep our country safe.' He laughed a high, musical laugh. 'But then, what need have I to tell *you* that? The fact is that I am commanded to inform you that my masters are most grateful to you, that they will rely upon you to make known to them at once any matters of a suspicious nature of which you become aware in the future.'

He saw confusion in Matthew's frown, followed the track along which his mind ran, half-expected him to ask if this were part of the conditions imposed on everyone buying an estate under present circumstances, and smiled still.

Well aware that if he were not careful he would sound as stupid as he felt, Matthew endeavoured to match Sir Edward's manner, and said pompously, knowingly, 'Yes, yes, of course. I – I quite understand . . .'

Robert leaned forward so that the rose perfume in which he had liberally drenched himself hit Matthew in a wave and said conspiratorially, 'Who better than you? Your letter concerning the Woodfalls came to hand most opportunely.'

Matthew gulped. His mother had assured him that no-one would ever suspect anything; that they – he – would be quite safe. His mouth opened, even though he willed it closed, and he repeated, 'Yes, yes, of course,' before he dared look into the dark face opposite, saw delicately raised eyebrows and stopped short, suddenly aware of the neatly laid trap into which he had fallen. Now it was too late he achieved silence, but to his visitor nothing seemed amiss.

From a pouch at his side Robert drew a small leather bag which chinked as he tossed it gracefully from one hand to the other and back again. 'I bring you this. Payment for services rendered.'

Matthew made one futile effort to cover wide-open tracks. 'But I have done nothing to earn . . . I thought you had come to bring . . .'

'Ah, the deeds you await so eagerly? That, I fear, is not my province. Too complicated by far. But I can assure you that they will arrive in due time. For now this – blood money – must suffice.'

Precisely Robert balanced the small bag on an arm of his chair and Matthew found himself unable to look away from it. This man of whom his mother had spoken so scathingly was no fool after all. The voice, affected as it was, held a note that brooked no argument, and Matthew felt himself begin to tremble.

'I do see your point of view, my dear fellow, and most commendable it is! You consider this house . . .' one hand gestured languidly round the fine room in which they sat, 'this and the lands that go with it, sufficient payment. It was, after all, your objective, was it not? When you sent this, I mean.' Although Matthew would have sworn that he did not move, with the air of a magician Robert had produced a single sheet of paper and at sight of it, whatever colour Matthew Stone possessed left his face.

'Take it, pray do!'

'Wha – what is it?'

'Why, the letter you sent to Sir Francis Walsingham denouncing the Woodfall family as traitors to the Crown. How can you have forgotten? Unless you send so many anonymous letters that you have overlooked this one?'

Robert's face showed no more than polite interest and his lips were still parted in a smile, yet Matthew knew beyond doubt that he was being played with, was cast in the role of mouse to a most superior and very cruel cat who was toying with him as he would.

He wiped sweat from his brow, clenched his hands between his knees and stared at them. It was another of the dreams he had had of late. If he refused to look up the tormentor would vanish, as the dreams did with the daylight.

'Come here!' It was no dream, and the voice had changed, was becoming impatient. Matthew obeyed as he would have obeyed his mother. The paper was held out towards him in a rock-steady hand. He recognized his disguised writing, remembered every word, could hear his mother dictating them in her high, malicious voice . . .

'Take it!' The voice still lisped but it had become ice cold, relentless, and Matthew panicked.

'No, no! I don't want it! I've never seen it before in my life! I don't want it!'

Hands that only a few days before had despatched a would-be assassin as easily as a man might snap a twig came out delicately towards him; they gripped his shoulders like steel springs, forcing him to his knees.

'Come now, Master Stone, enough of this play-acting! Anyone might suppose that I was accusing you of some crime. If you do not know what it is, why are you so sure you do not wish to examine it more closely? Do not spoil my belief in human nature by telling me that you have no curiosity in you at all.'

'It – it – you can't prove anything!' Matthew was blubbering now.

'You can't imagine that I came all this way on a wild-goose chase? Listen to me.' One hand shifted from his shoulder, fingers twisted tightly in his hair and pulled his face upwards until he was staring into grey eyes, wide open now, from which he could not look away. Who would have thought that this man possessed such strength? And still the voice was bored; its owner, it implied, was not used to wasting time on stupid yokels. Patiently it explained:

'The man to whom you entrusted your letter would be only too willing to identify you. You are too naive if you

375

suppose that he would be allowed to deliver such a document and proceed on his way unquestioned. If I remember correctly, he began to talk after less than five minutes.'

Matthew whimpered, 'Oh God, but – but I have done nothing wrong. They – they were guilty, the Woodfalls. The men who came found incriminating letters; they confessed and are convicted.'

Robert released head and shoulder, surveyed long, ringless fingers and rubbed them delicately together as if to rid himself of something dirty.

Kindly he said, 'How fortunate for you! Tell me, between ourselves, did you indeed expect that a family would be arrested and convicted on the word of an anonymous scribbler without any search being made? Or if you did know of the letters, perhaps I should suggest that you yourself be questioned?'

He paused for an answer that did not come, said, 'Take the blood money you have earned, Master Stone.' Now the money bag, taken up more swiftly than Matthew would have thought possible, dangled from a finger and swung tantalizingly towards him.

Gibbering with fear now, Matthew put out a shaking hand, but at the last moment the finger curled inwards on itself like some spring, holding him tethered. Sir Edward was gaining inordinate pleasure from his plight. Clutching desperately at the leather Matthew swore that he had known nothing, that he was always at Her Majesty's service.

'Splendid!' Mocking approval sounded in the lisping voice. 'We shall all sleep the better for knowing that.'

The purse was released and Matthew, still clutching at it, fell back into the stale rushes that covered the floor.

'What do you mean?' Despite what he had said earlier, he would have given much to have his mother there, if only that she might hear him curse her!

'You, Master Stone, are to be allowed to feast off your ill-gotten gains, as I think I have already told you, because the Crown has need of people who are ready to undertake work of a – less than pleasant nature. Our – cover, shall we say, has been somewhat sparse in this part of the country until now.'

Matthew remained still, fighting the impulse to clutch at the other's feet, to beg for mercy. His fingers tightened about the purse until his knuckles showed yellow below the skin.

'You do understand the price of a refusal to do as you are asked in the future?' There was no respite. 'A whisper in the right ear and men would ride up and arrest you as they did Sir Thomas. They might find letters somewhere. *He* is to be beheaded, but that comes of having friends in high places. I cannot imagine that you would be so pleasantly treated.'

'But they were guilty – *guilty!* They must have been – they found letters . . .'

Robert sighed. 'My dear Stone, I thought we had established that when you wrote to Sir Francis you did not know that. You were prepared to destroy a family for greed. This place would have come to you on your marriage but Edward Woodfall's land would have remained a thorn in your side, would it not? Hence your devious plan. If your part in this affair should chance to come to the Queen's ears, as it might should you fail us, you are lost, and so I warn you. Sir Thomas, no matter what he is now, was once her friend, and her memory is long.'

From what Robert had seen, Matthew Stone and his mother would take over Highwoods complete with all its furnishings, no doubt Abbey House too. The wall hangings were the same he had noticed when making sure that the building was safe to receive Her Majesty. Where were the Woodfalls living, and in what conditions? He doubted whether this grasping, miserable, snivelling apology for a man had imagination enough to envisage the treatment meted out to traitors, or how they were induced to confess. Therefore, in the next few minutes, all those things that had haunted his own life, the doings of the courteous clerk in the sunlit room, even more subtle interrogators in other places, the conditions experienced for as long as body and soul could withstand them by prisoners under question, and finally, every gory, pain-racked detail of hanging, drawing and quartering, of burning at the stake, of beheading, he whispered into the horrified ear in word pictures so graphic

377

that Stone heaved in physical sickness and great beads of water stood on his blotchy, yellow face.

'Wha – what must I do?' he squeaked. 'I will do anything – anything you say.'

'Nothing for the moment. You will be contacted as and when required.'

Robert was sitting back once more, to all appearances relaxed and comfortable. Cecil's errand was fulfilled; now he would use that same sanction for his own ends. Waving Matthew back to his chair he changed the subject with the rapidity that had surprised the truth out of cleverer men than the one he dealt with here.

'Her Majesty must soon allow your betrothed and her cousin to come home. You will have your wedding to plan.'

'My mother says – that is, I am thinking of . . . I may not marry Rose Woodfall after all. The daughter of a traitor . . .' Matthew faltered, his stumbling explanation drowned in the other's rippling laughter.

'Forgive me, Master Stone, but from – certain things – that were said when I mentioned your name in the village, I imagine that if you break your betrothal you might find it difficult to hold down this land, especially with people who loved Edward Woodfall. Misguided we may think them, adhering so strongly to traitors, but the womenfolk are innocent, after all, and affection for a family is not easily dispelled among such simple folk. It would not please my masters to discover that they had allowed you to be installed here only for you to be displaced in a twelve-month.'

Matthew found some courage, licked his lips. 'Then if I must take a Woodfall after all, it shall be Cecily. Now that that clodhopping cousin of hers is gone, there is no reason why . . .'

'*Rose!*' said Robert inexorably. 'Mistress Cecily is not for you.'

Matthew looked in earnest at his visitor then, and into the cold expression he saw he read what Robert had intended he should, so that he stammered, 'Oh, yes, yes, of course, Sir Edward. I understand. You yourself . . .'

He never knew how close he came to having Robert's hand hard across his loose mouth. But the charade was carried on with consummate ease.

'Then I need say no more. You will be taking up an honourable burden. Many will admire you for it. I imagine you intend Edward Woodfall's widow – you knew, of course, that he had died – to remain at Abbey House with her family? Most satisfactory.'

Bewildered by this swift disposal of his future, Matthew attempted to explain. 'My mother will live in Abbey House. What use will it be, large as it is, to Edward Woodfall's widow? She has only the young children now, and her sister-in-law, who is quite mad.'

'From all I hear, Benedicta Woodfall is a most capable lady. I hardly think you need lose sleep over her house-wifery, and she must have a bailiff to deal with outdoor management. But her sister – what is her name, now?'

'Agnes.' Matthew, beginning to envisage other difficulties, replied without undue thought.

'Mad, you said? Since when?'

'Oh, she seemed well enough until her brothers were arrested, although my mother says she has always been strange. Then, next day, she found the old man, Acres, she was so friendly with dead in his cottage. Now she wanders about at all times of day and night, muttering and calling, talking to people who aren't there.'

Matters were coming into focus, sharpening, providing horror that might last a lifetime, distracting Matthew from the frown that came to Robert's face at such news of Cecily's beloved aunt, the lady of the salve.

'Merciful God in heaven!' Matthew started to his feet, and an expression of horror that was almost comic contorted his face. He had reached a conclusion.

'My mother *and* Aunt Eleanor under one roof, with me? There must be some other way. It would be open warfare!'

'It is customary for a widowed mother to live with her daughter, I'm told. No doubt you will grow used to it.' Robert's tone was offhand, but he had received confirmation of what he had surmised all along. Master Stone had no more set in train the whole hideous plan that had brought him here than had one of the rabbits that lived in his warrens! Jealousy between sister and sister had caused the writing of that accursed letter, in an attempt to obtain the estates unencumbered by a marriage. It must have seemed well worth the gamble. Mother and son had acquired the land, but the price was still to pay – and not only in money.

'I shall be returning to London very soon, Master Stone. May I suggest that I carry a note from you to Mistress Rose? The poor girl sadly needs kindness, and not having heard from you for so long . . .'

It was an offer in phrasing; in tone it was an order. For one instant it occurred to Matthew to plead that he had no idea where in the house to find paper and ink but he did not. All that stretched before him was fear, unhappiness and worry. With what shreds of dignity were left him, he obeyed Sir Edward's order, would have folded his poor attempt but that Robert said, blandly, 'Unsealed, if you please,' and read it much as a schoolmaster an essay, before handing it back for sealing.

Robert rose to his feet to take hat, gloves and riding whip from the table on which Matthew had laid them. He felt stiffer than he would have expected, even after the hard riding of the past two days. His arm was hurting and he cursed Gregory's ghost. The dressing he had uncharacteristically ignored since the beginning of his journey was suddenly much too tight. He blinked to clear his head, realizing that the minor discomforts he had felt earlier had been the beginning of what was happening to him now. If he lapsed into delirium he might undo all he had accomplished. He hoped that Cecil's orders to his escort included ensuring his safe return to London, that they would really help him if he needed it.

Matthew Stone, intent on his own fate, noticed nothing of his visitor's distress and Robert forced himself onward. 'If you will beg your lady mother to spare me a few moments of her time I am willing to save you the unpleasant task of explaining our transactions to her.'

'She – she is not here, sir. The Woodfalls – all of them – are at Mistress Agnes's house. She – my mother – has gone to visit them.'

'A property of which you have not yet possessed yourself?'

The irony passed Matthew by. 'It is hers, every stick and stone,' he said sulkily. 'I cannot touch it. Much good may it do her.'

No need to stay longer. Well aware that in his eagerness to impress upon Matthew what he must do he had allowed his own voice to take the place of Sir Edward's, Robert paid close attention to his host and was satisfied. Stone would have been gnawing his fingernails had he been alone; certainly he showed no sign of suspicion at any change. All the same, Robert decided on one last impression. Sir Edward Linton should go out in his own inimitable style in what, if he had anything to do with it, would be his final incarnation in this place.

He set velvet cap, complete with enormous feather, at a jaunty angle upon his black curls and an expression of sheer horror crossed his face.

'My dear fellow, help me, do.' The lisp was back in earnest. 'My wig. Is it on straight, *really* straight, would you say?'

Matthew gaped and Robert giggled. 'You did not suppose all this hair to be of my own growing? I must tell you that Her Majesty likes such things. If ever you are called to court you would do well to bear it in mind. Now, find someone – your groom will do – to direct me to your mother and I'll take up no more of your time!'

Price was not summoned to show the visitor the door; Matthew performed that duty himself, gasping as they went, 'I swear that I will do as you ask, Sir Edward. Shall I report to you – to anyone – when all is settled?'

'No need to put yourself to such trouble.' The kindly, pitying smile beamed out at him for the last time. 'From now on we shall know precisely what you do and when, almost before you know it yourself, Master Stone. Useful you will most certainly be, but by treachery you have, so to speak, added your name to a list of men and women who bear watching.'

For all his aching head, Robert maintained his mincing gait out of the house and across the gravel. He knew, without looking back, that Master Stone's terrified eyes were on him still, and on the two large, dark-cloaked men who without a word fell in behind him as he rode away. Under his breath he swore at the necessity of meeting Edith Stone; if only he could keep his head clear until after that, he could rest for a time at least.

The guide provided by Matthew Stone ran alongside the men from London, with many an upward glance at their leader, until presently he tugged his forelock, said, 'There be Mistress Agnes's place, sir,' and was gone.

Robert, surveying the hunting lodge with its surrounding orchard, enclosed behind a high brick wall, on the edge of the woodlands that divided Highwoods from the grounds of Abbey House, was pleasantly surprised by its size. Before its gates a horse-drawn litter waited, its attendants lounging beside it. Edith Stone was giving herself the pleasure of gloating over her sister and her unfortunate family.

Throwing his horse's reins to one of the men, Robert made his leisurely way along the short, mossy path that divided track from house and knocked on the door with the handle of his whip. It was answered by a child who could have been none other than one of Cecily's young sisters: there was the brown complexion, the round face. Only the eyes were different, soft and brown. There was fear in them and Robert said swiftly, 'Ah, child, please present Sir Edward Linton's compliments to Mistress Stone and ask her to grant him a word in private.'

The child curtseyed, vanished, to be replaced by Edith Stone, fat and puffy, her determined mouth smiling. A representative from court was always welcome, though she had deemed it necessary to warn her son against emulating this one.

'If you will step inside, Sir Edward . . .'

Robert removed his hat with a flourish, bowed low. 'What I have to say is brief and most private, madam. We can deal with it very well outside.'

His tone was courteous and the lady followed him unsuspecting down the path. During the minutes that followed he was conscious of eyes that watched from a window to the right of the door, children's eyes, women's eyes. With an air of apology but most succinctly he told Mistress Stone what had brought him there, what her son had promised, what would happen to him – and to her – if ever he broke his word.

As Katharine Woodfall later said in high glee – and her mother had not the heart to rebuke her – she had never imagined that Mistress Stone knew how to *scuttle*. She went down the path leaving the caller standing, as if a fiend were after her, scrambled in most undignified fashion into her litter and was borne away without a word of farewell to kinsfolk or stranger. The one glimpse the watchers caught of her face as she passed the gateway showed it white and drawn, her mouth open and working. Whatever Sir Edward Linton had said had pleased her not at all; therefore it gave immense pleasure to the Woodfalls.

Robert went back to his horse, had one foot in the stirrup when there came voices from the doorway. One of the children was trying to run out to him, to ask for news of her lost ones. She was restrained by a woman whose voice sounded so familiar that before he glanced back he knew what he would see. Cecily, as she would be if she lived another twenty years, faded and growing old but not, please God, as grief-stricken as this woman, black-gowned and somehow, in spite of her plumpness, fragile-looking.

Without acknowledging her presence he mounted, even as Edward Woodfall's widow gathered her children to her in an open-armed gesture of despair.

'He is a stranger. He cannot help us, my love, no-one can!'

Her words rose into a cry of agony, and like an echo of that greater pain the wound in Robert Cooper's arm began to throb steadily, insistently. He had ignored its niggling for two days, determined that nothing should turn him from the course on which he was set. Now he shivered as if from cold, yet he felt burning hot, and some small, detached part of his mind registered that his arm was infected, that he must do something about it soon.

He had ridden some half a mile along the rutted track that led to what in dry weather passed in these parts for 'the road to London' when a woman stepped out of the wayside trees almost under the horses' hooves, so that Robert's mount reared and the woman reeled backwards, keeping her balance with a desperate effort.

His horse's antics pulled at his wounded arm and he had opened his mouth to advise her sharply to keep her mind on where she was going when he saw to his amazement that she had left her covered basket where it had fallen, was standing by the track staring at him with an expression of incredulous joy and arms outstretched in welcome. She was tall for a woman, tall and straight, so thin that she was mere skeleton, skin-covered, and the untended hair revealed by the falling back of her hood was long and white, but the thing he noticed first, and it made him curse beneath his breath, was that the unmistakable Woodfall eyes were blazing up at him, deep-sunken in their sockets.

'You have come back! I knew you would!' she cried.

From an eye corner Robert saw his attendants staring, straight-faced but intrigued. He tossed a coin to the nearer of them. 'There is an inn four miles or so along the road. Wait for me there.' They left willingly enough and Robert, turning back, had no need to ask for a name. Even had he not seen her when the Queen visited Highwoods, when she had been elegant and of a carriage equally regal as the royal visitor, he must have known Agnes Woodfall, who had become through misfortune the mad aunt of Stone's description.

'Robert, oh, Robert!'

He dropped heavily from his horse and faced her, frowning, intent only on making certain that she was unhurt before he went on his way. But twig-like fingers grasped at his clothing, would have taken his hand had he not moved aside to prevent it, gave him no time to become Linton once more.

'You do not remember me, Robert? But you *must!* I am Aglaia. *Aglaia!* All these years I have waited for you to come home.' Her voice was melodious; it thrilled with deep tenderness. 'What of the messages I sent? What of them?'

Moved by a last faint hope that he could trick her, he lisped politely, 'You mistake me for someone you know, madam.'

'You are Robert Emory, Rosamund's son. Your mother died in my arms. I suckled you.' Her voice sharpened, like a nurse instructing a small child. 'For heaven's sake talk properly, stand straight and take off that dreadful wig!'

Little point in dissembling; she knew who he was and he obeyed her, not ungratefully, as he must have many times long ago, if what she had just said was correct.

'Aglaia?' he echoed. One of the three Graces? Splendour and beauty, if he remembered correctly. She laughed like a young girl.

'That is my real name – the name my mother gave me. My everyday name is Agnes, but I told you the other and you repeated it many times until you remembered it. So small you were, so intent and so clever!'

Bluntly he said, 'I have received no messages and I do not know you.' No Grace had ever lightened his childhood dreams, only a small brown woman who was ordinary and comfortable.

Even in his own ears the words sounded ungracious. Something more was needed of him, some gesture towards a woman who by her own account – and he could not tell whether it were true or no – had cared for him as a babe. He put out a hand and holding it she looked him over from top to toe, carefully, critically, before she said, 'Your mother's son through and through. Have you brought Cecily with you?'

His head must be swimming again. Experienced as he was in dealing with the unexpected, in maintaining conversations on subjects about which he knew nothing without that fact becoming evident, he had difficulty in following this woman whose grasshopper mind jumped from one subject to another without connection and who appeared to know more about him than might be safe for either of them. She had gone through a serious illness recently, so much was apparent, but the eyes that never left his face were intelligent enough; no madness there.

To one side of the track, in a small, leaf-filled hollow, lay a tree, uprooted in some gale. It had been dragged out of the way, its smaller branches hacked off, but the trunk, with a huge tangle of earth-encrusted roots at one end, remained intact.

'Come!' She led him, unresisting, towards the shelter and dryness the tree afforded, where he tethered his horse, waited until she had seated herself on a thick branch and, leaning beside her, waited in silence. Lovingly she put out a hand, smoothed back his dark hair, freed now from the disfiguring wig, before she prompted him with facts she seemed certain he must remember.

And there, on a cold winter's day, with fever gnawing away at the edges of his brain, Robert heard for the first time the circumstances of his mother's death and his own early upbringing, told by a woman who frowned and laughed and clapped her hands in glee, as at some special cleverness, and who made it into a fairy tale for a child because, he realized with a pang of compassion, that was the only way in which she could face the past.

Almost at once it became apparent that although the madness was there, it was not entire. Her real self came and went, came and went, like the sun peeping out between hurrying clouds on a spring day. Her brain had been affected by some terrible trouble, a trouble in which he had been concerned, and he stood unmoving, except that almost without thinking he took one of her hands in his, and so comforted her.

'Once upon a time, Robert, I had a daughter. Her father raped me, and I carried her and gave birth in the hope that one day she would wreak revenge on him and on Thomas Woodfall who had abetted him.'

Her voice lost its note of anger, grew soft, crooning. 'So tiny she was, and so pretty. You might expect a babe conceived in hatred to be ugly, but she was not, she was not at all. Then, out of the storm came your mother, with you inside her shawl. She died in my arms that same night. I had not enough milk for two, Robert. What there was I shared between you and Angharad, and you were both unsatisfied.'

All emotion left her voice; as if it were the most natural thing in the world she said, 'I knew a boy would have a better chance of carrying out my plan, so you lived and Angharad died. I killed her for you.'

She half-turned on the log, peering up at Robert who listened in horror, explained: 'Then I fed you in her place and you weren't hungry any more. I thought there was no God but there is and He was angry. First He put it into Thomas's head to take you from me, then He arranged for you to disappear.'

Backwards and forwards she rocked herself, lost in memory. 'But I knew you were not drowned as they said. I stood by the river and your spirit was not there, so I knew. I knew.'

She laughed, fell silent, and Robert asked, 'And had I remained, what did you intend that I should do to bring about your vengeance?'

She looked at him in surprise, explained patiently, 'You would have killed Sir Thomas. Then, after you had married Cecily, you would have taken Highwoods and everything would have belonged to you, after Edward died.'

'In spite of Sir Thomas's wife and daughter?'

'There are ways of dealing with people. No-one would have suspected – ever. Eleanor is a wicked woman.'

'As wicked as her sister?' His tone was level, unrevealing. He must know whether this woman really had the gift of Sight.

'Edith Stone? What has she to do with it? She is stupid.'

So she knew nothing! Robert felt laughter rising wild within him and stifled it, but his aunt was sensitive to his mood, demanded to know what was amusing him. He reassured her, asked, 'Why choose Cecily for me, above all the others?'

It was the right question. 'Cecily is one of the golden ones, the brightest of the bright. None of the others are like her.' She leaned confidentially towards him. 'There was a problem with Lewis's boys, of course. But Wat had a dark cloud over his head, just as there had been over his father's. I knew he would not live long. I expect he is dead by now. About Martin I was never sure.' She frowned. 'He and Cecily were very close and I could not see what would happen to him, try as I would. Always he has been surrounded by a mist, neither good nor bad. His destiny, I believe, must depend on the actions of another.'

For all the world as if this narration of horrors were a normal conversation, Robert asked, 'And all these years you have known I would come back, have been waiting for me?'

'No! No!' she said impatiently, as if he were slow of understanding. 'I knew you were not dead, but Peter – Father Peter – said I must let you go, so I did, because Angharad's father came back inside Wat and I could fight no longer. It was the guilt, do you see? I had always known that I was a murderess and when that happened I could stand the pain no longer. I confessed and received absolution. My penance was to put aside my plan, to work without hope of reward for the poor of the district all my life long. Angharad is glad I did that. She tells me sometimes. Strange that such a small babe should talk so well, do you not think? Then my powers faded and of course Edward wanted Cecily to marry Martin, so all was turning out for the best.'

Brooding she sat there, and touched by immense pity Robert said, 'So that is what you are doing now, looking after the poor as you promised? And you had forgotten me?'

She drew away from him, clutching at her hair with skinny fingers until it seemed it must come out in handfuls, and stared straight before her, confronting a problem that had puzzled her poor mind over and over, night and day.

'He went away,' she said piteously. 'Peter went away. He died just as if he were an ordinary man, not a priest at all. He left me all alone.'

388

'Perhaps he thought you were strong enough to carry on until – until you meet again?'

'I am not, I am not! He should not have gone. I need him. As soon as he was not there to pray with me you began to creep back into my mind, but I must tell you that it is all too late. They took my brothers away because I am wicked and Cecily is gone, and young Martin too. So I have to send *them* messages now, many, every night.' Then, accusingly, 'You should not have come back. You are too late and it is wrong.'

Gently Robert said, 'I intend no harm to anyone. I am passing through the district, that is all.'

He glanced towards the basket lying beside the track. The cloth that covered it had fallen aside and withered leaves and twigs spilled from it. His head ached and his arm throbbed so that the conversation they were having made hideous sense. 'She is so clever with herbs and simples,' said Cecily's innocent voice. Heaven help Matthew Stone and his mother if ever she 'saw' what they had done! Aglaia indeed! Her mother had misnamed her. She was a Fate, not a Grace; cruel, inhuman and heartless, endeavouring to weave and strand the destinies of those about her to her own plan. Mad even in those far-off days, poor soul. Say Lachesis rather, or Atropos, since on her own admission the ending of life seemed to have little meaning for her. Any more than in the past it had for him, if he were honest.

He shook his head to clear it of the horror that boiled up within him, gazed at Agnes Woodfall whilst he tried to marshal thoughts that were attempting to get away from him. He was cold, so cold, yet sweat broke out on his face. He felt it run downwards to his chin, trickle inside his ruff. He could not leave matters so; could he have been suckled by a murderess? Was that why all his life the kinder human emotions had been denied him? Had darkness wrapped about him from the beginning? Before they parted he needed to know, for his own peace of mind. With skill born of long practice he began to put her at her ease.

'I fear I have understood little of what you said, madam. Will you tell me again, if I ask?'

Surprised she turned to him, smiled a smile that had something of Cecily's kindness about it.

'Of course, Robert.'

'My mother gave me to you and so that you might keep me you killed your little daughter? How did you do that?' Not by poison, he thought; dear God, not by poison. I cannot have that on my conscience too.

'You were both crying, but you were strong so I put you into the crib and took Angharad into my bed. And in the morning she was dead.'

For a moment relief absolute held him silent, then, 'You overlaid her, you mean? You did not intend her to die.'

The scorching blue eyes turned full upon him once more. 'Why, you are Father Peter in another skin, just as Wat was Gilbert! That's what he said when I confessed to him, and I began to believe it. But I *had* thought about it before that, when you were both crying so loudly that my head hurt, so my spirit must have done it when my body was asleep.'

Robert had not known that deep within him was the well of kindness that now reached out to this foster-mother of his. 'It was an accident, that is all, a sad, sad accident. No blame to you. As to what you thought of regarding Thomas and his family, that was only a dream, brought on by cruel treatment. You would never have done anything to harm your own brother, never.'

'Yes, Peter,' she said, and smiled. 'If you stay with me I shall remember that.'

Then, with one of the lightning turnabouts that characterized her now, she dismissed subject and Father Peter both; said viciously, 'You have no feelings for that pompous old bore, Sir Thomas, have you, Robert?'

There at least she was right; nevertheless he replied, 'My father, madam.'

She laughed at him then, pityingly. 'Why do you suppose your mother's dying wish was that you be named Robert?'

'I was named for her brother.'

'You were named for your father and no-one else.'

Robert swallowed between lips that were suddenly very dry. 'My father?'

'Robert Dudley. Your mother was a very beautiful woman for all she was a trollop. How could she fail to attract his attention during those long, dull months at Hatfield?'

'The Earl of Leicester? Are you sure?'

'Do you think that even your mother would lie with her dying breath? She came to Sir Thomas because Dudley would do nothing for her. She was only a pastime with him. He aimed higher, much higher, than a maid-in-waiting. Sir Thomas believed you his because he wanted to believe it. Only we two know the truth.'

As if he had been turned to stone Robert leaned there. He thought of Jerome telling him about Thomas Woodfall in an attempt to save him from the mortal sin of helping to bring his own father to his death; saw, too, Robert Dudley, middle-aged and portly, in intimate conversation with his queen and – some said – lover. It was possible; the man had always had a keen eye for pretty women, so long as they did not interfere with his ambitions.

But what came as a wrenching shock to Robert meant little to Agnes Woodfall. She had lived with the knowledge for years; of late it went round and round inside her with things she knew, things she had known and things invented. Dismissing them all she said, as if it had been a subject they were already discussing, 'Come home with me and I will dress that arm for you. Leave it longer and you will not reach London alive.'

'No!' The reply was sharp but she only nodded, fetched her basket without argument. 'Then I will do it here.'

No need to ask how she knew he was hurt; it must have been obvious that he held an aching arm somewhat stiffly. He removed his cloak and doublet; blood had seeped through the original dressing and stained his shirt, drying and hardening. She eased the cloth away from the wound, then produced from her basket a length of bandage and a pot of salve so like the one he had received from Cecily that it was on the tip of his tongue to say, 'You trained your niece well in your skills,' but the words were cut off in his throat, turning to something like a yelp and ending with an oath as Agnes's fingers came about his arm and dug deep

391

into swollen flesh. Swaying slightly he bent his head, saw pus spurt down his arm, was aware that she wiped it away, squeezed again, wiped once more, muttering a little beneath her breath as she worked, before she smeared salve on to the wound and bound it firmly about with fresh linen.

The paste felt cold on his skin, colder even than the wintry air that wrapped his naked body about. Almost before she had helped him back into his clothes it had soothed the fiery throbbing. She gave the pot and more strips of linen into his hands with instructions to renew the dressing night and morning until he was healed. That done, her attention wandered again.

'You received no messages, you say?'

For the first time her beautiful voice held a tentative note and unreasonable anger surged within him.

'How could I, mistress? No letters would have been allowed me, even had you known where to send them.'

Impatiently she said, 'Not letters, *messages*. Almost every night I spoke to you, felt sure you could hear me, that one day, when the time was ripe, you would return.'

'Witchcraft?' He hitched his cloak about him, sounding unimpressed, so that this woman who for years had skilfully trodden a tightrope between wise woman of medicine and witch, even to the extent of being scrupulously careful never to keep about her any animal that might be deemed to be her familiar, was surprised.

'Some call it so,' she admitted. 'It is a gift, passing from seventh child to seventh child among my people.'

'And unable to reach me, it would seem.'

She ignored the irony, said seriously, 'It would be because of the pain. I see that now. The barrier was too great.'

'The pain?'

'Not five minutes ago I saw the marks of beatings on your back. And these are not the worst scars you bear, I think.'

'All children are beaten.'

'And you do not believe in my gift?'

For a moment he would have said, 'No. If I believe in anything it is in the love of the woman I thought was my Aunt Benedicta. She came to me in my dreams sometimes, not you, never you.' But he did not. This woman had saved his newborn life at terrible cost to herself. Gently he said, 'I believe in your great skill with herbs and I am prepared to concede that you can tell without words whether those close to you are happy or not. Many people can do that. That is all.'

He raised his hands. 'No fingers crossed behind my back and no sign of the horns to ward off your power.'

She stood close beside him and looked into his eyes. She was the tallest woman he had ever encountered, the first who had not had to look up to him. For a long time glowing blue eyes looked directly into black-rimmed grey and Robert, frighteningly, found himself unable to move.

At last she released him and stepped back. Her shoulders were as rigidly straight as they had been when first she came to him; she bore her head like a queen. When she was young, Agnes Woodfall must have been a startlingly beautiful woman. But for all her stance there was something defeated about her now. Quietly she said, 'The mistake was mine. I should have searched for you. I knew you were not dead.'

'Then I am not a golden person after all?' Even as he spoke he regretted the foolish words.

Agnes Woodfall took her revenge, if revenge it were – he was never to be sure – in the same quiet way. 'Neither gold nor black, not even misted round like Martin. Robert Emory no longer exists – there is nothing behind your eyes, Robert *Cooper*, nothing at all.'

She picked up her basket and drew her cloak about her, saying brightly, as to some chance-met acquaintance, 'Goodbye, sir. There are many people living in my house at present and they will be looking out for me. When I see Peter again I will tell him we have met and that you are gone away for good,' and so left him.

He made no attempt to call her back. If she went home, said she had been talking to Robert Emory, who would believe her? Sir Edward Linton had passed briefly amongst them, no-one else. Robert Emory had been dead these twenty years and more and Agnes Woodfall had had one of her hallucinations.

Clumsily he untethered his horse. Leafless brambles pulled at his cloak, the remains of bracken fettered his heavy feet, but at last he hauled himself into the saddle and rode off, his head full of thoughts he could no longer control. He shivered; the glowing eyes had stared deep into him, had seen things no-one else had ever suspected. She was mad, no doubt of that, but she had said things that made him think she perhaps still had the gift of Sight. Wearily his head dropped forward on to his chest . . .

By the time he reached the small inn where his companions awaited him he was semi-conscious and they had to prise the fingers of his good arm loose from the pommel of his saddle and disentangle them from the curls of his tightly held wig. As they laid him in bed he had just sufficient sense left to instruct them on the dressing of his wound, to tell them that whatever his condition in the morning they must pack him on his horse and start for London.

Having, despite his suspicions, received no instructions to watch and report on his doings, the two men saw nothing strange in this. Their master employed them because they were efficient, and for the same reason he would have chosen this stranger for his errand. Therefore the following morning they re-dressed his arm, already considerably less swollen than it had been, well nigh lifted him on to his horse and set out on the homeward journey, keeping him in the saddle, where the road was wide enough and its surface good, by riding one on each side of him in case he should fall.

Robert Cooper remembered little of that journey. He stayed in the saddle by instinct, feeling the motion of the horse beneath him, but his mind was occupied by thoughts of Agnes Woodfall. As the pain lessened he sent silent thanks back to her for her help and apologies that he had not been kinder. He found himself hoping that the power of which she had spoken would enable her to receive them. If only for the sake of the vain, fleeting dream she had shown him: the Woodfall estate and Cecily together!

Mists gathered about him, swirled and thickened, and voices filled his ears, rose and fell, and were as quickly gone. 'Tell anybody where you comes from and Bill 'ere and me'll know for sure . . .' 'Cooper will do as well as any name . . .' 'Your name is Emory, Robert Emory. You talked in your fever . . .' 'Your father is Thomas Woodfall. Honour thy father . . .' 'Robert Dudley! Trust him as far as you can watch him . . .' 'Tell your master Sir Edward Linton requests . . .' The last voice was his own; it echoed round and round in his head, 'requests, requests, requests . . .' until Agnes Woodfall cut across all: 'Even your mother would not lie with her dying breath . . .' then finally, incisively, 'Robert Emory? No, Robert *Cooper!*' and the voices were gone, leaving a silence that rang louder than all the words and he startled his attendants by laughing aloud. She had had the Sight after all, the mad woman he had met in the woods. She had called him by the only name he would ever bear . . .

But the men who rode beside him only knew that his eyes were half-closed, that from time to time he muttered, 'I must lose no time. I must get back,' and once, very fiercely, 'No! I tell you *no!*' as if he were refusing something being offered to him, something he would have given much to accept.

They reached London in little more than the two and a half days the outward journey had taken them. Five of his eight days of grace were gone. The fever had broken and when Master Cecil's men delivered him at his door as they had been instructed, and Martha assisted him up to his own room, he fell into a long, dreamless, healing sleep, from which he wakened, weak and drained, but with the outline of a plan clear in his mind and the hardest part of it yet to accomplish.

CHAPTER XI

Complacently Rose Woodfall smoothed down her black gown and smiled the small, tight smile she had inherited from her mother. There were those to whom black was becoming, as herself, and those like her cousin whose complexion faded and died in its shade who, no matter how expensive the stuff from which their gowns were made, looked downright dowdy. Having appropriated the only chair in the room, she surveyed the small figure crouched, arms about knees, on the wide windowsill. An ebony carving could not have been more still, yet only moments earlier she had heard Cecily whimper. A small noise, reminiscent of a child in pain, but there none the less, and to Rose completely incomprehensible. During the past weeks, when they had been humiliated and scorned, Cecily had been strong and kind and Rose had come nearer to liking her than ever in her spoiled life. But now the ground was once more firm beneath her feet; she would soon be in a position to return favour for favour and could see no cause at all for Cecily's unhappiness. What was done was over and past. Far better, thought Rose, to be absolute ruler of her own small kingdom than an insignificant and disappointed member of a large one, as she had been here.

For the twelfth time at least she read through the ill-spelled lines delivered to her early that morning by Taylor who had, she averred, no idea who had brought them to the Palace. She was but the deliverer of what, her look plainly said, would undoubtedly have been bad tidings had she had any hand in the composing. The duress under which he had written notwithstanding, Matthew's message rang with high self-esteem and triumph:

'Dear Rose, Highwoods and all about it is mine. I am a man of my word and will marry you despite recent events. Matthew.'

Anyone who knew Master Stone would have said that he had perfectly transferred his innate lack of grace to paper, but Rose would not have changed it for the tenderest, most poetic love letter ever penned. It brought security, continuance of the wealth that all her life had wrapped her about, a guarantee of her due place in society.

Thus, when Cecily, summoned to Lady Patchett's room, had returned to break the news that Sir Thomas had that morning been beheaded, her reaction had been an honest one. 'Poor Father,' she said with as much feeling as if she had heard that he was suffering from a chill. 'Whoever will Mother find to bully now?' Most surely no longer a daughter who had a written promise of marriage from so rich a man.

To Cecily, who had walked as slowly as she could back to their bedchamber, wondering how best to break the news, this was unbelievable. She kept to herself Lady Patchett's words, intended to comfort, that the condemned man, untouched in body, was utterly broken in mind and spirit, had gone to his Maker with not the faintest notion of what was happening to him and without recognizing a single person about him.

Her Majesty, for the sake of past friendship, was pleased to allow the cousins to return home the following day in order that Sir Thomas's dishonoured body might receive burial in his family's vault, and here again it was Cecily who expressed proper gratitude; his daughter received the favour as no more than her due. In her mind she saw herself, her cousin and some nebulous escort – there must be an escort! – riding out in splendour, with herself pale and beautiful, on their way back to Highwoods, an estate which through marriage to Matthew Stone would so soon become hers.

Vaguely, somewhere in the background of this picture, she magnanimously found a place for Lady Woodfall, but it was, as Matthew had intended in regard to his own mother, very much in the second rank.

For the sake of Cecily's recent kindness, her Uncle Edward's family also should be taken care of. Her mother had inculcated scorn for them and all their doings into her ever since she had been old enough to understand such things, but provided they agreed not to trouble Mistress Rose, they should be housed and fed. Matthew himself she considered no more than she had when he was the boy to whom she had been promised from the cradle. Now he was a means to an even greater end and if, deep within herself, she owned surprise that a youth she knew to be mercenary and greedy in the extreme was prepared to ally himself to the daughter of a self-confessed traitor, she quickly passed over the thought. With the example of her mother's treatment of her father before her, Rose intended to dominate Matthew. But first things first! She must give orders to Taylor regarding the packing of her belongings . . .

Out of respect for her uncle Cecily had put on a black gown, a thing she had refused to do for her own father, whose happy soul had nothing to do with mourning and the black trappings of death. She had spent her last day in the Queen's service; Her Majesty, Lady Patchett had informed her kindly, was pleased to commend her for the way she had carried out her duties and had not forgotten earlier services rendered. What, her ladyship had gone so far as to ask, overcome by curiosity, could that mean? Cecily, for whom the first meeting with her monarch had been completely erased from her memory by subsequent events, had replied with transparent honesty that she had no idea, since she had done no more than any of the other maids.

She pressed her aching head against the cold stone of the window frame. Her father was dead, Uncle Thomas was dead and by now Martin, too, might be far beyond the reach of all those things she longed to say to him. No word had come from Robert Cooper, and she was glad. If he did arrange some drier place of confinement for Martin, what? Nothing but longer imprisonment, a slow, drawn-out decay, until bodily weakness, coupled to despair, took him to join his uncles. What right had she to wish for such a thing? The first and last act of love she could offer the man towards whom her feelings were now so obvious to her was to pray that he die as quickly as possible, that his suffering might be ended the sooner.

Ahead of her lay a lifetime of supporting her mother and sisters. Where, she wondered, would they live? Was any money left them, even so much as might allow them to move to a part of the country where no-one had ever heard the name Woodfall? But that was not to be considered; Woodfalls lived in Sussex, come what might. She had indeed whimpered as the numbness that had helped her endure all these weeks relaxed its grip at the prospect of the ending of her ordeal, the thought of seeing her mother once again.

She became aware of Taylor's voice, speaking to Rose with no attempt to conceal insolence. 'I've packed more chests in my lifetime than you can imagine, and for people of far higher degree. I need no overseeing, I thank you! Take a stroll in the gardens, do, and leave me to my work.'

Then, softened in tone, but still brisk: 'Mistress Cecily, will you listen to me! How many times must I tell you? Take your head off that cold wall at once. A fine thing to travel home with your nose streaming with cold!'

A large, hard hand pulled the unresisting girl upright; the advice to Rose to go walking was repeated, was ignored, and it was Cecily's cloak that Taylor held out, seemingly in no fear of a refusal from that quarter. Meekly Cecily allowed it to be draped about her shoulders and in the process Taylor's hand surreptitiously took one of hers, pressed into it a screw of paper. The woman's face signalled silence as clearly as if she had spoken aloud.

As she left the room, the paper clutched tightly, Cecily's mind registered with some surprise that Taylor had known exactly what she was doing. She had spoken to Rose in such a way as to ensure that there was no possibility of her obeying. For the first time it occurred to Cecily to wonder whether there was more to their serving woman than met the eye. And when, once established in a tree-sheltered corner, she unfolded the paper, she knew there was.

It carried no greeting, no signature; none was needed. The writing was carefully formed, so that even a child might read it, but she knew its tall characters to be Robert Cooper's. It was another example of the man's thoroughness. He had no idea whether or not she found reading easy and he would brook no small detail causing his order to go unanswered.

'Be in the Queen's chapel at five o'clock.'

Quietly, at the time appointed, she let herself through a side door into the chapel. She had been there often when it had been brightly lit, filled with splendidly dressed men and women and ringing with the sweet high sound of boys' voices. Although the more obviously Roman Catholic statues had been removed, here no-one had been allowed to pull down ornaments for destruction's own sake, to smash panels and carvings lovingly wrought to the glory of God by men whose only fault – to present-day eyes – had been that they used different words in their praise and acknowledged as head of their church a man who lived in a distant land. Her Majesty, Protestant though she might be, left splendour and panoply much as it had been and enjoyed it. Cecily, remembering the bare, gutted interior of the small church at home, the teaching of the puritanical Master Watson that all ornamentation was sin, was glad the Queen thought differently.

Today no candles in tall, golden holders struck sparks from the jewelled cross, picked out the elaborate carving of the reredos or made the red velvet altar frontal glow as it did during services. The glass of the east window showed dark, its pictures indecipherable, defeated by dusk and by the tiny lamp kept burning perpetually over the sanctuary. As her eyes became accustomed to the gloom, Cecily made out the shape of the Queen's great padded chair and the surrounding lower seats. For a moment she held her breath, listening, but there was no sound of human movement; she was alone. As she sank into the corner of a pew something small squeaked and scuttled away between her feet. After that the silence was broken only by the occasional crack and creak of settling timbers.

She reached into the small pouch at her waist, took out the piece of embroidery her mother had given her when she left home. Less than three months ago Cecily, as poor a needlewoman as her Aunt Agnes, would have laughed had anyone told her that her mother's everyday design of intertwined leaves in drab greens and greys would mean anything more than a dull task to be completed as quickly as possible. Now she held it first thing in the morning as she knelt to her prayers, touched it during the day whenever she had a free moment, and the crumpled and rather grimy material, fraying about its edges, sewn and unpicked, sewn and unpicked in so many attempts to bring it to somewhere near the high standard demanded by the Queen, brought close a feeling of home and family.

So many times of late she had slipped into one of the smaller, less ornate chapels of the Palace, had prayed desperately, asking for a miracle that had been denied. Now resignation filled her and made her old before her time. She awaited Robert Cooper with no feeling of hope; but neither was she any longer afraid. What more could happen to her family than had already happened? The small red light on which her gaze was fixed blurred and spikes of light darted out from it in the tears that suddenly filled her eyes. She blinked to clear her sight, found it impossible, and her sewing dropped to the floor unnoticed as she raised her hands to cover her face. So slowly that she was scarcely aware of it, the sleep she had found so difficult to win of late overtook her; she drew her legs up on to the seat and with her head pillowed on her arms relaxed, and knew no more.

Promptly to his time Robert Cooper arrived, silently closed and bolted the doors behind him, and stood accustoming his eyes to semi-darkness. In the all-pervading stillness Cecily's light, even breathing was not audible so that for one moment he thought she had not come. He took it as an omen, who all his life had believed nothing in such things. He was free to go, to forget the insane plan he had evolved following events earlier in the day. When he had given the note to Taylor it had seemed a good enough idea; now he wondered whether his lightheadedness had recurred.

As he hesitated he heard a sigh, moved softly forward along the aisle and found her, a small, curled-up shape, sound asleep. The Queen's little brown mouse in hibernation! Illogical pleasure flashed through him. After all that had happened at their last meeting she had still come at his bidding. For a moment he stood looking down at her. He would have gone as quietly as he had come, without troubling her, but as if suddenly aware of a watching presence she came awake as swiftly as any wild animal and was on her feet in front of him. In the gloom he saw only the pale, disembodied outline of a face tilted up towards him and two small hands clasped together. Cecily knew him more by height and the air of authority that hung about him than by recognition of features.

'You wanted to see me, sir?' and he, equally calmly, held out his hand, said, 'the paper, if you please,' with no doubt in his mind that she, whom he had taught himself to think of as 'child' as if that were protection in itself, would be scrupulously careful enough not to have left it lying about. When she gave it to him he tore it across and across until it was no more than a pile of tiny pieces, put them into his pouch, said, 'Sit down. We can at least talk in comfort.' Waiting until she had resumed her seat, he sat beside her.

Intent now only on getting away as soon as possible, he said, 'I am sorry to have left you so long without word after I promised, but work took me away for several days.'

To her horror she heard herself reply, 'I expected nothing else,' was aware that he bent forward to peer at her and in an attempt to put right an offence she had in truth not intended, whispered, 'I did not mean to sound discourteous, sir.' The ghost of a laugh reassured her.

She folded her hands decorously in her lap. 'Rose and I go home tomorrow. We have no further value, having been hostages for our fathers' behaviour.' She made no attempt to protest their innocence. Before too many people she had defended them and too many people had sneered. To the world the evidence was final and damning and she had ceased to fight openly against it.

He made no attempt to contradict her statement. 'I have been asked to oversee the arrangements for Sir Thomas's cortège. All will be ready for you to leave first thing in the morning.'

She bowed her head in acquiescence, and although she remained silent he knew that at any moment she would ask for news of Martin. Therefore, before she had time to draw breath, he said, 'I have news for you, mistress, not all of it pleasant. When the *Larkspur* docked at Plymouth she was under tow by one of her sister ships. Scarcely half a dozen of her crew remained alive. Contaminated water, it was said . . .'

'And Walter was not one of them.' So steadily she said it, as if she had already known.

'I fear not.'

Before her Cecily saw the handsome, laughing face of the cousin who had gone forth to make a fortune that should free him from the family he scorned. She shrank from memory of his love-making, designed to bind her by a promise he had no intention of honouring himself, so that the brother he despised should not win her. Despite! she thought abruptly, angrily; no, never that. Jealousy! That was the force that had driven him since childhood to fight, to lie, to demand his own undisciplined way. Jealousy of a brother who seemed to have so much less, yet who in coveting nothing had proved to be so much the richer.

'Aunt Agnes never liked him,' she said, and that was all. Robert interpreted the statement silently according to what he knew; neither mentioned him again.

Deliberately Robert said, 'Rose received a message from Matthew Stone this morning, but you will know more about that than I. From the man who brought it I have news of the rest of your family.'

He had all her attention now. The patient hands, unclasped, were held out towards him as in supplication.

403

'They are well,' he said gently. 'Your mother and sisters. I am told that you have an aunt who owns a house on what was your father's estate. All are living there.'

Cecily sighed in relief. 'Abigail is looking after them.'

'Another relative?'

'No. She is my Aunt Agnes's servant who has lived at the house for many years, she and her son.'

'I see. Lady Woodfall is there also.'

'Oh!' It was plain that even in present circumstances Cecily had little faith in her aunt adding much to the well being of the party. However: 'Better there than with her sister, Edith,' she added judicially. 'Father – Father always said those two were at each other's throats within moments whenever they met.'

So Matthew Stone's horror had not been exaggerated; the thought brought Robert some degree of contentment.

'There will be room for you, and for Mistress Rose also? At least until her marriage to Master Stone?'

'Of course.' Cecily was surprised at the idea that any member of her family might be turned away. 'I am glad Matthew is standing by her. She will be able to live as she always has.' As once before he marked no envy in her voice.

'You think he will make a good master for the estate?'

What need to consider? 'I do not!' said Cecily promptly, 'but it is of a piece with everything else. It does not surprise me.' She paused before she forced herself to ask, 'And Martin?' as if he were not of more consequence to her than all the others put together.

'He was alive this morning.'

He felt her stiffen at his seeming callousness, knew that because of it she would question no further and was glad. He had reached his decision. She must go back to her mother and Martin Woodfall must die. It would not take long, if he were any judge, and although she would never forget him, his memory would fade. There would be her family to tend and at length someone else to love and laugh with.

That being so, it was no longer necessary for him to remain and he had already risen to his feet to take his leave when Cecily said sharply, 'A moment, Master Cooper, if you please!'

'Mistress?'

Head tilted slightly to one side she said, 'You have told me nothing you could not have asked Taylor to pass on. You are too busy a man to waste your time carrying me news of a family I shall see within the week. What was your true reason for asking me here?'

He forced surprise into his voice, even a note of mockery. 'I owed you an explanation, therefore I made time.'

'You are in church, sir! In this of all places, you must not lie!' She broke off with an exclamation of exasperation. 'This will not do. Come with me.' She rose, brushed past him, walked up the aisle towards the chancel step and waited. All too slowly for her he followed, so that almost before he was within reach she put out a hand and taking him by one arm pulled him onwards. He missed his footing on the step and, stumbling, hit his left shoulder sharply against the carving of the priest's chair.

Accusingly Cecily said, 'You flinched.'

Sufficiently recovered to be amused by her severity – she had changed very little since the first time he had seen her, after all! – and at the same time angry with himself that he was allowing her to prolong the interview, he said abruptly, 'I have hurt my arm.'

'But not just now. You did not hit yourself hard enough for that.' Enlightenment dawned. 'You were favouring it the night we went to the Tower. Was that not so?'

Once more he chose mockery as the best form of self-defence. 'You have no salve to offer?'

Seriously she replied, 'I could fetch something, if I knew what was amiss. Is it a cut or a bruise?'

He laughed, a harsh sound in the semi-darkness. 'You are kind, mistress, but I need not trouble you. It has been attended to by experts.'

'Good!' she said crisply. 'Then stand beneath the light so that I can see you properly. Why did you bring me here?' As they faced each other, over Robert swept the feeling that if he delayed longer she would say, 'I am waiting

Cooper!' in much the way Jerome had done throughout his childhood.

But there was no amusement in the situation, none at all, and gravely he said, 'I have already told you.'

'And I do not believe you! There is more to the matter. I know it, I can feel it! I have a right to know.'

For a moment he felt his temper rising to match hers, then, against his better judgement, he gave in. 'This morning it seemed that there might be a possibility of releasing Martin Woodfall. I now know that it was a false hope.'

The air of command left her at the very thought, as he had known it would. With desperate hope she asked, 'Her Majesty might be prevailed upon to release him, after all?'

Robert found relief in a short bark of laughter. 'Mistress, unless you have spoken of him to the Queen I doubt if she knows of his existence. If he had left the Tower it would have been upon my assistance and mine alone that you must have relied.'

'And it is no longer possible?'

'The price for your family, for Woodfall – and especially for you – is too high, mistress. I see that now.'

'Since I am the sole representative of my family here, sir, surely I am the one to judge what is too high a price.'

Grimly Robert nodded. 'Very well, I will tell you. Your father and uncle are – were – beyond doubt guilty men. Nothing will ever change that. About Martin Woodfall, after hearing you together, I am not so certain, but if he is freed he can on no account go rampaging back to Highwoods obsessed with some mad scheme of reclaiming his own and trying to prove innocence that does not exist. He must go overseas and make a life where no-one will ever find him.'

In a small voice Cecily said, 'He will never agree to that – never!'

'He will if you go with him.'

The round face, stained by red lamplight, stared up at him in disbelief. Unable in the first euphoria to see any difficulties, she asked, 'I am to go with Martin?' and a smile came to her face. 'What sort of price is that? My mother will agree to it.'

'There, mistress, is the rub. As you yourself have observed, escape from the Tower is impossible. Woodfall must be deemed to have died in his cell and you – you will disappear. No trace must ever be found of either of you. Now do you understand what this means to you – to all of you?'

Cecily's bewilderment reached out to him like a tangible thing so that taking her by the shoulders he set himself to explain.

'If you are to join Martin you must leave your cousin during her homeward journey. Your family will receive news of what you have done from Mistress Rose. She will make the most of such a tale, of that you may be sure. It is your good name that must be sacrificed and they left to believe the worst.' All the more, he added silently to himself, because Sir Edward Linton has already put into Matthew Stone's head the idea that you are spoken for, and I doubt that that young man's tongue will remain silent!

'Either your mother and sisters receive your consolation, in which case Martin Woodfall dies where he – where you saw him – or you take him abroad and desert loved ones who have already borne too much. Now do you realize why I decided after all to leave you in ignorance? No-one should be asked to make such a choice, no-one!'

He felt her sway and quickly caught her beneath her arms lest she faint clean away. Placing her in the priest's chair, he stood ready to do what he could if she needed help, but she recovered and was silent, staring ahead into the darkness with lips tight pressed.

'Nor can I guarantee success, mistress. You will go your way not knowing if I have managed to save Woodfall or no, and since he must travel a different route to you, it will be days before you hear anything of him. He is weak from imprisonment; he may not withstand the journey even if I get him clear of the Tower. If that happens you still will be unable to return home. Think of your mother's sorrow, mistress; think of that. Be sure, very sure, of what you do.'

'You do not know them, sir. I could go back to them

407

after a year – after whatever time you care to name – and they would be glad, because they love me, and I them.'

'There would be questions, mistress, and talk when news of your return spread.' His voice rang hard. 'I must involve too many innocent people to be able to take such a risk.'

He stopped abruptly, waiting for her to voice the inevitable conclusion, wondering how he could bring himself to confirm it when she did. But he need not have worried; despite what had happened to her family expedient killings had no place in her innocent world. She sat before him for a long time with her head bowed, and when she looked up, although her voice trembled it held pride, determination and unwavering resolve.

'There is no choice, Master Cooper. I could not live with the knowledge that I was given a chance to help Martin and did not take it. It is what my father would have wanted, that I know. If – if things go wrong, I shall manage – I must!'

'So be it!' Robert strode swiftly into the small recess the Queen's confessor used for robing and returned carrying writing materials and a page torn from the back of some book.

He put a quill into her hand. 'You will write at my dictation. Begin, if you please, as you address your mother . . .' and kneeling on the floor, with her body leaning to one side so that all available light fell on the paper, Cecily wrote: 'I cannot return home whilst Martin is still in prison. I must do all I can to help him. My love and duty to you all. Cecily.'

Robert restored the priest's belongings to their place, said, 'Give this note to your cousin to deliver when you leave her. You are sure of what you would do? Once we leave here there can be no turning back.'

'Yes.'

'Then, come.' He reached out a hand, led her to the lectern where he transferred her hand to the heavy, ornate Bible. 'Swear, swear before Almighty God that you will accompany Martin Woodfall and will never communicate with your family again, on pain of their deaths and your own.'

She stared up at him, scarcely able to move within the circle of his arm; then she looked at the Book and when she spoke her voice was steadfast. Still she did not question. 'I do most solemnly swear.'

He released her so abruptly that she almost lost her balance. Without waiting for her he strode back into the body of the church.

Watching his dark shape and appalled by the action she had taken upon herself, almost she cried out, 'Put *your* hand upon the Book and swear before Almighty God that you believe my father and Uncle Thomas to be guilty men!' But although she opened her mouth no sound came out. Like her Aunt Agnes she had gained an insight into this man who held her life in his hands. One had said, 'There is nothing behind your eyes . . .' The other thought, 'He has no belief in God . . .'

She rejoined him by the pew in which they had earlier been sitting and asked, 'What if Martin refuses to swear?'

'He will swear, mistress. There is no doubt of that.'

A cold shiver of fear passed through her. She had accepted his offer; from now on the game was according to his rules.

Rapidly Robert gave her a list of instructions, then asked, 'You know what you must do?'

Committed, Cecily nodded. Then, as he would have turned to leave, asked, 'If – if my family seek me, what then?'

'A body, clothed in a gown you will give to Taylor, will be taken from the Thames in due time. News of your drowning will be sent to Sussex, the body may even be taken back there for burial if your mother so wishes.'

Cecily swallowed a sob. 'My – my mother, sir. She will stay with Aunt Agnes, do you think? That house will not be forfeit to Matthew Stone?'

'Most certainly it will not. Title to it belongs solely to your aunt.' His voice resumed its mocking lightness. 'And you reckon without Master Stone. So great a man as he plans to become can hardly leave his wife's family in penury. Think how badly it would reflect on his standing in the county! The noble, kindly Matthew Stone – no doubt to be *Sir* Matthew as soon as he can contrive it – intends that your mother shall return to Abbey House and live as heretofore. That I know for fact, mistress. His reward will be the admiration of those who assume he does it from compassion!'

His caustic tone softened. 'Goodbye, Mistress Cecily.' He kicked something soft that hampered him, stooped and picked up Cecily's forgotten embroidery.

'Yours, I think?' He pressed it into her hands, and the moment's hesitation gave Cecily her chance.

'Why?' she asked. 'Tell me why you are doing this. Martin and I are not the only ones who pay a price. You must put your own life into deadly danger.'

The light grey eyes looked steadily down at her. He was about to sever two young people from their family, perhaps for all time, by an oath he knew they would not break. If he did free Martin, and the Woodfall family went on into future generations through the two upon whom Edward Woodfall had set his heart, it would be under another name and in a distant land. And both, knowing and loving Edward Woodfall, would never believe him guilty of treason. Questions must arise in their minds, nor could he find it in himself to think that other than proper. Taylor had carried him news of the fight between Rose and Cecily when the former had accepted her father's guilt. From the very fury with which Cecily had rounded on her it had been apparent that she, too, doubted Sir Thomas; the perfect scapegoat was to hand. Nothing need be said directly to Cecily; the seed was there, would take root and grow if he said certain things to Martin and the boy, surviving, had half the brain he thought he had. For Cecily he would say what he now admitted was in his heart.

'What I do, I do for your sweet sake, because I am yours to command.'

Shock held her silent, open-mouthed; disbelief filled her round eyes. He went gracefully down on one knee before her, took her hand and pressed his forehead upon it. 'Go to your happiness, child. All will be well.' And although the gesture was consciously flamboyant, the words came from deep within and brought with them pain. 'I shall never forget you.'

Before she recovered he was once more on his feet, had unbolted the door, looked outside to make certain he was unobserved and was gone.

In the frosty stillness of next morning's dawn, Rose and Cecily Woodfall left the court of Elizabeth Tudor for ever. So busy had Rose been picturing her new life, planning a homeward journey that should show her, a sorrowing daughter, to best advantage, that she failed to notice how preoccupied was her cousin, that for once she, who never cried, had sobbed herself to sleep.

Lettice said farewell with reddened, downcast eyes that had nothing to do with the Woodfalls. Andrew Stratton was to command Sir Thomas's last escort and would not be returning to London. They had vowed undying love, although both knew that the Queen had dismissed him as a favour to Lord Pemberton, that probably within weeks Lettice would receive – and must accept – the addresses of a young nobleman of her father's choosing.

Two black-dressed attendants led the small procession that set off towards Sussex, followed by the cart containing the body of Thomas Woodfall in his lead-lined, black-velvet-draped coffin. Behind him rode his daughter, pale head held high, inexpressibly haughty, a goodly distance ahead of Andrew and Cecily, who came side by side. And behind them two more attendants and a servant with packhorses.

To Rose's immense satisfaction, the cortège created no small stir as it passed through early morning cobbled streets. Once into the countryside she would have reined back and joined her companions in amiable condescension, save that a backward glance showed her two grim faces that promised no pleasure at all. Her lonely, exalted position was best, she decided, and gave herself up to imagining the effect she would have on the next group of villagers they passed.

From time to time Andrew glanced sideways at Cecily's cold, pinched, unhappy face. He alone of the three had had a parting audience of the Queen, who had been pleased to be affable. He might well do worse, she had informed him, once his broken heart was less sore, than to look to Cecily Woodfall as a bride. Traitor's daughter she might be, but through no fault of her own. And once bring word of their betrothal, no doubt some post could be found for Master Stratton that should allow him to support a wife in comfort. Ignoring the hurdle of his parents' disapproval, Andrew admitted honestly to himself that the idea appealed to him. He might never feel towards Cecily as he did for Lettice, but they had always got on well together. He caught her eye and smiled . . .

He was still in his dream when a horseman waiting on the grass verge at a crossroads spurred forward and with upraised hand halted the party. Straight to Cecily he came, bowed, and in a voice that carried clearly to her companions, announced that his master awaited her, if she would be kind enough to accompany him.

He took the small bundle that was all she was allowed to carry into her new life: one change of clothes and the box containing her herbs. All the splendid gowns she had worn at court would go back to Highwoods, to be made over, no doubt, for the sisters she would never see again. She looked neither at Rose nor Andrew. To go without speaking was best; let them think what they would.

Surprisingly, it was Rose who showed not only surprise at the turn of events but genuine concern also and it was her voice, squeaky with fear, that Cecily heard as she turned away.

'Cecily, Cecily, don't leave me! Who is that man?'

The anonymous horseman pushed roughly between the cousins. 'On your way, mistress,' he said to Rose, 'unless you wish to return to London,' and at what sounded very much like a threat, Rose shrank aside whimpering, whilst Andrew, encountering the stranger's grim frown and noting the plain-hilted sword by his side that bespoke use rather than ornament, allowed discretion to overcome brief thoughts of impossible valour.

Into Cecily's throat rose a lump that made it impossible

for her to speak. Robert Cooper's warning of her family's interpretation began here, in Rose's shocked face, in Andrew's frowning eyes.

'Mistress, we are awaited.' The horseman's tone when he spoke to Cecily was deferential. The sooner they were on their way the better, it implied. Into Andrew's hand she pressed the folded paper of Robert's dictation – it would be safer with him than with Rose – and without a backward glance urged her horse on the way to a life she had chosen because she believed, as her father had taught her, in the future of the family into which she had been born.

CHAPTER XII

Feebly, lying in darkness and still more than half-asleep, Martin Woodfall pulled a rough woollen blanket up round his chin. He was warm; every bone in his body ached, as they always did these days, his wrists and ankles throbbed where the skin was chafed and festering and from head to toe he itched from the bites of innumerable lice, but he was warm. For a moment he savoured the feeling, a comfort that he had well nigh forgotten. Then, suddenly, he was wide awake, and fear, the fear that shamed him because it controlled him so completely, had him again in its grip, churning at his stomach so that he retched convulsively. It was a dream, pleasant this time, and therefore the harder to bear, coming when he had thought he was at last done with dreams, when for days he had known that nothing was left him but to sink down into blackness and cease to be.

Since he had been pushed, chained at wrist and ankle, into his underground cell, the door ground to, the key turned in the lock, he had been in darkness complete and impenetrable. Thereafter his solitude was broken only by the visit of a jailer who, from time to time, brought him a lump of rock-hard bread and some fetid water. There would come the sound of a man's tread, echoing along a stone-flagged passage, the jangle of keys, his door would open and food be pushed inside. It happened by the light of a lantern that seemed to Martin bright as the noonday sun. It flared before him so that always he must turn his eyes from its dazzle, the door closed, the footsteps retreated. The routine never varied; the man never spoke, and Martin ate and drank, as he dragged out the rest of his existence, in darkness. At first he had tried dividing his food into portions, conserving part of it until he felt hunger, in the hope that this would enable him to keep some track, no matter how vague, of the passing of time. But he was not alone in his imprisonment; small furry creatures that he could feel but not see came scuttling and snatched whatever he did not eat immediately so that, braving their snapping teeth, he learned to push whatever he was given into his mouth as fast as he could, to chew tasteless bread for which he had no saliva as if it were a king's banquet and he as hungry as after a hard day's work in the fields. Then the squeaking objects at which he lashed out with foot and chain took the crumbs he dropped and departed. Thereafter he was alone to shiver and dread their return. All his life he had hated rats. The days when Ben had taken him hunting them were among the worst he could recall and these seemed twice the size of any he had ever known.

Soon, as he lost count of time, shallow sleep was filled by vivid, half-waking dreams, in most of which he was back in his old life. But always had come an awakening to darkness, filth and hunger, the pain of his fetters and a numbing coldness which had eaten into his bones so that he thought he would never be warm again. But worst of all had been the fear. It pressed on him like some tangible weight; fear, at first, of physical agony as he waited to be fetched for questioning. Then, when no-one came near him except his jailer, an overpowering horror that he had vanished from the memory of living men and would spend the rest of his days buried alive in silence until the rats that came and went, squeaking and scuttling through his straw, sensed his ever-growing weakness and ate him alive, and the place became his tomb in very truth.

Or he might go mad. He saw the door to his cell flung open by men who had never known him and he a gibbering wreck, crouching bearded, naked, in one corner. He would have forgotten who he was; nothing had ever existed save darkness and cold and rats, and he began a litany designed to stave off that day. 'My name is Martin Woodfall of Abbey House, Highwoods, Sussex, my name is Martin Woodfall . . .' again and again until his tongue tripped over the words, they tangled themselves beyond his helping and he found himself unable to recite them in due order.

At first he had used up his not inconsiderable strength pacing out the length of his cell – it was so narrow that it was possible only to walk one way. Four chain-hampered strides from wall to wall as he kicked his way through foul straw and stumbled, if he were not careful, into the evil-smelling channel that ran along its middle. He forced his body onwards and slept whenever tiredness overcame him. Four paces back and forth, back and forth. He painted the scenery of his uncle's estate in his mind, worked and walked in fields and lanes, visited Master Acres. He held long, imaginary conversations with his family and friends; even recited Master Acres's lessons and smiled wryly when he realized how much he could recall when there was nothing to distract his mind, no more pleasing pastime to run away to. One day if ever – *when*, he corrected himself firmly – he got out of this place, he would tell the old man.

Here, with no-one to hear, he pledged Cecily his undying love and in return heard her explain that she could never be his because she was promised to Wat. Yet once she had come to him like a ministering angel, had wrapped him in a thick, woollen cloak, had comforted and kissed him and told him she loved him. But that too had been a figment of his overwrought brain, for the cloak had vanished when he later felt round for it, and he had put his head down on his arms and cried like a child at the pain.

Soon lack of food and the coldness that seeped out of the stones worked its way into his very bones, sapped even his young strength. He ceased to walk. At first he had gritted his teeth and forced himself onwards, crawling to and fro on hands and knees. When even that became too much, he spent more and more time huddled in the straw, telling himself that if he did not move he would die. Very well, he would move presently, when he had had a few more minutes' rest . . . Finally came the time when life no longer had any meaning and he longed for death. He apologized to his family; to the uncle who had hoped for him to carry on the estate, to his aunts who had loved him, to Cecily. But when he lay down and waited, death would not come to him – unless he was already dead and this was hell, cold, wet and dark; not burning as he had heard tell, but hell all the same.

Now he knew that he was awake. He pushed back a blanket and put wasted hands up to his face. Someone had visited him, had bound a thick pad of cloth tightly about his eyes. Anger flared inside him; there was no need for it. He was in darkness without a blindfold. Frenziedly he pulled at the knots that held it in place, but they were too firmly tied for him to undo. He shuddered and drew his legs up tight to his body, clutching his arms about his knees and trying not to cry out. What were they doing to him now? Would it never end?

After a time his bemused senses cleared a little, like the rolling back of a fog when the sun breaks through. He was in a much more open space than his cramped cell. The air about him was warmer! He was unable to believe, unwilling, lest it was but another dream after all, but this time it was not. The wet, foul straw was gone. He lay on a bed and someone had wrapped him in a weight of blankets. A sob broke from his lips and with an overwhelming effort of will he forced himself to relax, to stretch out his legs and lie full length.

He stayed quite still until he realized, with a sickening jolt at the pit of his stomach, that far away, but continuously and most insistently, he could hear the sounds of the everyday life of a town. Traffic creaked and bumped its way over cobbles and rutted earth, there was the jangle of horses' harness and the thud of hooves; men and women talked and shouted and once he picked out the laughter of a happy child. Then, somewhere almost directly beneath him, it seemed, a woman began to sing. Her voice was raucous and very much out of tune and the words were bawdy, but nevertheless she sang. After an eternity of silence he was back in the world of men! But how, and where? And why the enforced darkness?

He put his forearm to his mouth, bit hard into what little flesh remained. Nothing changed; his arm hurt, still he lay upon a narrow bed which, although hard, was – praise be – dry. Afraid even now that the noises would vanish, he raised his head and so became aware that somewhere nearby was food. He could smell real bread, and the fruity tang of wine such as he had not known since he was dragged away from home. He put out a trembling hand in hope of locating such luxuries and in that moment realized for the first time that the chains that had bound him for so long were gone, like the straw. His skin was raw and broken where they had cut into his flesh, but he could stretch out one arm without the other having to follow.

Slowly, painfully, he inched his way to the side of the bed. His hand hit the edge of a solid wooden table and he groped over its surface for whatever it held. A loaf of bread, despite his slow carefulness, fell to the floor and bounced away. Then his almost useless fingers touched the base of a round flagon and he tried to pull it towards him, whimpering for joy. Had he had the use of his eyes he would have seen that even in the grey winter light it glowed jewel-red, but it was enough that it smelled so good that he could hardly wait to get it to his mouth. It was useless; the vessel shot from between his hands. And in the same moment he drew himself too near the edge of the bed for recovery and fell to the floor. He lay there, gasping for breath, waiting for the flagon to crash down upon him, but it did not. High above him, too high for him to reach, he could hear it rolling backwards and forwards on the table. He groaned and became aware of wetness splashing down upon him, sweet and sticky upon fingers he licked in frenzy, anxious to lose no drop of what was spared him. He lay until the dripping stopped, puddled his fingers into the wet dust on the rough planks of the floor and stuffed them over and over again into his dry mouth.

Exhausted by the effort, he stayed where he was. Had

someone promised him a full flagon held to his lips and bread to go with it if he climbed back on to the bed, he could not have done so, but even the small amount he had managed to get into his mouth had tasted wonderful; he made no effort to search for the missing loaf.

Hazily he recalled his cell door grinding open, remembered guarding dazzled eyes against a light held by a darkly cloaked figure that was not that of his jailer. A man's voice said, 'Trust me.' And trust he had, largely because, in the depths to which he had sunk, whatever he did could bring nothing worse. He had drained to its dregs the liquid his visitor held to his mouth, a liquid that had rapidly brought an inability to move, followed by a gradual falling into soft, gentle sleep. After that he had known nothing until his awakening to this place that for all his inability to see it seemed, after his recent lodging, little short of paradise.

His twisting, turning thoughts were interrupted by the all-too-familiar noise of key in lock. He turned his head towards the sound, drew his legs up to his stomach in fear, and listened. The door closed, was re-locked, there was a thud as of something heavy being dropped to the floor, followed by a firm tread coming towards him.

Robert Cooper stood silently by the side of the huddled, filthy, blindfolded young man, looked from the overturned flagon teetering on the edge of the table to the bread on the floor.

'My apologies, Master Woodfall. I had intended to be here before you awakened. I trust you have not been unduly alarmed.'

The voice was familiar from the night before and, vaguely, from a time further back than that. Martin, the strength the wine had given him ebbing, coughed slightly. 'In God's name, who are you?'

He might as well have saved his breath, for he received no reply. Robert tossed his cloak across the foot of the bed, lifted Martin back on to the mattress and propped him into a sitting position before he picked up the loaf from the dusty floor, brushed it briefly with his hand and broke it into pieces. In the bulbous side of the overturned flagon was trapped a small amount of wine, which he poured into a tankard and, dipping the bread into it, waited whilst it soaked up the liquid. Then he fished out a sopping piece and held it to Martin's cracked lips.

'Eat!' he commanded, and it was the voice of authority. 'In the best of worlds you might stay here until you had regained your strength, but that is not possible. We must go as soon as you can move.'

At the words Martin, the first chunk of bread sliding softly, easily down his throat, choked, closed his mouth and turned his head away like an obstinate child. 'We must go . . .' Now he knew where he had heard the voice before and in whose company. This man was Cecily's – friend, she had called him – who had brought her to the Tower, he who had been afraid that wet straw would burst into flame!

Emotions that his imprisonment had long frozen swept through Martin. This unseen stranger with the deep, authoritative voice, whose body, in contrast to his own stinking carcass, gave off a pleasantly scented, freshly washed smell, was helping him for Cecily's sake.

Mistaking his reluctance, Robert, forcing himself to more patience than he felt, said, 'Come! Try again. The more you eat, the easier you will find it, and Heaven knows you need all the strength you can gather.'

With a supreme effort Martin accepted chunk after dripping chunk of bread from hands that, given a choice, he would have pushed away from him as hard as he could, until with a gasp he said, 'No more, no more . . .' and Robert put down the tankard, wiping his fingers on a large square of white linen.

In a voice that trembled for all his efforts at control, Martin begged, 'In the name of Heaven, have mercy. I cannot go on like this. Tell me where I am and why – why . . .' His voice faltered and he raised shaking hands to his bandaged eyes.

'You are free of the Tower for good, Master Woodfall, unless something goes sadly amiss with the remainder of my plan. As to the other thing – be assured you are not blind, if that is what you fear, or not for more than a few days at all events. Remember that you have been living in darkness for some weeks. To awaken to bright daylight after that would have been painful in the extreme; might even, I imagine, have damaged your eyes. Therefore I bound them, intending to be here early so that you would not be alarmed. I regret that I was detained on the way.' A note of grim amusement rang in Robert's voice. 'A funeral I attended took longer than I had made allowance for.'

As he spoke he watched Martin's tense body relax, heard the sobbing breath that shuddered between his teeth and, with more consideration than was his wont, continued talking, to give the boy time to pull himself together.

'I have seen such things happen before. If you take my advice you will keep your eyes shaded, except at night, for a week or so, accustoming them to light gradually. Then all will be well.'

Martin, one fear dispelled, grew ashamed, gave a shaky laugh. 'Then I shall not have to beg my bread on street corners, after all!'

'Not unless that is the life you choose,' agreed Robert Cooper coolly. 'Now, Master Woodfall, we have little time. I have brought you clothes and money to see you on your way but before you leave there are things I must tell you and you will attend to me better if you are warm. Lie back!'

Hands that had so capably ministered to Jerome over the years pulled covers once more up to Martin's chin before the impersonal voice continued.

'Much has happened to your family whilst you have been imprisoned, none of it good. You are now the only male Woodfall remaining alive. *Stay still, sir!*' as Martin, in horror, struggled upright.

'Your uncles are dead. Sir Thomas was beheaded for treason yesterday. Past friendship with Her Majesty saved him from the form of death common to most traitors. Edward Woodfall died naturally in his cell . . .' The lie came easily now, with repetition. 'You knew he was ill, of course.'

'*Executed!* For what?' Martin asked savagely. 'There has never been a traitor in our family, and never will be!'

'In your own case I believe that to be true or I would not have lifted a finger to help you. Sir Thomas, however, confessed, as did Edward Woodfall – with a remarkable degree of similarity in detail – to having been involved in a plot to place Mary Stuart on the throne of England. You are not the first person to have lived close by others without knowing all their dealings, believe me!'

'Under torture they confessed.' Martin's voice was hard. 'As would I have done – and doubtless you also, whoever you are!'

Robert had expected opposition: for Martin, newly delivered from solitary imprisonment, the news must come as a worse shock than it had to Cecily. She at least had known what was happening from day to day and had had a life which in some small measure had mitigated her agony. What he had not anticipated was the dislike aroused in him by the young man he had rescued, a dislike he felt returned in good measure every moment they were together! On his own part he put it down to the work he had done in the night just past, coupled to lack of sleep. He had not supposed himself to be so squeamish.

'No torture was necessary. The papers found at Highwoods were proof sufficient in themselves even before the confessions. The Sussex lands have been confiscated, of course.' He paused, added, 'They have gone to Matthew Stone.'

'Matthew . . .? Dear God in Heaven!' Martin gave a sudden crack of laughter. 'All his life he has coveted, and now to get them without marrying Rose! To think that he should be the one to come well out of this twisted business.'

Unable to believe in his own family's guilt, he sought desperately for an alternative, and hit upon the correct one. 'That that spotty youth should . . . Could it be that he . . .?' The question died unfinished on his lips, but its import was clear.

It was Robert's turn to laugh and his amusement sounded, perhaps even was, genuine. 'From what little I have heard of Master Stone I think it hardly likely that he could find his way from one village to the next unescorted! What do you suppose he could have done?' His voice mocked, laid part of the truth before Martin in such a way that it sounded unbelievable. 'You think he obtained genuinely treasonable letters, for so I assure you they were, planted them on your uncles and informed the authorities, so that he might reap his reward? Great as the shock is to you, and I honour you for your loyalty, you must accept that such a thing would be impossible. Guilty men were accused, guilty men were condemned. I have seen the evidence. There are agents throughout the country, especially in such times as these, on the look-out for anything suspicious, and they did their duty.

'And before you condemn Stone outright, I should tell you that he intends still to marry your cousin Rose, which I imagine will surprise you. Her mother will live with them. Your Aunt Benedicta and her family he will permit to return to Abbey House and resume their lives.'

One word and one only bit into Martin's horrified mind. '*Permit? He* will permit? You must think me a fool, my friend. This whole affair has a nasty stink to it, and whatever happens to me now, sooner or later I shall find out the truth, you may be sure of that.'

In grief and anger and the jealousy that tore him, he overlooked the hardening of Robert's so-patient voice, ignored the danger signs in the quiet 'You know the truth; the matter starts and ends there.'

'And I do not believe you!' Fleeting strength surged through Martin's thin body, once again brought him upright to face the disembodied voice that slandered his beloved family.

The words were barely out of his mouth before he was being forced back hard against his pillow by hands that bit like steel into his shoulders and, gasping, he quailed before a blazing fury the like of which he had never known.

'Curse you for an obstinate fool!' The words hissed between Robert Cooper's teeth. His breath came hard and panting and there was a white line about his mouth. Slowly, inexorably, his hands moved upwards and clamped about

423

the neck of the helpless man on the bed. Their pressure increased and Martin, after one feeble, useless gesture of resistance, waited for death.

'I tell you this, Master Woodfall,' continued the inhuman voice close to his ear, 'you will swear to me, here and now, never to do what you have just proposed. Do you understand? Well – do you?'

'And if I – if I will not – swear?'

'Then I have wasted a good deal of time and effort, for you must die.'

'What of – of Cecily? What – of her?'

'She will be no concern of yours.'

The fear that had chilled Cecily shuddered its way through every bone in Martin's body. Feeling the consciousness being throttled out of him, he made a slight gesture of surrender with his right hand, croaked, 'What – must I do?'

The cruel grip loosened. 'You will swear on *this* . . .' Into Martin's fingers he pushed a small, leather-bound book. 'You will swear to go exactly where I tell you and speak to no-one concerning what has happened.' And on Master Jerome's borrowed, aged copy of *The Aeneid* Martin Woodfall swore an oath similar in all respects to that Cecily had taken in the Queen's chapel a day earlier.

All fight gone out of him, with no thought for the wisdom or otherwise of such a disclosure, he said wearily, 'But I have a brother.'

'Walter is dead.' Robert's voice was once more expressionless.

'Dear God, not . . .?'

'Her Majesty's agents can scarcely be responsible for every death in the kingdom, whatever you may think,' said Robert drily, 'although I will not deny that when he died he was being sought for questioning.'

'But he has been at sea for years!'

'The men who deal with such things do a thorough job! Your mother's family has a strong Catholic background although I gather, fortunately for them, that they have not been implicated in this sorry mess. As things turned out, your brother's hot temper put him beyond the reach of any human questioner. He drew his dagger on a stronger man than himself in some dockside tavern in Plymouth. His pay from his last voyage disappeared in the fracas.'

It sounded like the Wat Martin had known all his life. In much the same way that Cecily had commented only obliquely on the news, he said, 'And Barndale? That also is confiscated?'

'Your grandfather being innocent, it is not. But you will no longer succeed to it. By the way, I told Mistress Cecily that your brother died on board ship from drinking contaminated water. It may seem to you, on reflection, a good idea not to tell her the truth. I do not know how much more pain she can bear.'

For a moment Martin lay silent. So he and Cecily were to meet again. Perhaps even now she was making her way towards this place, would see him thus, in comparison to his rescuer. Any pleasure he might have felt died, killed by the last thought. Harshly he said, 'You seem to know my cousin well.'

He heard his visitor move abruptly from the bedside, stride over to the window, then there was silence. With his eyes unbound he would have seen Robert Cooper pressing his face against the tiny casement, seeking comfort from the cold air that cut in through the ill-fitting horn panes, staring out unseeingly over the shabby aspect of rough-plastered houses and tumbledown thatched roofs, whilst his hands moved one against the other, washing, cleansing, getting rid of stains about which this boy could never know.

Martin pressed. 'It is for Cecily's sake that you have rescued me, that much I can work out for myself. She asked you.'

Robert's lips twisted. In Martin's world Cecily had only to ask for a thing for it to be granted.

'What is she to you?' Filthy, emaciated, so weak that he could hardly move, jealousy yet ran in Martin's voice. '*What is she to you?*'

Robert turned back into the room and for a moment the red glare that had shone in his eyes when he had come so near to killing this youth was there once more. He gripped his hands hard together behind his back.

'Mistress Cecily and I met at court and for lack of anyone else she asked my help. If he had possessed the key to your cell, she would have asked the devil himself!'

What had he said earlier, this man who had brought him here? 'I believed in your innocence,' or words to that effect. How fortunate that Cecily had beguiled a man of influence. And how unfortunate that not a word he said about her was to be believed! Harshly he asked, 'Since I cannot go home, what?'

'Your cousins left court this morning, Rose to escort her father's body home for burial, Cecily to journey to the coast and await you there. Since you cannot stay in this country, she agreed that France might prove a pleasant alternative.'

'All that way to say farewell? At this time of the year? Is it too late to stop her? I shall – I shall do well enough alone. She should be with Rose, on her way back to her mother and sisters, who need her.'

Robert sighed. 'You have not understood, Master Wood-fall. Your cousin has chosen to disappear at the same time as you. To the rest of her family, because the less they know the less they can tell if questioned, she will be dead. To become your wife is what she wants more than anything in the world.' Mockery sounded in the clipped, impersonal voice. 'You did ask her, I believe. What more could you desire? Freedom, and the woman you love by your side. She will nurse you back to health; she has a talent for such things! Oh, I know that she ran away from you once, but it is often not until we have lost a thing that we recognize its true worth. No sooner was she free of you than she knew that what she had rejected was the one thing she wanted. You are a fortunate man, Martin Woodfall, in spite of what you think at this moment!'

'And you will give her up to me, after all you have done for her?'

'In the name of Heaven, Woodfall, I have nothing to *give* up! Your imprisonment has addled your wits! Let there be an end to this tomfoolery!'

Martin drew up his knees and rested his head on them. He was young, he was delivered from prison and – most wonderful of all! – the woman he loved awaited his coming. The easy tears of bodily weakness started from his eyes, running down beneath his bandage. He remained unmoving until there came the thud of a bundle on the bed beside him and Robert's voice, once more perfectly under control, said, 'You look well nigh dead, what little I can see of you, but we have no more time to waste. I believe I have covered your tracks, but delay could be dangerous. It is a pity I can do nothing to clean you up. You will have to endure your dirt for a little longer. Hold out your arms so that I can get those filthy rags off you.'

Martin slid to the edge of the bed and, as he submitted to being dressed, said, because he could not bear the silence, 'I do not even know your name, Master – Master . . .'

'My name would mean nothing to you,' said Robert curtly. Cecily could supply the want any time Martin cared to ask, but the petty stubbornness, practised on a family not lacking in that quality, pleased him.

'And you yourself will not suffer for what you have done?'

'There is no need to concern yourself about me. I shall be safe enough. And no-one will look for you anywhere, Master Woodfall, unless you are extremely careless, because you died last night in your cell and I saw you buried this morning.' It had been the final hurdle overcome; not until he had seen the clods of earth cover the coffin had he been sure, quite sure, that his plan could succeed.

Astounded, Martin sat quiescent whilst the fingers that had once unlaced Cecily quickly fastened his shirt and the points of his hose. Before him rose a picture of the grim fortress he had left, as he had seen it in all the despair of his arrival there. He thought, despite Master Acres's teaching, of witchcraft and magic, and restrained a sudden impulse to cross himself. For Cecily's sake this man with the cold voice had somehow spirited him, who had barely strength to sit up, out of an impregnable prison. Not only that, but had apparently persuaded those in charge that he was dead!

'So it was my funeral you attended this morning! And you do not propose to tell me how you worked what seems to me to be a miracle?'

'I do not,' agreed Robert coolly. 'You will sleep better without the knowledge.'

As if the matter were thus closed, he picked up a pair of rough, old shoes. 'Hold out your feet,' he ordered, taking Martin by one ankle, only to find that for the first time in this whole affair he had misjudged. Martin's feet were long for his height and the fetters about his ankles had caused them to swell. With an exclamation of irritation Robert dragged a blanket from the bed, tore it into strips and, kneeling, bound them about Martin's feet. As he stood up, 'I should have made allowance for the size of a farmer's feet,' he said, and briefly there was a flicker of amusement between two young men not too far apart in age. It was gone immediately, as Robert went on, 'These bindings will suffice. You have no walking to do. Put your arms about my neck.'

But Martin made no effort to move. Firmly he said, 'When I have seen your face, and not before, sir.'

For reply he received a sharp laugh, then: 'Spoken like a true Woodfall!' Knots were loosened and the bandage fell about his neck. 'Keep your eyes closed for a moment,' Robert warned, and Martin felt a cloth being draped over his head.

'So! You have your back to the window and the blanket will keep the glare from your eyes. I kneel before you; look your fill.'

Martin opened stuck-together eyelids to daylight for the first time in weeks, slowly and carefully, and the world was a swirling red mist, shot through with flashes of vivid colour so that tears ran unchecked down his face and there was a sudden sharp ache across his forehead and down into the back of his throat. He put hands over his face, fighting, willing the mist to part, until gradually it settled, became less intense, was tinged with other smoking mists of grey and white. Then, out of the middle of the cloud, swimming towards him disembodied, he saw the face of the man who had saved him; thin, assured and handsome, with light grey eyes that looked forbidding.

For a moment Martin was filled with self-pitying despair. From one handsome man to another she went, he thought, and why not, blessed as she was, whilst he stood to one side, unconsidered save as a brother!

Then he recalled the debt he could never repay, forced to his face the tired remnant of the boyish smile that was so like his Uncle Edward's. 'I can never thank you for all you have done, sir, but . . .' He put out one filthy hand, which was taken in hard fingers and held whilst Robert made the only return he could.

'Cooper,' he said, and his voice was harsh, 'my name is Robert Cooper.'

With an understanding that had grown in him during the course of this one meeting Martin nodded. 'I shall not forget. Thank you – Master Cooper.'

His hand was released. 'Close your eyes. Remember what I said about keeping them covered. Come now, there is no more time to waste.'

Martin raised his arms, was wrapped in a thick cloak and picked up as easily as a child.

'A cart waits to take you on the first part of your journey. The driver knows where to drop you off and someone else will be awaiting you there. Tell me, do you or Mistress Cecily speak French?'

'No, sir,' and at Martin's meek, rueful tone, Robert laughed.

'I thought not. You have no need to worry; when you reach France you will be met and taken to a place where you can stay until you know enough of the language to make yourselves understood without attracting attention. One last thing: alter your name and do not be tempted to change it back. Choose something entirely unconnected with your past life, not your mother's maiden name or anything of that sort for sentiment's sake. From such small slips tragedy grows!'

In the pouch that hung from his belt was a heavy weight; Martin moved slightly in Robert's arms to feel it.

'Gold. Enough to give you a beginning. It is money honestly earned. Not blood money. Tell your cousin so if she asks.'

He wondered wryly whether Cecily's scruples would allow her to take it if she knew exactly where it had come from. Honestly earned it had been indeed – by someone – but before he relieved them of it just outside London the evening before, it had been on its way to the Queen's coffers in care of two very surprised tax collectors. The realm, he told himself, owed that much at least to the Woodfalls. Three bags of gold was small price to pay for family estates confiscated and two innocent men horribly slain; he was not inclined to include Walter.

Robert carried Martin down a narrow staircase, heaved him on to the seat of a sack-laden cart beside its smock-frocked driver and pulled a wide-brimmed hat firmly down on to his head before he stepped back. From his perch Martin turned once more in the direction of the man who had saved him from a lingering death and his mouth curved in the smile that no privations could rob of its charm. 'Thank you, sir,' he said simply, but received no answer. Had it not been for a curt word spoken to the cart's driver, he might have supposed Robert Cooper to have vanished.

By the door to the tumbledown house Robert stood watching until the clumsy vehicle turned a corner and was gone from sight, before slowly he went back up the stairs. In the bedchamber he set methodically about removing all signs of recent occupation, moving the table forward so that the winestains on the floor were covered. The dregs of wine and the bread he tipped from the casement, to the delight of a flock of starlings who quarrelled over it loudly and long. Martin's discarded rags and the useless shoes he gathered up into a bundle, but gradually his movements became slower until he stood immobile by the bed, head bowed, hands twisted tightly into folds of cloth.

The tearing of the rough wool between his gripping fingers brought him back to his senses. He eased his left arm cautiously against the sleeve of his doublet. The gash had healed cleanly, but the scar was tender. As well he

430

had come to the end of lifting and carrying members of the Woodfall family!

Wearily he straightened his shoulders and gave himself once again over to his training. He walked backwards to the door, swinging the remaining blanket across the floor so that all footmarks were obliterated. Then he tucked it under one arm and cast an expert glance over the chamber. To all intents and purposes it was as unused as when he had given the woman who lived downstairs the two silver pieces that had bought her silence, as it had at other times in the past.

He clattered down the stairs and was soon lost among the throng of people buying and selling at the stalls in the nearby street market.

CHAPTER XIII

She had listened open-mouthed to her father's tales about it, Wat had talked of it in his boastings, but never until she reached her journey's end had Cecily seen the sea. It was like looking off the end of the world; its dull winter's greyness met that of the sky with scarcely a line to mark the difference. To the tired girl who slipped from her horse in front of the clifftop cottage it was terrifying; at first even the thought of going near to it, let alone venturing upon it in a boat, as soon she must, horrified her. Yet on her second day, when the gale of the previous night dropped to a sharp breeze and a wintry sun poked long fingers of light from the clouds to make a dazzle of the wave tops, she took Patience True's advice and half-walked, half-slid down the path cut into the low cliffs. There, with her toes at the edge of the shingle, where the water pushed stones at her with a roar and then fell back with a not unfriendly *shush*, she found a measure of peace and schooled herself to wait for Martin. That he might never arrive she would not allow herself to consider.

Hour after hour, each day the weather was fine enough, she spent on the shore, warm and comfortable inside her thick, woollen cloak, its hood pulled over her ears. And under that – she smiled as she wondered what Martin would say when he saw her!

'Only one gown, m'dear!' Patience, who had probably never had more than one at a time in her whole life, had been scandalized at the paucity of the young lady's wardrobe. 'Well to be sure! How like a man to think that would do! No one will see ee 'ere; save your gown, get ee into these and be warm.' So saying, from an old wooden box she had produced a boy's doublet, hose and rough-soled shoes.

'Belonged to my eldest, they did,' she explained, seeing the look on the girl's face. 'Half your age he were but about your size. Nothin' catchin' took 'im, that I promise ee, unless 'twere the catchin' o' fish, for he drowned in the calmest summer sea I ever do remember.'

She cut short Cecily's words of sympathy, roughly but not unkindly. 'Happens, it does, as well ee must know and nothin' we that's left can do about it but go on wi'out lookin' over our shoulders too often 'cept in love.'

So she had turned the comfort to Cecily's own use and unless, before she left, Cecily found words to thank her, she would never know how much she had helped.

For two days and half of a third Cecily had ridden hard beside the horseman who had detached her from her cousin and Andrew with such scant ceremony. He was a man in his middle years, of few words, punctilious when it came to finding her decent accommodation for the night. They followed what was for him obviously an often-travelled route, for he never hesitated, and the first sight of her destination had been a column of smoke that appeared to come out of the ground at the end of a sandy clifftop path. 'A good job for them it's in a hollow,' her companion had said with one of his rare smiles, 'I've wondered often enough, as it is, how they keep the roof on in the winter gales!'

He rode away with the briefest of bows and without allowing her to utter a word of thanks, leaving her with Benjamin True, enormous, rough and hairy, a man very much in command of his own small world. His equally large wife, who meekly obeyed him in all things, asked Cecily no questions, but told her that they were fisherfolk. There were two young children, unschooled, tousleheaded, dirty and as quarrelsome as young puppies, who also obeyed their father instantly, but who obviously loved and were loved in return. The sight of their happiness brought a renewed ache to Cecily's sore heart and because of the forlorn look on her face, Patience True had taken her straight to the back room set aside for her use and lifted her on to the bed with a command to rest until she was recovered from her journey. In this tiny, two-roomed cottage she had almost half the space to herself and Patience, as she stooped to remove Cecily's shoes, said, 'They always stays 'ere when they comes.' On that cryptic remark Cecily had fallen asleep, wondering if 'they' included Robert Cooper.

On the morning of Cecily's fourth day of waiting, she was turned out by Patience, who said she most certainly had no work fit to give a young lady. Fresh air would bring roses back to her cheeks. Off she must go, and obediently she climbed out of the hollow in which the cottage lay, ran across the hard, cropped turf that separated it from the cliff edge and made her way down the steep, sandy path that led to the seashore. She sat, shielded from the wind by an old, upturned boat against which she rested her back, and stared across the glittering waters towards the foreign land she must soon call home. She clasped her hands about her knees and sat still as a stone image, so that the seagulls that had risen screaming to swoop and wheel at her arrival soon once more settled in their crevices in the chalky cliff or sat and bobbed on the sea. The very sight brought memories of home flooding back. In just the same way ducks had ridden the calm waters of the pond beyond the stable yard, clean and beautiful, quiet until disturbed, when their coarse, loud quacking had been enough to waken . . . She pulled up her thoughts with a sob. 'To waken the dead!' She had lived, as people did, surrounded by death – outbreaks of plague, smallpox and fevers of so many kinds for which there was no treatment were part of her life – but never had it struck so hard at her own family until this year, never in so cruel a form.

Her father, she had been told, rested peacefully in the tiny burial plot at the Tower, in a grave unmarked by stone or cross. That would not have worried him greatly, she thought, remembering how heartily he had laughed at the inscription raised in their village church to a man whose way of life had been the talk of the neighbourhood. 'A handsome payment to a stonemason turns an old devil into a saint!' No lavishly praising inscription for Edward Woodfall, not even a resting place in his own family vault, but that, his favourite daughter knew, would not have worried him either. Where his bones lay would have bothered him not one jot; no angry ghost would walk by his last resting place.

She closed her eyes against the glare off the water and her head drooped slowly forward, the sound of sea and birds combining to form a background to her increasingly drowsy thoughts. A moment more and she would have been asleep, but there came a scuffling and a falling of pebbles down the path. Billy and Mab True were slithering towards her as fast as they could come, grabbing and holding each other back.

'Me, me me!' shrieked the girl. 'Ma told *me* what to say!'

'Well, I'm going to say it!' retorted her brother, and still locked in combat they came to a sliding halt before Cecily who, with an unwonted feeling of excitement, had already half-risen to her feet.

'You'm to come at once, Ma says,' panted the boy, with his gap-toothed grin.

'Please. You'm to say *please*. You forgot that, fool!' snorted his sister in triumph, and grabbed Cecily's hand.

'Please!' they chanted in chorus, forgetting their differences, and began to pull her towards the cliff. But Cecily, her heart suddenly pounding, shook them off and was gone, running, climbing with desperate strength over the loose surface so that her youthful attendants were left behind.

Whenever she thought of Martin it was always as he had been at home, strong and thickset, his skin brown from the weather, with a smile lifting the corners of his mouth. She seldom pictured him as he had been in his cell – because she could not bear to – and never called to mind his quiet, withdrawn sternness in the days before she had left for court. So much had happened since then. Lives had ended, others had been put at risk to bring them together; he would accept her word that she had been untried and foolish, and all would be well.

What she now saw, propped against a water butt by the side of the small cottage's only door, was a bundle that at sound of her flying footsteps resolved itself into a huddled figure wrapped in a cloak. There was a downbent head beneath a battered, wide-brimmed hat and two feet wrapped in rags. Not for an instant did she hesitate. She sped towards him and a ghost of the voice she loved asked, in so tired a whisper that her heart contracted at sound of it, 'Cec?' She dropped to her knees at his side, pushed off the hat, found herself looking into the face of a man, gaunt, stubble-bearded and an unhealthy greyish-white, with a grubby cloth bound about his eyes, and she choked in fear.

'Martin! Oh, Martin!'

'Gently, Cec, gently. Take your time. Don't come too near. I stink! The Lord knows what sickness I carry!'

His warning went unheeded. Sobbing, she held him closely and he laid his head upon her shoulder, with the gesture of a weary traveller who has at last reached home.

'But your eyes. What has happened . . .'

'Nothing. The daylight is too bright yet, that is all.'

Wordlessly she clung to him, whilst the deeply interested children watched round-eyed and open-mouthed until Patience, arms akimbo, stood beside them and said calmly, 'The young gennleman's right, my dearie. 'E needs a bath and quick about it. Do ee bring 'im in.' She turned to the children. 'And ee,' she added fiercely, 'ee can run away, far, far away, until I shouts ee!'

Cecily stood, putting one arm about Martin to help him. 'Come, my dear,' she said. 'You have met Mistress True, I take it?'

Martin inclined his head weakly in the direction of the fisherman's wife. 'I was deposited at her feet by the carter like a sack of logs. Good day, mistress.'

The words took the last of his strength. He slumped suddenly, heavily, against Cecily and in that moment Patience took over.

'You'm been in the wars, to be sure, but I've dealt

wi' worse,' and she stooped, lifted Martin as if he had indeed been the sack to which he likened himself and slung him over her shoulder. In this ignominious fashion, closely followed by Cecily, holding on to one of his hands, unable to let him go for an instant, he entered the cottage that must shelter them both until he was well enough to journey further.

Mistress True placed her burden gently in a corner of the settle before the hearth. 'Now, sit ee still whiles I fetch the tub, and we'll clean ee up in no time.' Then, when Martin showed signs of feeble protest, 'And wi' all respect, sir, ee can be quiet. I've bathed men in my time, so ee'll not shock me, and I'm told this young lady'll be your wife, so there be nothing to worry about there!'

Mistress True dragged a large wooden tub into the room and filled it from the vast cauldron that heated water day and night over the fire; deftly and gently she stripped Martin of the clothes in which he had travelled. It was obvious from the way her large, capable hands moved that this was not the first time she had dealt with a broken body, but when Martin's clothes had been thrown outside the door and she lifted him bodily into the steaming water, even she stood there and surveyed him sombrely.

'Well, young sir,' she said in her slow drawl, 'somebody's treated ee bad, no mistake.'

Cecily, unable to help herself, uttered a cry and put her hands over her face, eyes closed to prevent the scalding tears brimming over. No false modesty beset her, she would do whatever was needful, but the state of his body, covered in sores and with every bone showing, called forth such an agony of pity that she did not know how to face him. Terror, too, came upon her when she saw the laboured way his chest rose and fell with each gasping breath. Suppose he had reached her at last, only to die. Desperately she prayed, 'Dear God, dear God, spare him to me, please, *please.*'

'Do ee stop that directly,' ordered Patience sternly. 'Wash your man whiles I get this stew stirred, or my Benjamin will be home to no food. Then I'll be 'ead down in that there water myself, I can tell ee!'

Cecily returned slowly to the tub, to the emaciated body, the closed, sunken eyes, and to Martin's voice, understanding, pleading. 'Help me, Cec, please help, if you can bear to come near me. I'll be right as a trivet once I'm clean.'

He flinched as Cecily touched him with the bar of rough soap Mistress True had provided and she drew back until he gasped, 'I'm alive from top to toe with the beastly things I picked up in that place. Scrub for all you're worth. I'd do it myself if I could.'

Her heart torn by his words, Cecily did as he asked until Patience True having lifted him, clean and towel-wrapped, from the tub, he subsided once more on to the settle.

'I think,' he managed to say carefully as Cecily dried his body, and his voice was a mere thread of sound, 'that – if I could lie down – lie down for . . .'

Between them the two women carried him, semi-conscious, into the tiny back room. Cecily fetched a rough woollen shirt from the bundle that had been awaiting his arrival and when they pulled it over his head he was too far gone to know or care what they were doing to him. His eyes they left unbound; even had they been open, which they were not, there was not enough light in the cottage to harm him.

For five long days he had lain prone in carts with all types of load, sometimes not even knowing when he had been lifted from one vehicle to another, and once, when all space was taken up by sacks, he had clung on to a high, swaying seat beside the driver until that worthy, with an extremely earthy comment, put arm and reins both about him to prevent his toppling on to the roadway. Later he would realize that he had been passed smoothly and efficiently along an organized chain of travel, but now he was utterly spent.

And so began the fight for Martin Woodfall's life. He lay on Cecily's bed and she never left his side. She dealt, with a competence that would have made Aunt Agnes proud of her, with all his bodily needs, she spooned cordial between his cracked and parched lips and dressed festering sores with salves from her box. Blanket upon rough blanket she piled upon him and held him close as he shook with the ague that his time in prison had given him, and on the fifth day, when Cecily awoke from a catnap on her chair to find his fever broken and his eyes, deep-sunken but lucid, watching her in the cold dimness of the tiny room, she knew that somewhere during this fight she had truly become his; for her, at least, no doubt remained.

As if her unspoken thought communicated itself to him he whispered, 'Cecily, Cecily,' as if in her name was everything he wanted or needed to say, and climbing on to the narrow bed, she put her brown head on the pillow beside his fair one and closed her eyes with a contented sigh.

Mistress True found them so when she looked in later. 'Your young lady hasn't hardly slept for nigh on four days on your account,' she told Martin. 'She'll make ee a good wife, I reckons.' She produced a hard, straw-packed pallet and laid it on the floor by Martin's bed. ' 'Tis warm enough, the little maid'll take no hurt. 'Sides, there be no other place for 'er,' and she lifted the unconscious Cecily on to the floor, where she slept without stirring for almost twelve hours.

Slowly Martin overcame his fever and a measure of strength returned to his body, but Patience True pronounced that he was in no state to undertake a sea voyage, not at this time of year, if he were to reach the other end of it alive, and a boat came and went without them.

Because there was nowhere else, Cecily and he shared the small room, he sleeping on the bed because she insisted and at first he had not the power to gainsay her, she on the pallet. Nor were they apart by day, this young man so painfully thin, stooped and pale, and the girl pinched and worn by sorrow and worry so that every shred of the life that had always radiated from her seemed lost.

At first they spoke little to each other, but Patience observed them always hand in hand, like two children who had been lost and had found each other again. Although Cecily doubted he would ever recover completely from his experiences, Martin was barely able to crawl before he must fetch and carry for her, look after her in all the small ways she had taken for granted over the years. He spoke gently of their family, reassuring her when she worried, cheering her when she grieved, yet himself from time to time fell prey to long, brooding silences and never once would he speak of their future. It seemed to Cecily that to live from day to day was all he could manage and she steeled herself to accept him so, to ask no questions until he was ready for them. Twice she broke her resolve, attempted to make plans. The first time Martin left her, wrenched himself up off the settle with more strength than she had thought he possessed and almost ran into the back room; the second time he stayed but he said, 'Not yet, Cecily, please,' so wearily that she fell silent. There seemed no way to reach beyond his refusal and she began to see in him less of the boy and more of the Martin of her last days at Abbey House, stern and withdrawn.

Small things set her worrying: never once had he called her 'little one', nor, after the first day when he had been half-delirious, had he shortened her name to Cec. Always she was 'Cecily' and there were times when the tone he used made her think she heard 'mistress' before it. Fear grew within her; he blamed her for her part in the oath Robert Cooper must have forced him to take or, worst of all, he no longer wanted her for his wife. What would happen if that were indeed so she could not bring herself to contemplate. That he might have transferred to Master Cooper the jealousy he had once felt for Wat never occurred to her.

She wondered, had even asked Benjamin True, whether their continued long presence in the cottage, isolated though it was, might be a danger to his little family, but he had only thrown back his head and laughed his mighty laugh. He could use the money, he said. Christmastide was over and the gales of the first half of January had blown themselves out when one day Martin said, 'Benjamin tells me that if the weather holds a boat will come tomorrow.'

That was all; nothing about the boat 'coming for us' and Cecily in her new-found sensitivity to his moods decided that the next move must be hers. 'If I take your arm, can you walk down to the beach?' she asked. 'We can be alone and it is sheltered. I should so like you to see it.' She, too, bit off the sentence, leaving it without 'before we go', and had no clear idea of why she did so.

Martin bowed slightly, mock-formally, once again making her aware of distance between them. By the time they reached the old upturned boat, he was panting for breath. Thankfully he sank down, leaned back and closed his eyes. Benjamin had trimmed his fair, curly hair, but he had kept a beard to hide the fading sores on his face, and it added to his older look, the look that put a man in place of the boy Cecily knew.

She pulled his cloak firmly about him and tucked it round his legs so that the breeze might not move it. It had come with the other clothes; it was long and black and there was a neatly mended tear in one shoulder. If it were not Robert Cooper's it was its twin, she thought, and sat down close to Martin. Still she wore the boy's clothes Patience had provided; never once had he, usually so forthright, commented upon them.

Without opening his eyes he said, 'Thank you. You'll make someone a good wife some day.' It had been an old joke of her father's whenever she had rendered some small service, and no matter how many times repeated, had always raised laughter, but not now. The expression on Martin's face said that the words had slipped out unthinkingly, that he would have given much to recall them.

But they gave Cecily the opening for which she had waited so long, and she took it. 'He was innocent, *innocent*, whatever they say, just as you are and – and . . .' Her voice trailed away as the thought she had tried so hard to suppress overcame her yet again. 'And Uncle Thomas,' she ended bravely.

'Was he?' The dry note in Martin's voice told her that she was not alone in her doubts. 'Uncle Thomas, I mean. Are you sure of that?'

'Martin!'

'When – when your friend, Master Cooper, set me on my way there were things he said that pointed me to the truth. I can hear him now – "it is possible to live all your life close by" – not *with* – "close by a person and know

441

nothing about them," he said. Well, we lived near to Uncle Thomas. Suppose someone came along and proposed that he lend a hand in a Stuart plot in return for promise of advancement . . .?'

'Such as what? He had the estate and more money than he needed.'

'Remember Aunt Eleanor! There he was, the same country gentleman she married twenty-odd years before. We all know he sent money to London regularly yet not once had preferment come his way. A few sneering words from Edith Stone, chancing just when the prospect of advancement offered from some other direction, and it's easy enough to imagine the rest.'

'He destroyed the family,' said Cecily sombrely. 'But Father wasn't guilty, any more than you, Martin.'

'We were near enough to Uncle Thomas to bear questioning. And the abbey ornaments found behind the panelling tipped the scales against Uncle Edward. I knew of them because he told me in case anything happened to him. They were there because of some promise made to the last abbot – the man who was executed. To be handed from generation to generation of whoever owned the abbey lands.'

'I didn't know that,' said Cecily gravely.

'The fewer people who did, the better. They were never used, not even by Father Peter, but in these days so small a thing warrants arrest and questioning at the least. As for me, my mother's family is staunch Roman Catholic to this day, and I had my schooling from a lapsed priest. Reason enough, to my way of thinking!'

'Master Cooper told you all this?'

Martin frowned, recalling and passing on what Robert had intended he should. 'He said – I remember now – that Uncle Thomas confessed and that your father's confession was identical in almost every detail. It's my belief they copied what Uncle Thomas said and gave it to Uncle Edward to sign when he was already dying.'

Cecily choked back a sob. 'But why, when he had done nothing?'

'Except to hide forbidden artefacts,' Martin reminded her

grimly. 'Suspicious in itself. They were making certain they cleared out what must have looked like a family of traitors. If only Uncle Thomas hadn't been so – so . . .'

'Wicked!' supplied Cecily viciously. 'Did you swear never to question what happened?'

'I did, and very nearly got strangled because I hesitated!' Martin's hands went to his throat at the memory of Robert Cooper's fury.

He watched her grieving at his side, forcing herself to accept harsh reality, but there was another subject that had lain undiscussed between them that could wait no longer.

'A man of some authority, your Master Cooper. Able to call for confessions at will and not used to being kept waiting! Who is he? How did you meet?'

For a moment Cecily hesitated. She was doing no more than marshalling her thoughts, yet Martin took it as confirmation of what he suspected.

'Well?' he prompted harshly.

Shaken by a tone he had seldom if ever used towards her, Cecily replied spiritedly, 'He is not *my* Master Cooper! I do not know who he is. You are right about the authority, of course. The night he brought me to the Tower we went in through the gates as if he owned the place. I met him when the Queen sent me with a message to Sir Francis Walsingham and he was there. He showed me the way back to the royal apartments.'

'And on the strength of that he agreed to rescue me?' asked Martin drily.

Instinct told her not to mention the day in the country. 'I – I met him once or twice more and he was kind. When I needed help I went to him because I could think of no-one else.'

'Not even the devil?'

'Whatever are you talking about?'

'Something he said about you asking the devil himself if he'd had the key to my cell.'

Cecily smiled. 'How strange – but I'm not sure that he wasn't right! In fact at first I wanted him to find Wat so

443

that *he* could help, but he couldn't because – because Wat never came home. You know about that.'

'Yes, I know.' Martin was no more expansive on the subject of his brother than Cecily herself had been on an earlier occasion. Let him lie, he thought; may he rest in peace.

'I'm sorry I hurt you so, Martin.' Cecily's voice was childlike. 'Please forgive me.'

A thin hand struggled out from the all-enveloping black cloak and took hers. It was carried to Martin's forehead in a gesture that reminded her so much of Robert Cooper at their last meeting that she pulled sharply away; in the embarrassment that swept over her she was not aware of the way her movement might be interpreted.

She came to her knees on the pebbles. 'How did Master Cooper get you out of the Tower? I can't wait any longer for you to tell me.'

Martin laughed, a hard, dry sound. 'Unless he tells you, you will never know. He drugged me, so much I remember, after which I knew nothing until I wakened next day in some house of his. But however important he is, he could hardly have thrown me over one shoulder and marched out through the gates!'

The words as well as the tone filled Cecily with unease. 'He put his life into great danger for your sake,' she said roundly.

Martin thought he had reached his decision. Cecily had trodden on him once when he offered his love, pride demanded that it should not happen a second time. He had determined to speak before she did; how could he have guessed that when the day came, self-sacrifice would be so hard to put into words? He had grown used to being with her all over again. She had always been part of his life and now he loved her more, it seemed to him, than ever he had. He tried to tell himself that he was losing nothing that had ever been his but he remembered far more of his talk with Master Cooper than the parts that had been intended to incriminate his Uncle Thomas. There had been a good deal, had there not, about Cecily wanting to go away with

444

him and what a fortunate fellow he was! Intended, it seemed to him, to get him to go on his way quietly! Therefore it was very much between clenched teeth that he said, 'We both know that whatever Cooper did for me was done because he loves you!'

Cecily blushed fiery red, catching her breath, covering hot cheeks with her hands, thankful that Martin did not know of a certain letter she had written the evening before she left London. For the first time she permitted herself to think of Master Cooper's parting gesture as more than kindliness, and because it worried her, said defensively, 'Nonsense! People at court say flowery things all the time!'

Martin pounced. 'So he did say such things to you!'

'Only, only once. It's a way they have, Martin, that's all. They don't mean one word of it.'

'To the Queen, perhaps.' Martin dismissed his monarch lightly. 'But not to you. For you only the truth is good enough.'

It was as courtly a compliment as ever he would pay her, but it passed unnoticed. Under the shock of what he was saying she gasped then, after a pause, asked rather stupidly, 'What are we going to do, Martin?'

'You *dare* to ask me that?' Anger that she should torment him thus rang through her cousin's voice. 'All has gone as you planned with Master Cooper, surely? Was he afraid that I might not fall in with his plan unless you were here to persuade me? You need have no fear, Cecily. You have nursed me back to health and I shall disappear overseas as I promised. You are free to go back to the man you love. I am not a fool, my girl!'

Bewildered, she stammered, 'But I am to go with you, that is what we arranged.' She knelt on the stones, staring at him as at a stranger, whilst he looked down at hands whose trembling he could not control and hated the thought of every moment she had spent with that dark, handsome young man.

'Do you expect me to believe that he would have taken such risks without promise of reward? *Do you?*'

She had never imagined that kind, gentle Martin could

445

speak to her so. Almost she clapped her hands over her ears to shut out the horror of it all before, in desperation, she threw her arms about his neck in one last attempt to save her happiness.

'No, Martin, no! It is you I love.'

His hands came up to break her grasp, to push her away and hold her at arms' length.

'You have been kind to me, so kind, since I arrived,' he said relentlessly, 'but then you must remember that I have known you a long time. You would have done as much for a sick stranger. I have not changed. I am the same person you rejected at home. Go back! I shall do well enough alone!'

With an action entirely uncharacteristic of him and so violent that she landed on her back in the shingle before him, he pushed her away and his voice rose in a despairing shout: 'In the name of Heaven, Cecily, what do you think I am made of? I cannot live with the ghost of Cooper constantly sneering at my elbow! First Wat, and now him!'

He buried his face in his hands and Cecily was left to pull herself up from her undignified position at his feet. She did so, knowing deep within herself that Martin was not even aware of the violence he had used. How she commanded her voice she never knew, but command it she did, and it was without a tremor that she said, 'Nor shall you, Martin. Robert Cooper was kind to me when I needed a friend. I do not love him and there was no bargain between us.'

She brushed sand off her dress. Her last hope for happiness was gone. Because of her behaviour when he had first declared his love, Martin was unable to believe her now. He was sending her away and the fault was her own. Quite steadily, with a dignity inherited from her mother, she said, 'It is the dearest wish of my heart to go with you, but it shall be as you choose. Goodbye, Martin. Good fortune go with you. My love always will.'

She had taken her first stumbling steps towards the cliff path, too numbed even to wonder where she might go and what the future could hold for her, when she heard a sound behind her, a broken, ragged cry; despite herself she stopped and looked back.

Martin was on his feet, trailing the old cloak from his shoulders. He reached out unsteady hands towards her. 'The dearest wish, little one?' he whispered. 'But Cooper has done so much for you and he is – he is . . .' He made an impatient gesture of comparison towards himself. 'I saw him. And smelled him for that matter – clean-washed and sweet. Just look at the state I'm in. How can you possibly choose me?'

The very boyishness of the words caught at Cecily's throat and, unable to help herself, she choked on a giggle. The stranger was gone and the Martin with whom she had lived and played all her life stood before her. The same Martin yet infinitely more dear.

'I do not know,' she whispered softly, 'but it is so.'

Like some black shadow the cloak dropped to the sand behind him unregarded and he came towards her with the shuffling, old man's gait that was all he could manage at present. Suddenly his eyes had regained something of the twinkle she had always loved, but his hands were by his sides and he made no attempt to touch her. Only, looking directly into the blue eyes that were so like his own, he said, with a tremor in his voice, 'But I thought . . .'

Through her tears, Cecily smiled. 'No you did not! That is just what you never did do! Robert Cooper asked for nothing and gave me all – because he sent you to me. For that I shall always remember him. But it is you I love, Martin, you and none other.'

'Then,' he asked quietly, 'will you become my wife, Cecily?'

In after years, she was wont to tease him by telling him that she never formally accepted his suit, and it was true, for in the next instant their arms were about each other and they were laughing, crying and kissing all at the same time.

Later, with one arm still about his neck, Cecily said, 'How foolish of me to take so long to find that it was you I wanted from the very beginning.'

She reached into the small pocket that hung from her waist and took from it the pearl set in silver her father had given her, cupping the precious thing in her palms and holding it out to the man she loved.

'This is for you now,' she said and gently, with bowed head, Martin accepted the token, responsibility for the future of the Woodfall family, and her love.

And as she spoke, from somewhere nearby she seemed to hear the echo of her father's laughter, contented and happy for her, although it was doubtless just the sound of the sea rushing in over the pebbles.

Firmly Martin said, 'I'll make a home fit for you, Mistress Norton; for you and a long line of little Nortons, until one day we take our own name again.'

Cecily pulled back and looked at him in astonishment. Bowing low, he said, 'You behold in me one Martin Norton, mistress. Master Cooper advised me to find a new name. Martin Woodfall, he said, lies dead and buried in the Tower of London. I asked one of the drivers who brought me here what his mother's name had been; it sounds well, I think?'

'Any name that belongs to you I shall be honoured to carry, sir,' said Cecily, curtseying, and neither of them at that moment gave a thought to Robert Cooper or how he had managed to dispose of the last of the Woodfall men without a dead body to show.

But he did, after all, come once more into their conversation that day, for Cecily asked, 'And now, tell me where you got that purse Patience found in your clothes.'

'You know very well where from, Cec. Gold, to give us a new beginning.'

His voice softened. In his new-found happiness he could afford to be generous, and pity for Robert Cooper swept away the last of his jealousy. How much he loves her, he thought, with the cruelty of young love, and she belongs to me! Aloud he said, 'Cec, my dearest little one . . .'

They came together again, their arms tightening about one another, and young Billy and Mab, coming to bid them to dinner, stopped short in their usual headlong race down the cliff path. The next moment they were running together back to the cottage, elbowing each other out of the way in their efforts to be first with the news.

'They can't come, not now they can't,' shrieked Billy, to his mother's amazement.

'He do be a-squeezin' 'er so much he'm like to break 'er into little pieces. Her's not big to begin wi', now is 'er?' added his sister in awe-struck tones, by way of explanation.

Mistress True threw back her head and gave vent to a hearty laugh. 'Well now,' she chortled, 'is 'e indeed! Not afore time! I do reckon as 'ow the stew can wait!'

CHAPTER XIV

Cecily had been gone from London for five days when Taylor called at the house in Trinity Street. She handed to Martha a letter left in her keeping, and Martha took it to Jerome who, after examining the folded and sealed paper, placed it on the study table to await Robert's coming. From time to time, as he tried to concentrate on his own writing, Jerome's eyes returned to it as if it called aloud to him; once he even took it in his hand, turning it this way and that. If it came whence he suspected – and Taylor had said nothing on that score – it would be as well destroyed. The child could have nothing of value to say. Robert must leave for France on the morrow and Jerome most earnestly wished him to travel with an easy mind. He knew – none better – how to open a seal, could refasten it so that not even Robert would detect his tampering. That delicate thing called personal honour was all that stood between the thought and the action.

Not a word regarding the Woodfall family had passed between Jerome and Robert recently although, from other sources, Jerome had heard of its miserable ending and had, in spite of having nothing to set against proven guilt, regretted it. One man lay buried at the Tower, the body of another was by now back at what had been his family's estate. He had gone accompanied by his daughter and the young cousin who had done all in her power to draw Robert into the toils that wound about them. The boy for whom she had been so anxious had died in his cell.

Jerome would as soon have told Robert the truth about his own relationship with his sister as ask his nephew's feelings for Cecily. He had, he thought grimly, no need to ask. Ever since his return from Sussex, weak from the effects of his wounded arm, yet never taking one day away from his work, Robert had spoken scarcely a word that had not been forced from him by politeness, sometimes not even that. He had gone about house and – for all Jerome knew – Palace, with a look on his face so rigid that to one who cared for him the conclusion was inescapable. That little brown girl had reached his heart after all.

One thing more he knew, which might have no connection at all with the Woodfalls. There had been a morning when Martha had come to him, white-faced and retching, to apologize that his meal was late and that there was no hot water because someone had been burning clothes, and ashes choked her kitchen grate. Eyes wide in horror, she had confided that they were undoubtedly Master Cooper's clothes and that – that . . . She stopped until prodded into further explanation by Jerome's stern instruction to continue. The parts that had not been burned but had doused her fire, were blood-soaked. It had taken Jerome all his time to placate her. Of course she had done right to tell him. No blame attached to her. It was careless of Master Cooper to have left such a job half finished (and more than careless! Whatever had he been up to?). He would have a word with him.

He had not, however. When Robert returned that evening he had looked so much as if all he wanted was to be alone that Jerome wondered why he had not gone straight up to the solitude of his own room. But that was not his way and perhaps, admit it or not, he had need of company, for he stayed long in his chair by the fire, eyes closed, unspeaking, and Jerome had made no attempt to leave him. If silent companionship would help, that the boy should have.

On this later day when Robert came in, slung his cloak over a chairback and dropped a tape-tied bundle of papers on the table, the letter was untouched, nor did Jerome draw his attention to it; only he watched from an eye corner as

451

Robert put out a hand. The writing meant nothing to him, there was no expectation of trouble in his face as, without examining it – and why should he? – he ran his thumbnail beneath the irregular, unmarked blob of sealing wax.

For a moment there was silence so that Jerome, seemingly intent on his book, peered even more closely. Two sheets of paper, and whatever they contained held the younger man unmoving until, with sudden violence, he screwed them together and twisted. He did not speak, he gave no exclamation, yet the pain in his face as he rose, blundered unseeingly round the table, was enough to make Jerome, who knew nothing but guessed at so much, wince in sympathy.

Robert stood for a moment by the hearth before, as if throwing off some burden, he shook his head, braced his shoulders, smoothed out between his hands the papers he had so tortured. In a surprisingly level voice he said, 'I beg your pardon, sir; this sheet is intended for you.'

It was the recipe for a salve of some kind, carefully written in a round, girlish hand. As Jerome looked up from it in surprise, Robert added, 'From Mistress Woodfall. It worked on your hands before,' and turned back to the fire.

The sheet he had retained he screwed up once more into a tight ball, tossed it into the heart of the fire and, taking up the long poker, stabbed at it again and again as if it were some living thing he would kill. Still he struck when nothing remained but a small mound of ash that might, for all anyone knew, have fallen off a burned log. If he had allowed his hands to be still they would have trembled, and every word that he sent so swiftly beyond retrieving, so as to deny his sudden insane impulse to carry it to his lips, he remembered as if it were burned on his brain:

'Dear Master Cooper, I enclose a copy of the recipe for Aunt Agnes's salve, so that when he needs it your foster-father can have some more made up. Now you have a Woodfall family secret! Use it wisely! I loved my father more than anyone in the world and it comforts me to know that you were with him so that he did not die alone. I shall remember you in my prayers. With respect and duty, sir, Cecily Woodfall.'

Had the letter been intercepted there was not one word that could not have been read aloud before the world, although the idea that his presence at her father's death-bed had been in guise of a comforter would have raised guffaws in certain quarters. Even in her kindness she had remembered her promise of secrecy.

The silence became intolerable. Once, just this once, Jerome told himself, he must be allowed an effort to break through the armour of this human being he had so largely formed. Folding Cecily's paper carefully, putting it on to the table beside him, he said calmly, 'A kind thought indeed. I hope Martha can be trusted to concoct it.'

The next moment the poker clattered to the hearth. Robert swung round, head bowed, then, as if someone had felled him from behind, dropped to his knees beside Jerome's chair, reaching up his hands as in supplication and resting his face on the older man's knee. As Jerome gripped and held both twisted, quivering hands in his one, a muffled voice said, 'I thought it was over.'

'Why did you not tell her you loved her? Why?'

Robert looked up, his face bleached of all colour in the candlelight.

'If only you knew how hard I fought against it. I would not allow myself to believe, and she – her heart was given to her cousin.'

Taking advantage of permission he had never received before, might never receive again, Jerome asked, 'The boy who died in the Tower? What is to stop you going after her, once her grief has worn away?'

Across Robert's face passed a shadow of the gentle smile Cecily had seen in the chapel. 'I shall survive,' he said, and the words that came to him were much the same that had come to Martin in his misery. 'I have lost nothing I ever possessed, after all! I apologize for embarrassing you, sir. It will not happen again.'

And it would not, thought Jerome, as the younger man

rose and pulled down his doublet. The moment of revelation, of close relationship, was over, would probably never return, and he accepted it as part of his penance.

Watching Robert pour wine into two goblets, hands steady once more, he turned the subject. 'I have completed one of Jenkins's miserable reports. If you have no plan for this evening perhaps you would be kind enough to deliver it for me. He has been harrying me for it this week and more.'

The state of affairs he might well find at Jenkins's house would jerk Robert out of his introspection and make him glad that on the morrow he would be on his way out of the country. Jerome allowed himself a moment of self-pity: leaving me to who knows how long of my own miserable company.

All unsuspecting, Robert knocked loudly on the door of Amos Jenkins's house. The woman who answered had been of the household as long as he could remember; Jenkins's mistress, they said, although he had never been interested enough to question. She was trustworthy, so much he knew, therefore he would have handed Jerome's package to her and gone on his way, but she stood back in the shadows and when she spoke the rough, deep voice trembled in what might have been fear, might have been excitement.

'He's in there, sir.' She jerked a thumb towards a door at the end of the passage.

Robert held out the package towards her, seeing no reason why he should deliver it in person, but she persisted. 'At the back, sir, if you please. And – and waiting for you.'

He shrugged. He knew what to expect; the man was drunk, and being drunk would be offensive as only he knew how to be. For the last time of asking, Robert thought, and if I let you vent your spite on me tonight it may make life easier for Jerome for a day or two.

Without knocking he opened the door the woman had indicated. A small room, even by the standards of this house, scarcely more than a closet. One chair by the hearth, a table holding the inevitable flagon and tankard, and a wooden box below the tiny window. The only light, apart from that given off by a miserably inadequate fire, came from one candle standing on that box and casting more light over wall and window than upon the room's occupant.

Robert stood for a moment in the doorway, accustoming his eyes to the gloom, fighting disgust at the smell of unwashed body and drink-sodden clothing that even at this distance came in waves off the man in the chair. He gave no thought to his own appearance, to what the sight of a tall figure swathed in black, hooded cloak might mean.

'*You!* They've sent *you!* I suppose I should feel honoured.'

Robert found that he was not, after all, in the mood to listen. He put Jerome's report on the table and turned to leave.

'I'm not getting out of the chair, if that's what you're trying for. Want to take me standing? Is that your game? The old bend backwards over the knee and crack goes the neck? Just like Gregory?'

Robert stopped in his tracks. There was panic in the stumbling voice and what Jerome had not told him the gabbled words made abundantly clear. Walsingham had replaced Jenkins! And a loose-mouthed drunkard with a head full of secrets could not be allowed to remain at large. He sat here waiting for the man his successor should send to kill him. As the woman had, Robert thought grimly. Both had taken him for the chosen assassin.

Jolted to the pit of his stomach for the second time that evening, he gave himself time to think by taking up the candle and carrying it over to Jenkins, who shrank from its light. Surprisingly, despite the smell, he was far more sober than anyone had known him for a long time. The tight-stretched skin of his face had the true drunkard's sheen, and atop that stood the sweat of fear, beads of water on brow and lip, trickling downwards to drip on to soiled linen. To see the terror of death on the face of anyone, even a man like this who had caused the deaths of so many and had enjoyed it, brought no pleasure at all to Robert. He indicated the flagon on the table.

'A drink would help,' he observed.

Eyes sunken into rolls of puffy flesh flickered sideways, came back to Robert's face almost immediately, with desperate bravado. 'Join me. No? But you'll give me time to drain mine?' He raised his voice. 'Doll! Another chair for – for – my guest! I tell her that she's nothing to fear. She goes with the house. Whoever comes will take her on. A good 'un is Doll.'

It seemed that the woman did not share her master's confidence in her future. She scuttled into the room and out again as fast as she could; never once did she look at either of them.

Robert sat down. Jenkins was sipping wine like some green boy afraid he might disgrace himself. He caught Robert's look and concentrated his attention on the tankard.

'I've a fancy to die sober,' he mumbled. 'Doll brought this in case I couldn't manage it.' He held out a shaking hand. 'And I'm not sure I shall. That's why I'm in this poky place. No space to run. I don't want one and all to hear that you had to chase me round and round the table, now do I? If – if you could find it in you to be quick, I'd be grateful. I taught you well enough.'

He grinned suddenly, with a disgusting display of black and yellow teeth. 'Suppose, just suppose I decided to take you on and make a run for it. I might get away. Think I couldn't?'

Coldly Robert said, 'I've not been sent here to kill you. You'll have to wait – just as all the poor devils you've dealt with over the years have waited.'

He sat back, surveyed as an object of curiosity a killer awaiting his own murder. He need not, he thought, have made that last remark.

Carefully Jenkins put down his tankard, seemingly reassured. 'So it's not you, young Cooper, but if someone opened the door this instant and told you to stand aside so that he could stab me, you'd do it without a second thought. And why?' Suddenly he was launched into the diatribe Robert had heard so many times before. It dated from the time when it had become obvious that he was to work for Burghley and not with Jenkins's bully boys.

'Because you're one of us, no matter what you think, that's why. You may look better than we do, and have book learning coming out of your ears, and spend your days among men folk like me bow low to, but if your master ordered you to torture information out of someone or plant damning papers on an innocent man, you'd do it, because that's what I trained you to. I said from the start that you were too nice and I was right, but I'm damned if I'll have you looking down on the rest of us!'

Robert held still, despite the rage that stirred in him at thought of an innocent family destroyed in hope of saving a drunkard's job and skin. There was truth in what Jenkins said, more than a little of it.

Jenkins subsided, his tone changed. 'They say dying men tell the truth, don't they? Not that I've ever relied on it. Well, much as it goes against the grain, Cooper, I have to admit that you *are* a gentleman fully fledged, as you might say. If I was a drinking man this evening, I'd pledge your health.' He raised an invisible tankard. 'To Master Robert Cooper, one of the coming men who's harnessed his horse to the right chariot. Master Cecil's a man to watch, no need to tell you that. Sent for me, he did, just after you'd left him.'

He laughed as Robert peered at him sharply. 'Oh, yes. Told me exactly what to expect if anything out of the ordinary, shall we say, happened to one of his employees – meaning you, Cooper, meaning you! Seemed to think I might be tempted! And me in a muck sweat, with Gregory lying in wait. The relief I felt when his body was found you can't imagine! Yet it hasn't given me much longer, has it? Must be a moral in that somewhere, must be.'

Robert leaned forward, filled up the other's tankard again, but Jenkins viewed it solemnly, making no move to take it up.

'Hear my confession!' he said, and suddenly he was desperately serious. 'You're as near to a priest as I shall ever come, you and your long face! Aye, as near now or afterwards, for they'll throw me in the river as the quickest

457

way, and never a word spoken over me. So you'll have to do. Either that or fetch Jerome. Now who would ever have thought he'd have outlasted me? I had him watched for years. Never put a foot wrong. Strange for one of them Popish creatures. Thought they were more fanatical.' He sat frowning over something that had obviously long perplexed him.

'Well, you it will have to be, Cooper, and maybe you can profit by what I say.' He leaned forward and his voice grew confidential. 'Listen, lad. They come back once you start to get old. You'll find that for yourself. They come back at night and watch you, all those men and women you delivered up for the good of the country and to earn a crust of bread. The drink makes them go away at first, then they get clever and stay. And you drink more and more and they laugh at you for thinking it'll work. And because you drink you can't do your job properly, so that pleases them as well. You'll see: that's how it is. It'll be just the same for you.'

Between horror and pity, Robert said, 'I think not,' and Jenkins laughed.

'Perhaps I'll stand at the end of *your* bed, who knows? If you die in bed, that is. Then you'll remember what I said. You'll remember . . .'

His voice died away as Robert stood up. Then: 'Is this it?'

Quietly Robert said, 'Goodbye, Jenkins. Drink what you've got there and ask Doll for more. It will be easier that way.'

He bowed slightly towards the man who had taught him the dark side of all he knew. He was almost at the door when Jenkins launched himself forward not, as Robert realized after his first involuntary defensive reaction, in anger, but in an agony of fear.

'Do it!' he blubbered. 'Be quick. I taught you. You owe it to me. I saved your life, remember? Jerome would have skinned you alive if I hadn't stopped him!'

His voice ended in a piteous, childlike whimpering and Robert bent to loosen clinging arms from about his legs. But terror gave the older man strength and he stood silent, shackled to the spot, as Jenkins realized that his pleas were in vain.

'Why not me? Why not? For pity's sake! You've not been so squeamish before! Promise I won't haunt you, promise I won't!' Silence, until as Robert still made no move, from the black twisted mouth in the dimly seen, upturned face, venom spewed at him.

'What a disappointment you must have been to Jerome, to be sure. Didn't want him, did you, for all his careful upbringing? I've seen the way he looks at you! But you – your tastes run in other directions. A baker woman old enough to be your mother, until she went off to an honest man. Not to mention her idiot son. Then a slut of a serving wench. Gregory's leavings, she is. A fine mother for your child, I don't think! And when a decent girl looks at you, what's it for? Please, sir, put my father out of his misery. And my cousin. Don't let them suffer, please, please. And you did it, didn't you? Two out of three! Hope she gave you your money's worth, her with her big blue eyes, before she rode off and . . .'

Livid with emotions he dared not analyze, Robert took the screaming man by the hair, wrenching him upright. For a moment he held him almost clear of the floor and Jenkins quietened, thinking that his time had come. But Robert only studied him as dispassionately as if he were an animal he were deciding whether or not to buy. 'What evil conjunction of stars brought you and Stone together, I wonder?' he asked, and with a blow from the back of one hand sent his victim spinning across the room, to fetch up beneath the window, half-stunned.

He had presence of mind, even as he trembled, to catch up Jerome's report before he left. He would deliver it direct to Walsingham's office. He needed a long, tiring walk and one direction was as good as another.

In the passage he met Doll, who cowered against the wall to let him pass. 'Look after him,' he said curtly and was gone before she had completed her curtsey.

He did not hear her quiet, 'Oh, I will, sir,' nor see the dagger she took from beneath her apron. Master

Cooper's visit had put Jenkins off-guard; her task would be easier now.

Robert strode in the direction of Whitehall and gradually, slowly, he regained his calm, forcing the thoughts that seethed within him to the back of his mind by composing the report he would so much have enjoyed leaving for Sir Francis along with Jerome's work.

'I have the honour to report that permission having been granted by Her Majesty for the corpse of Sir Thomas Woodfall to be returned to his home for burial, I took a cart to the Tower to collect the coffin, on his daughter's behalf, on the evening following his execution. The cart I left at the gatehouse and went to visit Martin Woodfall in his cell. Knowing him to be completely innocent of any crime, as were all his family, I had undertaken to rescue him for his fair cousin's sake.

'Finding him, as I expected, so weak from his treatment as to be incapable of helping in his own escape, I drugged him almost to the point of death and called his jailer. This worthy, one Will Smith, who is so gullible as to be unworthy of his miserable employment, agreed with me that the prisoner was dead and assisted in removing his chains. Thereupon, at my suggestion, Smith fetched a coffin to the chapel of St Peter Ad Vincula where the body, as that of a gentleman, might lie until its burial, without undue ceremony, the following morning. When we reached the chapel and the empty coffin lay side by side with the more ornate one of his lately executed uncle, I laid Woodfall down and suggested to the jailer that as he was no doubt eager to get back to the guardhouse brazier and better companionship than corpses, I would fasten Woodfall's body down if he would fetch my cart across the courtyard and help me load the late unlamented traitor, Sir Thomas, into it. He readily agreed and no sooner had he left than I prised open the lid of Sir Thomas's coffin, lifted out body and severed head, and placed both in his nephew's simpler box. Martin Woodfall's body I deposited in the coffin I was to take away. I had barely time to fasten down the two lids before Smith returned. He helped me load the escaping prisoner on to the cart, rode with me to the gatehouse and let me out.

'Sir Thomas was interred next morning in his nephew's stead. Knowing his high opinion of his own worth in life, it would not surprise me if his ghost were to walk the Tower complaining loudly of such unbecoming treatment.

'Martin Woodfall, still unconscious, I transported to a room in a house belonging to a woman who is beholden to me, where I transferred him to a bed. In his stead, I placed in the coffin the corpse of a beggar I had obtained earlier. This poor wretch's head I severed, lest anyone, on arrival at Highwoods, be foolish enough to open the coffin. The face was unrecognizable. This coffin, draped in black velvet, was duly escorted on its homeward journey by Mistress Rose Woodfall, daughter of the so-called traitor, and will no doubt shortly be interred in his family vault with due ceremony. Martin Woodfall is on his way overseas, and whoever the beggar was, he lies far more splendidly in death than ever in life.

'I consider this to be the best night's work of my life, despite its having cost me a suit of clothes I found it necessary to destroy.'

The grim humour sustained him until he reached Sir Francis's room. There the light still burned; papers littered the table. Jerome's report was received with a word of thanks, added almost abstractedly to a pile. Robert had made his bow, his hand was already on the door latch, when Walsingham said, in much the same words as had Jenkins, 'You go to one of the rising men of our world, Cooper.' The narrow, cunning face bent once more over the papers that, arriving from many counties, many countries, enabled him to keep fingers on the pulses of nations, to strive for England's peace, and his parting words were almost lost: 'Good fortune. If you wish to return at any time, you will be welcome.'

With nothing now to exorcize his demons, Robert made his way swiftly along flambeau-lighted corridors, passed impassive guards before the Queen's apartments where all

461

was quiet, drew aside to let pass late-night servants, who hurried about their final tasks before sleep.

He came at last, almost abstractedly, to a wide passageway at the end of which a door led into gardens, black and white under a moon which trailed silver-edged wisps of cloud like veils. There he had seen Cecily Woodfall laughing and talking, fetching and carrying at the Queen's behest, both in her tranquil first days at court and, later, when she had known of the shadow hanging over her family. Then still she had performed her duties with pride and a quiet bravery that had caught at more hearts and minds than his.

Tonight two things had happened that had brought him face to face with the self from whom he had always endeavoured to hide. Cecily Woodfall and Amos Jenkins had never seen one another, yet separated by many miles and the difference between good and evil, they had come together and shattered what peace of mind he had managed to cling to.

He had accepted that he would never see Cecily again, had been reasonably sure of his self-control until the belated receipt of an unexpected letter had torn away his guard. Despite rapid action with fire and poker, every word she had written was graven upon his brain. For a moment almost he hated her. '. . . and you were with him so that he did not die alone.' The little fool had seen the conditions in which her cousin was imprisoned. Did she think her father had died in the comfort of a featherbed? She would never hear, because no-one but he himself would ever know, the truth about her father's death. '. . . Now you have a Woodfall family secret . . .' I poisoned him, mistress. At the time it seemed merciful, you understand. A secret indeed!

Always he had known, and had told himself that it was for the country's good, that in the name of expediency things that were not spoken of aloud were condoned by men of far higher rank than would ever be his. In the midst of more pleasant work, he had directly or indirectly delivered men to prison, had attended interrogations, had himself questioned men dying after ill-treatment that would turn the stomach of any decent person. He had deceived, lied, impersonated and yet, despite what Jenkins thought, never until the last weeks had he killed a man with his own hands, save once. Sir Evelyn Talbot-Jones's dying face rose before him, wearing an absurdly surprised expression, as the youth he had thought easy game vanquished him with no difficulty at all.

And now, within the space of a few weeks, he had poisoned Edward Woodfall and had, by a carefully careless word, delivered the unknown and innocent Walter Woodfall to his death. The first might be considered a merciful release; the second most surely could not.

Jenkins's words crowded in on him. In all these years when the man had gone about his work seemingly untroubled, who would have guessed how many nights he had spent haunted and guilt-ridden? For the first time Robert wondered where this teacher of his had come from. Had there been a time when he had been hopeful and clean of spirit? Had he undertaken work he detested for what he believed to be a short time, and then again and again, until there was no turning back?

Until, as Robert had lately found to his own horror, killing became easy. What need to have broken Gregory's miserable neck? A sound beating – easily administered – would have sent him scuttling, yet he had killed as if the lad were no more than a rabbit for the stewpot.

About Martin Woodfall he could scarcely bring himself to think at all. The actual rescue had held something of the stimulation of an academic exercise – he had proved that it was possible, with luck, to remove a prisoner from the Tower without arousing suspicion. But when the defenceless young man had challenged him, he who had been so certain that he had his hot temper under control had been within an inch of snapping another neck. Until the actual day he died Martin would have no closer brush with death than he had had then. And why? Not because he had refused to swear the oath demanded of him. The reason, Cooper, the true reason? He forced himself onwards. For one uncontrolled, rage-filled moment he had been prepared to kill so that if

463

he himself could not have Cecily, neither should Martin Woodfall.

Tonight he had even lied to Jerome concerning Cecily herself. True, his 'I thought it was over' had been dragged from him, but he knew very well that it was not over, nor would it be until word reached him that she and Martin were safely abroad. If Martin died on his way to meet her, or before they left the country, weak as he was, the thing that neither cousin in their innocence had suspected would become inevitable. He had detached the girl from her family, firmly believed that whatever happened she would keep her oath never to return to them, but that was not sufficient safeguard. For the sake of his promise to Walsingham and Cecil and to protect those he had used, he could not leave her wandering until someone recognized her, or she became ill and babbled his secrets for all to hear. It might yet become imperative to kill her. Fool that he had been to allow her to persuade him to proceed with a plan that led to this. Would he have been able to kill her himself? he wondered. How fortunate, how very fortunate that he must set out for France next day, that he had been able to pass the task on to the dour man who had taken Cecily to the Trues' cottage. He could be trusted to do what he must as quickly and cleanly as might be if the need arose.

Robert shivered, and not from cold. If he was justified in helping Edward Woodfall from the world, why, as Jenkins pleaded, grovelling, for quick death had he responded with no more than an open-handed slap when a more sharply angled, cunning blow would have delivered him from what might be hours of terrifying waiting? In what way was he, who chose the objects of his compassion as they suited him, who could give orders for the killing of a girl he had told himself he loved, different from the quiet little man in the Tower who had terrified his boyhood?

Before him, strive against it as he might, was the line of night visitors of whom Jenkins had warned him. One day he too might sit in a room too small to allow him to run away and face ignominious death with the perverse bravado that had invested Jenkins. And in the meantime how many

464

times would there be when, for one reason or another, he killed when he need not? What had love to do with such as he, who was soiled and twisted to the depths of his soul?

He became aware of the coldness of the night air, frosty and clear about him, and came to a halt, having missed his way. Beneath his cloak he was wringing his hands together, washing them in invisible water, and he shrank from the spectre of madness. Water could not cleanse his hands but it might, after all, bring an end to the pain that was life. He had drowned when he was five years old, or so his family believed, if they were his family! What matter five or twenty-five?

He remembered a river rippling over stones and a pool, dark and deep, beneath the roots of an oak tree. Near it he had sat with a young girl and had deliberately sought, because it was his job, to destroy her life. He could plunge his dagger deep below his ribs and slide down into the cold, kindly depths beneath the roots. His body might be caught below the surface and never be found. No-one would wonder, after the first speculation, why he had vanished. He had no belief in an after-life. All he asked was everlasting, dreamless sleep; an end to the struggle that shamed and tore him apart.

Tomorrow he would make his way back to the wintry meadow, tomorrow for sure. Cecil could find some other man to work for him. He looked around him like a man awakening from deep sleep in some strange place. He was in a grassy opening, some way from the Palace. In its centre, surrounded by high, fancifully clipped yew hedges, was a deep pond with bulrushes. He sat down on its rim in the stillness and gazed deep into the water, seeing his head as a dark shape against the cloud-streaked sky. Gradually, in his over-tired mind, the pond merged with the pool under the oak trees. No need to wait until tomorrow. A mirthless laugh broke from him; these people had taken his soul, they should have his body to go with it. Without hesitation, without haste, he unlaced his doublet, drew his dagger and, holding it with both hands, deliberately put its point to a spot below his ribs . . .

CHAPTER XV

'Not in my pool, I thank you, sir!'

It was a woman's voice, harsh and commanding. Shock brought him back to his senses, the dagger clattered unnoticed on to the stone edge of the pool and he rose to his feet, swinging round in one lithe movement. She stood in a gap between two tall yews. For a moment, despite the authority in her words, he did not recognize her. A white lace cap topped a thin, fleshless face and about her bosom one ringless, clawlike hand held a somewhat dingy, fur-lined robe that was all she wore over a lace-trimmed nightshift. Then his numbness passed, he went down on one knee, head bowed.

'Your Majesty,' he said, and at the sound of the deep, pleasant voice the Queen frowned.

'Look up!' she said sharply, and as he obeyed the moon came out from behind its veil of cloud and threw a cold, clear light across his face. 'God's wounds, I know you! It is Master – Cooper, yes, Cooper, is it not? We met once in Burghley's rooms, I recall.'

She had a good memory! The better when he thought of the considerable effort he had made on that occasion to keep his head down, his face hidden!

'I had that honour, madam.'

'And now, it would appear, you intend to do me further honour by spilling your life's blood into my fish pool. *Stand up at once, sir!*'

As he came to his feet she moved forward into the small, sheltered space and Robert was surprised into saying, 'You are not alone, madam?' for all was silence about them. No other movement than theirs broke the stillness; there was no rustle of a lady's gown, no sign of a guard.

She inclined her head. 'I went to bed, Master Cooper, but sleep would not come and the moonlight was tempting. My ladies are snoring and I told the chamberers that if they so much as moved before I returned I would have their heads.' She cackled. 'That puts them into something of a quandary. If they disobey me they die, and if anything happens to me because they did nothing, they die!'

Alone in a vast garden that was open to the public she stood in darkness with an armed man and joked, showing no sign of fear.

'Then with your permission, I will leave you to the solitude you seek, Your Majesty.'

Robert bowed and was turning to retrieve his dagger, shaken out of his melancholy, self-pitying mood by this unexpected encounter, when she said, 'You will leave when I say so, and not before. Explain why you are here!'

Robert stiffened, hesitated. He could hardly say that he intended to end his life that night – although she appeared to have surmised so much – that had she not happened along when she did, by now he would have been floating face down among her carp. He murmured something which was incoherent even to himself about delivering papers to Sir Francis Walsingham and walking this way to think.

The Queen gave vent to a sharp and extremely unladylike expression. 'You lie! Do me the courtesy of not expecting to fool me by such a transparently false tale!'

With these words she made her way to a stone bench beneath the yew hedge. 'Come!' she ordered, seating herself. 'Sit beside me!' But he was slow to follow. She was his sovereign, but she was also an ageing woman – though he doubted very much if anyone would dare tell her so! – frail-looking and somehow not so formidable without her wig and fine clothes and with her face wiped clean of paint. He heard himself saying, 'Your Majesty, I cannot allow you to take so little care of yourself. The night air . . . Permit me.'

He fetched his cloak from the pool's edge and, she offering no objection, placed it about her shoulders; then he stripped off his doublet, folded it and placed it on the stone seat. 'If you will sit on this, madam, the stone will strike less chill.'

Meekly she did as she was bidden, pulling the cloak high about her shoulders. Observing him closely she was aware that for his queen he was only doing what he would have done for any other lady in such circumstances, making sure that she was safe and comfortable. There was no thought in him of achieving favour by playing the courtier. Looking up at him, thin and handsome in shirt and hose in the cold night air, she smiled a trifle maliciously and pressed him further.

'My feet are cold, sir,' she said and Robert felt his lips twitch in involuntary response as, obedient to her unspoken command, he stepped out of his shoes and laid them before her.

'You may put them on for me.' Still clearly diverted, she held out small bony feet, clad only in flimsy embroidered slippers.

Carefully, knowing that at any moment she might come to the end of her patience and tire of this game she had begun, he removed the damp slippers and hung his own much-too-large shoes on her feet. Then, encouraged by the fact that still she smiled, a smile that lightened her tired, stern face and stripped from it years in age, he looked down at her, said reflectively, 'I fear that that is the utmost of the help I can give, madam.'

She bowed her head gravely. 'And it is more than sufficient, I thank you. Now sit down, young man, here beside me, and let us hope that your constitution is strong enough to withstand the cold, stripped as you are!'

Robert sat down at a respectful distance from a Queen of England in her nightgown, but she snapped, 'I do not bite – sit down *beside me*, I said!' and then, more gently, as he moved along the seat until they were almost touching,

'I think we are both here for the same reason, Master Cooper. I am troubled and you, obviously, were about to solve your worries in a way that can only be called drastic in the extreme! Shall we see if, possibly, I can help you?'

'I would not presume,' he began slowly, feeling his way, and was not surprised to be told irascibly, 'I am not asking you to *presume*, man! I am offering you help. You should be honoured! What you mean with your "not presuming", I think, is that you would not trust me, your sovereign, with your problems. Is that not nearer the mark, sir? Eh?'

At her tone Robert made to rise, only to find bony fingers biting into his arm with surprising strength.

'In God's name will you stop bobbing up and down! Very well, if you will not trust me, I must give you a lead. I cannot sleep, nor have been able to do so recently because a personal problem I had thought trivial has intertwined itself with politics and gives me no rest. It hurts, Master Cooper, after all these years it still hurts.'

She felt him relax. 'The personal problem you know about, I think. The other it drags in its wake. When Sir Thomas Woodfall was young, he and I were friends. Apart from the fact that he *was* a friend – and that was all he was – never one of the fools who thought to share my throne or achieve advancement at my expense – I find it incomprehensible that after all these years he should have conspired to have me murdered. That I meet you of all people tonight seems almost like an omen, for you were in at the beginning. You questioned young Cecily Woodfall, did you not? Ah . . .!' as she felt her companion's arm stiffen beneath her hand. 'So the wind blows that way, does it? Well, your turn will come in a moment. I must know this, and I will have you swear on all you hold most dear – was Sir Thomas guilty or no?'

Quietly she awaited his answer, and for the space of a breath or two Robert Cooper held the safety of the realm in the palm of his hand. He had only to say, 'Your Majesty, the whole Woodfall family was innocent. There was a plot, engineered no matter by whom, and connived at by Walsingham, that you might be induced to sign Mary Stuart's death warrant.' There would be an uproar that would resound from one end of the kingdom to the other and he would have ensured that Martin Woodfall and his Cecily could return to their true home and pick up the threads of whatever was left of their old life. That he would have to explain his own part in what would be Martin's surprising return from the dead crossed his mind not at all.

The temptation was fleeting. For his country's good, for the sake of his given word, Robert looked steadily back into the Queen's pleading eyes and replied calmly, 'Sir Thomas was guilty, madam. I have seen the letters that were found. They are undoubtedly genuine. Sir Francis has them, and the confessions, in his keeping if you wish to see them.'

'And what, Master Cooper, do you swear by?'

He drew a deep breath. 'I swear by my love for – a certain young lady. If I have told you an untruth, may any hope I have of meeting her in heaven, for she can never be mine on this earth, disappear.' The oath, flamboyant beyond his nature, meaningless as far as he was concerned, was nicely calculated to please the Queen.

'That is sufficient, sir. Stupid, *stupid* Thomas! And he has heaped trouble and guilt upon my head with his tricks!'

'Madam?' Robert was committed now to play out the scene he had begun. She would never ask to see the evidence, of that he was convinced.

'Before long they – Burghley and Walsingham – my whole Council, will be upon me yet again to agree to the execution of Mary Stuart. Already there are whispers of another plot, bigger and no doubt better organized than Sir Thomas's. I shall hold out as long as I can, but how long will that be? Ah, they do not know what it means to me . . .' Her voice swelled in agony and her hands were clenched white talons in the moonlight. 'I know, Master Cooper, what it is to live in fear for my life from day to day. I have lived in dread of a powerful queen. I have woken to wonder whether a day would be my last. I know, as they cannot, what Mary Stuart thinks in the long, still night hours – plot she never so fiercely by daylight. Left alone she might

470

have been content to stay quiescent. It is men with their own interests at heart who push her, and she agrees. She has always been weak-minded, yet ambitious – a strange combination! It would be ironic, would it not, if she died because her life were so tedious that she agreed to anything that would break its monotony?'

The Queen's laugh was dreary, and her head, in its dainty white cap, drooped forward upon the borrowed cloak.

'Can she not see that in the end she must win, no matter what? She can never succeed me but her son most certainly will. That should please any natural mother, would you not say?'

Robert's own distress was forgotten, swallowed up in contemplation of a greater.

'Your Majesty may yet marry. Your suitors are many.'

That she had even mentioned the succession was amazing in itself, for she avoided the subject like the very plague, and for a moment he thought he had gone too far. Silence stretched between them, icy and long, and he waited for her to summon her guards, to order the arrest of a commoner who had spoken to her as an equal, who had dared to attempt to soothe her as he might had she been an ordinary woman in trouble. So sure was he of her reaction that he rose to his feet and stood waiting, feeling the coldness from the frost-whitening grass striking up through his stockinged feet, whilst his queen sat before him wrapped in his cloak and wearing his – on her – ridiculously large shoes.

But all she said as she looked up at him was, 'What is your name, your first name?'

'Robert, madam.'

'Then sit again beside me, Robert – another Robert, aye me. Your kindness is well-intentioned, I think. There will be no children of my blood to succeed me. I may enjoy the chase – or appear to – but that also is a matter of politics. I am a quarry that will never be caught.'

She stopped, a frown between her thin, reddish brows, as if she were seeing something visible only to her, something, to judge from her expression, that was not pleasant to contemplate. Then sharply she said, 'These are night words, sir. Never to be repeated!'

He bowed towards her, acknowledging a confidence, promising its sanctity.

'So now to you, Robert, my friend of the moonlight. This young lady by whom you swore. She is, I believe, my little brown mouse?'

'Aye, madam.' No thought of denying it crossed his mind. A confidence, be it never so small, for a confidence. He sat down again and his mouth twisted wryly. 'Cecily Woodfall. I dare say it will amuse you to know that I have reached the ripe age of five-and-twenty before falling in love. It comes the harder for its lateness!'

'Before you *allowed* yourself to love, I think you mean,' observed the Queen astutely. 'So your trouble also is founded on the Woodfalls. She is a good, kind child. I saw her father at a distance when I visited Thomas, but I cannot recall him.'

'Not very like in looks, madam. One of your sailors in his youth.'

'And allowed himself to be led astray – these family loyalties are the devil, Master Cooper. Did she refuse your suit?'

'There has been no suit, madam. A woman like Cecily needs a husband who can give her a settled home . . .' His voice trailed away.

'And she has returned to Sussex with that tiresome cousin of hers.' The Queen's tone sharpened. 'I was not impressed by what little I saw of Thomas's wife. Their daughter takes after her!'

Robert found himself forced to lie again. 'Aye, they have both returned home. To what little is left for either of them there. It is for the best.'

He looked down at his tightly linked hands and his mind slipped once again to the turmoil within him, so that the Queen's voice – and the question it asked – made him start.

'I recall that Sir Francis said Burghley had been responsible for your education. Who were your parents, boy?'

Who indeed? Was Agnes Woodfall speaking truth when she said that he was Dudley's by-blow or had it been some fantasy of her poor, twisted brain? And if Thomas Woodfall had sired him, how would Her Majesty take the news that he had helped hound his own father to the scaffold? He judged that she had reached the time of life, and had she not proved it this very night, when friendships made in youth assumed a roseate hue and became the more precious. But he had lied to her already and got away with it; therefore he said, 'I do not know, Your Majesty.'

With the words he looked her full in the face, with the practice of years of deception to aid him, and as he did so fear throbbed through every nerve in his body, fear such as he had never known in all his life. As he watched, her face changed from that of a tired, middle-aged woman seeking to relive her youth, to that of the Queen of England whose word had these many years been law. How it happened he could not have said, but that haggard, unpainted face, framed in wisps of faded hair, became regal and entirely unyielding. It did not matter what he said. As surely as had Edward Woodfall, she recognized him, and for the same reason. He had forgotten to veil the eyes that were his mother's legacy.

Something in the situation, some wild, sick humour, took him and he threw back his head with a shout of laughter. Peal after peal of the desperate sound echoed across the still, moonlit gardens whilst the Queen sat rigidly motionless by his side. Then, he knew not how, he was on his knees before her in the cold grass and the laughter had turned to tears. The relief he had spurned through years of loneliness came now and shook him from head to foot. Not an hour since he had come eagerly seeking death yet now, when it was inescapable, he knew that more than anything he wanted to live, on whatever terms. Some small, innately honest part of him wondered whether it was vile imprisonment he feared most or a death such as he had helped Edward Woodfall to avoid.

Crouched there he sobbed himself into silence, watched by his queen. At length he drew a deep, quivering breath

473

and rose unsteadily to his feet, groping in his pouch for a handkerchief. He stood with his head bowed, dishevelled, tear-stained and, had he but known it, looking more like an unhappy child than the man of blood he believed himself to be. Presently he pushed back the hair that had fallen over his forehead and dared to raise his eyes. Her Majesty was watching him intently; then, as he tried to nerve himself for what must come, she asked quietly, in genuine curiosity, 'How long have you known? About Sir Thomas, I mean.'

'Only these last weeks, madam. Not until it was too late to draw back.'

She nodded slowly, appraising him still, seeing honesty and a cold strength her country needed.

'You are a brave man, Robert Cooper. Such a duty would have brought down many.' Her smile held understanding.

With its dawning Robert realized that he had nothing to fear and in that same instant knew why this woman drew folk of all degrees to serve her. She might wander her garden at night mourning a friend of her youth untimely dead, even though he died a traitor, but England came first with her and always would, so that she accepted that that friend's son had helped to deliver up his guilty father to the authorities because it was his job, a job in which for him too the country came before any family ties. He saw not a queen to love but a queen to admire and respect for she, when it came to her turn, was herself prepared to make the sacrifices she expected of others.

Elizabeth Tudor wondered how much of her own part in his unhappy life this troubled young man knew or suspected, and was woman enough to hope that he knew nothing. Where he had been born and how he had so lately come by knowledge of his parentage she would not question. Some stones were better left unturned. Thomas had been a weak-willed man; he might well have given up a bastard son if that sour-faced wife of his had insisted. What mattered was that the child had grown into a man who could be of use. The Queen needed Robert Cooper to do the work he did, just as she needed servants, bodyguards, clerks, the thousand and one people who contributed in great or small measure to the running of her kingdom. Therefore she freed a hand from her wrappings and leaned forward to look into the pale eyes. Both of them, she thought shrewdly, had had enough of emotion and drama for one night, and it was as in a dream that he heard her voice, kindly once again, say, 'As I remember your mother, she was wilful in the extreme, but I think I never before nor since have had a maid as good-looking as she. Thank Heaven fasting, Master Cooper, that you favour her instead of your father. He ran sadly to fat!' She paused. 'We will leave the matter there. There is small profit in reopening old wounds. Do you not agree?'

'Most gladly, madam.'

'I may take it that you will not use your dagger – other than upon my enemies?' Her glance in the direction of the nearby fishpond was full of wry significance.

He went down on one knee. She must believe that it was only unrequited love for Cecily and the part he had played in bringing about Thomas Woodfall's downfall that had driven him to the brink of suicide. The other darker things were for him to bear alone. He bowed his head, so that his face was hidden from her.

'Come, sir, I will take your promise!'

He felt her hand lightly stroke his hair. 'Remember, Master Cooper, that some of us have difficult paths to tread. That should make us proud. If this land is to be kept safe I need the help of men I can trust. Not the lapdogs with whom I surround myself for amusement and to keep out the darkness, but men of inward strength who will do work that is not pleasant but that must be done. Such few, my boy, sacrifice themselves for the happiness of the many, and perhaps their reward is to be looked for in another life than this.'

Her voice died away, although her hand remained upon his head, and it was as if he were in some way drawing strength from her. It was his duty not to take the coward's way out but to go on serving Queen and country to the best of his ability. That way lay his expiation.

With a deep sigh he looked up into the face of a

woman who had understood and who had stooped to help him.

'To the end of my life, Majesty, that I swear,' and the smile that touched his face as he stood up was that of a man beginning at last to come to terms with what he was, so pleasant a smile that pain tugged at the heart of the woman before him.

As was her wont, she covered softer feelings with a show of sharpness. 'No doubt you would like your clothing returned to you, Master Cooper? And I must don my flimsy slippers again and wade through this clammy grass?'

Robert ventured all. 'The alternative, Your Majesty, would be to permit me the honour of carrying you to the door. No-one will see us, I think, and we shall thus ensure that you do not catch cold.'

Her Majesty hesitated not at all. 'Splendid!' she said, with a crack of laughter. 'You may begin your renewed vow of service thus. Have a care for my aching bones!' A smile that was almost a grin creased the thin, regal face. 'Take your shoes, Robert Cooper. Let us go!'

So Robert put on his shoes and, stooping, gently gathered the Queen of England, still wrapped in his cloak, into his arms. Swiftly and easily he carried her through the silent garden, his feet crunching on frozen grass, until they reached the door through which he had earlier wandered in such distress. There he set her on her feet, she pulled his cloak from her shoulders and held it out to him.

'I shall sleep now, I think, Master Cooper, as I hope you will. We shall meet again.' Intently she surveyed him. 'When next I see Walsingham I shall ask him why, when I needed an escort to Sussex, he sent that impossible Sir Edward Linton when he might have sent you. Do you know the man?'

Guilelessness rang through the question but Robert knew that she was not fooled, that she appreciated why he had found disguise necessary. Therefore he said, 'We have met, madam,' and heard her chuckle. When he straightened up from his deep bow she was gone.

Tired beyond belief, Robert leaned against the door jamb. It would not be any easier than ever it had been, the life he had this night sworn to uphold, but he would work as best he could for whatever time was left him. His dream of a small, brown-skinned, determined girl would fade until it became one with the pleasant memories he had of her mother.

He pushed himself upright, swung his cloak about him and set off across the garden to fetch his creased and crumpled doublet from the seat on which it had served as a queen's cushion.

The deep, quiet pool beneath the oak tree's roots could wait; it would always be there if he needed it.

THE END

LEGACY
by Susan Kay

May 1536: A turbulent love affair ends in murder, and a headless queen is laid to rest in a common arrow chest in the Tower of London. Behind her is left a small, silent girl who should have been a boy – legacy of the unholy union that shook the world.

Accusations of 'possession' were levelled at Elizabeth Tudor all her life, based on her incredible luck and her uncanny hold over the men who served her. LEGACY is the story of a Queen who sometimes thought herself possessed, who spent a lifetime in search of a master, and whose unparalleled love affair was with England, her country, for which she was prepared to lie, cheat, flatter and scheme.

'Remarkably accomplished, detailed and arresting'
Good Book Guide

'The story is vigorously told . . . a stirring read'
Jane Aiken Hodge

'The story of Elizabeth and the men who devoted their lives to her has been told and retold but rarely as well as by Susan Kay . . . long may Miss Kay, newly crowned queen of the historical novel reign!'
Daily Mail

'Quite simply, the most exciting, most moving, most passionate novel of Elizabeth I have ever read'
Diane Pearson

0 552 12720 5

I AM ENGLAND
by Patricia Wright

'I AM ENGLAND NOW LET THAT BE MY LIFE. THE FIRST QUEEN ELIZABETH SAID THAT, AND WAS LOVED BY HER PEOPLE FOR HER PRIDE IN ENGLISHNESS. THE REST OF US, WHO MADE THE LOOK AND FEEL OF ENGLAND, SHOULD ALSO BE REMEMBERED. WE ARE ENGLAND TOO.'

In this remarkable epic, which spans fifteen centuries from AD 70 to 1589, Furnace Green in the Weald of Sussex is England. Set about with great trees, abundant with deer and boar and wolves, the first people to come to the Ridge were the shy forest people, then Brac the ironsmith, who used a deer sign as his mark to express his love for his wild, strange wife.

Then came Edred, the Saxon, who left the Ridge to kill the hated Danes, and returned with a Danish slave girl with whom he could found a dynasty.

Their descendants, over many years, many calamitous events, continued to love and fight and build and pray on the Ridge. Robert the Falconer, doomed to die if he did not carve out a Fief by the Ridge, and Benedict, the priestly knight, fighting his last fight, and the Elizabethan yeoman who forged the cannon to defeat the Armada – these were the people of the Ridge – the people of England.

Winner of the Georgette Heyer Historical Novel Award

0 552 13290 X

A SELECTION OF TITLES AVAILABLE FROM CORGI BOOKS

THE PRICES SHOWN BELOW WERE CORRECT AT THE TIME OF GOING TO PRESS. HOWEVER TRANSWORLD PUBLISHERS RESERVE THE RIGHT TO SHOW NEW RETAIL PRICES ON COVERS WHICH MAY DIFFER FROM THOSE PREVIOUSLY ADVERTISED IN THE TEXT OR ELSEWHERE.

☐	12720 5	**Legacy**	*Susan Kay*	£3.99
☐	13292 6	**The Queen's Head**	*Edward Marston*	£2.99
☐	13293 4	**The Merry Devils**	*Edward Marston*	£2.99
☐	13520 8	**Heartsearch**	*Mary Napier*	£3.99
☐	10249 0	**Bride of Tancred**	*Diane Pearson*	£2.99
☐	10375 6	**Csardas**	*Diane Pearson*	£4.99
☐	10271 7	**The Marigold Field**	*Diane Pearson*	£2.99
☐	09140 5	**Sarah Whitman**	*Diane Pearson*	£3.50
☐	12641 1	**The Summer of The Barshinskeys**	*Diane Pearson*	£3.99
☐	13423 6	**I am England**	*Patricia Wright*	£2.95
☐	13379 5	**That Near and Distant Place**	*Patricia Wright*	£3.99

All Corgi/Bantam Books are available at your bookshop or newsagent, or can be ordered from the following address:

Corgi/Bantam Books,
Cash Sales Department,
P.O. Box 11, Falmouth, Cornwall TR10 9EN

Please send a cheque or postal order (no currency) and allow 80p for postage and packing for the first book plus 20p for each additional book ordered up to a maximum charge of £2.00 in UK.

B.F.P.O. consumers please allow 80p for the first book and 20p for each additional book.

Overseas customers, including Eire, please allow £1.50 for postage and packing for the first book, £1.00 for the second book, and 30p for each subsequent title ordered.

NAME (Block Letters) ....

ADDRESS ....

....